THE RECKLESS OATH
WE MADE

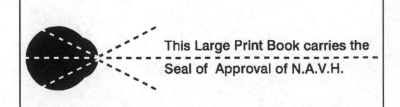

This Large Print Book carries the
Seal of Approval of N.A.V.H.

THE RECKLESS OATH WE MADE

BRYN GREENWOOD

THORNDIKE PRESS
A part of Gale, a Cengage Company

GALE
A Cengage Company

LIBRARY OF CONGRESS CIP DATA ON FILE.
CATALOGUING IN PUBLICATION FOR THIS BOOK
IS AVAILABLE FROM THE LIBRARY OF CONGRESS

ISBN-13: 978-1-4328-7292-2 (hardcover alk. paper)

Published in 2020 by arrangement with G. P. Putnam's Sons, an imprint of Penguin Publishing Group, a division of Penguin Random House, LLC

Printed in the United States of America
1 2 3 4 5 6 7 24 23 22 21 20

*For anyone who is struggling to build
their tower: may it be strong
and just tall enough*

CHAPTER 1
ZEE

People talk about having an angel on one shoulder and a devil on the other. I had a pair of imaginary bill collectors, so no matter which way I turned, there was somebody to remind me I needed money. That's how I ended up on a train at four o'clock in the morning with my nephew and a hundred pounds of weed.

We were hours behind schedule, but the westbound Southwest Chief was running on time. When the two trains met each other, they rattled back and forth, and the air that leaked in through the vents smelled like diesel and burning brakes. I could see into the other train's windows, where a few people were still awake. Usually, it made me feel lonely, seeing those people so close but separated from me.

This time felt different. Having Marcus' head resting in my lap reminded me I wasn't alone. He was small like his mother and dark-haired like his father, but when he was asleep, he was like me. Always running hot and trying to burrow his way into things. After hours of him sleeping on me, my hip hurt so much I kept hoping he would wake up, but he slept through the railroad crossing bells in every small town we went through. When he did wake up, rolling over and grinding his forehead into me, I didn't make him move. I smoothed his hair down and said, "Shh, it's okay. I'm here. Go back to sleep."

The trip to Trinidad had never been a big deal to me, but then I'd never had to take Marcus with me. I didn't have a choice, when LaReigne didn't come home, and twenty-four hours later, I was still waiting to hear from her. Waiting but dreading it, too, because there was no way I could keep lying to her. I would have to tell her about the weed, and she would have to get over it. She could be as mad as she wanted, but that wasn't going to pay the rent, and maybe it was time she knew where the extra cash came from. Sometimes she spent money like it magically appeared in our bank account. Like the gas money she burned up driving to El Dorado to volunteer at the prison.

Back before I started doing the Colorado run, LaReigne used to call Asher my *boy-*

friend, I guess because that was the only way me having sex with him made sense to her. She didn't understand it was just about the money. My hospital bills, the rent, the groceries, Mom's prescriptions, LaReigne's tuition, and whatever thing Marcus needed, because kids are money pits.

In my experience, you could fuck for money, or wait tables for money, or sit in an insurance office forty hours a week like La-Reigne did. However you get it, you need it, because money always decides whether things get better or worse. They never stay the same.

I was in too much pain to sleep, so I practiced in my head how I would explain all of that to LaReigne.

The thing that bothered me was that she didn't always come home on her volunteer nights, but she always texted. She always had an excuse. One time, exactly one time, she had completely flaked out on us. It was right after she'd filed for divorce, so Marcus had only been three. We'd been in our apartment for a month, and we didn't know where the next month's rent was coming from. We were living on potatoes and canned stuff from the food bank. One Thursday, LaReigne had gone out for a job interview and hadn't come home. I'd spent the whole weekend trying to find her, and gotten fired from my job for not showing up. LaReigne had finally come home on Sunday night, and we had a knock-down, drag-out fight. She never told me where she'd been, but she'd promised she would never do that again. And she hadn't.

Except where was she? If she'd lost her phone, she would have replaced it by now, so I couldn't keep pretending that's why she wasn't answering. For the first time, I let myself think about other reasons. Maybe she was dead. A car wreck. Some asshole with a gun who got her office and the Planned Parenthood clinic down the street confused. Her ex-husband was in jail in Texas, or I would've added him to the possible ways LaReigne could die. He'd threatened her enough times. Looking at one of the last texts I'd sent her, I wished I could take it back. *If you're not dead, I'm going to kill you.* What if I'd jinxed her?

A new text popped up, but it was only from Asher's lackey, Toby: *Why is the train so late?*

Engine problems

Ok well if there r cops at Newton ur on ur own

WTF are you talking about? Why would there be cops? I said.

10

The little dots flashed as Toby typed. When the answer came, I would have fallen down if I hadn't been sitting down: *This deal with your sister. Asher gonna murder u if the cops get his shit*

Panic washed over me, and my hands shook so hard I could barely type. *What are you talking about the shit with my sister???*

The thing out at the prison.

What thing at the prison???

Toby didn't answer.

I opened my Internet app to look at the *Wichita Eagle*'s website. While I waited for it to load, I couldn't tell if it was the train rocking back and forth or my stomach.

MANHUNT FOR ESCAPED INMATES was the top headline. Underneath that were grainy pictures of two guys in orange prison jumpsuits.

The smaller headline was *Two Guards Killed in Riot,* with pictures of the guards in their uniforms. Below that: *Night of rioting ends with three inmates injured and two volunteers taken hostage.* LaReigne was so unimportant, they mentioned her last. I didn't recognize the picture they used for her, so it was probably from her volunteer badge at the prison. She managed to look glamorous even in a mug shot–style picture.

11

Her hair in blond waves and her eyebrows drawn on perfectly. The other volunteer was a woman, too. Chubby and maybe fifty with short brown hair. Was it Molly, who LaReigne had stayed with a couple times when she had a migraine and didn't want to drive home?

I tried to find out more, but all the news sites had the same information. Rioting, low staffing, overcrowding, dead guards, escape, hostages. I was rereading it, over and over, when we pulled into Newton.

I was the last person off the train, practically carrying Marcus while the conductor tossed my suitcases out on the sidewalk. Marcus flopped down on the ground next to the bags, cried for about two minutes, and then fell asleep.

I almost cried, too, but I held it together while everybody was meeting up with their families and finding their rides. The whole time, Toby was standing in the shadows, watching me. Maybe he thought he was keeping a low profile, but he looked like a creeper.

"Do you want this shit or not?" I said, after the train pulled away.

"Keep your voice down."

"There aren't any cops." I raised my voice, same as always, because being mad felt safer than being scared. Toby came over and started towing my suitcases toward where he'd parked his car next to mine. After sitting for twelve hours, my hip felt like it was full of gravel, but I picked Marcus up and limped after Toby.

Usually Toby unloaded the suitcases into his trunk and gave them back to me, but when I got to his car, he was tossing them into the back seat. Those suitcases were serious business: matching, locking, hard-sided, polycarbonate, all-terrain wheels. The only place I'd ever taken them was Trinidad, Colorado, and the only thing I'd ever packed in them was Asher's weed. They'd cost me serious money, too, but right then didn't seem like a safe time to argue about them, so I set Marcus down and unlocked my car.

"Why the hell did you bring the kid anyway?" Toby said.

"Because I had to. Asher said if I didn't make the run tonight, he'd have you fuck me up."

Toby laughed and said, "You're already fucked up. What kinda person brings their kid on a run?"

"He's my nephew, and my sister didn't come home last night, which *you already know.* There was nobody else to watch him."

"Shit, for real? This is LaReigne's kid?" Toby looked at Marcus, who was asleep on his feet, leaning up against me. "So that's some crazy shit, huh? What do you think is —"

"Shut up, you asshole!" I said.

Even though Marcus was right there, Toby reached out and grabbed me by the neck. He pushed me back against my car, digging his thumb into my throat.

"You need to learn some fucking manners, Zee."

"Please," I said, which wasn't what I felt at all. "Don't say anything in front of him."

When Toby let go of me, I opened the door and lifted Marcus into his car seat. After I shut the door, I turned back to Toby with my arms crossed, so he wouldn't see me shivering. There was a reason Toby couldn't do the run to Colorado himself. He looked exactly like what he was: a drug-dealing thug with a neck tattoo and a squir-relly eye. He also happened to be one of the scariest people I knew. Him and Asher. Any time I got tempted by those blocks of cash, that was all I had to think about. Two hundred grand would pay off all my debts — hell, the debts of everybody I knew — but it would also get me killed.

"Jesus," Toby said. "I was gonna offer to

make things easier for you with Asher. Smooth things over."

I knew what he had in mind for payment for a favor like that, and I really wanted to be done paying for things with sex. I hoped I was never going to be that desperate again.

"Anyway, doesn't matter now. Asher told me to tell you you're cut off. You don't call him. You don't text him. He'll call you after this shit quiets down."

I probably should have got in the car and left, but I had bills to pay.

"My money?" I said.

Toby snorted, but he reached into his back pocket and took out an envelope. He held on to it for a couple seconds after I reached for it, but he finally let it go. I stuffed the money into my pocket and walked around to the driver's side of my car. When I opened the door, Toby was still watching me.

"Tell Asher he owes me for those suitcases," I said. "They weren't cheap."

CHAPTER 2
ZEE

When we were in grade school, LaReigne and I walked to and from school every day, separated by about ten feet or so, because she was too cool to walk with a *baby*. One day — I was in third grade and LaReigne was in sixth — when we got to our block, there were half a dozen cop cars parked in front of our house. I remember crying, even before I knew what had happened. I don't know when I learned to be afraid of the police, but I was. We all were. That day, La-Reigne took my hand, and we walked down the street to our house together. Mom stood on the front porch, screaming and sobbing, with a cop on either side of her. Dad was locked in the back seat of a police car, with his head turned so he wouldn't have to look at his wife or his daughters.

Now, driving past our apartment building and seeing a police car and a police van parked outside, I felt eight years old again.

Afraid and angry, but not ignorant or innocent anymore. I didn't dare stop. I had five ounces of weed in my backpack and a bunch of drops and edibles. Probably the smart thing to do was ditch the weed, but I couldn't afford to. I needed the money, and it was the only thing that really worked for my pain that didn't require a prescription.

I kept driving.

"You missed our turn," Marcus said. Five years old and he was already a backseat driver.

"We're not going home yet." I pulled up to the light at Central, white-knuckling the steering wheel to keep myself focused. In my side-view mirror, I could still see the cop car parked in front of our apartment.

"Where are we going?" he said.

"Grandma's house."

I should have gone somewhere else. Anywhere else. A motel. A park. A fucking church. Even going to Marcus' other grandparents' would have been a better terrible choice, if I was going to make a terrible choice. My mother's house was on a cul-de-sac that dead-ended where they had widened Kellogg into a six-lane highway, so when I turned down the street, I was already stuck. There were three news vans, plus half a dozen other cars. Once again my family was newsworthy.

Reporters didn't scare me the way cops did, so I pulled up at the end of the line of vehicles and parked. I got Marcus out of the car and led him across the neighbors' yards, but as soon as we reached the weedy edge of Mom's yard, the reporters saw us. Holding Marcus' hand tighter, I walked faster, keeping my eyes focused on Mom's front porch, which was piled up with old furniture and lawn tools.

"Are you a member of the Trego family?" said the first reporter that reached us.

"Do you know the family?" said another one.

A TV cameraman cut me off at the sidewalk, while more reporters shouted, "Do you know LaReigne Trego-Gill?"

Marcus started to cry, and then his hand slipped out of mine. My heart stuttered and I turned around, thinking it would be a reporter or a cop or . . . I didn't know who might grab Marcus.

Standing there, next to Marcus, was Gentry. Where had he come from? Had he followed me there? Of course; he followed me everywhere. Before I could think of what to say, Gentry picked Marcus up. What I would have done if my hip hadn't been hurting so much. Then Gentry reached past me and used his arm as a barrier between me and the cameraman who was nearly in my face.

"Let the lady pass!" Gentry bellowed. The cameraman backed up.

I ran the last ten feet to the porch, with Gentry behind me carrying Marcus. The screen door was only attached at one hinge, so you had to be really careful with it, and I wasn't. I was so freaked out, I jerked it open, and the glass panel on the top rattled into the bottom and almost fell out. I managed to shove the whole thing out of the way, but the front door was locked. I pulled my keys out of my pocket and got the deadbolt turned. When I pushed, the door opened, but only a few inches. For a second, I thought, *Mom has finally managed to block both doors. She's going to die trapped in there.*

"Has the family heard anything from La-Reigne? Do you have any news? Has there been a ransom demand? Are the police negotiating?" Reporters were shouting behind me, Marcus was sobbing, and I could hear Gentry breathing hard.

"Push," I said to Gentry, and I stepped as far off to the side as I could. Still holding Marcus, he put his free hand on the frame and leaned his whole body into the door.

There was a thump and a crash inside, and the door opened wide enough for us to squeeze through.

Inside, there was no room for us to do anything but stand packed together. Gentry slammed the door closed and set Marcus down on top of a half-collapsed stack of newspapers. I hugged Marcus tight, feeling his whole body quivering. I wondered if he understood why those strangers were shouting his mother's name.

"It's okay, buddy. I got you," I said. With this sick lurch, I realized that I was LaReigne now. Not just for Marcus, but for me. After Dad went to prison, right up until she left for college, LaReigne had been the adult in our family. After that I had to be my own adult, but now I would have to be one for Marcus, too.

"Zhorzha? Is that you, Zhorzha?" Mom yelled from the front room.

"Yeah, it's me. I have Marcus with me."

"What was that crash? What did you knock over?"

"I don't know. Whatever was behind the door. I almost couldn't get it open."

What had fallen over was a cardboard box full of ballerina figurines, too high on the stack to be the ones LaReigne had as a kid. There was also a tumbled-over pile of romance novels, a broken laundry basket with a half-finished quilt in it, and two wooden boxes that maybe were for silver-ware. I knew she got stuff off Craigslist and eBay, but I didn't have a clue where most of the new stuff came from.

I turned around, intending to make sure the door was locked, and there was Gentry, looking the way he always did. Like one of Marcus' Lego people. Not very tall, but a solid block, dressed in a black T-shirt, cargo shorts, and Timberlands. He had his back pressed against the door, his head down, and his hands resting on the back of his neck. He didn't look at me — he never looked me in the eye — so at least I didn't have to hide the horrified look on my face when I realized what I'd done.

I'd invited my stalker into my mother's house.

CHAPTER 3
GENTRY

I brought Lady Zhorzha and her little page
safe through the throng of knaves, but 'twas
no great task for the many months I was set
to watch over her. To guard the threshold
like a dog would give me joy, but my lady
needed me to carry the boy.

I set him down, and my lady embraced
him while I made fast the door. I saw no
clear path from that place, and I would not
give offense, so I waited to hear my lady's
bidding. I felt her gaze upon me, but knew
not how to meet it. 'Twas rare I kenned her,
nor she me.

From deep within the cottage, the air
rumbled with a great voice, heavy and
coarse with age. It called my lady's name
and stirred all the voices in me.

"Come in," Lady Zhorzha said. "Come in
and meet my mother."

Marcus led the way, clambering like a goat
down narrow passages. On all sides heaped

up weren manuscripts and folios, and great cupboards filled with platters and goblets. Our footsteps set them to rattle.

"How long has it been like this?" Lady Zhorzha called.

"They've been here since yesterday. And calling and calling. I had to unplug the phone."

"Oh my god, Mom. I tried to call you a bunch of times. Why didn't you call me if you were going to unplug the phone?"

First Marcus and then Lady Zhorzha withdrew through a doorway, flanked upon each side by mounds of chests and baskets. I followed, and at last, afound the answer to the question I asked of the Witch many a time. 'Twas my bounden duty to protect Lady Zhorzha, for she was descended of dragons.

There, in the inner chamber, reclined upon a throne of red leather that scarce contained her serpentine hugeness, was the dragon Lady Zhorzha called Mother. My lady was blessed with a great mane of fire that ne comb ne blade might tame. Mayhap in the dragon's youth, she had worn such a mantle, but in her age, her hairs weren grayed.

Fearless, Marcus approached the throne and flung himself upon the lady dragon. For a time, there was kissing and lamenting, for they weren greatly distressed with the fate of my lady's sister. The dragon clapped the little boy to her and succored him. Then she raised herself upon one red-scaled elbow and with a plume of white smoke spake: "I was calling you all day yesterday! I was about to report you and Marcus missing to the police."

"I had my cellphone on all day yesterday. What number were you calling?"

"Your apartment number."

"We don't have a landline anymore, Mom. You have to call my cellphone. And you can't smoke around Marcus," Lady Zhorzha said, but the dragon exhaled another blast of smoke.

"Who is this?"

I felt the dragon's gaze fall upon me.

"Hark, little knight," Gawen said. "She would eat thee."

"Filth and the Mother of Filth," Hildegard said.

Tho none but I could hear them, I would not support their uncourtesy, and heeded them not.

"This is Gentry," Lady Zhorzha said.

"Gentry, I suppose we'll have to introduce ourselves, since she can't be bothered to."

"I'm sorry," Lady Zhorzha said. "Gentry,

this is my mother, Dorothy Trego. Mother, this is Gentry Frank."

The dragon offered one sharp-taloned hand to me, and I took it. I would go upon my knee, but the dragon's hoard was too close upon her. I bowed over her hand to show my admiration.

"And who are you, Gentry?" she said.

"My lady, I am thy daughter's champion."

The dragon laughed like a clap of thunder and pressed my hand.

"Oh, he's charming. Nicholas was good-looking, but he had no sense of humor. I never could —"

"Seriously, Mom? That's what we're talking about right now? Because I can think of a few things that are more important than my ex-boyfriend."

"Little pitchers have big ears," the dragon said.

"You're thirsty, aren't you, Gentry? Don't you need a drink?" Lady Zhorzha said, but I kenned not her intention. "Marcus, why don't you take Gentry and get him a pop out of the fridge?"

"Okay." Marcus came down from the dragon's throne and led me further into the maze. The dragon's hoard trespassed even into the scullery, platters and goblets piled upon the cabinets until the cupboards above opened not. So high weren the things heaped up there, I saw not the spigot.

We passed through another door and into the garage, where great towers of chests and crates rose to the rafters. In the midst of them was a small icebox with a small oven stacked upon it. Marcus opened the door and shew me what was within. I wished not for a sweet drink, but would do as my lady bid.

"What do you want? There's Coke or orange," Marcus said.

"I would have an orange drink, Master Marcus."

"You talk funny," he said. " 'Twas always thus."

"Are you Aunt Zee's boyfriend? You always park outside our apartment."

"I am her champion. I watch that I might her serve."

He brought from the icebox two cans, and we sat upon the threshold to the house and drank.

"Do you know where my mommy is?" he said.

"Nay, I know not." Yet I knew what caused my lady's distress.

Always in the hall where we ate what was our midday meal, the Duke of Bombardier allowed his vassals to see the news. The night past, I had seen the visage of my lady's sister. I knew her straight away, for oft I saw her with my lady and with Marcus. *Taken,* the news had said of the lady LaReigne, by knaves locked up in the gaol at El Dorado. Certs they weren men of ill intent, but mayhap my lady's sister still lived, tho there was no word of her fate.

When the hour of my leaving Bombardier had come that morning, I went not home, but to my lady's house. There I saw the sheriff's men. I perceived not their task, but as I kept watch, Lady Zhorzha had passed and stopped not.

"Soon," the Witch had said for nigh two years. "Soon Lady Zhorzha shall have need of thee." As I sat beside young Marcus, the Witch spake again, saying, "They aren under thy protection now. Take them to thy keep."

"To my father's keep?" I asked.

"Nay, to thine own."

I kenned her not, for my keep lay in chaos, a field of stones, and no fit place for my lady, tho oft I dreamt it.

"I don't like being out here," Marcus said.

"Dread thee nought. Thine aunt and thee, ye aren under my protection."

The boy put his hand into mine and I took it as the Witch's surety. She oft spake in riddles, but I trusted her. If she said 'twas to be, it was.

CHAPTER 4
ZEE

"Have you heard anything from your sister?" Mom said, as soon as we were alone.

"Not since Monday." I took out my phone, meaning to show her the texts, but then I looked at them and changed my mind.

Remember you're getting Marcus from school today. LaReigne had texted that at one forty-five, when I was still at the restaurant.

I remember. She acted like I didn't have a calendar on my phone to remind me.

Please don't get high tonight ok? She sent that with a little sad, disappointed emoji, which wasn't even fair. Who kept all the bills paid? Good old stoner Zee. So why did I get the sad, disappointed emoji?

I never get high when I'm watching him, I'd answered.

Right it's for "pain relief" but you won't even TRY the guided meditation I use. You know I had Marcus through natural childbirth using that. No pain meds, no spinal block.

I know. Because she never got tired of telling me.

Just please don't get high tonight.

It was useless explaining to LaReigne that there's no natural childbirth equivalent to hitting a highway at sixty-five miles an hour, dislocating your hip, and breaking your leg in two places. Lamaze won't get you through that.

"The last time she texted me was at like six o'clock on Monday," I said. "She always lets me know when she gets to the prison, and when she's leaving, but she didn't."

I'd texted her at ten to see where she was, but she never answered. Same at midnight, and, by then, Asher had told me to make the trip to Colorado.

"Well, where have you been?" Mom said, like an accusation.

"I had to do a favor for a friend of mine, so I took Marcus with me, and I thought LaReigne maybe just flaked out. Only she didn't come back."

Saying it out loud, it finally hit me. LaReigne had been kidnapped. Taken hostage. Whatever you called it, I didn't have any idea if she was safe or if they were going to hurt her or when I was going to see her again. Maybe we didn't always get along,

30

but she was my sister. She was the person who held my hand on two of the worst days of my life.

"Oh, baby, I know." Mom opened her arms and I went to her the same way Marcus did. I put my knee up on the reinforced arm of her chair, and leaned against her to bury my face in her shoulder. I couldn't remember the last time I'd hugged her. Not put my arms around her to leverage her in and out of her chair, or the toilet, but to hug her.

"What do we do? What's going to happen?" I said. Mom's hand was warm on my back, rubbing slow circles, while I cried all over her shoulder. I wanted to stay there, but I knew I couldn't. That was even more true than it had been when I was sixteen. I pulled myself together and stood up. "Should we call the police? They have to tell us something, right?"

"They've come by twice now, but I couldn't answer the door." *I couldn't* meant a lot of things to Mom. Maybe she'd been too scared to talk to the police. Maybe she couldn't get out of her chair and answer the door. "Now that you're here, though, we'll call them. And they'll tell us whatever they know."

I got the phone plugged back in, and

Mom dialed. She was put on hold three times, and every time she had to tell someone new who she was. Then she finally got someone on the line who knew something, because she listened and nodded.

When she started crying, I had to sit down on the arm of her chair. The worst, that was what I expected. The very worst. After a minute Mom went back to nodding, and then she said, "Yes, I understand. That's fine."

"What did they say?" I said after she hung up.

"They're going to send someone to talk to us."

"What does that mean? Do they have any news?"

"They didn't tell me anything." Mom started crying again.

"Have you talked to Emma or Aunt Shelly?" I said. They were practically the only family we had left. Aunt Shelly had been married to Mom's brother, Tim.

"Not Shelly, but Emma. I talked to her yesterday, just for a minute. Before everything got so crazy."

"And?"

"We had a little fight. You know, in their minds this is somehow your father's fault. Or LaReigne's fault, which is ridiculous."

"Well, not like she's completely innocent, either," I said.

Not that anybody would take me as an example of how to be a good person. Like Toby said, *What kind of person takes a kid on a drug run?* But what made LaReigne want to do something goody-goody like volunteer at the prison? Hadn't we already put in our time? Before he died, our father spent twelve years in prison, and we went to see him almost every single week. Wasn't that enough for LaReigne?

The door to the garage opened, and I heard Gentry and Marcus coming up the steps into the kitchen.

"Yea, I am a knight," Gentry was telling Marcus. He said it with the *k,* k-night, and Marcus parroted it back to him that way.

"But k-nights have swords. Do you have a sword?"

"I have more than one sword."

"You do?" Marcus said.

"What does that mean? *Not completely in-nocent?*" Mom said.

"Shh." I didn't want to get into it with her when Marcus might overhear us. "There goes my plan to ask Emma to watch Marcus for a little bit. The police were up at the apartment, so I don't know if we'll be able to stay there."

"You should stay here."

"How? There's not even any place for us to sit down, let alone lie down."

"That's not true. You know there's a sofa bed in the sunroom."

The way Mom said it, so sure of herself, it gave me goosebumps. Even if you could get in the sunroom — you couldn't — I doubted there was a sofa you'd want to sleep on. I stood up, because the whole house was quicksand, and I could feel it sucking me in.

"Probably we'll get a motel room tonight," I said.

"That's silly to spend money on a motel. We can figure out something here."

"No, I think it'd be better to take Marcus somewhere else. I don't like all those reporters out there."

"My lady," Gentry said from the kitchen doorway. "I offer thee and thy page sanctuary at my father's keep."

"Okay." I didn't hesitate, because I had to get away from the quicksand. After I escaped, I could figure out what to do.

"Are we going?" Marcus said.

"Not yet, buddy. Grandma has some people coming over who need to talk to her."

Marcus crawled up into the spot on

34

Mom's chair I'd just pried myself out of. He kissed her cheek and said, "When's Mommy coming?"

"Soon, sugar pie. Soon," Mom said. How many times had she told us that lie about Dad? *Soon,* when what she really meant was *Never.*

"Do you want to watch a video?" I asked Marcus. He didn't move from where he was lying against Mom's side, but he nodded.

"Gentry, do you mind taking Marcus back out to the garage? Just for a little while?"

"Nay, my lady," he said. " 'Tis my honor."

"It's not too warm out there, is it?"

"Nay, 'tis pleasant enough."

Whether it was pleasant or not, I didn't want Marcus there when we talked to the police. I got the iPad out of my backpack and gave it to Marcus, who followed Gentry out to the garage, even though he didn't look very happy about it.

"He's very charming," Mom said.

"Who?"

"Gentry. He's very charming. Where did you find him?"

"Oh god," I said. "It's complicated."

CHAPTER 5
ZEE

Where did I find Gentry?

At a physical therapy clinic about three months after Nicholas and I had our huge fight, and I laid his Harley down in rush-hour traffic on Kellogg.

Right after the wreck, while I was still in the hospital, Nicholas had moved home to his parents' in Merriam. I couldn't go back to our apartment by myself. Hell, I couldn't even afford it by myself. I couldn't move in with Mom, because you could barely walk through her house *without* a cast on your leg. I was back to being the kind of homeless I'd been since I was sixteen.

LaReigne rescued me. She had come to the hospital while my leg was still in traction. She took my hand, just like when I was little, and she'd said, "I'm taking you home." So I'd moved in with her and Loudon, which was so delightful I used to fantasize about falling down the stairs and breaking my neck. Marcus had been only two and a half then, and I was sleeping on the other twin bed in his room and listening to his parents fight nonstop.

Two months after the wreck, I was out of my leg cast, but still in a brace and walking on crutches. Twice a week, LaReigne had dropped me off for PT and picked me up after, because I wasn't cleared to drive. Even if I had been, my car got repo'd after the wreck, because I lost my job and stopped paying on the loan.

The day I met Gentry, LaReigne didn't show up after my appointment. Every time I texted her, she'd said, *I'm sorry, I'll be there in a little bit.* After I'd been sitting in the clinic lobby for three hours, I got the text I'd known was coming. *I'm sorry, Z. Loudon took the car and I don't know where he is. Can you get an Uber or something?*

I didn't have money for a cab, so I'd looked up bus routes on my phone, but the closest the bus could get me was two miles from the condo. Two miles on crutches. I went out to the parking lot, and there was a guy standing next to his truck. I'd seen him in the waiting room a bunch of times. In the beginning, he'd had his arm in a sling, but at this point he just had athletic tape on his arm and shoulder. He was a nondescript white guy. Cargo shorts, tank top, stocky, medium height, dark hair. I never would have recognized him, except he had the worst haircut I'd ever seen on another human being. Not like he'd cut it himself, but like he'd let a toddler cut it with a pair of garden shears, repeatedly.

As I came down the sidewalk, he stepped away from his truck and bowed to me. I will never forget what he said: "My lady. Thy servant."

I stopped, because there was nobody else he could be talking to, but I had no idea what he meant. He straightened up, but kept his eyes down.

"My lady. If thou wilt allow me to help thee," he said. When I didn't answer, he got down on one knee, like he meant to propose to me. " 'Tis my honor to carry thee whither thou desirest."

I was staring at him, but he never looked up. He stayed there with his bare knee on the asphalt, one hand over his heart and the other offered to me palm up. Was I supposed to take it?

He looked off to his left and nodded.

"Yea. I see, man. I am not blind," he said. Then he went back to looking at my legs. "Thou art wounded, my lady, and I would thee serve."

I almost kept walking, because the level of crazy there was so high, but then I'd remembered my fantasy about falling down the stairs. If this guy was a serial killer, it would save me the trouble of breaking my own neck.

"Is this your truck?" I said, because I didn't speak *whither thou desirest.*

"My lady, 'tis." He stood up and opened the passenger door for me. Even though he offered his hand for me to get up in the cab, he looked shocked when I put my hand on his shoulder for leverage. Once I was in the cab, he tucked my crutches behind the seat and closed the door.

When he went around and got into the driver's seat, I snuck a picture of him and sent it to LaReigne. *If I get murdered, this is the guy who gave me a ride.*

"What's your name?" I said.

"I am called Gentry Frank." He glanced over at me for about half a second.

"I'm Zhorzha. Rhymes with Borgia," I said, like always. "You can call me Zee."

"Lady Zhorzha, whither goest thou?"

"Okay, you're cracking me up with that. I need to go past Twenty-ninth and Rock, if that's not too far."

I guessed it wasn't because he took me all the way home. I would have had him drop me off at the front gate of the complex, but I was so tired I didn't care. I told him the gate code and had him drive me up to the building. He pulled in and parked next to LaReigne's car. Either she'd lied to me about Loudon taking the car or the dick-head had just come home.

While I was trying to get myself out of the truck, Gentry came around and got my crutches out. He held out his arm for me to take, but I used the doorframe instead, because he'd seemed so freaked out about me touching him.

"My lady, shall I help thee?"

"No, my good sir," I said, trying to get into it, to be nice. "Thank you, though. I appreciate it."

"If thou needest aught." He'd bowed and held something out to me: an appointment card from the PT clinic with his phone number written on the back. I turned it over and looked at his appointment time. Half an hour before mine. So he'd waited all that time for me to walk out of the clinic. Waiting to give me that card? The corners were damp and worn down like he'd been worrying it in his hand.

"Um, thank you," I said, but I'd put the card in my back pocket, thinking like hell was I ever going to call him.

In the condo, LaReigne and Loudon were having a shouting match while Marcus hid in the bedroom. As soon as I walked in, the fight turned into *Your fucking sister here all the time and she doesn't even pay rent!* Which was pretty goddamn rich coming from Loudon, who didn't pay rent, either. His parents paid for everything.

"Don't you talk that way about my sister!" LaReigne always said, and I'd end up offering to leave, even though there was no place for me to go. Sometimes I'd spend a night at my cousin Emma's, and sometimes with my high school buddy Shelton, but he was homeless about half the time, too. I always ended up back with LaReigne and Loudon.

The next week, I'd seen Gentry at PT again. Waiting for me. I didn't waste any energy pretending I didn't need a ride. After all, that's why he was hanging around, and it saved me the trouble of getting LaReigne to pick me up. The week after that, Gentry had started taking me to my appointments, waiting while I did PT, and then taking me home. By then he wasn't even doing PT anymore, and I felt like a mooch. Not that I wasn't used to feeling like a mooch, but I was always trying to start over being a better person. So I offered to buy him lunch before he took me home. I thought he'd

41

relax, and I'd feel better about the whole situation. Except we didn't talk much and he ended up paying for lunch.

Next week, same thing. Him sitting in the waiting room with his head down over a book, then lunch again. I forced myself to make small talk.

"Are you in school?"

"Nay, my lady."

"Where do you work?"

"I am a vassal of the Duke of Bombardier," he said.

"Wait. Bombardier?" I got the giggles, and even though it was probably wrong, I said, "Verily, thou doth build flying machines?"

Some little light went on in him. He smiled and looked at me. Just for a second.

"Yea, my lady. 'Tis my duty to rivet wings upon Learjets."

"So how did you hurt your shoulder?"

"I was wounded in a joust," he said.

"Really? Well, obviously, really." He said so little, and I only understood part of it, so right then I'd decided to take whatever he said at face value.

The day I was officially crutch free and brace free, I did a happy dance in the PT clinic parking lot. Gentry stood next to his truck, smiling, watching my little celebration. I didn't even think about what I was doing. I was so happy to be walking again that I kissed him. Well, I tried to kiss him. He was so surprised that he pulled back from me like I'd tried to bite him. Maybe *surprised* was the wrong word. Horrified? I got into the truck cab and slammed the door, feeling totally embarrassed. For half a minute he stood there, with a blank look on his face, and then he walked around to the back of the truck.

I watched him in the side-view mirror having a whole conversation with himself. Talking, nodding, shaking his head, gesturing with his left hand, while he rested the right one on top of his head. After a few minutes of that, he came around and got in the truck. He cleared his throat, started the truck, cleared his throat again.

"Look," I said. "I'm sorry about that. Just a misunderstanding. No big deal."

"Nay, my lady. Thy kiss offendeth me not."

I'd only tried to kiss him because it seemed like the next step to whatever was going on. I never understood romance, but I knew what it looked like from the outside well enough to fake it when I needed to. I'd faked almost my whole relationship with Nicholas, because I couldn't get ahead by myself on minimum wage.

Gentry, though, he was . . . I guess the word is *chivalrous,* but he wasn't romantic. That whole *my lady, thy servant* wasn't going to turn into *my lady, thy boyfriend.*

We drove to the condo without talking, and, when we got there, I figured that was the end of things. He came around to open the door for me, even though I didn't need help with my crutches anymore.

"When cometh again thy physic?" he said. My next appointment, he meant.

"It's okay. You don't have to keep taking me. It's only a few more weeks, and I can walk to the bus now."

"Nay. 'Tis my honor —"

"I know. It's your honor to help me. But for how long? One of these days I'll be all healed up." I hoped that was true. I was counting on being able to get a job and get the hell out of Loudon's house.

"For always, my lady," Gentry said. When I didn't respond to that, he asked me again about my next appointment, so I told him.

I didn't try to kiss him again, and I didn't suggest lunch anymore. He took me to PT; he took me home. We made polite small talk. *How farest thee? Good, how was your day?* I guess so we could feel friendly, even though we weren't really friends.

Things got worse with Loudon and, at

what turned out to be my last PT session, LaReigne texted me to say, *Do you have somewhere else you can stay tonight?* I didn't.

Sitting in the truck, waiting for Gentry to go around to the driver's side, I started to cry. My hip still hurt, and probably it always would, and I couldn't afford the prescription for my pain meds, and I was homeless again.

"My lady," Gentry said when he got in the truck. "Thou art unwell?"

"I just can't go home right now. I guess you can take me . . ." To my mother's house or my cousin Emma's, because I didn't have money for a motel. I texted Emma first, but she didn't answer.

"If thou art willing, couldst come to my mother's keep," Gentry said.

That was how I'd ended up meeting his family.

Ranked in order of evilness and stupidity:

Vicky, his youngest sister. Hot Topic's Number-One Customer. Typical teenager. Bad attitude about everything and under the impression that makeup is the great equalizer. Hint: it's not.

Miranda, his mother. An overgrown teenager. She hadn't looked old enough to be Gentry's mother, and when I tried to shake her hand, she giggled and just looked at me. I wasn't surprised her other kids had such terrible manners. It was more surprising that Gentry didn't.

Marla, his middle sister. Mean. Bone mean. Even at our shittiest petty teenage worst, LaReigne and I never talked to each other the way Marla talked to Vicky.

Brand, his younger brother. Two prison tattoos short of a hate crime, and about to be too old to be charged as a juvenile. He wore a Confederate flag T-shirt, which was such bullshit because Kansas was a free state.

"Oh, holy shit," Brand said when Gentry introduced me. "Dude got himself a real live girl."

"Plot twist," Vicky said. "Lady Zhorzha turns out to be a real person. I did not see that coming."

"I thought she'd look like a princess," Marla said. "And not a —"

"Are you going to get dinner?" Miranda said.

"If it thee liketh, my lady."

Gentry went on being polite, and they went on being assholes. It's not like I'm Miss Manners or anything, but I never ordered anybody around the way Gentry's family ordered him around. To take out the

46

trash, while the rest of them sat on their asses watching TV. To go get them dinner, from fucking Taco Bell. To get up and refill Miranda's wineglass. To get Marla a different kind of hot sauce from the fridge.

While we ate, Marla and Vicky were texting on their phones, and then Marla looked up and said, "Can I go meet Lilah at the mall?"

Miranda shrugged and said, "I'm not driving you."

"Gentry will take me." They pronounced it *Gent-ree.* He pronounced it *Gen-tree.*

"I wanna go," Vicky said.

"You're not going."

"Mom!"

"Take your sister," Miranda said.

"I fucking hate you, zit face," Marla said to Vicky. Then she turned to Gentry, who still hadn't finished eating in between all his other errands, and said, "Take me to the mall."

"There's this word you maybe haven't heard of," I said. *"Please."*

"Fuck you, Lady Thunderthighs."

"Oh, ow. My feelings."

"Spew not thy venom on Lady Zhorzha," Gentry said.

"Spew not thy venom," Marla said in that shitty teenage voice.

47

"We should start buying lottery tickets, Marla," I said. "If we win, I can get lipo on my thighs and you can get a plastic surgeon to fix your ugly nose."

"Fuck you!" Marla started crying, but I didn't feel even a little bit bad.

"You think you're so much better than us," Miranda said. "Just like Gentry. You've been looking down at us since you walked in here."

I was a guest in her house, and on another day, I would've kept my mouth shut and made nice. My whole existence since I left home at sixteen was built on being polite to strangers, but I'd reached the end of the line that day. I stood up and put my backpack on.

"I don't *think* I'm better than you. I *am* better than you," I said. Then I felt bad. "I'm really sorry, Gentry."

"Well, fuck you," Brand said. "You're nobody special, you bitch."

"Nay, I may not," Gentry had said to the person he sometimes talked to on his left. He clenched his hand into a fist. "Truly they aren queds, but they aren my kin."

"Oh my god, Little Lord Fauntleroy and his invisible friend," Miranda said.

His own mother said that, and the rest of them laughed.

48

When I walked out, Gentry followed me. We stood in the street, him scratching the back of his neck with both hands. I didn't know him that well, but I knew that meant he was upset.

"It's okay," I said. "You don't need to worry about me. I can get the bus home." Anywhere was better than there. Even a homeless shelter. It wouldn't have been the first time I stayed in one.

"Nay, my lady."

He walked over and opened the passenger door on his truck for me. I don't even remember discussing it, just that Gentry drove us to a motel. I wasn't sure what it would mean for us to get a motel room together, because that stupid kiss was still hanging over me. Whatever happened, I decided, that was up to him. Once we were in the room, he knelt in front of me where I sat on the edge of the bed.

He took my hand — the first time he'd ever touched me — and he didn't seem too sure about how to hold it. I expected his hand to be sweaty. Nervous. But it was dry and steady.

"Lady Zhorzha, canst thou forgive me? I am shamed that my family was uncourteous to thee."

"It's okay. You don't get to choose your

family." I squeezed his hand, to let him know I didn't take it personally, and maybe as an invitation to something else. He squeezed back for a second, and then he let go and stood up.

"I must leave thee," he said. "For I serve the Duke of Bombardier this night. I shall see thee in the morn."

He went and I stayed. Somewhere around one A.M., LaReigne called me, not to tell me I could come home, but to tell me Loudon had kicked her out and what should she do?

In the morning, when Gentry had come back, there I was with Marcus and LaReigne, camped out in a motel room he'd paid for. Even while I was trying to let Gentry off the hook, I was dragging him in deeper. Like I was quicksand, too.

It scared me, because of how awful his family was, and how he put up with it. *My lady, thy servant* started to look like an invitation to use him, and I was afraid I wasn't good enough to resist that temptation. I knew I had to walk away after I borrowed a thousand bucks from him to pay the deposit on an apartment for LaReigne, Marcus, and me. I had mooched off so many people over the years, and I couldn't bring myself to do it to him.

That was why I agreed to do the Trinidad run for Asher the first time. Money from waiting tables got spent as fast as I could make it, but I walked away from that first run with two thousand in cash. After Toby dropped me off, I sat out on the apartment building's steps, waiting for Gentry to show up, like he did most mornings. I hadn't talked to him since I borrowed the money, and I figured that would be the last time. I walked over to his truck and, when he rolled down the window, handed him the thousand dollars. I thanked him and said goodbye. Then I went inside.

Two minutes later, he knocked on the apartment door, and handed me the cash back.

" 'Twas a present, my lady," he said.

I never tried to give him the money again. I used it to buy the piece-of-shit car that was still getting me from one lousy waitressing job to another.

After that, I thought he would go his way, and I'd go mine. We'd never had a relationship or anything, but apparently we had something, because he kept coming around. He never tried to talk to me, but he kept driving by the apartment and the restaurants where I worked. For a while, I worked at this Cantonese place, and Gentry started

coming in and ordering food to go. Sometimes for a bunch of people — his shitty
family, I guessed — but usually just for
himself. After I left that job and went to
work at a Mediterranean place, he started
getting food from there. No matter where I
went, he eventually showed up and got take-
out.

If I'd been afraid of him, I would have felt
differently about the whole thing, but he'd
never said or done anything that seemed
threatening. He'd only touched me that one
time, and he'd never given me so much as a
hard look. After a while, I got used to it. He
became a fixture in my life. LaReigne
started calling him *your stalker,* which stuck,
even though I hated it. As in, "My car
wouldn't start this morning, but your stalker
jumped my battery."

"Maybe he'll start stalking you," I said.

"Please. He was all business. Didn't even
try to flirt with me. He's in love with *you.*"

She didn't believe me that we'd never had
that kind of relationship, and I was sorry
I'd let her joke about him. Yes, he was weird,
but he'd rescued LaReigne, Marcus, and
me, and never asked for anything in return.

Now he'd rescued me again, standing
there in the middle of my mother's wrecked

house, and all I could think of to say about him was "It's complicated."

CHAPTER 6
DOTTIE

My late husband was tall and handsome, the sort of man who draws women's attention everywhere he goes. Our girls both took after Leroy in their own way, LaReigne because she was beautiful and Zhorzha because she was tall. In fact, she was taller than her new boyfriend and both of the federal marshals who came to talk with us.

Mansur, who did most of the talking, was an older black man, quite stout around the middle. Smith, who didn't talk much, was a younger white man, wearing a suit like a bowl of oatmeal. They introduced themselves but didn't offer to shake hands. Not that Zhorzha gave any indication that would be acceptable. She stood there with her arms crossed over her chest, prickly as a cactus.

The marshals started out very polite, letting me know how concerned they were about finding LaReigne safe. They were polite until I started asking questions.

"There is very little information I can give out right now, because of our investigation and ongoing security issues at the facility," Mansur said.

"Well, goodness, I'm not asking you to tell me how they broke out or where the secret tunnels are. Imagine!"

"The fact is, we didn't come here to brief you. We're hoping you might be able to tell us something about your daughter that will help us find her."

"What do you think we can tell you?" Zhorzha said. "My mother just wants to know *something*. Is — is LaReigne alive?"

"We have no reason to suspect that she's been harmed," Mansur said.

"Well, thank you for that," I said. Zhorzha snorted and turned her back on the marshals.

"Did she ever talk to you about the inmates she volunteered with?" Smith said.

"I asked her if it was safe," I said. "These aren't men like my husband. He was a good man. Of course, yes, he was involved in that robbery, but he was not a violent man."

"Did she ever mention these men to you?" Smith asked. "Tague Barnwell. Conrad Ligett?"

"Which is the younger one? The handsome one?"

Zhorzha scowled at me, but with regards to LaReigne, it was certainly a valid question. She'd never been interested in homely men, and why should she be when she looked like that?

"Barnwell is in his thirties. Ligett is in his forties," Mansur said. "I'm not sure I would describe either of them as handsome."

"Well, Ligett is bald," Smith said, which was at least useful information. I couldn't imagine LaReigne falling in love with a bald man, and, after all, that's what they were insinuating. Why would they question us unless they thought LaReigne was involved somehow? And why would LaReigne be involved unless there was a handsome man? That's the kind of girl she was. She got that from me.

"Does the name *Craig Van Eck* ring any bells for you? He's serving a life sentence for murdering a police officer and his family," Mansur said.

"Yes, he was a friend of my husband's. He had flowers sent to me after Leroy passed away." I'd never asked why Craig was in prison. He was Leroy's friend; that was enough for me.

"What did these guys do? Barnwell and Ligett," Zhorzha said. "Why were they in prison?"

"They're both serving life sentences for that shooting at the Muslim student center five or six years ago." Mansur looked at his notebook as though he needed to look that up, whereas I knew it perfectly well from watching the news. They'd mentioned it dozens of times.

"So the prison let her volunteer with murderers?" Zhorzha paced into the kitchen, and when she came back she stayed behind my chair, where I couldn't see her. Her breathing sounded sniffly, like she was trying not to cry.

"Did she ever talk to you about these men?" Apparently that was the only thing Smith knew how to say.

"I recognize the name *Tague*. Not the other one," Zhorzha said. "And she talked about a few of the volunteers. This woman named Molly. LaReigne stayed at her house a few times, when she had a headache and didn't want to drive home at night. So you're telling me you don't know anything yet? Two prisoners can escape, and there's no surveillance footage or anything?"

"Actually," Mansur said. "We have surveillance footage. It shows your sister driving away with the escapees and the other volunteer."

"So you at least know the make and model of the car they're in?" I said.

"Ma'am, it was her own car. That's one of the reasons we'd like to know if she ever talked about Barnwell or Ligett."

"What's that supposed to mean?" Zhorzha said. "Yes, she knew the one guy. Yes, she talked about him. That doesn't mean she helped him escape."

"Miss Trego, you understand, we have to follow all possible leads. There are —"

"That's fucking bullshit. Why aren't you out looking for my sister?"

"Zhorzha, there's no need for that kind of language," I said. "Don't be such a hot-head." Just as she was about to open her mouth and spill out another heap of curses, the door to the garage opened, and Gentry came stomping into the room.

"My lady," he said. "These knaves outragen thee?"

"I'm fine. I just lost my temper," she said.

I'd thought it was charming at first, but it was really too much that he talked that way in front of the marshals. There was a time for that sort of thing, and this was not it. Still, he stood in between her and the marshals, looking uneasy but defensive. Zhorzha was overdue for a man who wanted to protect her.

"And who is this?" Mansur said.

"A friend of mine, who also doesn't know anything," she said.

The four of them stood in the middle of the living room, Zhorzha towering over the three men. She may have gotten her height from her father, but I don't know where she got her red hair or her temper.

"Mrs. Trego," Mansur said. "Like you, our goal is to get LaReigne back safely, and recapture two dangerous men. If you or your daughter think of anything that might be useful, and, obviously, if you hear from LaReigne, definitely give us a call. Here's my card." Instead of handing it to me, he tossed it onto the side table.

"We can show ourselves out," Smith said, but Gentry followed them to the door, and I heard him bolt it after them.

Once they were gone, Zhorzha went out to the garage and brought Marcus back inside.

"I think we're going to go now," she said. "Give Grandma a hug, buddy."

"Who are all those people outside, Grandma?" he said, as he climbed up on my lap.

"Oh, some people who want to talk to me, but I don't feel like talking to them right now."

"Why not? When's Mommy coming home?"

"Soon, sweetie," I said, but it broke my heart to tell him that same old lie.

CHAPTER 7
ZEE

All I cared about was getting past the reporters, and getting Marcus out of there. Gentry piggybacked him out the front door and down the street to where his truck was parked behind my car. Before I realized what he intended, he'd opened the truck's passenger door and lifted Marcus in. The reporters were already coming, dragging their equipment with them, so I got in after Marcus, while Gentry went around to the driver's side. With the doors closed and locked, I tried to think clearly, and I thought about Gentry's horrible family.

"I think I'll get a motel room for me and Marcus," I said.

"I would that ye comen with me. That I might keep you safe."

"I don't think I can take your family right now."

"Nay, my lady. 'Tis well," he said. "I spake with my father. Ye two aren welcome."

Before I could answer, he started the truck and backed it down the block, leaving the reporters behind us. Gentry drove, not to Miranda's house, which was down off Harry, but to one of those twisty neighborhoods northeast of Rock and Kellogg.

I wondered if maybe Miranda had won the lottery, right up until we went inside, and a woman who definitely wasn't Miranda came to meet us.

"My mother, Lady Charlene," Gentry said. "Mother, this be Lady Zhorzha. And her nephew, Master Marcus."

"It's so lovely to finally meet you, Lady Zhorzha! We've heard so much about you." The woman put out her hand and I took it, but I was too confused to say anything.

First of all, she was the only person to ever pronounce my name right the first time.

Second of all, Gentry had apparently traded in his old family for a new one. Because Miranda was a scrawny white woman with bleached hair. This version of his mother was a black woman in reading glasses with white hair pulled up on top of her head with three big curls the size of Coke cans.

While I was trying to figure all that out, the realization kicked in that Gentry's new mother said my name right, because they'd *heard so much about me.*

"You're his mother?" I said. I didn't know what kind of look I had on my face, but Charlene started laughing and squeezed my hand tighter.

"Oh, I forgot you must have met Miranda. You didn't tell her, Gentry?"

"Nay, my lady," he said with his chin tucked down almost to his chest.

Of course, he hadn't told me anything, because he hadn't spoken to me in two years, except to order food. Did Charlene not know that? She couldn't know that, could she?

"Miranda's his biological mother. A few years ago, he decided he wanted to try having a relationship with her and his half siblings. That would have been close to the same time he met you."

"Oh. I did not know that," I said. It was the only polite thing I could think of. "It's so nice to meet you."

"Aunt Zee." Marcus pulled on my arm. "I gotta go."

"Could we use your bathroom?"

"Lord, yes. Here I am keeping you standing in the foyer. Come all the way in. Bathroom is down the hall, second door on the right," Charlene said.

The house was one of those long 1950s

ranches. Left off the foyer was a great room with a vaulted ceiling, a fireplace, and sliding glass doors onto a patio. On the right was the hallway to the bedrooms. We went down the hall, wrestling Marcus out of his backpack along the way. I got him through the door and found the light switch, but when I went to step outside and close the door, he was standing there with a sad look on his face. The front of his blue jeans was a lot darker than the rest.

"Oh, fuck," I said, because I was the worst aunt in the world. He started crying.

"I'm sorry, Aunt Zee."

"No. I'm sorry. It's okay." I got down on my knees and hugged him, wet pants and all. Then I backtracked to the hallway and grabbed his book bag. We got him cleaned up and into dry pants.

When we came out of the bathroom, Charlene was waiting in the hall.

"Is everything okay?" she said.

"Just a little accident. Could I get a plastic bag?"

Before I knew what she was going to do, she reached out and took Marcus' wet pants from me. In her bare hand, like a woman who has raised boys.

"Let's just run these through the washer." I followed her down the hallway, with Marcus coming after me all hangdog. We passed Gentry at the kitchen counter with a whole row of knives laid out in front of him. Marcus stopped to look.

"Don't you sharpen my knives down to nothing. If you're feeling anxious, you sharpen your own knives," Charlene said. "Gentry, are you hearing me?"

"I hear thee, my lady," was his answer.

"If it's too much trouble, we can go," I said, once I was alone with her in the laundry room. "I don't want to be a bother."

"Do you have somewhere else to go?" She started the washer and pitched Marcus' clothes in.

I had money for a motel room, but for how long? And what if I needed that money for something else?

"Not really," I said.

"Well, I'd say that answers that."

"I'm sorry." I may not have peed my pants in her house, but I kind of felt that way.

"The words you're looking for are *thank you.*"

"I'm sorry. Thank you." I thought she'd said it to scold me, but she laughed and patted my shoulder.

"That was close. And you're very welcome."

In the kitchen, Gentry was sharpening

knives while Marcus watched.

"Now that you've sharpened my knives, shall we cook dinner?" Charlene said.

"Gladly," Gentry said.

"Can I help with something?" I said.

"Oh, no. He'll have these knives so sharp you'd likely lose a finger. Besides, I cannot imagine he would permit the lady Zhorzha to dirty her hands with scullery work."

"You can call me Zee. Everybody does."

"Well, I have it from the lady's mouth then." Charlene leaned in close to me and fake whispered, "Most people actually call me Charlene, not Lady Charlene."

Gentry made a few more swipes across the whetstone, until Charlene reached out and tapped her nail on the counter. He immediately laid the knife down and started scratching the back of his neck.

"We're going to make some chicken stew. Do you like herbes de Provence, Marcus?"

"What is that?" I was glad he seemed interested in Gentry and his knives, because up til then he'd just looked sad and confused.

"Well, we cheat and put in some spices the people in Provence don't use, but it's a nice stew with chicken and potatoes. Do you like chicken and potatoes?"

Marcus nodded.

"Good. Why don't you sit up here and have a snack while I wash vegetables?"

"What can I do to help?" I said, after I got Marcus seated on one of the stools at the kitchen island.

"Not a thing, hon. Do you want a Capri Sun?"

"Yes!" Marcus said.

"What about you, Zee?"

"Water's fine for me."

Charlene set three pouches on the countertop anyway. I put a straw in one for Marcus, one for Gentry, and then one for myself.

"I thought so," she said. "You sit here and have a snack while Gentry tries to impress you."

I took the stool next to Marcus, where Charlene had laid out a plate of cheese, lunch meat, and crackers.

Marcus and Gentry took a sip out of their straws, so I took one, too, trying not to smile like a dope. It was my favorite thing, that first night staying with a friend, when everything was new, and everyone was being polite, and I could sit there drinking my Capri Sun and wait for someone to feed me and give me a place to sleep. It was pathetic, but those were some of my happiest memories.

"Thou needst not tell me again. 'Twas of no matter the first time and groweth less so with each telling," Gentry said, and he sounded pissed off.

"You can finish that conversation later," Charlene said. "Right now, you have work to do." She opened the fridge and handed Gentry an entire chicken wrapped in plastic.

He laid a couple of knives out next to the cutting board. Rearranged them. Nodded. Then he eviscerated that chicken. Took every bit of meat off the bones, and cubed it up. That went into a big skillet with oil to cook, while Gentry got out a clean cutting board and another set of knives. He started with onions and garlic, shucking them and dicing them to go in with the chicken.

Charlene stood at the sink washing vegetables: potatoes, carrots, peppers, zucchini, celery. Once she had a pile of potatoes accumulated, Gentry carried them to the counter. He peeled them with a paring knife, faster than my mother could with a peeler. Round and around, so that most of the peels came off in one piece. The carrots he stripped with the flat of the blade. He cored the peppers, took the ends off the zucchini and the celery.

"Go ahead, show off," Charlene said.

Gentry lifted his head and smiled. He took

the first potato and halved it, halved it again lengthwise, then cubed it. All in about five seconds. He went through the rest of the stuff like he was a goddamn Cuisinart, until there was an avalanche of vegetables on the counter. By then the chicken was cooked, and everything went into a big Crock-Pot with seasonings. If I was supposed to be impressed, I was. And convinced that Charlene was his real family. Miranda and her monsters may have been his biological mother and siblings, but they were strictly Taco Bell people.

"What did you think of that?" I asked Marcus, but he was sitting there like an owl.

"I see somebody who needs a nap," Charlene said. "Actually, I see three somebodies who need naps. Gentry, get some sheets and help your lady make up the guest room."

The phrase *your lady* made me uneasy, like I was there under false pretenses, but I was too tired to deal with any of it. I got Marcus by the hand and followed Gentry down the hallway to the guest room. He opened the closet and said, "Which thee liketh best? Blue or green?"

It struck me as a really funny thing to ask, but I said, "Green."

While Marcus stood in the middle of the bedroom, Gentry and I made the two twin beds with green sheets. All those years of sleeping on people's couches and floors had done a number on my bed-making skills. Mine ended up looking slept in from the start, but the one Gentry made for Marcus had hospital corners.

"If thou needest aught, I am in the chamber next," Gentry said as he bowed. Then he went out and shut the door.

Sometimes you had to talk Marcus down to a nap, but he was so tired all I had to do was take off his shoes. I was out almost as fast.

I woke up to a sound I couldn't identify. Whacking and grunting, and every once in a while a thud and a shout. The light in the room had changed, from bright to soft yellow. I almost didn't understand what that meant, because I never got to take naps in the afternoon. It felt more like waking up in a different universe than like time had passed. I reached for my phone, but I'd forgotten to plug it in, and it was dead.

The whacking and grunting had stopped, so that I wondered if I'd dreamt it. Marcus was still sleeping, and even me kissing his forehead didn't wake him up, so I left him there. There was nobody out in the great room or in the kitchen, but I could smell dinner cooking. I was about to go look in the dining room when the patio door opened and Gentry walked in. His hair was dripping wet and he was wearing something that looked like quilted pajamas.

"Is it raining out?" I said. It didn't make sense to me, because I hadn't heard rain, but I couldn't come up with any other reason that he would be soaking wet.

"Nay." Before he could say anything else, a kid walked through the door behind him.

"Oh, wow! You're Lady Zhorzha," the kid said. He was maybe fifteen, Asian, a little taller than Gentry. Also damp and wearing quilted pajamas.

"My brother Trang," Gentry said.

We were about to shake hands when Charlene called from the dining room, "You boys take those nasty, sweaty clothes off!"

Not rain. Sweat. I pulled my hand back and Trang grinned at me.

"Sorry, we were jousting," he said, which I remembered was how Gentry had injured his shoulder.

Charlene came in carrying a laundry hamper, and the two of them stripped down to T-shirts and running shorts that were plastered to them with sweat.

"Dinner's almost ready, so you two need to get cleaned up," she said.

"Can I do anything to help?" I said.

71

"No, come and meet my husband."

I followed her into the dining room and shook hands with her husband, Bill, who was a big bald white guy with a gray beard.

"Well, we are honored to have you here, Lady Zhorzha," he said. I couldn't tell whether they were being serious with that.

"Thank you for having me." How many times had I said that to how many people? How many friends' parents' houses where I tried to be as polite and invisible as I could?

"Bill." Charlene tilted her head toward the table. He reached out and folded over the newspaper in front of him. Today's paper. With LaReigne's face now hidden. That jolted me back to reality. I took a step backward and almost fell over on top of a little girl in a wheelchair who'd come up behind me. She was so tiny I couldn't guess how old she was — maybe four or five — but she wore great big glasses and her hair in a pair of afro puffs.

"Oh god, I'm sorry," I said.

"And this is Elana, Gentry's sister," Charlene said.

"Lady Elana," the girl said.

"Well, Lady Elana, this is Lady Zhorzha," Bill said.

I didn't know what to make of the fact that she looked starstruck. She held out her hand, so I took it very gently, because it seemed too fragile to shake.

"It's nice to meet you, Lady Elana," I said.

The starstruck fell off that fast. She squinted at me and pulled her hand back.

"You're not really Lady Zhorzha. You don't talk right at all."

I looked at Charlene and Bill, hoping for some help, but she rolled her eyes and he was trying not to laugh.

"I'm sorry, but I really am Zhorzha," I said. Elana wasn't convinced.

"Dinner's about ready. Why don't you get Marcus up and herd the boys this way?" Charlene said.

Marcus came awake the way he always did, as belligerent as a prizefighter, but I rousted him out and got him to the bathroom. Just like Gentry had said, his room was next to mine. Because Charlene had told me to "herd the boys" to dinner, I knocked, but the door wasn't latched, and it swung open.

The room was almost identical to the guest room. Two twin beds. Two nightstands. Only it wasn't a bedroom. It was an armory with beds in it. All over the walls, hanging off hooks and sitting on shelves, were swords and helmets and shields and pieces of armor I didn't know the names for. Chain mail shirts and big metal gloves. And more swords. And knives. And an axe. And a thing that looked like an axe on a long pole.

"My lady," Gentry said, as he stood up from the foot of his bed, wearing nothing but boxers. Of course, because he'd just taken a shower, and I'd barged into his room without being invited. At least Trang was dressed.

"I'm sorry. I wasn't expecting the door —"

"You do have swords," Marcus said. He pushed past me so I couldn't close the door, and stood there as saucer-eyed as I felt, staring at all the glittering blades.

"I have, Master Marcus." With us there as an audience, Gentry pulled on a T-shirt and shorts. Still barefoot, he stepped up onto his bed, lifted the biggest sword off the wall, and brought it down to us. It was a two-handed sword, and it must have been heavy, but Gentry didn't have any trouble with it.

"It's big," Marcus said. It was taller than him. He stared at it with the kind of amazement that was usually reserved for giant Christmas trees and people in superhero costumes.

"Yea," Gentry said. He looked off to his

left and laughed. "A bastard sword for a bastard."

CHAPTER 8
CHARLENE

Zee was not quite what I expected. White and redheaded, that much I knew, because Gentry had described her as "flame-haired and fair." Nobody had had the sense to put the girl in a hat when she was little, and she was freckled all across her cheeks and down to her décolletage. She was taller than Gentry by several inches, at least five eleven. I'd imagined her as a delicate Arthurian princess, but she was solid, with a broad, nervous smile. Trying hard to be polite, but the kind of girl who puts on her good manners like clean, white church gloves. Not the sort of thing you wear all the time.

Because we had guests, I made dinner milder than usual. So many kids weren't used to eating anything but chicken nuggets, and Marcus did pick out and eat some chicken and potatoes, but most of his dinner was the cheese toast I served on the side. Zee, I got the impression, would have eaten anything I put in front of her, to be polite. The only way to tell she didn't care for it was that she turned down seconds.

Gentry of course didn't. As he was coming back to the table with his and Trang's bowls, Elana whispered to him, "You said her hair was *pretty.*"

Gentry hesitated, setting the bowls down before he answered her: " 'Tis."

" 'Tis not."

"Elana. We do not talk about our guests." I gave her a warning look, but the little sass box ignored me.

" 'Tis not," she said.

Gentry sat down and picked up his spoon. Then he put it back down.

"Sister, thou shalt make me wroth if thou art uncourteous to Lady Zhorzha," he said.

"It's okay," Zee said.

"He said your hair was red, but it's orange," Elana said.

"It's from eating too many carrots." Zee reached over and took a chunk of carrot out of Elana's bowl and ate it. That made Elana giggle. Gentry smiled, and then Elana couldn't decide whether she liked Zee or was jealous.

We usually watched a little TV before Elana's bedtime, but there was an immediate problem when Zee sat on the couch next to

Marcus, and Gentry sat on the floor in front of her. I could tell the whole day was wearing on him, because as soon as he sat down, he started stimming. One hand at first, scratching his neck. Then after a few minutes, both hands scratching his shoulders, so that his arms were pressed up near his ears with his elbows pointed up.

"Does your back itch?" Zee said. "I can scratch it for you. If you want."

I thought it would go nowhere. Sometimes he went so far away when he was stimming that it was hard to get him back. After a few minutes, though, he nodded and scooted back far enough that he could have leaned against her legs.

Zee started scratching his shoulders, just below the seams of his T-shirt. I couldn't see the look on his face, but Bill and Trang were both looking at him. They glanced at each other, then at me. I gave a very small shrug, because I didn't want Zee to notice that we were all watching and waiting to see what would happen.

"That's not fair! Why does she get to scratch your back?" Elana said, and that put an end to that. Zee jerked her hands back, and Gentry jumped up.

"Child, it must be your bedtime," I said. "Why don't you boys go to bed, too?"

Elana put up some crying and fussing, but I finally got her down to sleep. Coming back past Trang and Gentry's room, the light was off, but I could hear them talking. Swords and armor? Or love and ladies? It was always one or the other with them.

Bill had turned over to the news, and that's what we were watching when Zee came back from putting Marcus to bed. She sat down to watch with us, but it was only a few minutes before the news cycle came back around to the situation at the prison. Bill reached for the remote.

"No, it's okay," Zee said. "I feel a little better seeing her. It lets me think she's maybe okay."

"I'm sure she is," I said. "You both seem like strong girls."

We watched, but there was nothing new to the story. *Manhunt continues,* that was the sum total of it.

"Would you like a little wine? I thought I might have a glass before bed," I offered.

That was how I lured her into the dining room, with a glass of that cheap sparkling peach wine I liked. She didn't seem like a girl with expensive taste, either.

"So, tell me about yourself. I think you can guess getting information from Gentry isn't all that reliable, since he didn't tell you about Miranda."

Zee took a sip of her wine, and then a swallow. She had nice fingernails. Not painted, but clean, neat ovals. Good nails for scratching.

"Well, you know. My sister is Wiccan, like they said on the news. She's part of a volunteer ministry at the prison." She was embarrassed, which I hadn't intended. I reached over to put my hand on hers, and she let me.

"What about you, honey? I know you're working as a waitress. It's the only reason Gentry would ever eat at a restaurant. Are you in school?"

"No. My sister's taking some classes to finish her degree, but I never — I'm not good at that kind of thing."

"Not everybody is. So, you had a motorcycle wreck? That's how you and Gentry met?" I tried. I appreciated that she was more comfortable talking about her sister, but I felt like I deserved to know more about her, considering I'd waited two years to meet her.

"Ma'am, I — I feel like I owe you an explanation about me and Gentry. I don't really — we're not dating or anything. I don't know what he's told you and I don't want to be rude but —"

I had to get ahold of both her hands and squeeze them before she quit trying to explain. I did my best, but couldn't stop myself from laughing.

"Oh, honey. It's okay. I know you and Gentry aren't dating. I'm not sure he — I'm not sure how that would go," I said.

"It was awkward." Zee gave me an embarrassed smile.

Then it was my turn to be surprised, because I didn't know there'd been *dating*. I'd laughed at the very idea. I let go of her hands so that we could have a drink of our wine.

"A few times, I tried to convince him to take you flowers, but he didn't think it would be appropriate, because you might think he was pursuing you."

"Except after we broke up or whatever happened, after I met his other family, he kept coming by my house, and where I work," she said. I felt bad for both of them, because obviously she was confused.

"He hasn't told you why?" I said.

She shook her head, so I took the plunge I'd taken with a few other girls: I explained about his autism, which she seemed to have figured out on her own. Then I told her about the voices he'd been hearing since he was a boy. Gawen, who was like an overgrown playmate, but a bit of a bully. Hildegard, who was pious but awfully judgmental.

"And the Witch, who is sort of Gentry's spiritual adviser," I said.

"Really? A witch?"

Zee laughed, which was new to me. Most people didn't find any of it funny. She wasn't the first girl I'd explained Gentry's voices to. I wasn't proud of myself, but with a few girls, I used the explanation to get rid of them. Girls who seemed needy or inclined to take advantage of his good nature.

With the Navarro girl from church, I'd had higher hopes. I'd imagined that if I explained carefully, she wouldn't be nervous about all of Gentry's side conversations. I was half right. She stopped being nervous, but her interest in Gentry immediately turned from romantic to pitying. Not that he noticed either way.

Of course, all those girls came along before the Witch pointed to Zhorzha in the physical therapy clinic and said, *There she is. That's the girl I've been telling you about.*

"The Witch has been telling him for years that he has a special duty," I said. "It turns out you're his special duty."

"I don't understand," Zee said.

"The Witch told him he was supposed to protect you, so that's what he's been trying to do. He didn't mention that to you?"

"I don't know. Maybe he did. Honestly, I don't always understand what he says. I got a C in English in high school, and we never got to Shakespeare. I wasn't in the advanced class."

I hadn't been sure what I thought of her until then. She wasn't stupid, but a lot of people won't admit their own ignorance. I could respect that.

"Do you know what a champion is?" I said.

"Yeah. It's like a knight who defends a lady, right? But in romance novels it's more romantic, I guess."

"Well, he means it in the chivalric sense. In the knightly tradition, a champion is a knight in service of a lady. Gentry only wants to protect you, so you don't need to worry about him or his intentions. Today was pretty important for him, that he was able to help you. I want you to know that."

"And there isn't anything they can do to keep him from hearing those voices?" she said. It was what people asked: *can't he be treated or cured?*

"Oh, honey, no. Plenty of people hear voices, a lot more than you might imagine. The only ones who ever make the news are the ones who have a serious untreated mental illness. The rest of them just go on with their lives. Mostly, I think Gentry's voices are useful to him. They help him navigate the world, when that's not easy for him."

"But why me? Why is he supposed to be my champion?"

"Oh, you'd have to ask the Witch about that. But why not you? Didn't you need a champion today?"

"I guess I did. I didn't know he was so into this medieval stuff. Being a k-night," Zee said. I laughed to let her know it was okay to think that was a weird way to say it.

"Oh, yes. Ever since he learned to read, he's been obsessed with knights and castles. You should ask to borrow some of his books. I know he'd be happy to have you read them."

"But he's serious, like with the swords and everything."

"He's always been serious about it. Enough that it's caused some problems. When he was eleven, he ran away because he wanted to become a knight. His older brother, Carlees, was on a Boy Scout camping trip that weekend, and Gentry really wanted to go, but we didn't feel he was ready yet. Socially. Instead, we told him he could camp at home. My sister, Bernice, had given him a little pup tent that he set up in the backyard.

"We were getting ready to host a barbecue for Memorial Day weekend. Bill went out to light the grill, and Gentry was gone. He'd packed up his camp and left. Bless us, I think we actually laughed about it a little. When the guests came, we went out walking around the neighborhood, figuring we'd find him at the park or the school playground. Someplace obvious. Then it got dark and we panicked. Called the police. Our pastor."

"Where was he?" Zee said.

"Oh, we didn't find him that night. Or the next night. A ranger up at El Dorado State Park came across his camp five days later. Gentry had walked all the way there, cross-country. Pitched his little tent, built himself a fire, picked some berries, and caught a fish for dinner."

"Oh my god. And he was how old?"

"Not quite twelve. It's a funny story now, but there were a few days where I thought we might lose custody of him. We'd had him since he was three, as a foster, before we adopted him. After that we had to be much stricter with him."

"Why did he run away?"

"He didn't even see it that way. He and

Gawen were on an adventure. There was this book, his favorite book at the time — I don't remember the title of it, as embarrassing as that is."

"One of those Barbara Leonie Picard books," Bill called. He'd been listening all along.

"If you say so. A historical book anyway. About a young boy in medieval times who runs away and becomes a knight. That's what Gentry was planning to do. After that, we were off the deep end into all the medieval romances. Gawain and Yvain and Arthur and Lancelot. Then we took him to a meeting for the SCA — the Society for Creative Anachronism — and he found a knight who was willing to take him on as a page.

"Until then, he'd struggled with speaking, but learning Middle English took a lot of the pressure off, because everyone starts on the same footing. Except Gentry. Even when he was twelve, he spoke better than most of the adults at those get-togethers. Of course, his voices speak in Middle English so, in some ways, it's his native language."

"That's kind of cool," Zee said, which I thought was sweet. I appreciated that she seemed interested.

"Then after he graduated high school, he

got very serious about historical medieval battle, with the swords and the armor, which I am not fond of. He's been injured a few times, as you know, but no more gallivanting around in search of knightly adventures. We like to keep him close to home."

From the front room, over the drone of the television, I heard Bill say, "Hey there, little man."

Then Marcus said, "Mommy! Aunt Zee, Mommy's on TV." When all the blood drained out of Zee's face, I could see how much she looked like her sister.

She jumped up and ran toward the family room, and I went after her.

CHAPTER 9
MARCUS

I wanted to stay and watch Mommy on TV, but Aunt Zee took me back to the bedroom.

"Mommy's famous now!" I said.

"I guess, kind of. Come here. Get in bed."

"Is that why Mommy isn't home yet? Because she's on TV?"

"Yeah, that's part of why Mommy can't come home yet. Look, I need you to listen to me for a minute." She made me get in bed, and pulled the covers up over me.

"Can I call Mommy?" I said.

"Not right now you can't."

"Why not?"

Aunt Zee put her hands up over her face, so I knew I was talking too much and making her head hurt.

"You know how Mommy is busy on Monday nights, right?" she said.

"Yeah, because she's volunteer." I didn't know what *volunteer* was, but she didn't come home til after my bedtime on Monday nights.

"Right. She volunteers at the prison. Remember how she told you it's the prison where your granddad Leroy used to be, right?"

"Because he did a bad thing. He stole something. That's why it's not okay to steal things. You can go to prison." There were lots of things you weren't supposed to do. Daddy went to prison, too, because Mommy said he made a bad decision. You could go to prison for that.

"Well, something happened at the prison on Monday. Some bad guys made Mommy go somewhere with them," Aunt Zee said.

"What bad guys? Did they steal something? Why did Mommy go with them?"

"She didn't want to. She wanted to come home, but they made her go with them. That's why she can't come home yet."

"When is she coming home?" I said.

"I don't know."

"But if she's on real TV, she can come home, right? If she's on real TV, she's somewhere," I said. We talked about that at school, how some stuff on TV is real and some stuff on TV is not real. Like *Sponge-Bob* and *My Little Pony.* They're not real.

"Well, yeah, she's somewhere. I don't

know where, but the police are going to find her and bring her home," Aunt Zee said.

"When are they bringing her home?"

"I don't know, buddy."

I didn't like Mommy being gone. Or bad guys taking her with them. Aunt Zee didn't like it, either, and I didn't like her to cry. I sat up so I could hug her.

"But why?" I said.

"I don't know. I wish I had more answers, but you should go back to sleep now. Maybe we'll know more tomorrow." Aunt Zee pulled the covers up over me again.

"What if Mommy calls and we don't answer because we're asleep?"

"My phone is on. If she calls, it'll wake us up. I promise."

"What if — what if —" I wanted to be brave, but it made me so scared I cried. "What if bad guys come while I'm asleep and take you?"

"Me? No. Nobody's gonna kidnap me. I'm so big, how would they carry me away?" Aunt Zee said.

"But what if it was someone bigger than you?"

"Then I would scream for help. Gentry's right next door, and he has his swords. He would come and protect us from the bad guys. Remember how he picked you up when those guys were bothering us at Grandma's house?"

I nodded, but I wondered if Gentry was big enough to pick Aunt Zee up like he did me. Because maybe he could take her away.

"I'm going to stay right here with you, okay? So you know I'm here," Aunt Zee said.

"Okay."

It was a little bed like mine at home, but Aunt Zee laid down next to me and put her head on my pillow. Her hair was all long, and it tickled my face. I tried to go to sleep, but every time I closed my eyes, I saw bad guys coming to kidnap her away.

CHAPTER 10
GENTRY

'Twas long my habit, after a night's labor for the Duke of Bombardier, to pass the keep where Lady Zhorzha dwelled with her sister. As they weren not there, I passed instead by the dragon's lair. All was still, but there was a man in a car that was strange to me. When I came to his door, he looked at me not, tho I stood before him. His window was open to release the smoke from his cigarettes. From the leavings upon the ground, he had smoked for many hours.

"What is thy purpose here?" 'Twas ill-mannered of me, but there was no reason he should be there unless he meant harm.

"None of your goddamn business, kid," he said.

"Certs 'tis."

"Public street. I can park here if I want." He closed his window.

I walked back to my truck and thought upon what to do. Behind the seat lay several weapons — a sword, a mace, a dagger — but they could not serve me for the nonce. I returned to the man's car with my phone that I might make an image of his license plate. Then he would leave, making a wanton sign with his hand ere he drove thence.

For a time, I stood in the street and thought of the lady dragon enthroned upon her hoard, alone. More alone than I, for when I departed the dragon's lair, I followed a clear path to my father's keep, where my lady mother prepared the morning meal at the hearth. There also, in the safety of my father's household, was Lady Zhorzha. Lest Gawen should mock me, I held the thought for only a moment, but she glowed as ember in a heap of ash.

"Good morrow. Slept ye well?" I asked, upon finding my parents breaking their fast.

"Well enough," my father said. "That CPAP may save my life yet."

"If only because I won't be tempted to smother you with a pillow," my mother said.

"And the lady? How fared she?" I dared not speak her name, for she was still an ember to me, and I felt the warmth of her presence unseen.

"She had a hard time getting the little man settled down," my father said. "He was pretty upset."

"They must be exhausted, and the news about her sister isn't great," my mother said. "They found her car abandoned near the Nebraska border."

"Her sister yet liveth?" I believed not that my parents possessed sure knowledge, but I longed to hear they held some hope for my lady's sister.

"Well, it seems to me that if they'd done something to her they would've left her with the car when they ditched it. So I think that's promising," my father said.

'Twas my habit to bathe ere I broke my fast, but as I went down the passage, Lady Zhorzha opened the door of the guest chamber and stepped out. She wore naught but a blouse and her braies. I would spare her my gaze, but mine eyes caught upon the sight of her bare legs. Her right thigh was covered in black markings that graved her pale flesh. I knew not why. As a punishment? As a claim upon her?

"Oh, hey," she said. "I was going to take a shower, but if you need the bathroom first, that's cool. I can wait."

"My lady." I would assure her that she might do as she wished, but words came not to my tongue. Fearing that I gave offense, I bowed to her, but she retreated to her chamber.

Before my staring eyes, as she turned from me, the marking upon her shank gained the form of a fantastical beast — the hindquarters and tail of a dragon. In the strike of my heart, she leapt from ember to flame.

"Scarred like a pagan," Hildegard said.

"Like a pagan priestess." Gawen was right, for there was power in such graving.

In the bath, I opened the spigot and chastised myself for the heat in my blood. Hildegard lashed me, saying, "Art thou ashamed for thine eyes' offense?"

"I averted my gaze," I said.

"Wert thou pure of heart, thou wouldst not need to avert thine eyes. Thou couldst look upon her naked without shame."

I protested not, tho 'twas untrue. I might do no such thing with a pure heart.

"She is thine to protect and no further," Hildegard said, but the Witch said naught.

Gawen laughed and said, "The lady inflameth thy liver. Thou shalt have no relief but by thine own hand."

Sooth, he was right.

CHAPTER 11
ZEE

People say, "Stay as long as you need," but they don't mean that literally. Most people don't even mean it past a week. No matter how good a guest you are, how cheerfully you help out around the house, eventually, your host starts to frown at the pile of blankets you try to keep out of sight when you're not actually sleeping on the couch.

Even with LaReigne, I sometimes felt like she was giving me that look: *Oh, you're still here, sitting on the couch, waiting for me to go to bed so you can go to bed, even though I'd like to finish watching this movie.*

Except for the year I was with Nicholas, I'd been living like that since I left home. Even before that, I felt like an invisible guest in Mom's house. Our house had always been cluttered with her stuff, but it got a lot worse after Dad went to prison. By the time LaReigne graduated from high school, Mom was off the deep end into hoarding.

Like if she couldn't keep LaReigne at home, she was going to collect stuff that couldn't leave her.

LaReigne went off to Seward County Community College on a cheerleading scholarship, while I stayed at home trying to keep Mom's stuff at bay. My living space was a twin bed, while the rest of my room got taken over by boxes of collectibles and books and craft projects. I had to start keeping my clothes in a canvas bag hung on a hook from the ceiling above my bed. Otherwise, I'd come home from school and have to dig it out from under whatever new treasures Mom was "just storing" in my bedroom.

When the sink faucet stopped working, Mom wouldn't let a plumber in the house, and we couldn't take showers, because of the stuff stacked in one end of the tub. I'd fill up a bucket from the kitchen sink to brush my teeth and take what Mom called a *whore's bath* with a washrag.

Then one day at the beginning of my junior year, I came home from school and, after squeezing through the gap in my bedroom door and crawling over the beaver dam of clothes and magazines, I found that my bed had been taken over by three plastic bins of old bridesmaids dresses and half a dozen cardboard shipping boxes. Mom had put them there because my bed was one of the last empty spaces in the house.

At first my friend Mindy and her family were cool with the fact that I was "having trouble at home," but that only lasted a week. Then I was out on my ass, toting my sleeping bag back to my mother's house, where I slept one night in the hallway, wedged in between the wall and stacks of magazines all the way up to the ceiling. I couldn't even turn over, so I laid there all night like a mummy with my arms tucked across my chest, listening to mice scurry around.

I burned through eleven friendships in high school. Eight my junior year. Three my senior year. Those were the early days, before I figured out that people didn't mean I could stay as long as I needed. Before I figured out that sex made a difference. It's harder for people to kick you out when you're having sex with them. Or their dad. Or whatever.

One of the first things you learn from sleeping over at people's houses is that everybody's family is weird. Maybe not your family's kind of weird, but weird.

So Gentry's family was super nice, and it was great to have my own bed, and for Marcus and me to have our own room, but I knew Charlene didn't really mean we could stay as long as we needed. Plus, living with LaReigne for the past two years, I'd forgotten how much hard work it was being a guest.

I missed having the option of going back to sleep. That was the trade-off to being a perpetual guest. You got to eat and not worry about where it came from, but you didn't get to lie in somebody's guest bed all day and cry. You had to get up.

I had to get up.

I guessed Gentry had just come home from work, because he was wearing steel-toed work boots and jeans instead of cargo shorts. I was wearing the T-shirt and panties I slept in. So that was awkward. After he finished in the bathroom, I took a shower and put on the last pair of clean clothes I had. That was the first thing I needed to do: go by the apartment to get clean clothes for me and Marcus. Before that, I had to get Marcus up, which, considering he'd been up half the night crying and having bad dreams, was almost impossible. It was only eight o'clock, though, so I had a couple hours before work. If I could get him up and take him to Mom's house by then, it would be okay.

When I went out to the front room, Elana was there watching some kind of educational video, and Charlene was in the kitchen.

"Good morning, hon. How do you feel about French toast for breakfast?" she said.

"Oh, you don't need to fix me anything."

"Well, it's already cooking, so you might as well have some. Does Marcus like French toast?"

"Yeah," I said. "He's just having a hard time getting up this morning."

"That's all right. I'll fix him some breakfast when he gets up. Go on, sit down, and I'll bring it to you."

In the dining room, Gentry was reading the newspaper, but he folded it up when I sat down.

"How slept thou, Lady Zhorzha?" he said.

"Oh, okay."

"My mother said thou passed the night ill, that thy nephew was much distressed, and for that I am sorry."

I don't think Gentry understood I was trying to tell a polite lie. "Well, he had to find out eventually, I guess." That was what I said, but then I spent a whole minute trying not to cry.

Charlene carried in a baking pan with these huge, fluffy slabs of French toast on

100

it. It was the most beautiful French toast I had ever seen. Golden brown and bubbly and dusted with powdered sugar. After the first bite, I cut a second one, but didn't eat it. I stuck the syrupy mess in the middle of my palm and stood up.

"It thee liketh not?" Gentry said, and he actually looked at me, so I knew I was acting pretty kooky.

"It's perfect. It's the most amazing French toast I've ever had."

It was so incredible, I carried it down the hallway to Marcus, and waved it under his nose.

"If you get up now, you get French toast," I said. "Otherwise, you're getting oatmeal for breakfast."

That probably wasn't true, but it got him up. I led him down the hallway with the bite of French toast like bait on a hook.

"Look who decided to get out of bed," Charlene said.

He ate two whole pieces without saying a word, which was a record for him. After he finished the second piece, he said, "When can I go see Mommy?"

I'd been thinking about having a second piece of French toast, too, but that killed the urge. I felt like the whole night had been a terrible dream, and I was going to have to live it again. Like *Groundhog Day.*

"Buddy, I don't know."

"But you said the police were going to bring her home. When?" He had a little mustache of syrup and powdered sugar that was so cute I would have laughed, but it was just fucking sad right then.

"They are," I said. "They're gonna find her and bring her home, but I don't know when. I hope really, really soon." All the same stuff I'd told him last night.

"Can we go to the prison and look for her?"

"She's not there. I told you, they took her away. We're gonna go to Grandma —"

"You don't know she's not there if you didn't go look," Marcus said. It was the kind of thing LaReigne told him when he'd lost a toy. *How do you know it's not there if you didn't look?* I guess he thought it worked for everything. He sniffled, but instead of crying, he shouted, "You don't know! You don't know!"

"Master Marcus, be not wroth with thine aunt," Gentry said. I wanted to tell him to mind his own business, but I was a guest in his house. Plus Marcus stopped yelling and looked at Gentry, who took the newspaper and unfolded it. " 'Tis here, writ in the paper. Canst thou read?"

"No. I can only do my alphabet."

Marcus was still sniffling, but he got up on his knees in his chair to look at the paper. Gentry cleared his throat and started reading: "As the manhunt for escaped inmates Tague Barnwell and Conrad Ligett enters the third day, authorities have widened the scope of their search, following the discovery of hostage LaReigne Trego-Gill's car in a rural area near the Nebraska state line."

More than a few times I'd wondered if Gentry ever spoke modern English, but I wasn't sure if this counted. After all, he was reading the newspaper, not making up the sentences himself.

I'd never thought of letting Marcus hear all the news, I guess because I was trying to protect him. Plus, normally, when you read him a story, he asked a hundred questions, and I didn't have answers. He listened to Gentry read the article all the way through in the same slow, steady voice. When Gentry finished, he pushed the paper across the table so Marcus could look at it. Marcus put his finger on LaReigne's picture, and I waited for him to ask something, anything, but he started crying.

I pulled him onto my lap and let him cry. I put my cheek down on the top of his head and took a deep breath. He always smelled like my two favorite things about grade school: recess and art.

Gentry got up and started clearing the dishes. By the time he came back with a rag to wipe off the table, Marcus had mostly calmed down, and I helped him blow his nose on a napkin.

"My lady, I am sorry if I caused him pain," Gentry said.

"It's okay. He needed to hear it. I don't know." I didn't even know what I didn't know. "I need to go to work. Could you take us back to my mom's house, so I can get my car?"

"I shall take thee wheresoever thou wishest. 'Tis my honor."

"I just need to get my car so I can go to work," I said.

"Is it safe, my lady?"

I laughed, because LaReigne had been kidnapped by a couple of Wikkkans, and Gentry was asking if it was safe for me to go to work.

"Why doesn't Marcus stay here for the day?" Charlene said. She was standing in the doorway wearing a professional, concerned smile. I hadn't asked what she did for a living, but she had to be a social worker or something. I wondered whether

Gentry had told her my mother was a hoarder. "Unless you'd rather he stayed with your mother."

"Are you sure? I don't want to be any trouble." It was comfortable to fall back into that. To let someone else make decisions.

"I'm sure Elana would like the company. She has schoolwork this morning, but then we'll probably do a craft project."

"I don't want you to go," Marcus said.

"I'm sorry, buddy, but I need to take care of some things, and I don't want you to have to wait around." I wanted to talk him into agreeing with me, but I'd already made up my mind. Leaving him at Mom's house was almost as reckless as taking him to Colorado. "Besides, Gentry is going with me, so I'll be safe, and you'll be safe here. I'll come back this afternoon, and if you need to check on me, Mrs. Frank can help you call me, okay?"

I worried he was going to cry again, but he nodded and said, "Okay."

At least the reporters were gone when Gentry dropped me off at Mom's. They'd left a bunch of trash. Drink cups, burger wrappers, and cigarette butts right out in front of the house. Assholes.

I wished I could get in my car and leave, but I knew I had to go inside and see Mom.

She was in her chair, watching TV, and the only way I could tell she'd gotten up at all was that her dinner trash was piled next to her chair. A loaf of cheesy garlic bread and a frozen lasagna with a two-liter of Diet Coke. She used to make that when I was younger, but for the three of us to share. Before things got so bad for her.

"Where's Marcus?" she said. "Did you end up staying with Emma?"

"No. We stayed with Gentry's parents. That's where Marcus is."

"You left him with strangers? You should have brought him with you." Mom planted her hands on the arms of her chair, like she was going to get up, but she didn't.

"They're not strangers," I said, which was basically a lie. "They're good people. Besides, I have to go to work."

"At a time like this?" Like there were days I didn't have to work.

"I can't afford to sit around and wait for something to happen."

"That's what you think I'm doing, isn't it? Just sitting around, like some pathetic lump."

Mom pushed against the armrests of her chair, so I went over and got my arms around her. I had to put my foot up on the edge of the chair to get enough leverage to help her stand. My lower back and hip gave off this twangy shudder that I knew I was going to feel for my whole shift. Maybe for the whole week.

"Oh, I'm fine, Zhorzha!" she snapped. "You know, I do manage to get up without your help when you're not here."

Sure, she managed to get up by herself, but there was a dank, sour smell on her that told me she wasn't always making it up in time to get to the bathroom.

"Mom, please, can we not fight?"

"You should have brought Marcus here. I could have watched him while you were at work."

"I'm sorry, but Gentry has a little sister about Marcus' age, and I thought it would be less stressful for him there. Because of all those reporters yesterday. All you're doing is watching the news, and he can't keep seeing that."

"They found your sister's car," Mom said.

"I heard."

I gathered up her dinner trash, carried it to the kitchen, and added it to a plastic bag of what I hoped was trash.

While she was in the bathroom, I sat down in her recliner, but the news hadn't cycled back to anything about the prison-break story yet. I decided to leave before Mom could quiz me about the bag of trash, or accuse me of sneaking around and throwing out valuable things.

"I'm gonna go to work," I yelled. "I love you."

"I love you," she called.

Outside, I took a big breath of fresh air, and carried the plastic bag over to the trash cart. Gentry had pulled his truck around and parked it in front of my car. He was standing there, sort of at attention, watching me, except like always, when I got close to him, he lowered his head and didn't look at me.

"You really don't need to —" I remembered what Charlene had said, about how important helping me was to him, and I felt shitty for trying to get rid of him. "Thank you, Gentry. I really appreciate you looking out for Marcus and me yesterday, and bringing me to get my car. Thanks."

" 'Tis my honor."

"But aren't you tired?" I said. "You should go home and sleep. I'm just gonna go to work."

"Be full of care, my lady. And if thou needest aught, call for me."

"Okay. I will."

I waited until he got in his truck and drove away, because I had a feeling he might follow me otherwise. After he was gone, I checked my phone. Another voicemail from Marcus' other grandparents, the Gills. They'd called last night, too, but I ignored it. I'd messaged a few people about buying some weed, and I had an answer from a woman who wanted to buy half an ounce.

We met at the mall and sat in her car to do the deal. Her little girl was buckled into a car seat in back and, for a second, I thought some really judgmental shit about that, before I reminded myself I'd taken Marcus on a drug deal, too. While the woman counted out a hundred bucks in tip money, the little girl told me all about her American Girl doll. I assumed the woman was a dancer, because I didn't know any waitresses with acrylic nails, and, after we did our deal, I'm guessing she went to drop her kid off at school.

I did another meet-up to make a sale, and then I went to our apartment, where the cops had taped the door shut like it was a crime scene. Seeing the police tape made me glad I'd taken Marcus to Colorado. Otherwise we would have been there when the cops came.

Inside, the police had gone through everything. Every cupboard, every drawer, the closets, the medicine cabinet, even the damn cabinet under the bathroom sink. I felt so sick I spent a few minutes thinking I might puke up my French toast. It wasn't that they'd left a terrible mess — they had — but knowing some fucking cop had even opened my stupid box of tampons and looked through them made me furious. Everything I owned in the world was in two Rubbermaid tubs, and the cops had stirred my clothes together with some old pastel drawings I'd kept from high school. All my clothes were smudged with chalk.

There was no way Marcus and I could sleep there until I cleaned up. That's what I was trying to do when the apartment manager walked in and said, "What are you doing here?"

"Dude. I live here. You know me," I said.

"The owner doesn't want the police coming around here. You can't stay here."

"You can't kick us out. My sister getting kidnapped doesn't break the lease." It pissed me off, because I always paid the rent on time.

"Except you're not on the lease," he said.

LaReigne was the only one on the lease, because I'd had this fantasy that I would eventually move out. That never happened, because I couldn't afford to pay rent on two places. All of a sudden, now that the police

110

had been there, management cared about me sleeping on LaReigne's couch.

"So my sister got kidnapped and you're making me and my nephew homeless?"

"That's not my problem," the manager said. "You can't be here."

I didn't know anything about how the law worked with me not being on the lease, so I got a trash bag and gathered up some of our stuff: mostly clothes and a few toys for Marcus. The manager followed me around the apartment while I did it.

"You can take your stuff," he said, like he was doing me a favor. "But you have to give me the key."

I dragged the bag of stuff I'd gathered down the stairs and loaded it into my car. The manager followed me, waiting for me to give him the apartment key, mumbling about how he didn't want to call security. I took the key off my ring, and I was about to hand it to him, when I decided I was done playing meek and mild.

"Go fetch, asshole," I said. I threw the key as far as I could, over the wrought-iron fence and into traffic on Rock Road.

CHAPTER 12
ZEE

After I left the apartment, I went to work, because that was all I knew how to do. If somebody dropped a nuclear bomb on Wichita, I'd probably still show up at work. The twinge in my hip had turned into a stabbing pain, and I was in the locker room sticking a CBD patch on my lower back when Julia walked in and gasped.

"Oh my god, Zee! You don't need to be here," she said. I was standing there with my pants unzipped and my shirt untucked, but she hugged me. It wasn't like we were close friends, but I didn't want to be rude, so I hugged her back. That's when the owner, Lance, walked in. He wasn't supposed to be in there, because it was part of the ladies' room, but that never stopped him.

"Zhorzha, my dear," he said. "I agree with Julia. There's no need for you to be here.

This must be a trying time for you and your family."

Just like we couldn't keep him out of the locker room, we couldn't stop him from hugging and patting and squeezing us. He was the owner. I scrambled to zip my jeans before he swooped in for a hug that was way too close.

"I'm scheduled to work, right?" I said.

"But we never imagined you'd come. I already asked Kristi to cover for you."

"Do they know anything?" Julia said. "I mean, do the police have any news for you? I heard they found her car. Is there — do you —"

"They don't tell us anything except what's on the news. And I'd rather work today," I said. I got away from Lance, but he and Julia stared at me while I pulled my hair up and put my apron on. They could hug me all they wanted, but they hadn't offered to pay me for not working.

"I went to Colorado earlier this week." I usually waited for people to ask, but I wasn't in the mood for subtle hints. "I kind of need to get rid of it. I could let you have an ounce for two hundred."

Normally I got seventy for a quarter ounce, but I didn't want to carry it around any longer than I had to. It was a good call, because by the time we opened for lunch, Lance had bought half an ounce, Julia's boyfriend came by with enough cash for an ounce, and I sold half an ounce each to the other two servers. It wasn't anything close to what I usually made, but at least it covered what I paid out, and it meant I wasn't toting around felony-level quantities of weed.

The lunch rush was the lunch rush. Too many split checks and shitty tips, but I could get through it. I always got through it, even when I was in worse pain than I was in. I'd just picked up drinks for the double four-top in back when I saw the TV behind the bar out of the corner of my eye. *Nebraska Body May Be Hostage* the graphic on the screen said. The volume was off, and all I meant to do was ask Lance to turn up the sound, but I moved too fast.

A glass of iced tea tilted and I tried to get it back upright, but my hands were shaking. The glass went over the edge of my tray — the first dish I'd broken in ages — and once it fell, I couldn't get the tray balanced. The newscaster was moving his lips and the graphic still said *Nebraska Body May Be Hostage.*

I tried to level the tray with my other hand, but the whole thing went sideways, and I dumped four Pepsis and a Sierra Mist on the floor after the iced tea.

I couldn't move. I felt like if I didn't do anything, none of it would be true. I'd be frozen there forever, but I'd never have to know.

"Zhorzha!" Lance shouted.

"Can you turn that up? The TV — will you turn it up?" I said.

By the time he got the remote, it was too late. They'd already gone to a different story. Somebody was dead, maybe my sister was dead, and it was only worth sixty seconds on the news. I was standing in the middle of a bunch of broken glass and everyone in the bar area was staring at me. I should have started cleaning it up, but I took out my phone and pulled up a news website.

"Julia, will you get this cleaned up, and get those drinks, since Zhorzha is busy with other things?" Lance said. He sounded pissed, but I had to know.

"It's okay," Julia said and started sweeping up the glass.

BREAKING NEWS: Body Found in Falls City, Nebraska. May be hostage from El Dorado prison escape. That was all I could find. No other details.

"I think you should go home," Lance said.

I wanted to argue, because I still had bills to pay, but I could barely hold the phone steady enough to read it.

"Until things are less stressful for you," Julia said.

Right then it felt like that would never happen, and whatever Julia meant, I knew what Lance meant. I was fired.

I went out to my car, still feeling shaky, and forced myself to do what I was supposed to do. I called Mom, hoping she wouldn't answer, but she picked up on the second ring.

"Yes, I saw," she said. "And it's not LaReigne."

"Did the police tell you it's not her?"

"I don't need the police to tell me. I would know. If it were her, I would know."

"I think you should call what's his name, Mansur. He left you his card. You should call him and —"

"I'm not calling him!" she yelled. For a minute, neither of us said anything, but I could hear her panting, like she was going to have an asthma attack.

"Do you want me to come —"

"I'm telling you, it's not her. You wouldn't understand, but I'm her mother, and a mother knows. If my baby were dead, I would know."

I let her have the last word, because there was nothing for me to say. After all, I wouldn't understand. Besides, LaReigne was the one who got along with Mom. When Mom was upset, LaReigne calmed her down. When Mom was being stubborn, LaReigne talked her around. All Mom and I ever did was fight.

I went to the only place I had left to go: the Franks' house. The woman who answered the door wasn't Charlene, but she looked so much like her that she had to be her sister.

"You must be Gentry's friend," she said. "I'm his aunt Bernice."

I followed her inside, where Charlene was at the kitchen bar. I could see she and Bernice must have been sitting there together talking, because there were two coffee mugs, and the TV was off. Charlene hadn't been watching the news. She didn't know.

"Hon, you don't need to ring the bell," Charlene said, when she saw me.

"I didn't want to just barge in." I'd worried I was taking advantage of Gentry's family, but it was such a relief to walk into a calm and quiet house. Too quiet. Elana was there, working on a coloring book at a tabletop set up across her wheelchair.

"Barge all you want. A closed door never stops Bernice."

Bernice swatted Charlene's arm and they laughed at each other.

"How was Marcus today?" I said, but what I meant was *where* was he?

"He was mostly fine. A few tears at lunch, but a nap put him back to rights. The boys are in the backyard, if you want to go out," Charlene said.

More than anything I wanted to see Marcus and make sure he was okay. In the yard, he was holding a little wooden sword and shield. He had on a chain mail shirt that came down to his knees, and on either side of him stood Gentry and Trang. Their swords were wood, too, but other than that, they were done up like something out of a movie. Big shields and all kinds of armor plates on their arms and legs. Trang's armor was mismatched pieces, but Gentry's was black and silver, top to bottom. In the grass next to them were their helmets, like a pair of metal buckets.

I'd planned to walk down and hug Marcus, but he was totally focused on Gentry. That didn't surprise me so much as the fact that Gentry was focused on Marcus. He was leaning down to talk to him, really paying attention to him.

"Now that thou hast seen brother Trang and I fighten," Gentry was saying, "tell me what thou learnt, Master Marcus. With thine own sword, canst thou touch me?"

Marcus hesitated, but he reached out and tapped his little sword against Gentry's chest. It thunked against his armor.

" 'Tis good," Gentry said. "A fair touch. Again."

He had Marcus poke him with the sword four or five times, and then the next time, Gentry shifted his own sword and pushed Marcus' away.

"Ah, I stopt thee. How?"

"You hit my sword with yours."

"Yea, Master Marcus. 'Tis called a *parry.* Again."

Marcus tried to touch him again, but not quite as sure of himself as he had been, and Gentry pushed his sword away again.

"And if I touch thee?" Gentry reached out and tapped his sword in the middle of Marcus' chest. It made me flinch, but Marcus giggled. Gentry did it again and got more giggles.

"Thou carest not that I stab thee, Master Marcus? Wilt thou not parry me?"

The next time Gentry tried to tap him, Marcus put his hand up and pushed the sword away.

119

"Ah, but a true sword is sharp. 'Tis not safe to grasp with thy bare hand. Canst thou parry my sword with thine?" This time, Marcus brought his little sword up and tapped Gentry's. Not really hard enough to push it away, but Gentry let him.

"Well done, Master Marcus. Again. And now canst use thy shield?"

In another couple minutes, he had Marcus doing something that looked like sword fighting to me. Trang, who'd been watching Gentry, too, looked up and saw me standing on the patio.

"Behold, 'tis Lady Zhorzha," he said.

"Aunt Zee! Aunt Zee! I'm gonna be a k-night!" Marcus ran across the yard, dragging his sword. He slammed into me so hard that I almost fell backward, but I managed to bend my knees in time. The chain mail was cool against my arms where I hugged him, but under it he was hot and sweaty. Holding on to him made me feel better and worse at the same time. He was safe and he was Marcus and I loved him, but what if he was never going to see LaReigne again? Was I enough?

As fast as he'd run to hug me, he let go and started telling me everything about being a k-night, which included about a hundred words I didn't know, including

120

greaves and *gorget* and *gauntlet.* I smiled and nodded, fighting to keep a calm look on my face. When Gentry reached the patio, he went down on one knee, with his sword held across his chest, the way he'd knelt to me the day we met. Seeing it done in full armor was somehow less bizarre than seeing it done in cargo shorts and a T-shirt. It made sense with the sword and the armor.

"Lady Zhorzha," he said. "Thy servant."

"Sir Gentry," I said, which surprised him enough that he looked up and made eye contact with me. Then he dropped his head and a whole rainfall of sweat droplets fell out of his hair onto the patio and my shoes. It must have been hot as hell under all that gear.

"Master Marcus, 'twas well done for thy first lesson, but let us disarm thee," he said. " 'Tis hot and thou art not accustomed."

Marcus gave up his armor, sword, and shield, and we went into the house, where I offered to help Charlene do something, anything, but she told me to sit down and color with Elana and Marcus. She and Bernice went back to the kitchen bar, and it sounded like they were planning an event for something at church. I tried to turn my brain off, to just be there coloring, but I felt like my head was full of bees. After a while,

I heard that weird grunting and thunking noise I'd heard the day before and, when I looked out the patio doors, I saw Gentry and Trang, swinging swords at each other. Not the low-key back and forth he'd done with Marcus, but really whaling on each other.

When I glanced back at Charlene and Bernice, they had their heads together over a cellphone. Bernice looked at me and then away, like I'd caught her at something. All the sudden, they both got up and went into the laundry room. I could hear them whispering for probably ten minutes, before Charlene came out and gestured for me. I felt light-headed when I stood up. Some of that was from not eating anything since breakfast, but the rest of it was fear.

"Have you seen the news?" Charlene whispered when I got to the laundry room. Bernice had the phone in her hand, and she looked as nervous as I felt.

"Before. Earlier. Have they —" I leaned against the washer. Even though the vibrating made me queasy, I needed the support. "Do they know who it is?"

"No, they haven't said, but I wanted to be sure you'd heard," Charlene said.

I nodded and limped back out to the front room. I didn't want to be rude, but I couldn't talk about it. After a few minutes, Charlene walked Bernice to the front door. I could hear bits and pieces of what they said: *remember to get the ham — need to put the rug back — Gentry can help — did you find the curtain rods?* Just boring everyday stuff, but full of the kind of shorthand you use with someone you know really well. Someone like your sister. There was a little bit of silence, which must have been them hugging, and then: *love you, baby girl — love you, too — see you on Sunday.* I colored harder, trying not to cry.

When Bill came home, Charlene and Gentry cooked dinner, which was taco salad, complete with every kind of thing you could imagine to put on it. I got the impression meals at Gentry's house always involved lots of things to be sliced and diced. I was relieved not to get the impression that I'd overstayed my welcome.

Toward the end of dinner, my phone vibrated. I slipped it out of my pocket and looked at it under the table. The Gills. Calling me for the third time that day.

"You're not allowed to have your phone at the table," Elana said.

"Last I checked, you weren't the dinner table police," Charlene said.

"I'm sorry. I need to take this." I pushed

my chair back and answered as I was walking away from the table.

"This is Harold Gill," he said, so I knew it was serious. So serious it made my taco salad go wobbly in my stomach. He never called. It was always Winnie.

"Hey. I'm sorry I haven't returned your calls, but obviously things are kind of crazy right now." I mostly wasn't in the business of apologizing to assholes, but I wanted to play nice. Harold didn't.

"It has come to my attention that Marcus has not been in school since Monday," he said.

"It has come to your attention?" I said it like a question, but I knew how he knew. They'd called the school and, since they were on the approved list of people, the office secretary must have told them that Marcus hadn't been in class.

"I do not feel it's appropriate for him to be out of school," Harold said.

"His mother has been kidnapped and maybe she's — and you think going to school is the most important thing right now? Because I kind of thought it might be better to wait for some news." I hadn't really thought it through at all, but fucked if I was telling Harold that.

"I expect my grandson to be in school

tomorrow. Especially during such a chaotic time, he needs routine." Oh, now Harold was an expert on childhood psychology. "This is not an idle threat. If I call tomorrow and he is not in class, I will get my lawyer involved. You are not a custodial parent. You do not have the right to make the decision to keep him out of school."

I took the phone away from my ear, because I didn't trust myself not to curse or cry or yell. When I was calm enough, I put the phone back to my ear and said, "Of course. He'll go to school tomorrow."

"I'm glad to hear it. Goodbye."

That's what kind of an asshole *Grandy* Harold was. Not a drop of concern about LaReigne. She could be dead in a morgue drawer in Nebraska with pictures of her corpse on the ten o'clock news, and he would call me and say, "Be sure to take my grandson to school tomorrow, or I'll have to get my lawyer involved."

"Motherfucker." I said it under my breath about ten times while I paced up and down in the front hall trying to get my temper under control.

"My lady," Gentry said. He'd snuck up on me and was standing in the doorway. "Thou art troubled? Hast thou news?"

"No. I'm fine. And no news." I didn't want

to get into it with him about how messed up everything was. I hadn't noticed before, but the wood-paneled walls of the front hall were covered in framed photos of Gentry's family. In the picture hanging next to where he stood, Gentry was an awkward teenager with long, shaggy hair. He had his head down and his arms crossed over his chest. Bill was sitting in a chair, and Charlene stood behind him with a hand on his shoulder. Trang was maybe five or six, and he looked like a grinning elf. There were two older kids, a boy and a girl, who looked like they might be Bill and Charlene's biological children, because unlike Trang and Gentry, they were black.

A nice family. A happy family.

"Who's this?" I said, pointing to the picture.

"My mother and father, and brother Trang —"

"I kinda guessed those. Who are they?" I put my fingers up almost close enough to touch the glass.

"She is my sister Janae, who is three years my elder. And he is my brother Carlees who is but one year my elder," Gentry said. "He is a teacher in the city of St. Louis. She studieth to become a veterinarian."

"That's cool."

"My father has declared that we shall have no television this night, but that we shall play games. Wilt thou join us?"

"Sure," I said. My first choice would have been curling up in a little ball somewhere, but my second choice was definitely just pretending that my sister wasn't maybe dead.

CHAPTER 13
ZEE

At Marcus' school, I realized I didn't know how drop-off worked, because I was always picking him up. I almost pulled in the wrong drive, and in the right drive, there was a sign that said NO PARKING, but I was already late. I got Marcus unbuckled and grabbed his book bag and the lunch Charlene had packed for him.

"You can't park here, ma'am," the school resource officer said. He came down the sidewalk with his gun belt rattling. I never knew what to think about that. Was Marcus any safer because a cop with a gun was on duty at the front door?

"I'm sorry. I don't usually drop him off, so I don't really know what I'm doing." I gave the cop what I hoped was a friendly smile.

As soon as I got his book bag strapped on and his lunch in his hand, Marcus ran up the sidewalk to the front door. I was going to call him back and hug him, but the SRO was frowning about where I was parked, so I yelled, "I'll see you at three-thirty!"

As I was pulling away from the school, my phone rang. Mom. I'd missed a call from her while I was getting Marcus out of the car, too.

"The police are here again," she said, as soon as I answered.

"They came by again? Or they're there now?"

"They're here now."

"What do they want?" I put on my signal and got into the turn lane to go to Mom's house.

"I don't know. I didn't answer the door."

I wanted to say, *You can't hide in your house like a turtle and hope this all goes away,* but she'd pretty much done exactly that since Dad died. Instead, I said, "Okay, well, I'm on my way to your house, so I'll talk to them."

When I got there, two patrol cars were parked in the street, and a police van was parked at the bottom of the driveway. Two guys in suits and three uniformed cops were standing on the front porch. I think I was too exhausted from worrying, because I didn't feel anything as I got out of the car. As I came up the sidewalk, though, I saw

129

that one of the cops was holding a goddamn battering ram, which I guess they were planning to use to knock the door down. I broke into a jog, wishing I didn't have to do the whole day on nothing but two stupid ibuprofen pills for the pain. One of the uniformed cops turned and held up his hand.

"Miss, you can't be —"

"I'm her daughter. Is there a problem?" I said.

I'd thought it would be the police coming to give Mom bad news, but when the guys in suits turned around, it was the U.S. marshals, Mansur and Smith.

"Miss Trego," Mansur said. "We're a little concerned about your mother. We've been here almost twenty minutes, knocking on the door, and she hasn't answered."

"She's fine. I talked to her on the phone. It's hard for her to answer the door. She's an invalid, okay? You met her." I didn't intend for it to come out like an accusation, but it was. They'd met her. They had to know how difficult it was for her to get up and come to the door.

"We're going to need you to let us in." Mansur had an ink stain on the pocket of his dress shirt, and I focused on that. On remembering that he was a federal marshal, but still just a person.

130

"Do you have some news for us?" I said, even though my mouth had gone totally dry. I mean, how could they not know? LaReigne was thirty and a petite blonde. The other woman, Molly, was fifty-something and a brunette. I could have looked at the hands for two seconds and known if it was LaReigne. As soon as I thought that, I was glad I hadn't eaten any breakfast.

"I'm sorry, we don't," Mansur said.

"Then I'd rather you didn't come in. You're just upsetting her."

"I'm afraid that's not an option." The whole time, Mansur had been holding a sheet of paper folded up in thirds. He held it up real casually, like it wasn't any big deal. "We have a warrant to search the house."

"A warrant. To search this house?" I pointed at the screen door that was still canted off to one side. "This house?"

"Miss Trego, is there a problem?"

"You saw it yesterday, and you want to search that mess? What do you think is in there?"

"The search warrant explains what we're looking for. Now, if you'll unlock the door, I'd prefer to do this with a minimum of distress for your mother."

"That's not even possible. Just wait here," I said, but when I unlocked the door and pushed it open, Mansur stepped in right behind me.

"Zhorzha? Are the police still here?" Mom yelled.

"You remember the marshals? Mansur and Smith?" I said. "They're here with me. They have a search warrant."

I waited in the front hall, because I wanted her to have a minute to pull herself together before she had to face the cops, but also because I didn't want to see the look on her face once she knew what was about to happen.

Mansur was getting impatient, so I started toward the front room as slowly as I could, with him following me. When I got to Mom, she was sitting upright in her chair with her inhaler in her hand.

"Oh my god," she said in a breathy voice, so I knew she hadn't used her inhaler yet. Her hand was shaking too much. I took the inhaler, put it up to her lips, and gave her a dose.

"Mrs. Trego, I'm here to serve a search warrant for this house. We're going to need you to go outside, so we can conduct it," Mansur said. He'd been standing back a few feet, but he came close enough to hand Mom the search warrant.

"You bastard." Mom hadn't quite gotten

132

her breath back, but by the time I got her out of her chair and put her robe on over her nightgown, she was saying it in a much louder voice. I knelt down and tied her shoes while Mansur waited, and then I guided her toward the front door. It took a good twenty minutes to get her to the front porch and, when she stepped out into the daylight, where the other cops were waiting, she'd worked up some real venom.

"You bastards," she told them. And then, as they helped her down the front steps: "You heartless goddamn bastards. Searching my house when my daughter is still missing!"

"You need to get her something to sit on," I said to one of the uniforms. There was no way Mom could stand outside until they were done. She was already shaky from walking that far, and who knew what was going on with her blood sugar? I didn't dare ask her, either, or she'd bite my head off about minding my own business.

"I think we've got a folding chair," the cop said.

"Are you stupid? A folding chair won't hold her." I didn't even bother saying it quietly, because Mom wasn't paying attention to me. She was staring at the front door of her house, moving her lips. I wasn't sure what she was saying, but I guessed it included the word *bastard.*

We were still standing there ten minutes later, when my cousin Emma pulled up. As she walked around the end of the police van to reach the sidewalk, she acted like it was radioactive, and she was afraid to get close to it.

"Are you okay, Aunt Dot?" she said.

"Oh, sweetie, thank you for coming," Mom said. "Zhorzha was dropping Marcus off at school; that's why I couldn't get ahold of her."

I took a step back, so Mom and Emma could hug each other, and it was a relief to have someone else holding Mom up for a while.

"What are they doing?" Emma said.

About half a dozen uniformed cops had gone into the house with Mansur and Smith. I wasn't even sure where they could all be standing, but they'd left one cop on the front porch.

"They have a warrant to search the house," I said.

"I can't imagine what they think they'll find." Mom sounded annoyed, but I had to purse my lips not to laugh, because I was trying to imagine what they wouldn't find.

Then I remembered the search warrant.

When I reached for it, Mom let me have it. I didn't understand all the legal crap, but there was a list of items they were searching for, which included the money from the first bank robbery my father and Uncle Alva committed. That didn't surprise me, even though they'd searched the house for it eighteen years ago. Probably the cops just used that to be sure the judge would give them the warrant. Since the money had never been recovered, it was a perpetual free pass to harass my mother.

What surprised me was the cops were also searching for guns, "correspondence or other communications" between LaReigne, Tague Barnwell, Conrad Ligett, and Molly Verbansky, and "components for improvised explosive devices."

I was staring at that last line when a cop stepped out the front door carrying three cardboard boxes stacked on top of one another. At some point, I guess they'd decided the air in my mother's house was too dangerous, because he was wearing a dust mask and rubber gloves. As soon as the first cop cleared the porch, another came out, then another, until all six uniforms had come out. They carried boxes to the edge of the driveway, where the police van was, and lined them up.

"Be careful!" Mom called. "There are valuable collectibles in those boxes!"

A couple cops turned and looked at her. Because of the dust masks I couldn't tell what kind of look it was, but I guessed contempt. Then they went back into the house and carried out more boxes. Some of it looked like kitchen things.

"I swear, if they damage anything, I'm going to hire a lawyer," Mom said. "There are a lot of valuable things in there."

"Just like old times," I said to nobody in particular, because Mom and Emma weren't paying attention to me.

Mansur came out of the house, carrying a single cardboard box, and started talking to the cop who was in charge of the van. She was wearing some kind of a paper jumpsuit and writing on a clipboard.

I walked toward them, but Mansur shook his head and gestured for me to stop.

"What is this?" I held up the search warrant.

"Miss Trego, I do need you to stay back."

"Will you tell them to be careful, Zhorzha?" Mom yelled.

Mansur walked back toward the house before I could say anything else. The cop in the paper suit started rubbing something that looked like gauze pads on the boxes that were lined up.

It went on for another hour at least, like watching ants evacuate a den. I stayed where Mansur had stopped me, no closer, no farther. When the sun came up over the roofline I was still in the shade, but it hit Mom and Emma full in the face. I walked back to them, planning to ask Mom how she was doing, but it was a stupid question. She was standing in front of her house in her bathrobe, watching the police drag all of her shit out on the front lawn.

"I can't do this again, Leroy," she was saying under her breath. Over and over.

I put my hand on her arm. Her skin was clammy. Emma stood there like a mannequin, like I'd been doing for the last hour. I turned around and walked toward the front porch, so that a cop who was carrying out more boxes had to dodge me.

"Ma'am, you've been told to stay back," he said.

"And I told you that my mother needs to sit down." I didn't know if I'd told that particular cop, but I'd told one of them, and they hadn't done a damn thing about it.

I made it all the way to the porch, but the cop on duty there put out his hand in this way I recognized. This badge-wearing Toby

137

way, so I knew he wasn't afraid to hurt me. The Tobies of the world, they all end up as thugs or cops.

"I want to talk to Mansur," I said. "Right now."

"Will you tell him?" the Toby cop said to one of the box-carrying cops.

I waited at least five minutes. Then I put one foot up on the bottom porch step.

"Ma'am. I will cuff you, if you don't stay back," Officer Toby said.

"Tell Mansur he better go ahead and call an ambulance, because if he leaves my mother standing out there in the sun any longer, she's going to need one."

"He's coming. You can tell him yourself."

When Mansur finally came outside, he was empty-handed, but now he didn't just have an ink stain on his dress shirt. He was covered in dust and cobwebs and all the other things that were hiding in the corners of my mother's house.

"Miss Trego. I would —"

"Do you see my mother out there? Standing in the sun?" I said. I stood up on the second-to-top step so that Mansur and I were eye to eye. If Officer Toby touched me, I was going to deck him, and to hell with the consequences. "She hasn't eaten breakfast so her blood sugar is probably rock-bottom. She has high blood pressure. And phlebitis. And lymphedema. I told them she needs a chair. Something that will hold her. If you're going to keep at this, you need to bring her recliner out here, so she can sit down."

"I'm sorry, Miss Trego," Mansur said. "Of course, we can arrange that."

"Can you arrange it before she faints and you need a hydraulic lift to get her up off the ground? I'm not kidding. You need to get her chair or an ambulance."

"My apologies. We'll get her chair."

It took them another ten minutes to clear the front hall, but finally two cops came out carrying her recliner. They staggered down the front steps and carried it to a patch of shade under the ash tree. In another hour, they'd have to move it again to get shade, but in the meantime, Mom was able to sit down. She slumped forward and put her elbows on her knees, panting.

"Do you want me to get you something to eat?" I said.

"No. I'm okay."

"I don't think you are."

"What about some water?" Emma said.

"Miss Trego." Mansur again, coming across the lawn toward me. "Could I ask you to come inside?"

It was that or argue with Mom, so I went with him. I still had the search warrant in my back pocket, so I took it out and unfolded it.

"Are you serious with this shit?" I said. *"Components for improvised explosive devices?* Do you think my mother is building bombs?"

"We have reason to believe that associates of Ligett and Barnwell may be planning to use pressure cooker bombs in a repeat of their attack on the Muslim student center. So far we've recovered three pressure cookers."

"Oh my god," I said. "My mother is a hoarder. I bet she has three bread machines, too. She has five goddamn microwaves, even though only one of them works."

"Miss Trego, if you'll help us with something, we can finish this more quickly."

They'd cleared the front hall and half the crap out of the kitchen. I could see the hesitation marks — like a suicide attempt — where they'd been trying to decide what to do in the front room and the sunroom. Where they wanted my help, though, was in the hallway to the bedrooms.

"Do you know what's in this room?" Mansur said, pointing to the first bedroom door.

"Like specifically or do you mean in a —

a —" It took me a second to get the word. "In an archaeological sense?"

"Excuse me?"

"I mean, I don't know exactly what's in there, but most of it dates to about 1999 to 2002. It used to be the guest room, but Mom started filling it up with craft projects and books after my dad went to prison."

Mansur took a couple of steps backward and pointed at the next bedroom door. I laughed, because I was in danger of crying. I shifted all my weight to my right foot, and the pain in my hip sobered me up pretty quickly.

"That used to be my bedroom."

"Do you know what's — archaeologically speaking, can you tell me what's in there?"

"Yeah, sure," I said. The cops had managed to get the door open about four or five inches. Most of what I could see were cardboard boxes and plastic bags, but at the bottom, there was a swatch of purple-striped fabric that I thought was a hand-me-down night-gown from Emma.

"Miss Trego?"

"Um, 1993 to 1999, it's mostly my stuff. Clothes and stuffed animals and books and things like — you know, when the feds searched the house in '99, after the bank robberies, they were convinced the bookcase in my room was a hidden door or something, because it was built in. So they got in there with pry bars and tore it off the wall." I wanted to unload on Mansur. Dump absolutely everything on him, but I knew I wouldn't be able to do it without crying, and fuck him. Fuck him and Officer Toby. I wasn't going to cry.

"1999 to maybe 2004, it's a mix of my clothes and shoes, plus romance novels and my mother's craft projects, and then by 2005, mostly her crap. Dolls and quilts and dishes and stuff."

"What about after that?" Mansur said. He was shining a flashlight into the gap in the door. With the room piled up to the ceiling no daylight could come through the windows.

"I'd guess nobody's been in there for at least five years. The last time I could actually get in there to sleep was 2007. That's where the bed is, archaeologically. Hey, if you're gonna excavate, somewhere in there is this really sweet Dusty Rhodes action figure my uncle Alva gave me. I would love to get that back."

Mansur turned and gave me a blank look.

"You know? Dusty Rhodes. The wrestler. The American Dream?" I said.

"I see." I don't think he did see, though.

He went back to shining his flashlight into my room. "Which one was LaReigne's room?"

"That one. She moved out in 2005, so Mom filled her room up first. I doubt there's anything in there that'll help you. Unless you think she was plotting to make bombs with white supremacists back in 2005. That's why you're here, right? You think LaReigne met up with these guys' friends or something? You don't see how stupid that is? Nobody comes here. Except me and LaReigne."

"And your nephew and your boyfriend and —"

"He's not my boyfriend, and yesterday was the first time he'd ever been in the house," I snapped. "Look around. Do you really think terrorists could meet here and build bombs? God, I can't even find a place to sit down when I come over. You did this to her."

"I did this?"

"You cops, searching the house. That's what fucked her up."

"It certainly wasn't us," Smith said. He'd been lurking in the hallway behind us.

"Yeah, you're so different from the marshals who searched it back then. What about after you're done pawing through all her

143

shit and swabbing it for whatever? You're gonna leave it out on the lawn and it'll be my problem how to get it back in the house."

"Maybe that's not such a bad thing. Maybe it'd be a good idea if you didn't bring it back in here," Smith said.

"Fuck you, you fucking judgmental motherfucker."

I had totally lost it, like I had flames shooting out of my head. I turned around and walked toward the front door, the first time in years I'd been able to do it without climbing over a bunch of shit.

Mansur came after me and, as I was about to step outside, Officer Toby said, "Marshal, that other search warrant you've been waiting on just came."

I knew what it would be, even before he said it. What else was there to search? They'd searched the apartment. They'd searched Mom's house. Of course, my car was next.

"How long are you going to take it for?" I said, when Mansur asked for the keys.

"It won't be too long."

"A day? Two days? You know, I have things to take care of."

"Let's say two days. Max," Mansur said. I put the keys in his hand and he passed them to the cop who'd brought the warrant. Just like that I was homeless, jobless, carless. Fucked.

I went outside and walked across the lawn to Emma and Mom. Emma had gotten Mom a bottle of water from somewhere, and when I reached them, she said, "Do you want some water, Zee? I've got more in my car."

She put her hand on my arm, so I knew she wanted me to come with her, but she didn't say anything until we got to her car. When she popped the trunk, this chill went down my back. Because they'd found LaReigne's car, and now they'd found a body. For all I knew, it was LaReigne, and I could see it. I could imagine her dead and stuffed in the trunk of her own car.

Of course, all Emma had in her trunk was a case of bottled water and a roadside kit. She passed me a bottle and, when I reached for it, both our hands were unsteady.

"Can you do me a favor?" I said, trying to shake that chill.

"I only came because Aunt Dot sounded hysterical. She didn't know where you were, and I didn't want to leave her alone. That's it. I can't do anything for you. This is all too much." Emma started crying, I guess because she was freaked out about the

145

police. She said, "Please, don't call me again. I won't answer the next time. And please, don't drag my mother into this."

"Who's dragging your mother into anything?" I squeezed the water bottle until the plastic crackled in my fist. It was weirdly satisfying and it made me feel less shaky.

"I just don't want my mother getting upset. You know she's not in good health," Emma said. "I'm sorry, but we don't want to be involved anymore. Nothing personal, but we don't want to be part of the Trego family mess anymore. It's too much."

I didn't believe Aunt Shelly's health had anything to do with her not coming to see Mom. They hadn't seen each other in years. They'd had a huge fight at Uncle Tim's funeral, over some family heirlooms Mom thought she should have. They'd gone to Uncle Tim and, after he was dead, his wife, my aunt Shelly, refused to give them to Mom, because Emma had just as much right to them as me or LaReigne. One of those stupid fights that aren't even about anything important, but that ended with Aunt Shelly cutting off all contact except for the family Christmas letter. That was Mom and Aunt Shelly both. Some great-great-grandmother's wedding china was more important to them than actual family members.

I couldn't blame Emma. If I had the option of walking away, wouldn't I? Mom's neighbors were standing out on their porches, and pretty soon reporters would show up, because who could resist watching a six-hundred-pound woman being publicly humiliated in front of the giant trash heap that was her home? Why would Emma want anyone to know we were her family?

"Yeah, well, thanks for coming anyway," I said.

"Sure. I hope everything turns out okay."

"I guess you'll hear about it on the news, one way or another."

"I'm sorry." She stood there all wet-eyed, like she was going to hug me. In case that's what she was thinking, I took a couple steps backward and held up the bottle of water.

"Thanks for this." Then I walked back to where Mom was sitting in her recliner. She straightened up a little.

"Where's Emma?"

"She had to go," I said. As pissed as I was, I didn't want Mom to know that her brother's family had written us off.

When the tow truck came and loaded my car, Mom was so fixated on the cops carrying things out of the house that she didn't notice. I was glad for that.

We'd been there another hour, and Mom had finished her bottle of water and half of mine, when she started coughing. I checked my pockets, and then the pockets on the recliner, but all I found was the TV remote and a bunch of romance novels.

"Mom, where's your inhaler?"

She couldn't stop coughing long enough to answer me, so I patted the pockets of her bathrobe, but all I found was tissues and Mentholatum. I'd had the inhaler in the house. I'd taken it out of her hand. What did I do with it? I couldn't remember. Did I give it back to her? Did I lay it down somewhere? That was an amateur move. I knew not to set anything down in her house.

I crossed the lawn and, before Officer Toby could sneer at me, I said, "You need to find her inhaler. How much stuff have they taken out of the front room? Her side table, have they moved that?"

"Do I look like I know? I've been standing out here."

"Then I need to talk to somebody who does know. It's an asthma inhaler. Do you —"

Mom stopped coughing. Just stopped. I turned to look at her, and even from that far away, I could tell something was wrong. Her face was bright red and her mouth was open, but no sound was coming out.

"You need to call an ambulance," I said.

"What's the —"

"Call for an ambulance. Right now!" I pulled his radio off his shoulder and put it in his hand. Then I ran back across the yard. When I got to Mom, she had her hand over her heart.

"I can't breathe," she said. "I can't breathe."

CHAPTER 14
GENTRY

'Twas as tho my heart lay upon the table aside my bed, for I woke an instant ere my phone buzzed.

If you're not sleeping, I need a favor, was Lady Zhorzha's message.

I answered *I am awake, my lady,* and a moment after, she called me.

"I'm sorry if I woke you up," she said. "I just — my mother had a — I don't know. Maybe a heart attack. They're taking her to the hospital, but the police impounded my car."

"Shall I fetch thee?"

"If you don't mind, yeah, that would be great."

"Gladly," I said. I had bathed ere I lay down to sleep, so I rose, dressed, and went straightaway to the dragon's lair. There, a great many of the sheriff's men gathered all 'round the dragon's hoard that they had heaped up under the open sky. I was hard struck to see it and confounded, for what hoped they to gain of such a thing?

Near hand upon the road stood the ambulance, and beyond weren the knaves and scoundrels that came upon the first day. They had come again to inquire and stare.

In the midst of it all, the lady dragon lay upon a cart, and a physician spake sharply and pressed upon her side. My lady was there, and I think much wroth with the sheriff's men, most especially the one called Mansur.

His deputies weren armed like soldiers, and he commanded that they should clear the knaves that the physician might take the lady dragon to the hospital. I joined them, for there was one qued who would make an image of the lady dragon as she was put into the ambulance.

I pushed him hence, but a deputy laid his hand upon my arm and, tho it me liked not, I retreated not.

"I come for Lady Zhorzha Trego. She called for me."

"Jesus Christ! Will you let him through?" my lady called to the deputies. To Mansur, she said, "I told you she wasn't well. This is your fault."

"Miss Trego. I need you to calm down and —"

151

"Do not tell me to calm down. Whatever happens to her, it's on you."

"All I'm asking you to do is come inside for a few minutes and have a calm discussion with me," Mansur said.

"To hell with you." She turned to me, and the heat of her gaze fell full upon me. "Gentry, will you give me a ride over to Wesley?"

"My lady, I stand ready." I beckoned her accompany me, for the ambulance prepared to depart.

"Please, Miss Trego," Mansur said. "If we go in and talk right now, I'll give you a police escort to the hospital as soon as we're done."

"You could give me a police escort right now, but instead you're playing this game."

"Miss Trego. I do not want to take you down to the police station to have this conversation. I would really rather —"

"Are you threatening to arrest me, you asshole?"

My lady raised her hand and I feared she meant to strike him. Hot dread filled my breast, and I knew not what to do. I laid my hands upon my neck, but found no relief.

"Thou art all that stands between them," the Witch said.

"Better a shield than a sword," said the

black knight.

I stepped between Lady Zhorzha and Mansur.

"My lady," I said. "Mayhap 'tis better to cede to him."

"You should listen to your friend," Mansur said.

"Fine. Fucking fine. Let's go in and talk."

My lady spake in a great dragon voice, all damped smoke and fury, and I feared for her. She wore her anger like a cloak of fire that burned none but herself.

CHAPTER 15
ZEE

The cops had emptied out almost the whole front room. Only a few pieces of furniture were left: a big bookcase; one of those particleboard pantries, which had disintegrated when they tried to move it; and, in Mom's "craft corner," there was a dining room table I didn't remember ever eating at. It had a sag in the middle like a swaybacked horse, from all those years of being piled high with stuff.

"Please, sit down, Miss Trego," Mansur said. "I don't want to keep you any longer than necessary. I know you're worried about your mother."

There was a rug under the dining room table, but I couldn't tell what color it was, because it had twenty years of dirt worked into it. I was embarrassed. Not for me, but for Mom, having people come in and see her house like that. When I was a kid, she'd always insisted that the house was cluttered, but clean. Even when I was a kid, I knew that was wishful thinking. You can't keep a house clean when you can't actually get to the floor. Or the walls. Or the furniture.

The problem wasn't that I hadn't imagined Mom's house emptied out like that, but that I'd always imagined LaReigne would be there with me, cleaning it out, after Mom died. Now everything was turned upside down, and maybe LaReigne was dead.

Mansur pulled out a chair for me and, after I sat down, he and Smith sat down across from me. Smith had a file folder that he laid on the table between us. Close enough that I could have reached for it, if I wanted to. I didn't.

"All we want to do is eliminate any possibility that you or your mother have any involvement," Mansur said. "That will help our investigation go forward in the right direction."

"If I'd been involved, I wouldn't be stupid enough to be here talking to you," I said.

"Well, I'm glad you're talking with us. So let's figure out what the situation is with your sister."

"The situation? She's been kidnapped by a pair of Nazis. Or maybe she's dead. And what are you doing about it? Because this

155

—" I held my arms out to try to include the whole idea of searching my mother's house. "This is not helping."

"I appreciate that to you this seems like a step backward, but it lets us check off this box. And let me be blunt, there are a couple of things that don't add up for us." Mansur took the leaky pen out of his pocket and flipped open his notebook. "When the police arrived at your apartment at six A.M. on Tuesday, May second, you and your nephew weren't there. Where were you?"

"At a friend's house."

"Wasn't Marcus supposed to be in school later that morning?"

"Would you take your nephew to school if his mother had been kidnapped?" I said.

"Except that information hadn't been released yet. Did you know LaReigne wasn't coming home?"

"She already wasn't home at two A.M.," I said. "Which was when I needed to go to my friend's. LaReigne wasn't answering her phone, and I couldn't leave Marcus alone, could I? So I took him with me."

I'd always thought of myself as a pretty good liar, but I'd never had to lie about actual criminal shit to a pair of federal marshals while I was freaking out about my mother maybe having a heart attack and my

156

sister maybe being dead.

Mansur put down his pen and rested his elbows on the table.

"We know they had help after they abandoned your sister's car. So you can understand why it's important that we know where you were. Because if I were trying to help my boyfriend break out of prison, it would be convenient if my sister could meet us and drive us somewhere else. Lose the trail."

"Like hell I would ever help a couple of white supremacists escape from prison," I said.

"It would be a lot easier to take what you say at face value, if you would be more specific about where you were Monday night. Let's start with your friend's name and address."

No way was I going to drop a dime on Asher or his Colorado contacts, but I had to tell the marshals something.

"I was at home with my nephew until two in the morning. Then we drove to Newton and got on the train. The Southwest Chief leaves at two forty-five. We went to Trinidad, Colorado, and I visited a friend of mine. We came back the next day. I think being on the train both days gives me a pretty solid alibi without dragging my friend into it."

"So that was a quick trip. All the way out to Colorado to visit a friend for a day?"

Smith and Mansur smiled at each other, because when you put it that way, it was obvious I'd gone to Colorado to buy weed. I should have asked for a lawyer, except as long as the marshals thought I was worth bothering, they were going to bother me. And if I got a lawyer, I would look like I was worth bothering.

"Let me go check with Amtrak," Smith said, and pushed his chair back from the table.

"Okay. But it won't be under my name."

"Excuse me?"

"I didn't buy the tickets under my name," I said. "It's under Debbie Jackson. And Marcus Jackson."

"Now why would you do that?" Mansur said.

"Because I can. Amtrak never checks your ID. Between the Amish and the Mexicans, a lot of people on the train don't even have IDs. It's no big deal. It's like when you give a fake name at Starbucks."

"You give a fake name at Starbucks?" Smith said.

"Yeah, Mr. Smith. Because my name is *Zhorzha Trego*. Do you know how hard it is to get people to understand that?"

"You do realize that interstate trafficking of marijuana is a federal offense," Mansur said.

"It's never come up." I tried to make my brain be quiet. They couldn't prove anything, and the only weed I had was in my backpack at the Franks' house.

"You frowned there a little, Miss Trego. Are you wondering how clean your car is?"

"Not really." I frowned harder, because there was no sense trying to hide it. "I'm mostly wondering when we'll be done here so I can go see my mother, and when you'll have some news about my sister."

Smith wrote something in his notebook and got up to leave.

"While he checks on that, I'd like you to look at a few things and tell me what you think they mean," Mansur said. Smith had left behind the file folder.

I braced myself, but all Mansur took out of the folder was a stack of color photocopies. I'd seen enough letters from my dad, I knew what they were copies of: prison letters. Written on cheap notebook paper in blue ballpoint pen, each one two or three sheets, double-sided, and written in perfect penmanship by a man who needed to kill sixteen hours a day in a cell with nothing to do except rewrite a letter until it was perfect.

Mansur laid them out for me, like he was going to read my tarot in prison love letters.

"While you look at those, do you mind if I take a look at your bag and your phone?"

"I really do," I said.

"I think you know I can get a search warrant if necessary, but if I have to do that, it's going to take longer for you to go to the hospital. Do you understand?"

I never kept weed in my purse, so that didn't worry me. As for my phone, I always deleted my texts with Toby and Asher, and it wasn't like I took pictures of myself with suitcases full of pot or stacks of cash. Still, it made my skin crawl when I slid my purse across to him. The first thing he did was empty it out on the table and turn it inside out.

There was nothing I could do while he snooped through my purse, except read the letters.

My Queen, that was how they all started, and they were full of the usual kind of stuff. Descriptions of perfect days, ideal lives, fantasies, philosophy, romance. Bullshit.

"So you've got some letters," I said, when Mansur finished snooping through my purse and phone. I'd only looked at the first few letters, but it was more than enough.

"Those letters are Barnwell's. We've

matched the penmanship with some drafts that he left in his cell."

"If you've got all these letters from him, they've got to be more useful than anything I know. Because all I know is that LaReigne volunteered on Monday nights. And now she's been kidnapped. That's. All. I. Know."

"Six months' worth of romantic, intimate letters from Tague Barnwell, that LaReigne stored in a flowery little box under her bed. Or are they yours?" Mansur said.

"They could be anybody's. She has a post office box, and probably half the people in that ministry use her post office box to exchange letters with their inmate pen pals. You don't give them your real address. She even lets the volunteers in the Muslim and Christian ministries use her post office box. For all you know those are letters she was storing for that Molly woman. She volunteers with one of the evangelical ministries. That's what LaReigne said."

"Oh, we know who Molly's pen pal was, but at least one of these letters was definitely written to your sister." Mansur reached over and slid one of the pages in front of me.

Dear La Reigne,
  The first thing I want to say to you is that I don't want you to take my letter

161

the wrong way. I'm sure you get so many letters from the guys here, telling you how beautiful you are. You are beautiful, but that's not why I'm writing you. I felt like, when we talked at the ritual, that there was a spiritual connection between us, and I'll understand if you didn't feel the same way, but I still wanted to reach out to you. Because the truth is, I'm alone in here. I'm supposed to have these friends, and people who support me, but I can feel myself changing, and they're not people who like change.

The second thing I want to say to you is that I'm not the man you think I am. It's brave and generous of you to come here every month to work with us and give us a chance to worship, and I don't blame you at all if you think I'm exactly like the guy you've probably read about in the newspaper. I did those terrible things. I hurt people. That's true, but I'm not that guy anymore. I've grown so much in the last four years, and I want to keep growing. What I need is a friend who is outside this circle of hate and destruction that I find myself trapped in, because I don't want to be part of that anymore, but here in prison, there's no way out.

I don't want to say anything negative about Conrad, because honestly, he has been a good friend to me. I was just a kid when he took me under his wing, and maybe that more than anything is why I went along with what he planned. I'm not saying that to deny my responsibility for what I did. I should have refused to be part of it, but I looked up to him like a father and it was hard for me to say no. In here, he's one of my only friends. Him and Craig Van Eck and Craig's crowd, and I think you know enough about them to know they aren't the best people for me to be around. They're trying to drag me back down. To keep me trapped in the same old thinking that brought me here. I don't want to keep being that person, but I can't get away from them either.

As much as I want to change, I need protection. There's no safety for someone like me alone in here. Especially with all these gangbangers in here. They would be happy to get at me. To hurt me or kill me. I know I've done terrible things, and you may even think that I am a racist (I truly am not!) but they hate white people. It would give them bragging rights to bring me down. So

163

whether I want to be part of Craig's group or not, whether I feel like part of that circle, I have to have friends in here to watch my back.

Thank you for reading all this, and if you feel like you can, a letter from you would mean so much to me. Just to know that someone out there has heard me and believes that I can be a better man.

Merry meet,
Tague

"So he wrote her a bullshit letter," I said. "Inmates are bullshit artists."

"Maybe you'd be more interested in the love letters your sister sent to Barnwell?"

"Not really."

Mansur didn't care. He pushed another stack of photocopied letters across the table to me, but I ignored them.

"You don't seem surprised at the suggestion that your sister sent love letters to Barnwell."

"These aren't even love letters," I said, after I'd looked at the first few. LaReigne was a romantic sap, and those letters weren't even all that gushy.

Next to the stack of letters, Mansur laid out a couple of Polaroids. Your standard sad prison visitation photos. Grainy, under fluorescent lights, everybody looking a little green and smiling awkwardly, posing against cinder block walls, or, somehow more depressing: a fake outdoor backdrop as cheap and cheesy as a Sears portrait studio. The kind of family photos that made up a lot of my childhood.

The pictures had been taken on the same night, probably only a few seconds apart. LaReigne was wearing a blush pink sweater. Modest, because you have to follow dress code for prison visitation, but nice. She looked pretty, standing next to Tague Barnwell in his prison scrubs.

You couldn't tell from his mug shot in the news, but Tague was good-looking. Tall. Broad in the shoulders. Light brown hair and a mustache. Super white teeth flashing at the camera. Maybe even better looking than Loudon, if you go for guys with prison-gang tattoos on their forearms. I couldn't make out the details, but from the shape of it, I knew what it was. A green-and-white number fourteen pool ball with the legs of a swastika peeking out around the edges. If you didn't know what you were looking at, it might take you a while to notice it, but it was exactly like the one my father got while he was in prison. Dad had always worn long sleeves on visitation day, but when I claimed his body, I'd seen the tattoo.

"This one came out of your sister's box of letters." Mansur tapped one of the pictures. "The other one came out of Barnwell's cell. He had it pinned up over his bunk, like the last thing he looked at before he fell asleep every night."

"Everybody needs something to get them through."

"Suddenly, it seems like you know a lot more than you thought you did."

"I don't," I said. "Here's what I know. La-Reigne can fall in love at the drop of a hat. Every guy is her one true love, and she has terrible taste in men. Also, some women really like lifers, because you always know where they are. When your man is in prison, he's not out cheating on you or spending your money or coming home drunk and smacking you around. He's locked up nice and safe somewhere, and he has time to write you love letters."

Mansur actually chuckled. Like I was funny. Like he was having fun.

"That sounds like the voice of experience," he said.

"Not mine. I don't do romance, and I definitely don't do romance with guys in prison. My mother, she was a hundred percent faithful to my father, even though he was never coming home. He used to send her three letters a week and he called every Thursday. Maybe to LaReigne that looked better than how her marriage turned out."

"Did you know LaReigne was in love with Barnwell?"

"No," I said. "But even if she is, that doesn't mean she helped him escape. Because maybe he tricked her. It doesn't mean she's not in danger. It doesn't mean he wouldn't hurt her."

I couldn't bring myself to say, *It doesn't mean he didn't kill her.*

"It certainly makes her look a little less innocent, though, doesn't it?" Mansur said. "If she was letting an inmate romance her. But then, that runs in your family."

"You know, not everybody thinks people in prison are scum."

"So white supremacist murderers? Not scum in your book?"

"That's not what I'm talking about." I hated how he'd backed me around and gotten me to say something he could use like that. My hands were in fists under the table, and I forced myself to relax them. I couldn't have another temper tantrum. I laid my hands on the table and laced my fingers together.

"So, tell me about this Asatru business," Mansur said. "How did your sister get involved with them?"

"She's not Asatru! She's Wiccan."

"But Barnwell is Asatru, if I understand my pagan denominations."

"I don't care what he is. There's only one pagan ministry at the prison, so all the guys are in it, no matter what they believe. LaReigne is not a white supremacist."

"What about your father?" Mansur said. "When he was at El Dorado Correctional Facility, he was a member of the White Circle, wasn't he? That's a known white supremacist gang. Run by his *friend* Craig Van Eck. And your mother stood by your father after he killed that bank guard. To me, it looks like your family doesn't have a problem with white supremacists or murderers."

I'd been feeling a little calmer, but the way he said it made me so angry I couldn't even talk. I sat there staring at Mansur. He stared back, waiting. For me to break? For me to cry? I stretched my leg out under the table, trying to loosen up my hip, but it didn't work. I was going to have to stand up soon or I wouldn't be able to. Slowly, I worked my way back out of that rage. I figured out what I wanted to say, what I

168

wanted Mansur to hear.

"When my father went to prison, I was eight. LaReigne was twelve. After he left, my mother fell down in this hole. Look around you. Seriously, fucking look around. This is the hole she fell into, and she never got back out. It was like we lost both our parents. Like we'd been abandoned. All we had was each other, and we survived it together. LaReigne would *never* abandon her son. She would never do to him what was done to us. You can show me all the love letters in the world, but I will never believe that. Do you hear me?"

"I hear you." Mansur closed the file folder and set his pen down. "I spoke to the medical examiner in Nebraska just before we had to call the ambulance for your mother."

He paused, I think, just to watch me suffer. He'd had news this whole time and kept it to himself. This was LaReigne's life, and he was playing games.

"They've identified the body in Nebraska," he said. "It's Molly Verbansky. Not LaReigne."

I wanted to be the tough bitch LaReigne always said I was, but I laid my head down on that dirty table and cried. Because she wasn't dead, but she wasn't safe. I opened my purse and got out a tissue, while Mansur watched me.

We were sitting there not talking when Smith came back.

"Debbie Jackson and Marcus Jackson. Left from Newton on Tuesday morning. Had return tickets to Newton on Wednesday evening," Smith said. "I imagine we'll be able to find some Amtrak employees who remember you. That hair's pretty memorable. How much marijuana do you think a person could bring back on the train like that?"

"A couple suitcases, I imagine," Mansur said. "Enough for federal charges."

"I went to visit a friend. Do you not have any friends?" I said. "Did you interrogate Molly's husband like this? Did you search his house?"

"What makes you say that? What do you know about Peter Verbansky?" Mansur said. He and Smith exchanged a *look.*

"Nothing, except that apparently his wife is dead, because these assholes murdered her. My sister is still in danger, and you're here making jokes about drug smuggling."

Mansur made a few notes before he looked at me. Like he was giving me an old-fashioned stare-down lie-detector test.

"Is there anything else you'd like to tell us?" he said.

"I can't think of anything."

I stood up, and a long, hot wire of pain ran from my foot up to my hip. I'd just wanted some relief, but Mansur didn't seem concerned, so I knew it was over.

I picked up my purse.

"Now hold on," Smith said.

"Am I under arrest?" I said. "I would like to go see my mother now. So unless you arrest me, I'm going to the hospital."

"Let me get you that escort," Mansur said.

If I'd left five minutes sooner, I could have walked out of my mother's house. Instead I got to limp out while Mansur and Smith watched me.

CHAPTER 16
CHARLENE

Bill and I had worked hard to build our family so that Gentry would feel like an insider. He had enough of being an outsider at school. Over the years, he'd made some friends through the SCA, people who were willing to expand their world enough to welcome him, but I knew at work he ate his lunch alone.

So it was strange to see him with Zee in the hospital waiting room. She was sitting with her hands squeezed between her knees, staring off into space. Gentry was sitting next to her, protectively, like a buffer between her and everyone else. A circle for two. Seeing that, I felt this motherly twinge, proud but a little nervous. He was growing up.

"Have either of you eaten since breakfast?" I said. "It's only sandwiches and chips, but you need to eat."

"I thank thee." Gentry stood up and

bowed to me.

"Oh, you didn't have to do that," Zee said.

"I don't think you should eat hospital vending machine sandwiches if you have any other option." Chivalrous as ever, Gentry pulled up a chair for me in their little corner and unpacked the food I'd brought. "Double-check yours, Zee. It should be turkey and bacon. His is some horrid thing with rare roast beef and cream cheese and pickled peppers. I don't know who taught him to eat that, but it wasn't me."

"I shall fetch us a drink," he said, after he laid out the food on a little side table.

"A Diet Coke, please," I said.

"Lady Zhorzha, what drinkest thou?"

"I already have —" Zee picked up a plastic water bottle, but it was empty. "Just water is fine."

"How are you doing, hon?" I said, after Gentry left.

"They've got her hooked up to a bunch of monitors to see what's going on. They don't think it was a heart attack. Maybe it was a panic attack."

"Under the circumstances, that would not surprise me. I imagine I would have a panic attack if I'd been through what your mother has. I saw on the news, about the other woman. The other hostage."

173

Zee nodded and fidgeted with the tassel on her purse zipper. We weren't talking when Gentry returned with drinks from the vending machine, and he wouldn't add to the conversation if there was food. He ate the way he always did, with his full attention. Like he was getting paid for the work. Zee took a few bites of her sandwich, but she was distracted.

"Miss Trego?" It was one of the nurses. "If you want to come back, I think we're going to be able to discharge your mother soon."

Zee jumped up, and in that way everything goes wrong on the same day, her purse fell off her lap and spilled all over the floor.

Gentry immediately stood up, so he *was* paying attention. He looked at her things scattered around on the linoleum, but he didn't look at her. I did. I recognized the expression on her face from the years I'd spent working for the family court. Not panicked, but resigned to the world heaping misery on her.

"You go on," I said. "We'll pick this up." She hesitated, one hand going to push her hair back, the other patting at her front pockets for something. Then she turned and followed the nurse.

After Zee was gone, we gathered up her

things and put them back in her purse. Gentry picked up with one hand, while he rested his other hand on the back of his neck. Not stimming yet, but thinking about it.

"How are you doing?" I said, but he only nodded. Tired, I imagined, and over-whelmed. "Are you going down to Bryn Carreg tonight?"

"I know not, for I would not leave the lady." He looked at his watch, probably thinking about how late in the day it was. It said a lot about his commitment to being there for Zee. He went down to his keep every weekend that he could. It was our compromise on knightly adventures. Out in the woods, but somewhere safe, so that we knew where he was.

Zee came back a few minutes later, frowning at some paperwork, and said, "What a goddamn nightmare."

"Is there anything I can do for you? Or for your mother?" I said.

"Did he tell you?" Zee swiveled to look at Gentry, but he didn't answer, so she looked back at me.

"Well, he told me the police searched your mother's house and impounded your car," I said.

"And I got fired and evicted. This week

175

has been a real shit show, but at least Marcus is in school, so he didn't have to see any of it." Zee gave a pathetic little laugh and took a sip from her bottle of water.

"My lady, if thou wilt, thou and thy nephew aren welcome in all ways to come with me to my keep," Gentry said.

I thought it was nicely done, but I felt that twinge again, of being proud of him and a touch scared, too. This wasn't the first time he had risked himself on another person, and so often it ended in disappointment.

"Or if you don't feel like camping, you're both welcome to keep staying with us," I said.

"I don't know what to do about my mother," Zee said.

"What in the world makes you think you need to do anything about me?" That was Zee's mother, who'd arrived in one of those extra-wide wheelchairs, pushed by a nurse who looked like he'd been a linebacker in high school. He was a little darker than my son Carlees, but with one of those wild black beards.

"This is your daughter?" he said.

"One of my daughters," Mrs. Trego said. "The one who made me come to the hospital even though I told her it was just heartburn."

"The hell you did," Zee said. "You were clutching your chest and saying *I can't breathe.*"

"So melodramatic. And I told you. I told you it wasn't LaReigne. A mother knows."

"I know. You were right."

I could see they were both exhausted, but Mrs. Trego had a fierceness in her eyes. Something like anger and triumph. I thought they might hug each other, but Zee went to get her purse from Gentry. Mrs. Trego put her hands on the chair arms and made a motion like she intended to stand up, but I don't think she could without assistance. Of course, Gentry hadn't told me how big she was, because it didn't occur to him. Like it hadn't occurred to him to tell Elana that Zee had pretty hair. Elana had asked and he'd answered, *Is her hair pretty? Yea, 'tis pretty.* If I had asked about Zee's mother, he would have answered, but he wouldn't think to offer the information on his own.

"I can walk from here," Mrs. Trego said.

"No, ma'am, you cannot," the nurse said. "Hospital policy requires you to get a ride out the front doors."

"I've got to make a call," Zee said, looking at her phone. "She's eligible for paratransit, but I didn't know she'd be ready to go so soon, or I would have called them already."

"That's ridiculous," Mrs. Trego said. "I'm not a charity case!"

"It's not charity, Mom. It's fucking social services, okay?"

"Excuse me," someone said behind me. I turned around to find a white man frowning at me. "Could she please watch her language?"

"Everyone deals with stress in their own way," I said. "And I know the Lord didn't send you here today to lecture her about her language."

"It's just that we have children here."

"Maybe this is not the best place for children then." Before he could answer, I turned back to Zee. "If it helps at all, I'm here in our van. It has a lift and a ramp for Elana's chair so it's more than equipped. It's no trouble."

"And who are you?" Mrs. Trego said.

"Oh god, I'm sorry." Zee stuffed her phone back in her purse and made a little gesture between me and her mother. "This is Charlene Frank. This is Gentry's mother. This is my mother, Dorothy Trego."

"Gentry's mother?" For a moment I thought maybe Mrs. Trego had met Miranda, too, but no, her confusion was the

usual sort. *But you're black and he's white!*
Or when I met Trang's friends: *But you're black and he's Asian!*

"I'll get the van and meet you out front." I gave the nurse's arm a pat, and he nodded.

"Thank you," Zee said. I was proud of her for not prefacing it with an apology.

CHAPTER 17
ZEE

All I wanted was five goddamn minutes to feel something about LaReigne not being dead in Nebraska, but I couldn't get them. Instead, I got a free lecture from the ER doctor about how it wasn't too late for me to lose weight, and some dick in the waiting room asking me to watch my language. Then Mom had to sign a bunch of discharge paperwork for things I was going to spend the rest of my life paying for. Medicaid would cover some of it, but not all of it, and Mom didn't have a dime. Just one more boulder on top of my mountain of debt.

When we got Mom home, the police van was still parked in the drive, and Mansur and Smith were on the front porch talking to the cop in the paper jumpsuit. Pure rage was pretty much the only thing that got Mom out of the van under her own power. While she went shuffling across the lawn, I turned to Charlene, feeling that old desperate itch. The need to get rid of people once they've witnessed my mother and her house.

"Thank you so much for all your help," I said. I was ashamed of myself for being ashamed.

"Do you need anything else?"

"No, we're fine. I don't want to keep you any longer. I doubt this was how you planned to spend your afternoon. But thank you."

*Thank-you*s were a superpower. They moved people along with the sheer force of gratitude. While I was getting Charlene back into her van, I could hear Mom shouting at the cops.

"Are you done tearing up my house and breaking my things and piling them out on the lawn for the whole world to look at?" She bent over to dig through one of the boxes, somewhere between crying and cursing. With all my heart, I wanted to beg Charlene to take me with her. Just get in her van like a stray dog, and leave my mother behind. I made myself say one last *thank you,* and then I walked over to where Mom was. Gentry stood a few feet away from her with his arms crossed, standing guard over the whole mess.

"My lady," he said, when I got there.

Mansur and Smith came down the front

181

steps as Charlene pulled away. For a couple minutes, they watched Mom and talked to each other. Then they put on their sunglasses and walked toward us.

"Everything okay, Mrs. Trego?" Mansur said.

"Does it look like everything is okay?" Mom said.

"I meant healthwise. Are you okay?"

"Don't act as though you care. Now you're going to go off and leave me to deal with this giant mess *you* made."

"Mom, it's okay," I said. "We'll get it put back." I had no idea if that was even possible.

"Will you be staying here tonight?" Mansur said.

"Of course, I'll be staying here. It's my home," Mom said.

"Mrs. Trego, if you think of anything." Mansur held out another business card, but this time, Mom grabbed it out of his hand, crumpled it up, and threw it on the ground.

"You go to hell," she said.

Mansur nodded at me, and then he and Smith left. Mom grabbed a box, trying to pick it up, but the whole side ripped out. A bunch of books and little Snowbabies figurines spilled out onto the grass. She started gathering them up into her arms, already panting like she couldn't catch her breath. The police van pulled away. A couple of the figurines slid out of Mom's arms. She tried to pile them back on, but others fell off as soon as she did.

"If you'll sit down and rest, I'll go find you some better boxes to put this stuff in," I said.

"I'm fine!" she snapped.

"My lady, I shall bear her throne within that she might rest," Gentry said. Her *throne*.

"Yeah, let's do that. Mom, we're going to take your recliner inside, okay?"

She ignored us, and went on trying to gather up knickknacks. I was grateful for Gentry, because he did the hard work, lifting the heaviest part of the recliner. I carried the head and guided us up the stairs and into the front room. Seeing the house in full afternoon light, when I wasn't in a panic, I felt sick. The hardwood floors were ruined. Stained and gouged and, worse than that, saggy and bouncy from having so much stuff piled on them for so long. We were lucky the cops hadn't called out the fire marshal or the city inspector. The house probably would have been condemned.

"My lady, how might I help?" Gentry said.

"Is there any way you think the two of us

can get the bigger pieces of furniture back inside?"

"Certs, it can be done. I shall go and think on it." In the middle of that mess, he bowed to me.

"Okay. I'm going to find a broom and try to sweep up a little bit."

I looked for a broom but didn't find one, and ended up back in the front room feeling helpless. The biggest of the china hutches had been blocking off the phone nook that was between the living area and the dining area. It was a weird little alcove that had shelves and a built-in seat. A long time ago, Mom had filled the alcove up with books, and then once it got full, she put the china hutch in front of it. The cops had emptied it out, and for a minute of calm, I stepped inside. It was like a coffin.

When I was a kid, Mom had hung up a sheet of poster board on the wall over the bench. She was so vain she hated to wear glasses, so she'd made these huge signs instead of using an address book. A newer one hung on the wall next to her recliner, but the original was still in the phone nook. It was so old my grandparents' address and phone number was there. And Uncle Alva and Aunt Tess'. That's how old the posters were. Aunt Tess was still alive and Uncle

Alva was anybody Mom would have called.

I pulled out my cellphone and punched in the number. Three rings later, someone answered.

"Yep." That was all he said. Older and raspier, but I still recognized his voice. He sounded how I remembered my father.

"Uncle Alva? It's me, Zhorzha," I said.

"Girl, what kind of fool are you? Don't call me again."

He hung up before I could say anything. The timer on my phone showed the call had lasted seventeen seconds. So fast it was like it hadn't happened. I put my phone back in my pocket and went outside to see what Gentry had figured out about the china hutches.

The answer was nothing. He was standing in the middle of the yard, holding a cardboard box. My mother was picking through another box and putting things in the one Gentry held.

"Mom, why don't you go inside and sit down? Gentry and I are going to try to bring in the china hutches and —"

"I don't need to sit down," she said. "Stop nagging at me."

"Okay, fine. You do whatever. We're going to try to move the hutches back inside."

The cops had carried them out with

everything in them, but they'd had a dolly and half a dozen men. Gentry and I were going to have to empty the hutches to move them. As soon as we opened the doors on the biggest hutch, Mom started going through everything in it.

"Oh, look, this is the champagne glass your father won for me at the state fair. I think it was the ring toss. He won two, but the other one got broken.

"Your grandmother liked to collect all these little blown-glass animals. She'd get them on all our family vacations. Oh, the little elephant's trunk is broken! I knew it. I knew the police would break things. They have no respect for anything."

Just like that we weren't emptying the hutch. We were taking a stroll down memory lane with occasional side trips to saying really harsh things about the cops. After fifteen minutes of that, I reached past Mom and started taking things out of the cabinet.

"Mom, we need to get this stuff moved inside," I said. "Anything you want to keep."

"What the hell does that mean?"

Me and my big mouth. Of course, she wasn't going to get rid of anything. It was all going back in the house.

"Fine, but it needs to go inside. Can we

do that without looking at every single thing?"

"There's no need to get snippy with me," Mom said. "You're welcome to go and do whatever you like. I'll have this all cleaned up by the time you get back."

I didn't know what to say to that, because Mom was delusional. It was going to take weeks to deal with what the cops had done.

She put something else into the cardboard box that Gentry had been holding. The bottom was about to give out, and she'd jammed it full of a bunch of random crap including those chipped and stained Snowbabies. The whole thing was so pathetic, I couldn't stand to watch.

"Oh, here are LaReigne's baby dishes. Look at how cute they are. It's the whole set: a plate, a bowl, and the little cup."

"Mom, I can't spend all day at this. I need to pick Marcus up from school and find a place for us to stay tonight."

"Well, you can stay here now."

"We can't stay here," I said.

"Why in the world not? You can sleep in your old bedroom and Marcus can sleep in LaReigne's room. There's plenty of space."

"Just because the police emptied those rooms doesn't mean we can stay in them. The mouse shit in my room is ankle deep."

"Well, whose fault is that? You were always leaving food in your room," Mom said.

"Oh my god. How is it my fault? I haven't lived here in ten years. I had to leave home, because I couldn't get to my bed. I was sixteen years old and you buried my bed under all your fucking crap."

"Don't you swear at me! You're responsible for the condition of this house, too. You never help —"

"You won't even let me take the trash out without checking it, because you think I'm throwing away your treasures!" I hated myself for getting sucked into the same old argument. I knew better.

"You're always breaking things," Mom said. "You're as bad as the police. You're just a big hoyden, always stomping around and breaking things. You broke that whole box of good crystal, and that can't be —"

"I was twelve! And you had it stacked on the edge of the fucking bathtub! I was trying to take a bath, and I accidentally knocked it off, which I wouldn't have done if you hadn't set a fucking box of fucking dishes on the edge of the fucking bathtub. I cut my foot open, and you're still blaming me for —"

"Because you don't have any respect for anything!"

"For this shit?" I grabbed the nearest thing: the box of figurines Gentry was holding. "I don't respect this because it's shit. And you care more about this than you do about your family. You'd rather pile this shit up than have Marcus come stay with you. So fuck all of this shit."

I dumped the box on the sidewalk, but that wasn't enough, so I stomped on it, too. Right while I was in the middle of trying to annihilate all those little Snowbabies, I realized it was the wrong box. It wasn't the box of chipped thrift-store figurines. It was Mom's treasures. The champagne glass Dad won for her. The little animals she'd inherited from her mother. LaReigne's baby dishes. I bent over, meaning to salvage something, but Mom laid into me. Slapped my head, pulled my hair, the whole time screaming. I didn't even put up my hands to defend myself, because I deserved it.

Gentry stepped in between us, which I hated for him to do. I honestly would rather have taken my beating than have Mom smack him. From where I was bent over, I heard the sound of her open palm on his back and shoulders.

"I'm sorry," I said. "Please stop. I'm sorry."

"You hateful, selfish girl! All you care

189

about is yourself."

At least she wore herself out pretty fast. She stopped hitting Gentry, and trying to hit me, because she couldn't catch her breath. For a minute or so, I stayed where I was, crouched down with Gentry bent over me protectively. When he straightened up, I stood up and tried to apologize again.

"I didn't mean to, Mom. I thought that box was something else."

"Get away from me. I don't want you here." She was rocking back and forth, taking big shaky breaths, and then in this soft voice, she said, "I want LaReigne."

I wanted LaReigne, too. I wanted the La-Reigne who had held my hand when I was eight years old. The LaReigne who could make Mom listen to her. I wanted her to come and help me figure out what to do, and that wasn't going to happen. LaReigne wasn't going to come save me. Maybe I was going to have to go save her.

"You don't want to be here, and now you don't ever have to come here again," Mom said.

It was true that I didn't want to be there, and I wished the other part was true, too.

Gentry stood between my mother and me, scratching the back of his neck. I could tell he was upset, but after a minute, he put his hands down and said, "Thy nephew, my lady?"

If it hadn't been for Gentry, I don't know what I would have done, because I staggered toward the street kind of in shock, and followed him to his truck.

"I'm sorry about my mother hitting you. I'm sorry about all of this. You probably need to sleep before you go to work," I said, as Gentry opened the passenger door for me.

"Nay. I labor not on Friday even."

"Oh, I forgot it was Friday. But you've been up since last night, haven't you?"

"Nay, I slept this morn," he said. By my math, maybe he'd gotten three hours of sleep before he showed up to rescue me again. That was all he said, and I couldn't think of anything that wasn't another apology, so we didn't talk on the drive.

At the school, I was late enough that the buses had already left. There were a couple of kids waiting to be picked up out front, but Marcus wasn't one of them.

In the main office, nobody was at the front desk, so I rang the bell.

"I'm here to pick up Marcus Gill," I said, when the secretary came out of the back room. "Is he still in his classroom?"

"No, I think he got picked up before lunch."

"You let somebody else pick him up?"

I didn't feel calm, and I must not have sounded very calm, because the secretary got the logbook and brought it to the front counter.

"It's okay. We wouldn't let anyone who wasn't authorized pick him up." She flipped through the logbook until she got to a form with Marcus' name on it. "See, his grandmother picked him up before lunch. Oh, it says a family emergency. I hope everything's okay. Is everything okay?"

I stared at the form that Winnie Gill had signed and knew everything was not okay. There was an envelope clipped to the bottom of the form. *Zorza Trego,* it said. Probably misspelled on purpose.

I tore it open as I walked out of the front office and read it while I waited at the curb for Gentry. The letter from the Gills' lawyer was only a paragraph long, basically telling me to read the other thing in the envelope, which was a court order from a judge granting them "temporary emergency custody" due to "parental abandonment."

CHAPTER 18
MARCUS

"You're going to stay with us from now on," Grammy Winnie said.

"Until Mommy comes home, right?"

"Maybe you'll get to stay with us for good."

"I don't want to stay for good," I said.

"Well, why don't you change clothes and then we'll have lunch. I have chicken nuggets for you."

At their house, I was supposed to wear *nice clothes,* instead of my regular clothes. They weren't very comfortable because the shirt buttoned all up to my neck, and I wasn't supposed to get them dirty. If I stayed there for longer, would I have to wear nice clothes all the time?

"Does Aunt Zee know I'm staying here?" I said.

"Your aunt knows. Don't you worry about her," Grammy said.

After lunch, Grammy and me went out on

the sunporch, and she gave me a new coloring book and a new box of crayons. I never got to have crayons at her house before, because it was messy, she said. It was hard to color and not make a mess.

I was being really careful coloring when somebody rang the doorbell, and Grammy got up to see who it was.

I heard her open the door and say, "I don't want you to come here again. I left you that letter to explain the situation."

"I don't care about your stupid letter. I want to see him." It was Aunt Zee!

Grammy was a lying liar pants on fire. Aunt Zee didn't know I was staying there. I got up and went inside the house to see her.

"We're well within our legal rights," Grammy said. "My husband will be home from work soon, so you need to leave."

"I'm not scared of you. People like you always think you can get your way just because you have money." Aunt Zee was mad and shouting, so I ran down the hallway to the front door.

"We're good Christian people, unlike you and your family. Marcus should have been with us all along, and now he will be."

When Grammy saw me coming, she shut the door and turned the lock.

"Aunt Zee!" I yelled. I grabbed the doorknob, but Grammy leaned against the door so it wouldn't open.

"Let me out! I wanna see Aunt Zee!"

"No, you may not," she said.

I wanted to hit her, but Mommy says I'm not allowed to hit girls. Even if she was old and bigger than me, I guessed Grammy Winnie was a girl.

I ran back to the sunporch, but the only door outside went into the backyard. I thought maybe I would push one of the screens out. I did that once, kind of on accident, and got in trouble.

Aunt Zee was standing on the sidewalk with Sir Gentry, and she was real mad.

"That bitch. *Good people.* Who says that? *We're good Christians.* If you have to say that, you probably aren't."

"Sooth, my lady," Sir Gentry said. "Those that would recommend themselves by their own testament have no good deeds to recommend them."

I didn't understand what that meant, but she laughed.

"Aunt Zee!" I yelled.

She turned around and saw me and waved with both her hands.

I heard Grammy yelling from the front door again. "You need to leave, or I will call the police. You're trespassing."

Aunt Zee ran across the lawn and put her hands up on the screen. She smiled at me.

"It's okay, buddy. You're gonna stay with your grandparents for a while. You'll come home soon, though, okay?"

"When Mommy comes home?"

"Exactly. As soon as Mommy comes home, you'll come home, too."

"And we'll be all together?" I said.

"I promise. Cross my heart." She drew an X on her heart. "I love you, buddy."

"I love you, too."

"Gimme a kiss," she said, and she put her lips on the screen. I put my lips on the screen, too, and pressed them against hers. It was so funny it made me laugh.

"I will call the police," Grammy said. She came up behind Aunt Zee on the sidewalk next to the house. I stuck my tongue out at her and pressed it on the screen.

"I'm going. But don't kid yourself. You're not a good person. Or at least you're not any better than I am," Aunt Zee said.

I don't know why Grammy said she wasn't a good person. Aunt Zee was my favorite person after Mommy.

"You need to go home and not come back here. If I see you again, I'll call the police." Grammy looked at me. "Stop licking the

screen and go inside the house."
I licked the screen again anyway.

CHAPTER 19
ZEE

I didn't have anywhere else to go, so Gentry took me to his parents' house, where his family treated me like an invalid. I wasn't doing a good job of pretending to be okay, because they acted like I was made out of glass. Charlene did my laundry, while I took a shower to get the dirt from Mom's house off me. Then Elana braided my hair while Gentry packed. There was packing required to go to Bryn Carreg, which was Gentry's *keep.* His house actually had a name, and that was where we were going. If it had been up to me, I would have gone to bed and stayed there, but I was a guest. So I sat on the front porch with my backpack, while Gentry worked.

It made me nervous watching him load things into his truck. There were Rubbermaid tubs, some kind of tent, and an ice chest. It felt very end-times.

"It's only an hour away," Bill said. "If you

decide you'd rather come back to town, Gentry can bring you."

"I think you understand that now, don't you?" Charlene said. "He'll do whatever he can for you." It sounded like a warning, and I could see how with someone as good as Gentry, she'd be worried about him.

They stood out on the porch, waving as we drove away, which made me feel like crying. Sometimes nice people are too nice. It reminded me of this whole fantasy I had when I was younger. Dad would come home from prison and Mom would get better, and we'd be a normal family, like Emma's family. Right up until Uncle Tim died, the three of them went on vacations together and bowled together. At Aunt Shelly's house, she had a whole wall of pictures of them together, like Gentry's family had. The hours I wasted on that fantasy as a kid. Imagining exactly what we'd talk about at dinner. What kind of sheets I would have on my bed when Mom tucked me in at night. How I would have sleepovers with the girls at school. The ones who wouldn't even sit with me at lunch.

Things had gone so sideways, I didn't even have a fantasy life anymore.

I wasn't going to cry. Especially because we drove in total silence. It weirded me out a little, so I worked up my nerve to ask if I could turn on the radio. Gentry said yes, but there weren't any stations programmed. I hit the SEEK button and it spun through until we got a station playing eighties music.

Bill had said Bryn Carreg was an hour away, but by my phone, it was closer to an hour and a half. We passed through a tiny town called Cedar Vale and, somewhere on the other side, we left the highway and drove north on a county road. Further on, we turned off onto a dirt road and then another, and at that point, the only reason I knew which direction we were going was that the sun was starting to set in the west. When we finally pulled up and parked, it was where the road dead-ended in a bunch of woods and hills. There was a metal garage and a carport, with a little Toyota truck parked under it.

Maybe some other time I would have been nervous about the whole thing, but I was too tired to care. It reminded me of that first day when Gentry gave me a ride home from physical therapy. Sure, maybe he was driving me out into the country to murder me, but his family was so nice, and getting murdered would solve a lot of my problems.

I got out of the truck and pulled my backpack on, while he went around to drop the tailgate and open the topper glass. I watched him pull out all the stuff he'd packed, wondering how much of it I'd have to carry and how far. I hadn't had any pain meds for my hip all day, so I decided I was going to take a big dose when we got wherever we were going. Enough to knock out a bear.

There was the big bundle that I'd guessed was a tent — a bunch of white canvas wrapped around some long poles — and two baskets full of everything else, including the ice chest. Gentry pulled the tent out until it was balanced half on the tailgate and half off.

"How much further are we going?" I said.

" 'Tis not far, but up the hill."

He squatted, got the tent balanced on his right shoulder, and lifted it up. Then he squatted again and looped one basket on the end of the poles. He turned and a third squat got the second basket on the poles.

"Do you need me to carry something?" I said.

"Nay."

"I'm strong enough to help."

"My lady, I doubt not thy virtue, but thou art weary, and 'tis my custom to bear it thus," he said.

"I don't know what that has to do with

my virtue."

He frowned. I was going to at least offer to close the tailgate and topper but he did a slow rotation so he could reach them with his left hand.

"Thy virtue. Thy strength."

"Is that what *virtue* means? I thought it meant something else," I said, but he didn't explain.

All that stuff must have weighed a lot. Enough that his right arm where he was using it to stabilize the weight on his shoulder was flexed tight.

"I didn't know you were taking me to the gun show." As soon as I said it, I could tell he didn't understand. He turned and tilted his head in that cute, doggy look of confusion.

"My lady?" He was standing there holding all that stuff, waiting for me to explain.

"Gun show, like your arms are your guns. It's just a saying. I only meant because your arms are so big. Whatever."

For a few seconds he looked even more confused, and then he smiled and turned back around.

" 'Tis nigh dark. Thou must admire my arms and walk in the same while," he said.

I hoped it was a joke, because I laughed. Walking behind him at dusk, it wasn't like I could see his arms, but going up the hill it was hard not to notice that he had calf muscles like softballs.

As we came up the path, I could see a bonfire and some sort of a Hobbit house with a grass roof. I hadn't known what to expect, but I wasn't sure why we needed a tent, if there was a house. When we got to the fire, two people stood up to greet us. A man and a woman, who was wearing a nightgown.

"Sir Gentry!" the man said. "Ever true to your word. We had begun to worry that you were delayed."

Then they saw me.

"You brought a guest!" the woman said.

Even with all that stuff balanced on his shoulder, Gentry bowed and said, "I present to you Lady Zhorzha. My lady, these folk been Sir Edrard, long my friend and brother-in-arms, and his wife, Dame Rosalinda."

"Lady Zhorzha! Welcome!" they said.

When Sir Edrard came around the fire, I put out my hand, meaning to shake, but he took it and bowed over it, the same way Gentry did. Dame Rosalinda curtseyed to me, and since I didn't know how that worked, I waved.

"I shall make ready the pavilion," Gentry said.

I would have been just as happy to help set up the tent, but I stayed there and made polite conversation. Sitting around the fire, I could see Edrard and Rosalinda a little better. Gentry wasn't all that tall, but they were adorable little gnome people. Edrard had a thick curly mustache and beard, and Rosalinda had Princess Leia hair.

I took the water they offered me and, when I asked, Rosalinda led me into the woods, where I expected to have to squat, but there was an actual outhouse. When we got back to the fire, Gentry was talking to Edrard about *sledging stones.* Or I thought that's what I heard.

By then, the sun was down, and we sat around the fire talking until I couldn't anymore.

"If it's okay, can I go to sleep?" I hated having to ask, but there I was, like always, a guest in someone else's house . . . ish.

"My lady, I am sorry thou hast waited and art weary." Gentry stood up and bowed to Edrard and Rosalinda. Then he gestured for me to come with him into the woods, further away from civilization. Twice I had to stop, because going up the hill made my hip feel like it might give out on me. The second time, Gentry held out his hand. I took it, because I wasn't sure I was going to make it otherwise. I didn't know how he felt about holding hands, but he held on to me the whole way up.

At the end of the path, where he let go of my hand, stood the tent. *Pavilion,* that was what he'd called it and, standing alone in the woods, under the moonlight, it looked like something out of a Robin Hood movie. Or like a miniature circus tent. I was so relieved when he pulled back the flap for me to go in. There were pillows and sheets, and he'd hauled all that up the hill and set it up by himself.

He handed me the little LED lantern he'd used to light the way, and bowed to me.

"If thou needest aught, I am without, my lady."

"Where are you going to sleep?" I said, because the bed was big enough for two. Sort of. Two people who knew each other better than we did.

He pointed over his shoulder to the out-side and then closed the tent flap and left me alone. I took off my shoes so I wouldn't get the bed or carpet dirty. Then I took off my jeans and my bra, and sat down on the bed to dig through my backpack for my THC drops and a pain patch. I didn't usually double up, but I didn't want the pain to keep me awake thinking. After I took my dose and put the patch on, I turned off the lantern and laid back on the bed.

Then I turned the light back on. Sometimes all I wanted was to be alone, but now that I was alone, I was miserable. I missed Marcus and LaReigne.

"Gentry?" I said.

"My lady?" he answered.

"Nothing. I just wanted to be sure you were there."

"I am here."

"Thanks."

I turned the lantern off again and pulled the top sheet over me. I wasn't cold, but I wanted something on me for protection. I thought about getting up and putting my jeans back on. I thought about calling for Gentry again, but I fell asleep before I could do either.

I dreamt I was in a long hallway, with gray-tiled floors and walls. In real life, the hall wasn't nearly as dark or as creepy, but in my dreams it was like something out of a horror movie. I'd only been there once, when I went to claim Dad's body, after he died. I was twenty, and while LaReigne was off playing Air Force wife with Loudon, and Mom was having a nervous breakdown, I was the one who arranged for the undertaker, picked out the coffin, and planned the funeral.

In the dream, sometimes the hallway turned into my old high school, and I was going to take a test I hadn't studied for. Other times, I was waiting to see Dad's body, while the prison chaplain tried to comfort me. When one of the doors opened, I knew I was supposed to go in, but I guess my brain decided I'd had enough of that particular dream and woke me up.

For a few minutes I didn't remember where I was. I sat up and looked around, because it wasn't completely dark. The walls glowed white, almost like there was a streetlight outside, but it had to be the moon.

I got up, stepped around the tent's center pole, and opened the flap to look outside. Gentry was lying there, sleeping right on the ground.

"My lady, art thou well?" he said. While I stood there like a dope, looking at him, he'd been awake, looking back at me.

"I'm fine. You surprised me. I thought you were asleep."

"Nay. Needest aught?"

"No. I'm just restless."

I didn't know what to say, so I tied the screen flap to keep the bugs out, and went back to bed. Having the outside flap open let in a lot more moonlight, and I could hear Gentry breathing. I felt better knowing he was there. Like being alone, but not *alone.*

CHAPTER 20
ZEE

In the morning, the way the light came through the tent canvas was so beautiful, I felt a little buzzed, even though I was sober. The roof of the tent was held up by something that looked like a wagon wheel, balanced on top of the central pole. It reminded me of the parachute we used to play with in PE class in grade school.

I wondered if this was what it felt like to jump out of a plane, because I felt like I was free-falling. I was helpless, and there was nothing holding me. Marcus was with the Gills. Mom had disowned me. I didn't know where LaReigne was. I'd lost my job, my apartment, and my car.

I'd felt that way after my wreck, when I was in the hospital with nothing to do except lie there. For a while it was peaceful, but eventually I crashed into the ground. I lost the baby. Nicholas abandoned me. I had no place to go. LaReigne rescued me, but living with her and Loudon was like Thunderdome with the fighting. Then the bills started coming, and the giant shit show that was my life returned to regular programming.

Thinking about all that crap ruined my little moment of calm, so I sat up and found my phone. I called Mom first, but it went to voicemail. Probably she was still mad at me. Or she couldn't find the phone. Or she'd tried to carry things back inside and had an actual heart attack.

After I hung up, I looked at my call log, at that seventeen-second phone call to Uncle Alva. I didn't even know why I'd called him, but the more I thought about it, the more tempted I was to call him again. He'd said, *Don't call me again,* and I kept turning that over in my head. I hadn't done anything for him to be mad at me. The last time I saw him, I was eight years old, right before he and Dad robbed that second bank. The one that got them caught. The one where my father killed a bank guard.

Uncle Alva had spent six years in the penitentiary at El Dorado. The same place my father had served. The same place LaReigne volunteered. I wondered how much had changed at El Dorado in the twelve years since Uncle Alva got paroled. It wasn't that long ago, and there were lifers there. Men who'd been there before Uncle Alva and who were still there. Men who might know something.

He'd told me not to call, but maybe he was worried about his phone line being tapped. Maybe his phone line *was* tapped. Ours had been for years after Dad went to prison. One more reason not to have a landline.

I closed the phone app and opened my browser to check a few news sites, but they were rehashing what I already knew. They'd dug up some new photos, including one of those portrait studio shots. They'd blurred out Loudon and Marcus, but there was La-Reigne with a big smile on her face. I don't know why I kept looking, burning up my data, knowing that eventually I'd stumble across the video of Mom being loaded into the ambulance. At the end of the news clip, Gentry stepped in from the left of the screen and put his hand over the reporter's camera lens.

All I was doing was sitting around feeling helpless, so I got up and got dressed. The braids Elana had put in my hair had come halfway out, so I took them the rest of the way out, but didn't bother trying to comb the mess. I stepped outside and looked around at what I hadn't been able to make out in the dark. The tent was surrounded by trees with a fire ring about twenty feet away, and the ice chest was strung up between two trees, to keep it away from animals, I guessed. In the night, I'd thought we were hiking over rough terrain to get there, but in daylight, I could see there was a trail that led back down to the main camp.

I followed the path, and found Rosalinda beside the fire, stirring something in a pot. Last night, I'd thought she was wearing a nightgown, but now I could see it was some kind of Ren Faire outfit. A long dress under a bustier, and a head scarf. She stood up and waved at me.

"Good morrow, Lady Zhorzha."

"Hi. Is Gentry around?"

"Sir Gentry, as he is known, hath gone a'hunting with mine husband, Sir Edrard. They shall return anon. What strange garb ye do wear. If ye would care to dress in a manner more suited, Sir Gentry hath provided garments for ye."

I stared at her for a couple seconds, thinking *Oh shit. We're going full-on Medieval Times.* I was used to the way Gentry talked, but she sounded like she was auditioning for a cheesy movie with her fake English accent. He didn't sound like he was acting at all. He sounded sincere.

I must have spent too long staring at Rosalinda, because next thing I knew she was coming at me with this big wad of fabric. The whole getup was three layers deep, and it didn't look much like hers, so apparently we were time travelers from different centuries. It started with a long white sleeveless thing like a nightgown, and over that went a long-sleeved dress that laced up the back. On top of that was another sleeveless dress that was half apron, half douchebag gym-rat T-shirt with the armholes cut out big. I couldn't figure out what to do with the dress sleeves, because they flapped open when I moved my arms. While I was standing there trying to find a way to cuff them back, Rosalinda brought out a needle and thread, and sewed me into the dress from my wrists to my elbows.

"Thank you for, uh, loaning me some clothes," I said. Never mind I had my own clothes that she'd more or less forced me to take off out in broad daylight.

"Nay, lady. Sir Gentry had this cotehardie made for ye and of the very best quality."

Honestly, it spooked me a little. There was a time when Gentry could have legit planned to invite me for his Camelot camping adventure, but that window was small and long past. He'd been waiting two years for this, or he'd made plans on the off chance that someday he would need to rescue me. It made LaReigne's joke about him being my stalker less funny, and it hadn't been that funny to begin with.

I managed what I hoped looked like a smile, because what else was I going to do? In Wichita I was homeless, and at least here, Gentry was making decisions for me. Even if he was a stalker, he wasn't a creep. Creeps didn't let you sleep unmolested in their tents while they slept outdoors. My creep ex-brother-in-law didn't even let me sleep on his couch without trying to mess with me.

I spent the morning hanging out with Rosalinda, making half-hearted efforts to participate in what she called *huswifery*. I stirred a pot over the fire that smelled like nasty soup but turned out to be soap. Then I helped hem a dress, which was about a million stitches and made my fingertips raw. At first the whole situation was like a hell dimension of camping and home econom-ics, but after a while it was soothing. Plus Rosalinda seemed super happy about me being there.

"I confess it, lady. We did betime wonder if ye weren't a fancy of Sir Gentry's imagination. To see ye art real, 'tis a delight. I hope ye will come again."

"Well, it's complicated." That seemed to be my go-to for Gentry, but I didn't want to embarrass him by telling his friends we weren't dating, if they thought we were. I settled for: "We'll see if he invites me again."

"Sooth, 'tis a joy to have another lady to while the time with," Rosalinda said.

"Do they usually just leave you here?"

"Oh, ay. There are ladies who enjoy the knightly life, but I am not inclined to tromp after the lads upon the hunt."

I was 99 percent sure she didn't mean "hunt" literally — like the way LaReigne called grocery shopping "foraging" — right up until Gentry walked into camp carrying a rabbit and three pheasants. He was dressed up all Ren Faire, too. A big poofy blouse with a vest over it, a pair of pants that only came to his knees, and soft leather boots that came up over his ankles. Seeing me by the fire in my *huswife* getup, I think he didn't know what to do. He waited until Edrard caught up with him before he came to the fire.

"I see ye have had a successful hunt," Rosalinda said, and then in this straight-up medieval Peg Bundy voice: "More so than mine own husband."

Edrard rolled his eyes and ducked into Mud Manor, which by then I knew was their house. That was why Gentry had a pavilion.

"For a common meal among friends," Gentry said, as he took off what he had slung over his back, which was a goddamn bow and a bag of arrows.

"You seriously killed three pheasants and the Easter bunny with a bow and arrows?" I said. Gentry looked down at his homemade instruments of death. Was he embarrassed?

"Oh, ay. Sir Gentry is a skilled hunter," Rosalinda said.

"I'm impressed." I really was. Less so with the actual dead things, but that he'd got them dead with arrows. I was even more impressed that he was the one who cleaned them, brought them back to the fire without their fur and feathers, and put them on a spit to roast. I'd worried that might turn out to be *huswifery,* and I didn't want to skin and gut a rabbit. My people are citified white trash. We're more familiar with opening dented cans of off-brand Spam from the food bank than skinning varmints.

Once the animal parts were cooking, Rosalinda put some actual soup on to cook, and Gentry chopped up some vegetables. I hoped it would turn out to be edible, because I'd apparently time traveled too late in the day to get breakfast.

While we waited for lunch to cook, Gentry sat down beside me on the log bench I'd been occupying all morning.

"Thou art well, Lady Zhorzha?" he said.

I was tempted to answer with Rosalinda's *"Oh, ay,"* but I didn't want him to think I was making fun of her. Even though I was.

"I'm okay. Thanks. And thanks for this, um, dress thing, I guess. I mean, thanks for sure, but I can't remember what it's called. I'm gonna shut up now."

" 'Tis a cotehardie. And hearen thy voice me liketh. Thou seemest well," he said down into his chest. "Wouldst eat of an apple?"

"Oh god, yes. I'm starving." I was so hungry I couldn't even be polite about it.

"Dame Rosalinda offered thee no bread to break thy fast?"

He didn't make me answer, because it was obviously no. He took a knife off his belt and an apple out of his pocket. He cut it in half, flicked the core into the fire, and pared a slice off for me. While I ate, he kept cutting slices and passing them to me on the tip of his knife.

"You don't want any?" I said, as I scarfed another piece.

"Nay, lady. I regret thou wast famished

217

this day. 'Twas not my wish."

"It's okay. I'm fine."

Right then it was true. I ate the whole apple, and I sat in front of the fire, not thinking about anything. After the meat was cooked, everything got ladled into bowls, and I could see that our medieval midday meal was ramen. Seriously. Ramen noodles in soup with grilled vegetables and meat on top.

Since there wasn't a table, I spent a few minutes watching Gentry's technique, which was resting the bowl on his leg while he used chopsticks for noodles and things. In between he picked the bowl up and drank the soup.

"So, did they have chopsticks in medieval times?" I said.

"I should think in Asia they did, though certainly neither Saxon nor Dane had them. We take an ecumenical approach to our reenactment," Edrard said, which didn't exactly answer my question and added a vocabulary word I didn't know.

"I thank thee, Dame Rosalinda, for this meal," Gentry said.

"Nay. I thank thee, Sir Gentry, for having secured meat for our soup," she said.

"I declare this mystery meat ramen most excellent," Edrard said.

"It's not exactly a mystery," I said, even though I'd been trying not to think about that.

"A staple of medieval Japanese cuisine: phabbit ramen. And now for a recitation. Things which Sir Gentry hath killed and eaten, parts one through nineteen." Edrard hummed a little note and then half recited, half sang: "Pheasant, rabbit, bison, songbird. Prairie chicken, lesser and greater. Catfish, trout, carp, duck, duck, goose. Rattlesnake, quail, vole, elk, deer, moose. Unicorn, selkie, ogre, dragon. Pegasus, phoenix, elf, and griffin."

"Nay, Sir Edrard. Thou makest me a great villain. I have ne killed ne eaten so many creatures," Gentry said, but he was laughing. That was new. He was normally pretty serious around me.

After lunch, I got to see the inside of Mud Manor, when I helped Gentry wash dishes. It was sort of half hut, half trailer park. The inside walls were made of the same mud-looking stuff as the outside, except they were painted white. There was a fridge and a kitchen sink, but no stove, unless I counted the fireplace. Helping Gentry mostly involved me standing there with my sleeves sewn closed while he washed and rinsed. I took the chance to do a little spying, and looked in at the bedroom. They had a futon and a cupboard. Little nooks and crannies were set into the mud walls, and they were full of books and bottles and crystals and shit. Except for the shelf where there was shampoo and toothpaste and a box of tampons. It hit me then: Edrard and Rosalinda *lived* there. They weren't camping out. It was their home all the time.

"My lady," Gentry said behind me. Even after all the times I'd snooped in other people's homes, I was embarrassed to get caught. "Wilt thou walk with me?"

"Yeah. Let's take a walk."

We went up to our camp first, and he put a blanket, a jug of water, and a book into a basket, so I grabbed the book I'd borrowed from him. The one about the boy who runs away to become a knight.

Our walk was more like a hike. Across a meadow and up another hill. The path wasn't clear-cut, and long skirts aren't great for hiking, but Gentry did what he'd done the night before, and pulled me up the steepest parts of it. I thought there must be another hill, because I could see a limestone embankment through the trees, but it wasn't a hill. It was a stone house.

Not a house. A castle. A castle in progress.

"Lady Zhorzha, I welcome thee to Bryn

Carreg," he said.

"This is yours? Your house?"

"Yea. 'Tis my keep. Tho I have many labors before me."

"Wait. You're building this? *You* are building it?"

"Yea. Stone by stone," he said.

My mind was blown, because that was a lot of stones to be building one by one. The walls were taller than me, and on the end closest to where we had come up the hill, the tower was probably three stories high. There was a gate there, big enough to drive a car through, and that was where we went in.

The walls were probably three feet thick and made out of blocks of limestone. I laid my hand on it as we walked through, and it was warm from the sun shining on it. Inside the tower, there was a door that led out to the courtyard, and a bank of stone stairs that went up in a spiral around the outer wall. Where there would have been a roof, there were blue tarps stretched across big wooden beams. The whole thing was probably forty feet across.

I put my hand on the wall again, because it was so familiar.

"Have you been to Colorado?" I said. "There's this guy. I don't remember his name. It's not that far from the Royal Gorge and —"

"Bishop Castle," Gentry said. "My lady, yes, I have seen it. It — it — it —"

I got to laughing, because that's how excited he was; he couldn't get any words out. He had to set down the basket he was carrying, so he could scratch his shoulders with both hands.

"It's amazing!" I said. "*This* is amazing! I can't believe you're building a castle."

"I saw Bishop Castle when I was a boy of ten, no more. Thou hast the book I read in thy hand. I would not rest til I had seen a castle. My father took me thither. Us alone, for brother Trang was yet a babe and my mother stayed home and — wilt thou come up?"

Of course, I would. We went up the stairs, even though there was no railing, and I remembered that about Bishop Castle, too. How in some places you were going up stairs with nothing to stop you from falling off, or standing with your back against the castle wall with the wind whipping around you. This wasn't anywhere near that tall, but it was closer to four stories than three. When we got to the top, Gentry pulled back the tarp so we could poke our heads out, and I could see why it was worth all the walking to have built up on the hill.

There was a long rolling slope down to a creek, and above the creek, three ponds stair-stepped down the hill. A big one and two small ones. Two of them were mossy-looking with lily pads and grass along the edges. The third one was lined with stones, so the water was clear.

Beyond that were hills and more hills, all the way to the interstate. From up there, it felt like I could see the whole state of Kansas.

I could also see what Gentry meant to do with the castle. There would be three towers, all connected with walls to make a courtyard in the middle. The one we were in was tallest, with the second one only about fifteen feet high, and the third one just a foundation with a couple rows of stones.

"How big is it going to be?" I said.

"Each tower shall stand five and forty feet. The curtain walls shall be eighteen feet. This be the gate tower. T'other two towers shall have no gate but to the bailey, and two chambers above the lower. Along the south shall be the scullery and the bath, for I buried the septic below."

"Septic? Your castle's going to have flush toilets? That's pretty damn fancy." For a second I was worried I'd offended him, because he frowned, but then he smiled and nodded.

"Elsewise, methinks it would like thee not," he said.

Unless I was wrong about how Middle English worked, he was building a castle based on what he thought I would like.

"How long have you been working on it?"

"This summer shall be my fifth year."

"How old are you?" I'd always assumed he was younger than me.

"I am four and twenty years, my lady."

"And you own the land?" He nodded. "So you bought it when you were nineteen? And started building a castle?"

"Yea, but my debt will not be paid for nigh a score of years. And mayhap ne will my keep be built ere I have paid it."

"But still." It deflated my excitement, not for him, but for me, because it was a reminder that I was twenty-six years old and I had nothing to show for it, except debt. I didn't own a house, and my car — the only real thing I owned — Gentry had paid for half of that.

We rested our elbows on top of the wall and looked down at all of his hard work, with the sun shining on us and the tarp flapping, until he yawned.

"When do you sleep?" I said, because I couldn't figure it out.

"Now I shall sleep." He yawned again, and after I went down the stairs, he fastened the tarp back. I figured we would go back to the tent for him to sleep, but he carried the basket around to the south side of the castle, where there were two giant oak trees at the edge of a bluff. He laid the blanket out there in the shade, but that was just for me. He stepped out into full sun and sat down in the grass to take off his boots. Then he took off his shirt, rolled it up to make himself a little pillow, laid back in the grass half naked, and fell asleep.

I sat on the blanket, knowing I wouldn't be able to sleep. My brain was too busy, and it seemed strange sleeping outside like that. Gentry was completely sacked out, though. He rolled over a few times, switching between cooking his front and his back. Once, a bee landed on his back and walked around, so I used the book to fan it away.

While he slept, I read. It was a kid's book, but super serious. This poor kid, Stephen, was taking it on the chin from all sides. People being shitty to him, and every time he'd rise above it, the world crapped on him again. His brothers were assholes, then he had to kill his dog, and he got sent away to become a priest, even though he didn't want to be one. So he ran away and took up with a knight, like Charlene had said Gentry tried to do, but then the knight got killed. Stephen had all these troubles, and then in the end, he went back and became a priest anyway. It was really fucking sad, especially for a kid like Gentry to have read when he was only ten.

I felt the same kind of sad when I thought about Marcus being with the Gills. They weren't mean to him, but I never felt like they loved him for who he was. More like he was something they liked to keep around to show off. Their only grandson. They were always trying to mold him, how he talked and dressed. What bothered me most was that however they treated him was probably how they treated Loudon, and he turned out to be an epic asshole. Thinking about that made me cry, for Marcus, for the kid in the book, for Gentry, for Mom and LaReigne, for Dad. At least that dress had plenty of fabric to dry my eyes on. I was curled up sniveling like a baby when Gentry woke up and stretched.

He carried his shirt and boots over to the blanket. My little spot in the shade had shrunk so small, I'd crossed my legs to keep my toes out of the sun. While I dried my eyes, Gentry got out the bottle of water and took a long drink. Then he sat down on the blanket and offered the bottle to me. I only took a few sips, because I was nice and cool in the shade with a breeze on me. Gentry, on the other hand, had sweated so much his chest hair was wet. I could feel the heat radiating off him.

"Did you sleep okay?" I was shocked he could sleep that way at all.

"Yea. I ne'er sleep so well as I do here. How farest thou, my lady?"

"Oh, I rested and read a little. This is a sad book."

" 'Tis?" He had his head down, unrolling his shirt like he was going to put it on, but he stopped and frowned.

"A lot of sad things happen to Stephen. Did you really run away looking for a knight when you were a little boy?"

"My mother told thee?"

Instead of putting his shirt on, he flopped back on the blanket and laughed. Honestly, I didn't mind looking at him. He wasn't chiseled like a guy who spends hours lifting weights, but he was solid, like a guy who spends his weekends building a castle. His body hair had perfect margins. Black hair on his forearms and his knuckles, but nowhere else on his arms. Same deal with his chest: a perfect butterfly shape of hair, but none on his shoulders or back. He had a little bit of a gut — at his age, it could have been baby fat or beer — and that was where all the sweat had run off him and soaked into the waist of his pants.

I recognized the surgical scar on his right shoulder from physical therapy, but on his left forearm, he had a bunch of old puncture scars, white against his tan. An even dozen, I guessed, because scars like that come in sets of four. He had more on his left shoulder, and a set of them up high on his throat under his chin.

"Wow," I said. "That must have been a big dog."

"A fair-sized dog, and I was a small boy. 'Twas thus I came to live with my mother and father. The judge would not leave me return to the house where Miranda dwelt, for the dogs remained there."

The dogs remained there. He'd gone into foster care, because his own mother wasn't willing to get rid of her dogs after he was bitten?

"Is it okay if I touch you?" I said.

"My lady, I am thy servant."

"Is that a *yes*? When you say that, it doesn't sound like *yes* to me."

He propped himself up on his elbow, so

228

he was facing me, but he didn't look at me. There was some stray grass on the blanket, and he flicked it away.

"My lady," he said and cleared his throat. "Yes. Thou mayest touch me."

I hadn't intended to turn it into a big deal, and with anybody else, I wouldn't have even asked. With him facing me, I settled for putting my fingertips on the top of his shoulder.

"I wondered if you were hot to the touch, and you are. I don't know how you can stand that." When I took my fingers away, he put his hand up to his neck.

"It troubleth me not, tho sooth thy hand is cool. Come August, when the sun is nearer, I shall ask thee share thy bit of shade with me," he said, like that was a given, that I was going to be there in August. "Let us go down and see if Sir Rhys hath come."

When we got down to the main camp, Sir Rhys had come. He was a taller guy, maybe six-two, blond, and good-looking, even if I wasn't a fan of goatees.

"Here you are at last, Sir Gentry. I was starting to think I'd come out here for nothing, but I can see you were otherwise occupied," he said, grinning at Gentry and then at me.

Rosalinda gave us such a weird look that I turned and looked at Gentry. He'd come around the fire to shake Rhys' hand, and he wasn't doing anything unusual for him. Except he hadn't tucked his shirt in all the way or laced it back up. I was basically sewn into my dress, but with his shirt hanging off one shoulder and open down to his belly button, Gentry looked like the cover of a romance novel. If he were a foot taller, with rock-hard abs and a chiseled jawline.

"Nay, thou art many hours late," Gentry said. "This be Lady Zhorzha. My lady, this be Sir Rhys of Vatavia."

"That's what I've been hearing, that we've finally been honored with a visit from Lady Zhorzha." Rhys put out his hand like we were going to shake, but when I gave him mine, he kissed it.

"Sir Rhys is the Porthos to our Athos and Aramis," Edrard said. I didn't have a clue what that meant, but I laughed anyway, and he looked happy.

"Nay, is he Porthos?" Gentry said.

"Well, I'm certainly no Aramis," Rhys said. " 'Tis thee through and through."

"Prithee, if ye must speak of such things, wait until after we sup," Rosalinda said.

"Camest thou to joust?" Gentry said. "Or wilt thou surrender ere we taken up weapons?"

"One-track mind. It's late. Let's joust tomorrow."

Gentry wasn't having any of that. Maybe I didn't get their jokes, but I could see that much.

CHAPTER 21
RHYS

For the longest time, Gentry, Rosalinda, and Edrard had a pseudo love triangle going on. She followed Gentry around like a puppy, and Edrard followed her, and Gentry was oblivious to all of it.

Eventually Rosalinda gave up on Gentry and settled for Edrard, and everybody lived happily ever after. Not that she wasn't carrying a torch for Gentry, but there was something desperate and sad about her that gave me the impression she would have settled for the first guy who offered to take her. It helped that Edrard went on being Gentry's sidekick and Gentry went on being Edrard's patron. Rosalinda and Edrard didn't pay him anything to live on his land.

By the time I showed up on Saturday afternoon, the triangle dynamic had undergone a major geometrical shift. Rosalinda didn't even give me a chance to figure it out on my own.

"You're in luck," she said as soon as I walked into camp. "Lady Zhorzha has graced us with her presence."

"You're serious?"

"As a heart attack." It was so serious Rosalinda had lost her ridiculous accent, and didn't manage to find it again all weekend.

"She's actually real? And that's actually her name?"

"I don't know why you two have to be that way," Edrard said.

"You didn't think she was real either," Rosalinda said.

"I was willing to give him the benefit of the doubt."

"Really? In light of Gawen and Hildegard and the Witch, you think I should give him the benefit of the doubt of assuming his friends aren't invisible?" I said.

"Well, she is definitely visible." Edrard pointed toward the path to Bryn Carreg, where I could see Gentry coming down, followed by a girl in a green dress. A redhead, that was all I could make out from that distance.

Up close, she was a Rosalinda, albeit a higher-quality one. Taller and more hourglass than apple, but still, one of those big girls who hope a corset will hide the fact that her cleavage is more fat than tits. It must have burned Rosalinda that Gentry had basically picked a prettier version of her.

Anyway, Zhorzha was a Rosalinda until she opened her mouth and said "Hey, man" in this surprisingly sexy, rough voice. Honestly, if she dropped fifty or sixty pounds, she would be pretty hot.

The kicker was that Zhorzha *was* her real name, but she went by Zee. She seemed surprised, but not all that curious to find out we weren't really Edrard, Rosalinda, and Rhys.

"What's Gentry's other name?" she said.

"Oh, he's Gentry everywhere. He joined the SCA as a kid, so I guess his mundane name just stuck. Or maybe he never picked a court name or a fighting name. He is a knight errant."

"Okay," was Zee's answer.

I tried all the usual questions with her and got one- or two-word answers. Wichita. Waitress. Physical therapy. Motorcycle wreck. We'd all assumed she was a figment of Gentry's imagination for so long that we were scrambling to come up with some sort of backstory for her. She was not interested in supplying it.

"What do you think of Gentry's castle?" I tried.

"It's really cool. I didn't know you could just build a castle."

"Well, our Gentry can." I kind of creeped myself out with that. I'd never been in a pseudo love triangle before, but I was seriously considering it, especially since Gentry more or less served her up to me. He hadn't bothered to stake any claim on Zee. Not even a *my girlfriend.*

All he wanted to do was joust, because why worry about girls when there were swords and armor? That was how Gentry saw the world, so we walked over to the fighting grounds and started dressing out.

The reviewing stand was a log bench off to one side of the field where we practiced. The girls sat there, Rosalinda wearing her usual greedy look and Zee looking mildly curious. I often wondered if that was Rosalinda's porn. When she was having sex with Edrard, did she fantasize about Gentry beating the shit out of him?

As always, I was ready first, because Edrard was a doughy bumbler, and Gentry was so goddamn ritualistic about everything. No variation allowed. Everything done in the exact same order every time. God help you if you had to fight him when he was wearing a new piece of armor. You'd spend more time waiting for him to get it the way he wanted it than you spent fighting.

To kill time, I went over to chat with the ladies.

"Gentry made that?" Zee said, pointing at my shield.

"How did you know?"

"That's what he does, right? Rivets airplanes?"

"Correct. So what do you think of our little idyll?" I don't think she knew what the word meant, because she didn't answer. "Do you like our little camp?"

"I'm not convinced about this dress business, but the rest of it's nice," she said.

"Well, I brought steaks for dinner, so you don't have to try your stomach on whatever random animal Gentry manages to kill."

"Art 'ou ready, Sir Rhys?" Gentry called.

"Wish me luck," I said.

"As though you need luck," Rosalinda said.

"Mayhap you would be kind enough to offer me your favor, Lady Zhorzha?"

Again, either she didn't know what I meant, or not answering was her thing, because she just looked at me.

"Traditionally," I said, in case she didn't understand, "when a knight was going to joust in a tournament, a lady would give him a scarf or a glove, as a gesture of her favor. He would wear it around his arm or his neck, and return it to her after winning. You could give me your headband." She was wearing a completely anachronistic zebra-striped scrap of fabric to keep her hair out of her face.

"Okay, I don't know how to speak Middle English," she said. Instead of looking at me, she was staring across at where Gentry was helping Edrard adjust his pauldrons. "But I have read about a thousand romance novels, so I know what a *favor* is. I know a lady only gives something like that to her champion, and you aren't mine. So either you're trying to pull some kind of trick on me. Or you're trying to pull something on Gentry."

She stood up and walked across the field, pulling the headband out of her hair as she went. When she got to Gentry, she said something and he answered. Then she tied her headband around his arm. By the time she got back to where I was standing, I was still trying to come up with something clever to say. I settled for, "Well played, Lady Zhorzha."

The kicker was that Gentry beat me. It wasn't rare, but he usually got me with brute force, because he was pretty tireless, but he actually won on strategy that day. He kept swinging at my legs, until I got into a rhythm. Before I knew what he was doing, he slammed his shield down on top of mine and pinned it to the ground. Then he swung his sword right into the gap between my gorget and pauldron, and tore a buckle loose there. He followed it up with a round-house blow with his blade under the edge of my helm, hard enough it popped up against my chin.

That was our fifth or sixth bout, and he'd already finished Edrard like an appetizer, so when I went down, it was over.

"My brother, art 'ou well? I meant not hit thee so hard." He knelt down next to me, pulled off his gauntlet, and reached for the buckle under my helm. I pushed his hand back and unfastened it myself. I was going to have a bruise on my jaw.

"You really got my number," I said.

"The black knight says thou art too much inclined to guard thy leg over thy shoulder."

"Isn't that cheating, him getting coaching advice during our fight?" I said to Edrard, mostly joking.

"It's not poker," Edrard said. "It doesn't require cheating to notice you kept leaving yourself open."

Zee's headband was still tied around the

cannon of Gentry's vambrace, and before we walked back to camp, he returned it to her.

"I thank thee for thy favor, my lady," he said.

If it were me, I would have gone in for a kiss, because that was kind of the whole point of all the chivalry crap, but he bowed to her. I'd been telling him for years he could make bank with the ladies, but he never did.

"You're welcome," Zee said. "You did good, I think. You won, right?"

"Most assuredly, your champion prevailed," I said.

"Thou fought bravely, Sir Rhys." Gentry bowed to me, too, and then slung his armor on his shoulder, and followed Edrard and Rosalinda back to camp. Zee fell behind while she put her hair up, so I dropped back and let Gentry get ahead of us.

"Looks like you chose your champion wisely," I said. She rolled her eyes at me.

"My dad always told me you should dance with the one what brung ya."

CHAPTER 22
ZEE

"You can't blame me for trying," Rhys said, as we walked back to the main camp. "Plus, it's not like Gentry even notices stuff like that. We could be back here making out and he wouldn't care."

"I'm pretty sure you were trying to usurp the one job he does care about."

"Oh! *Usurp!* Damn. Lady Zhorzha dropping the big words on me."

"Gentry," I said. He was ahead of us, close enough to hear us, but he wasn't paying attention.

"Good luck with that. He's gone off the grid. You can't get through to him when he's like that. Come on, though, am I really being so terrible?"

"No, it's cool. You're being about average."

"Ow! Thou dost wound me, lady," Rhys said, and gave me what I guessed was the smile that usually worked on medieval maidens. I didn't have the energy for witty banter. It wore me out.

"Gentry!" I yelled. His head came up and he turned to look at me.

"My lady?"

"This knave is bothering me."

"Sir Rhys, leave the lady be. Thou art little better than Gawen."

Gentry fell back to walk next to me, but Rhys stuck with us.

"Do you know about Gawen?" he said. "About Gentry's invisible friends?"

"Is this what you usually do when you come out here?" I said to Gentry. "Work on your castle and have sword fights?"

"Yea, my lady. And sleep." He gave me a little smile.

"He's still training like he wants to qualify for Battle of the Nations, but you've pretty much given up on that, right?" Rhys said.

"What's Battle of the Nations?" I said, but Rhys didn't give Gentry a chance to answer.

"Essentially, it's the Olympics of historical medieval combat. Full armor, real fighting. Instead of using wooden swords, it's fought with actual medieval weaponry. Obviously, not with sharp edges. The blades are re-bated, but even with all the pointy bits knocked off a mace, it can still do some damage, right, Gentry?"

"Is that what happened to your shoulder?" I said.

"Yeah, before he hurt his shoulder, we were training to go to the tryouts for the American team. Then last year was a no-go. What about this year?"

" 'Twas last week. In Spain," Gentry said, the first thing Rhys let him get in.

"I guess it's lucky for me you didn't go this year," I said.

"How's that?" Rhys said.

"Because I needed him this week, and I was really glad he was here." I got a nod from Gentry, which seemed funny, since I was trying to thank him.

"Yeah, well, he's not actually ever going to Battle of the Nations. No way would his mother let him go to Europe." Rhys laughed. "She put her foot down pretty damn fast, as soon as he started talking seriously about it last year."

Rhys talked the whole way back to Mud Manor and, when we got there, he started dropping hints about going skinny-dipping in the pond. When I refused, the three guys went off to go swimming, and honestly, they needed it. Jousting was sweaty business.

"Don't take it the wrong way," Rosalinda said once we were alone. "Rhys is a terrible flirt, but he doesn't mean anything by it."

"It's nice to meet Gentry's friends." Habits are hard to break. Maybe Rosalinda's house was a mud shack and a fire pit, but it was still her house, so I wanted to be polite.

"Well, you know, Gentry is special to us." In case I didn't get the warning, Rosalinda followed up with, "I don't want you to be disappointed."

"About what?" I said.

"About Gentry. Do you know what a *paladin* is?"

I shook my head, because apparently it was Point Out the Gaping Holes in Zee's Education weekend.

"Let's just say that Gentry really is noble. It's not something he's playing at. He's a Christian, and not in the sense that he just goes to church every Sunday, but that he really believes in the chivalric code."

"I know he's a good guy."

"It's more than that, though," Rosalinda said. "So don't be surprised when you find out he can't be seduced."

I laughed, probably a lot louder than I should have, because the whole situation was funny. I wondered if I'd misunderstood about Edrard and Rosalinda being married, because she was acting kind of jealous. Did I look like I was planning to seduce Gentry?

"I'm just saying, I don't know of any girl

who's ever made it to second base with him." Rosalinda stood up with this prim little smile on her face and shook out her skirt.

I didn't know how to answer her, because she was being serious, and all I could think of were jokes. *He seems more like a short stop to me. Have any boys made it to second base with him?*

I settled for saying, "Did they have baseball in the Middle Ages?"

CHAPTER 23
ROSALINDA

All weekend it was *Lady Zhorzha this* and *Lady Zhorzha that,* while I got treated like a draft mule. The story of my life. The worst part was her flirting with Rhys while showboating about Gentry being her champion. Or maybe the worst part was Gentry acting like her servant. Her steak had to be cooked just right, and he cut it up for her like she was a baby.

After dinner, Edrard brought out his mandolin and we sang, which was our frequent amusement in the evenings, but then Zee stood up and said, "Not to ruin the illusion here, but I need to make a call. Is there any place that has better reception?"

In an instant, Gentry and Rhys were on their feet.

"My lady, yon hill is the place of fair to middling reception," Rhys said.

"I shall walk thee," Gentry said.

No matter how helpless Zee was with sewing and cooking, I assumed she could walk uphill without an escort, but I think she had something more than a phone call in mind, because she took Gentry with her. I'd warned her he wasn't that kind of man, but she probably took it as a challenge. She wouldn't be the first girl who decided she was going to be the one who finally hooked up with him, and she would be wrong like the rest of them. My mother always told me that men prefer to do the chasing, and they prefer a woman who's never been caught.

Zee and Gentry were gone so long that Rhys joked about some mischief befalling them, but the only thing likely to befall them was Zee making a fool of herself. When they came back at sunset, it was obvious she'd been crying. Of course, Rhys noticed that Zee seemed a bit down, and then he and Gentry were having a chivalry-off. *Did my lady want some more mead? Was my lady warm enough? Too warm?*

"Do you guys ever smoke up?" Zee said, after they'd moved the big log bench about five inches further from the fire for her.

"No," I said. "Cigarettes are as much an anachronism as cellphones."

"I don't know what that means, but I wasn't talking about cigarettes. Do you like to get high?"

246

The answer should have been no, but Edrard ignored the look I gave him and said, "I'm not opposed to partaking of a little medicinal herb."

"Hear hear. This party needs a fun injection," Rhys said.

I expected Gentry to be on my side, but he went up to his pavilion and brought down a zippered makeup pouch that belonged to Zee. I wouldn't have minded so much if they'd only smoked a little, but they kept passing Zee's pipe around until they were all stoned. Including Gentry. I assumed that was her doing, but when I asked him when he'd started smoking marijuana, he said, "My brother Carlees, when we weren in school, we smoked, tho it my mother liketh not."

While they smoked, I sang, but after they got stoned, Edrard sang a bawdy song, which meant Rhys had to sing a vulgar one.

"What about you? Do you sing, too?" Zee said to Gentry.

"My lady, Sir Gentry is a warrior, not a bard," Edrard said.

Gentry laughed. He was lounging at Zee's feet, but he sat up and cleared his throat.

"Needest thou a note to tune thy voice?" Edrard said, which made us all laugh.

Out of absolutely nowhere, Gentry sang.

Or anyway he made a joke of singing.

"Roxanne! Thou needst not hang that lantern tonight. Roxanne! Ne wearen that cotehardie tonight."

"Oh my god, that is such shit!" Rhys said, but Edrard and Zee laughed like hyenas. "I call foul. That is clearly the work of Gawen."

"Nay, 'tis mine own devising." Gentry smiled and leaned his head back against the bench, almost close enough to touch Zee's leg.

"It's totally his. We heard that song on the drive down yesterday," Zee said.

"Yes, but if Gentry heard it, Gawen heard it, too. Think of Gawen as Gentry's conjoined twin," Rhys said. "His evil invisible conjoined twin."

"Nay, he be no brother of mine," Gentry said.

"Then what is he?" Before Gentry could answer, Rhys went back to talking to Zee like he was narrating a nature documentary. "Since he was a kid, he's been hearing these voices, right? And before you say schizophrenia —"

"I wasn't going to say schizophrenia," Zee said. "But I was going to ask who's where, Gentry, because I'm not always sure who you're talking to."

"Oh, you really only need to know about

the trinity," Rhys said. "The Lion, the Witch, and the Wardrobe."

Gentry laughed, but he sat up straighter and pointed them out, the way his mother had done for me. "The Witch," above his head. "Hildegard," a little to his left, and "Gawen," who was behind his left shoulder. Then he said something I'd never heard before, so it must have been for Zee's benefit: "Hag, Nag, Douchebag."

Everybody thought that was so clever. Zee laughed and tossed her head forward so that her hair fell across Gentry's shoulder. He was laughing too much to notice.

"Nooo. He's not a douchebag. We love Gawen!" Edrard said. "He makes us merry and doth often slay us with laughter."

"Yea, he would slay me. His japery is unceasing, such that I cannot bear to frig myself upon the left, and must take it upon my right." Gentry made a gesture like he was masturbating, right there in mixed company.

Zee stopped laughing long enough to say, "Are you seriously telling me you had to change which hand you stroke off with, because this guy is always talking to you?"

"Lady, in my youth, it distressed me mightily."

Everybody went on laughing, but I hated

for Gentry to act that way to impress Zee. It was clearly about her, because he'd never said anything that crude in the whole time I'd known him. He'd always spoken like a gentleman. Also, I felt sorry for Zee. Apparently her mother had never told her that a man won't respect a woman who allows that kind of familiarity.

They went on joking and laughing, until Zee picked up Gentry's tankard of mead and took the last swallow.

"Wouldst take more?" he said.

"No, at this point all I need is a bath and to sleep for like twelve hours."

"We ladies are due a turn in the bathing pool. I shall be ready soon enough." I went into the house to finish a few chores, but when I came out ten minutes later with a towel and a fresh dress, only Rhys and Edrard were at the fire. I said, "Where are Zee and Sir Gentry?"

"He walked her to the pond," Rhys said. "I guess she's not completely averse to skinny-dipping."

"That's rude. I was going to go with them."

"I'm not sure they wanted company."

"Well, I wanted a bath."

"Do you want me to walk with you?" Edrard said, but he didn't get up. If I insisted, he would, but he only offered so he could say he had.

"No. Unlike Zee, I'm not afraid of the dark."

"Meow," Rhys said, which was ridiculous. It was not catty to expect people to be polite and inclusive.

As I went up the path toward the ponds, I heard Zee and Gentry coming toward me.

"But what if I'd drowned?" she was saying.

"My lady, certs thou art taller than I, and I never drowned. And thou must not forget Melusine."

"Who?"

"Melusine, that was spied upon in her bath by her husband. I would not meet his fate."

"Did he catch her shaving?"

" 'Twas far worse," Gentry said. "If it liketh thee, I shall tell the tale."

"Good even!" I called, since we'd nearly reached each other.

"He had to cut me out of this dress," Zee said. "I'm not a fan of that."

"There's no need to be melodramatic about it. It's a common way to make the sleeves of a cotehardie fit tight, without buttons. You snip the thread and it all comes loose."

"Okay, but I don't usually need a man with a sharp knife to undress me."

I doubted it usually took that much effort to get her out of her clothes. She hadn't even gotten redressed. She was walking through the woods wearing nothing but a wet linen chemise, carrying her cotehardie and surcoat over her arm.

"If you'd waited for me, I could have helped you," I said. "I hope you didn't damage the fabric."

"Nay, as thou sayest, 'twas easily undone. Ne cloth rent ne blood shed," Gentry said. The moon was bright enough that I could see his hair was dry. He hadn't gone in for a swim with Zee.

"Sir Gentry, would you be so kind as to walk me up so I'm not bathing alone?" I said.

He hesitated, which was a first. He had always offered his help freely when I asked for it.

"If it giveth thee no trouble, Lady Zhorzha?" he said.

"Oh, I don't want to keep Lady Zhorzha standing out here with her wet hair," I said. "She can take my lantern to find her way."

"I think I know which way the tent is." She turned and pointed. "That way, and then up the path where the 1871 fence post is, right?"

"Yea, my lady. True as an arrow."

"Here, my lady." I held out my flashlight and she looped it over her wrist.

"Just so you know, Rosalinda, he's a lousy lifeguard. He didn't keep an eye on me at all." Zee laughed as she went down the path, singing "Roxanne" like a drunk tavern wench.

CHAPTER 24
ZEE

Rosalinda could disapprove all she wanted, but I felt better after I got high, and I laughed so much my face hurt. After I took my bath, I hiked back to the tent singing to myself, which I almost never did. I'd used the chemise as my towel, so I hung it up to dry. In the summer, it was probably scorching hot in the tent, but right then, it felt good to lie there naked.

When I heard footsteps out by the fire ring, I yanked my nightgown on and said, "Are you coming to tell me a story?"

"Sure, I can tell you a story. What do you want to hear? 'Goldilocks and the Three Medieval Bears'?" Rhys, not Gentry. I smoothed out my nightgown, before he opened the flap on the tent and looked in at me.

"I thought you were Gentry," I said.

"I thought *you* were Gentry."

"Rosalinda didn't want to swim by herself,

so he's waiting on her."

"I guess she's not done flirting with him after all." Rhys obviously wanted me to ask about that, so I kept my mouth shut. "Is it okay if I wait for him?"

"Knock yourself out," I said.

"Cool." He started to step into the tent, so I shook my head at him.

"You can wait out there. I'm going to sleep."

Once he pulled the tent flap closed, I turned off the light to keep him from bothering me. I must have drifted off, because I woke up to Gentry laughing and saying, "Thou art a knave." To Rhys? I guessed not, because nobody answered before Gentry said, "The lady sleepeth and hath not said I might wake her. Nay. My greatest wish is that thou stint thy clappe."

"Gentry," I called.

"My lady."

I turned the lantern on and got up to look outside. He was squatted next to the fire ring arranging a pile of logs.

"Are you coming to tell me the story about the lady whose husband spied on her taking a bath?" I said. He came over to the tent, but when I stepped back to let him in, he hesitated. I held up my hands and made little scratchy movements. "I'll scratch your back for you."

Gentry ducked and stepped inside. Then we were standing in the tent together, me looking at him and him looking at my bare feet. His hands hung down at his sides, but relaxed like he didn't know what to do with them. Now that I'd seen him fight, I wondered if when he clenched his hand up, he imagined he was gripping a sword. Something familiar to do with his hands.

"If you were someone else, I would kiss you now," I said.

"I am naught but myself."

"I didn't mean it that way. I meant, I would kiss you, except I know you didn't like it the last time I tried it."

"Nay, my lady. Thy kiss was no outrage upon me. 'Twas only that I knew not what thou . . ." That was all the words he got out.

He kept his head down, so I couldn't see his face, but he clenched his right hand around his invisible sword. Was that anger? Or nervousness? Or something else?

"Is it okay if I kiss you now?" I said. I knew flirting with him was stupid, but I was still high, and I didn't want to be alone. Plus I liked watching him fight, and that he laughed so hard at his own jokes.

"Where?" he said, which gave me the giggles.

"I thought I'd start with your lips. And then maybe your jaw, next to your ear. And then a little bit lower, on your neck." I'd never been asked before where I was going to kiss somebody, so I thought it was better to be really specific. I waited for follow-up questions, but he nodded and raised his head enough that he was looking at my lips.

I leaned in, still feeling giggly, and kissed him on the corner of his mouth. Since he didn't seem to mind that, I centered the next one. Then, like I'd told him I would, I kissed his jaw, right where it met his ear. A little bit below that was apparently the sweet spot, because when I kissed him there, he made this sound — I swear, the sexiest sound I ever heard a man make — this involuntary groan that I don't think he even knew he could make.

I took half a step back to give him some space, but he brought his right hand up to my jaw, so his thumb touched my chin. His other hand hovered like he couldn't decide where to put it, but he finally settled on my arm, below my elbow.

I thought, *Is he actually going to kiss me?* right before he did. Whatever base that was, he had definitely Frenched somebody before, because he knew the basics. It lasted about thirty seconds before he dropped his hands and took a step back, almost into the side of the tent.

"My lady —" He was going to apologize.

"You're okay. It's okay. Come sit down and tell me the story." I sat down on the bed and patted the space next to me, but he stayed standing where he was.

" 'Twas many years past," he said. Then he took a deep breath and started over.

" 'Twas many hundred years past and the king of Alba was a man called Elynas. One day he rode out hunting into the greenwood, where he came upon a lady called Pressyne. So fair was she, her lips bedewed, that he bade her marry him. The lady assented but bade him swear never come into her chamber while she bathed or birthed."

"Birthed? He wasn't supposed to see her bathing or giving birth?" I hated to interrupt him, but I wasn't sure I understood.

"Nay, and he swore this oath. Ere they weren wed many years, she bore Elynas three daughters. Palatyne, Melior, and Melusine."

"Uh-oh."

"Tho the king swore, as holy a troth as his marriage vow, suspicion entered his heart. What secret kept the lady from him? And wherefore? Soon he broke his vow. At the door of the lady Pressyne's chamber, he knelt and looked through the keyhole."

Gentry acted it out, kneeling down and putting his hand up to his eye like it was a keyhole. It was so cute, I laughed. Then he started giggling.

"You're stoned," I said. He shook his head. Then he nodded, still laughing.

"I am happy, my lady, but shamed it is at the cost of thine own happiness."

"How do you figure?"

"Thou art here only because of thy distress, but thou art here."

"How long have you been planning to bring me here?"

"From the day the Witch told me I was to be thy champion."

He was still smiling when he brought both his hands up and started scratching. First his neck, then his shoulders. After a minute or so, he stopped scratching and put his hands flat on the tops of his thighs.

"Lo, the king looked and saw Pressyne disporting in her bath —"

"Disporting?"

"The lady was playing in the water, but she was no lady."

I bit my tongue, even though I had a bunch of questions. If she wasn't a lady, how had she given birth to three daughters?

"Above her navel, she was like as any lady. Soft of shoulder. Full of breast. But below her navel, she had a great split tail atwinkle with silvered scales. The king meant to spy her in secret but, in his surprise, he cried out. Pressyne heard his cry and knew he betrayed his hest to keep the privacy of her bath. In a fury, she flew thence. She carried her three daughters to the enchanted Isle of Avalon, and swore King Elynas never see her nor them again."

"Okay. Wait. Pressyne —" Those crazy names, like my mother was in charge of naming mysterious women from the forest. "I thought Melusine was the one whose husband spied on her while she was taking a bath, but it's Pressyne with the spying husband? I'm confused."

Gentry scratched at his neck and his shoulders again, frowning the whole time.

"Nay," he said, but nothing else. I felt like I'd screwed up the whole thing, the story and him being there with me. Like I'd peeked through the keyhole at him taking a bath. I wished we could go back to the part where he was laughing at his own jokes.

CHAPTER 25
GENTRY

"I promised to scratch your back while you told me a story. Come lie down," Lady Zhorzha said.

By such enticement she drew me on, but I withstood. Upon my knees, beside the pallet I made for her, I was reminded of my proper place. When she saw I would not lie with her, she rose before me, her hair about her like a cloak, and reached for me with her dragon's talons. I meant to take no more than was offered, but she scoured my shoulders in slow circles so that I lost the thread of my tale. I gained upon her til my brow rested against her belly, and all that lay between us was the cloth of her chemise. Soon, twixt her flesh and mine, there was kindred warmth. I breathed upon her and breathed her in. She smelled of darkness and cool water and full sun all at once.

"Why don't you put out that light and come to bed?" she said.

"Nay, I shall keep the watch this night."

"So you liked kissing me, but you don't want to sleep with me?"

"Wert thou only a woman, and I only a man, I would swive thee." I drew back from her, for I would be ruled by the oath I swore to protect her, and not by my desire.

"You would what?" she said.

"Wert thou a doe and I a stag in rut, I would mount thee." I spake plainly that she might ken me.

"Wow, Gentry. I don't know if you're reciting poetry or talking dirty to me. But what am I, if I'm not a woman?"

"Thou art the daughter of a dragon, and above all, thou art the lady I swore to protect and champion."

"You think my mother's a dragon?" She laughed in a voice that carried the truth: deep and full of smoke. With one finger, she lifted her chemise til half her thigh was bared. "Or because of this?"

"Yea, my lady, and —" I could discover no more words, for she drew her chemise higher. Tho she held me not, I was tranced.

"It's not a dragon, you know."

"Is it not?" My voice was thin as water.

"It's a phoenix. Do you know what a phoenix is?"

" 'Tis a token of the Resurrection."

"It is? I just know it's a bird that rises from the ashes and is born again. Oh! The Resurrection. That makes sense."

Higher she raised her chemise, that I might see the feathered tail and haunch of the beast laid to bone by fire and graved in black. She turned and bared her buttock, where wings arched in flames against the white of her flesh. She turned further and the beast's sharp-hooked beak emerged in a raging fire upon her back.

Ere she let the chemise fall, I saw the bright flame flash of hair twixt her thighs. The thing that rose in my breast was a tangled skein of bravery and lust. I pledged fealty with my lips upon the place where the fire bird's black claw carved blood-ready into her pale skin.

Quick as 'twas done, I needed none to tell me I presumed too far.

"Forgive me," I said.

I sat back upon my heels that I might rise and leave her, but Lady Zhorzha returned her hand to my shoulder. She slipped it into my blouse, so that skin kissed skin, her palm to my breast. My breath caught and my heart stammered, too sharp to bear. I pushed her hand away.

"Did you just parry me?" she said. She stepped back and sat herself down upon the pallet. With her hands gone from me, my heart calmed and I perceived my villainy.

"Lady, I meant no offense."

"I'm not offended, but it's not a sword fight. All you had to say was *no.* Or *nay.*"

"I said not nay."

"Then what? You brought me here and fed me your food and put me in your bed. Why?"

"Little knight, she is nigh naked for thee," said Gawen. "Thou hast seen and smelt the hair of her cunt. Lady or no, dragon or no, she offereth herself to thee."

"Like a bitch in heat," Hildegard said. "Thou art of no import to her. The slattern would open her legs to any man."

"And he runneth like a frighted whelp."

"I am no coward," I said.

"I know you're not," Lady Zhorzha said, laughing.

"But I am more fitted to battle than bower. I shall go, for I would not offend thee further."

"Wilt thou leave her to Sir Rhys? He would not retreat thus," Gawen said. "If not afraid, art thou unable?"

"I am able."

"Unwilling to fight leaveth a man as dead as unable to fight. Show her thou hast some fire."

" 'Tis not fire," Hildegard said. " 'Tis filthy lust. She hath no shame, and thou must have it for ye both."

I would hear the Witch's wisdom, but she was silent.

"Stay and finish the story," Lady Zhorzha said. "I promise I won't touch you again. Unless you want me to."

"Lady, thy lips are soft and thy breath is sweet." I longed to have her ken me, but I kenned not myself.

"I wager her cunt is soft and sweet," Gawen said.

"Yea, and were the deed done, mayhap 'twould all turn to bitterness," I said.

"What does Gawen say?" she said, for I could not conceal it from her.

"I care not, my lady. I would not have thee despise me."

"Oh," she said upon a sigh. "Like I haven't had sex with people I despised."

"I would not be numbered among them. Where aren they? Standen they ready to take up a sword to defend thee?"

"No, they're long gone."

"And when thou scorneth me, wilt thou allow me to stay? I think thou wilt send me from thee."

"What if I promised not to send you away?"

"Wilt thou? Swear such a vow?"

"Sure," she said, tho she smiled. I knew not if 'twas in jest.

"Sooth? Thou wilt not send me away from thee?"

"I won't. I promise." Her voice was soft, and so by a venture she spake truth. "But how do you know you'll be ready to defend me with your sword if you haven't tried it?"

"She meaneth thy prick," Gawen said.

"Yea, I ken she meaneth my prick."

"What about your prick?" she said much amused, for I misspoke to her.

I knew not how to answer, for certs I was able, but was I willing?

"Finish your story, Gentry. So what about Pressyne? What the heck was she?"

"Some say Pressyne and Melusine alike weren water nymphs, like as the Lady of the Lake that stole Sir Lancelot when he was a babe."

"A water nymph!" Lady Zhorzha laughed and coiled upon her side that I might see the phoenix burning upon her limb. I looked, tho Hildegard said, "Filth" and "Slut."

I took up the tale again, tho ne my liver ne mine heart weren at peace.

" 'Twas Melusine first among Pressyne's daughters who learned why they lived exiled in Avalon. Quick as she knew it, she was wroth and swore to revenge her father's slight against her mother. She betook her sisters to the place of their birth in Alba, whence they kidnapped King Elynas. They also took his riches, and secured them in a cavern until they might devise their revenge.

"When their mother heard what they had done, she was full wroth. For tho she loved him no more, tho she forgave him not, she would not that his own daughters shew him uncourtesy. She cast them three out and cursed them, but most especially Melusine that had plotted this act against her father. Melusine, like her mother, was cursed to take the form of a monstrous sea serpent, not only in her bath or in birth, but upon each Saturday, from sunup to sundown.

"Exiled from Alba and from Avalon, Melusine and her sisters wandered til, one day, they came upon a lone huntsman in the forest of Poitiers. He was distraught and unburdened himself of his sad tale. That morn, he and the Duke of Poitiers, that was his uncle, had made up a party of twenty men for hunting, and rode into the forest. During the hunt, they became lost. The duke and the young man, who was called Raymondin, weren alone together.

"The boar they sought to hunt burst from

the trees. Raymondin raised his blade to strike it dead, but misstruck and swung again. When the boar lay dead at his feet, Raymondin saw that the first hit of his sword slew his uncle the duke. The boar and the nobleman lay side by side, both dead. In grief and confusion Raymondin wandered the forest until he found Melusine and her sisters beside a stream.

"*What,* he asked of Melusine, *ought I do?*

"*Go,* she said, *and ride out of the woods. Pretend thou knowest naught of thy kinsman's fate. Say only that ye two weren parted as well. None shall suspect thee.*

"The lady was right, for in the confusion of the hunt, none had seen Raymondin and the duke together. The huntsmen returned to the wood and found the duke. *He slew the boar and the boar slew him,* they said. They took his body to the cathedral and laid him out. Some days after, Raymondin returned to the forest to thank the lady and entreated her be his bride. She assented but bade him swear never enter her chamber while she was under her mother's curse."

"Well, crap. Like mother, like daughter," Lady Zhorzha said. She prostrated herself and lay her hand upon her eyes as tho she would shut out some horrible vision.

"Yea, my lady. 'Twas many years that Melusine and Raymondin weren steadfast in marriage. She built him up a great castle with mighty fortifications that still stand, called Lusignan. Because of this, Raymondin was made Count of Poitou. Melusine gave him also many sons. All weren strong and clever, but each was in some way disfigured. One with a great tusk like a boar's. One with ears like a donkey's. One called Horrible with a third eye upon his forehead. And so on.

"Raymondin loved her, but soon his brothers, who coveted his castle and his crown, cast into his ears suspicion that Melusine's secret Sabbaths were of evil intent. That mayhap 'twas the devil's work that her sons weren ugly. Tho he vowed never do it, Raymondin crept to her bedchamber one Saturday and looked into the keyhole. There she was, like her mother before her."

"Disporting in the bath?" said my lady.

"Yea. Disporting in her bath. Raymondin gazed upon her monstrous tail and her white neck and her glistering scales and her high, round breasts. He saw and he loved her no less. For she was this mysterious creature, and yet she consented to love him and share his bed six days of each week. He went from her bedchamber with all care and silence, and for many years hence, spake no word of what he had seen, and would hear no more accusations against her.

"The sons of Raymondin and Melusine grew to manhood, and weren known as brave knights, most especially he of the boar's tusk, that was called Geoffrey Big-Tooth. In a while, there arose a quarrel twixt Geoffrey and his pious brother Froymond. Geoffrey would not see Froymond taken into a monastery, for he scorned monks and feared they held sway over Froymond. In a great fury, Geoffrey fired the monastery. It burned and with it, the monks and his own brother.

"When the dire news reached Lusignan, Raymondin wept to hear the evil deeds of Geoffrey, and Melusine took herself to his side to succor him upon her white neck. In his grief, Raymondin remembered how it was that Geoffrey was birthed, from the great scaled nether parts of Melusine. He pushed her from him and cried out, *Touch me not, odious serpent!*

"Melusine's grief and anger weren much at war, but she withdrew from Raymondin and said, *Thou hast broken the only vow I asked of thee on our wedding day. By cause of the curse upon me, I must renounce thee.* Tears upon her cheeks, knowing that the curse must part her from her dear husband, she transformed. Her tail lay in full view before all of the court at Lusignan, and from her back furled two great wings, scaled alike as her tail. Leaving behind two young sons in their cradle, she thrice flew about the castle ramparts, and cried out in grief. She flew thence and was nevermore seen by Raymondin."

My lady was quiet, and for a nonce I thought she slept, for I feared my tale was not to her liking. Then she drew her hand from her eyes and looked at me, so that I averted my gaze.

"That's really kind of horrible," she said. "How hard was it for him to keep that one promise? I mean, it's not like he thought she was grotesque. He still loved her after he knew she was a monster. They were still making babies, but then he had to throw that in her face. That's cruel. Her son was dead, too."

'Twas true, but I had no answer.

" 'Tis late, my lady. I wish thee good night," I said.

"Good night, Gentry."

As I rose to go, the Witch's breath fell cold upon my head.

"Art thou content to be a bloodless priest?" she said. "Another Froymond, who felt no heat til the church burned round his

271

ears? This mayhap is the last path that lies smooth afore you. I gave her into thy protection believing thy blood was hot and thine heart strong."

"Always he proveth his virtue, but he showeth the lady no faith," the black knight said. I startled to hear him, for ere that night he spake to me only when I was in the joust.

Gawen and Hildegard discorded over his meaning, and argued til the Witch made them silent.

"Sooth," she said. "The lady hath proved her trust in thee, but thou givest not of thine own trust."

"Nay. I trust her."

"By thy word, not thy deed," the black knight said. "Many things binden two. Love, fear, a common enemy. Ye two haven not these things. If ye would be bound, it must be with trust."

"And ye would tell the boy to build trust with fornication?" Hildegard said.

"Trust is built as a tower is built. One stone upon another," the Witch said. "The lady hath laid her stone. Thou must lay thine atop it."

"Gentry?" 'Twas Lady Zhorzha, and I knew not how long she said my name and I heard her not. "Are you okay?"

"Yea, my lady." I laid my stone. "If thou

consentest, I would kiss thee."

"Yes, you can kiss me."

Many times had I dreamt she might come to be there within my pavilion, under my protection, but I never imagined it thus. She lay upon the bed, waiting to receive me. Where the fire bird touched her not, her legs weren white as cream, and the flesh of her arms was not yet scaled like her mother's.

"If thou givest thy heart in fire, thou shalt not fail her when the time comes," the Witch said.

I was drawn tight as a bow when I leant down over Lady Zhorzha and pressed my lips to hers. We kissed us. Soft at first and then with great heat.

"You can touch me," she said.

"Where?" 'Twas only half in jest, but she laughed.

"Wherever you want."

Through the fabric of her chemise, her breasts weren round and cool as river rock, but warmed to my hand. I pressed my lips to her throat, where the sun had kissed her before me.

She laid her hand upon my neck, and I retreated, for 'twas always thus with me. My armor stripped away, and my skin with it, til I was raw and atremble.

I braced for her curses, but she said, "It's okay. You can say stop, if you want to stop. Or wait, if you want to wait."

She rose upon one elbow, and her other hand made to cover her legs. Quick as the phoenix was hidden, I longed to see it again. I returned to her and lifted her chemise that I might lay my hand upon her bare thigh. When I was not burned, I made my pilgrimage. From her thigh to her broad hip, and from thence to her belly and again to her bosom, drawing alongside her chemise so that she was naked neath my hand. Ere I could falter or quail, I kissed her mouth, her throat, and at last her breast.

She gave a great sigh of surprise but chastened me not.

Soon enough, I lost my armor, and everywhere our skin touched was like fire to me. I drew back that I might gather some maille about me for protection. Tho I set my nails upon my shoulders, 'twas some time ere I lost my unrestfulness. She sat up before me and waited, her hair all fire about her shoulders.

"More?" she said.

From the black knight's words, I had prepared myself that swiving was akin to fighting. 'Twas not. Never would I ask quarter of another knight, but I asked it of

Lady Zhorzha again and again. Each time, she me granted mercy.

CHAPTER 26
ZEE

I thought he was only going to kiss me, so when he touched my breasts, I was about as shocked as he must have been that day in the physical therapy clinic parking lot. There I was thinking we'd go slow and figure things out, but the time from kissing my mouth to kissing my breasts was a minute, tops.

As fast as we got started, it was over. He pushed himself back up on his knees, and I wondered if he was having another discussion with his voices. I sat up in front of him and said, "Can I touch you?"

I thought he was going to say *no* or *where,* but he said, "Yea, dear lady."

I followed the same route he'd taken on me, running my hand up his thigh and over his belly. He was fully dressed, which didn't seem fair, so I took ahold of the front of his blouse with both hands and untucked it. I leaned in and kissed him, while I ran my hands over his bare chest.

He turned his head to break the kiss and said, "Wait."

Wait, which was not *stop.*

I'd promised that was all he had to say, so I took my hands out from under his shirt. For a few seconds he pressed his hands flat on his thighs, and then he put them up to his shoulders and started scratching.

I waited, calm at first and then, when I realized what was going to happen when he finished scratching, kind of excited. I pulled off my nightgown and laid back on the bed. He stopped scratching. He looked at me and squeezed his hand in a fist so tight his knuckles went white.

"Watching you do that gets me a little wet," I said. I did not know what constituted medieval dirty talk, but that was true. He had great hands.

He leaned down and started kissing me again. It was this weirdly urgent kiss, considering I was lying there naked and he wasn't even touching me. Part of what made it so good was that I knew it wouldn't last. In another minute, he was going to pull away like my lips were burning him. Maybe they were. A virtuous Christian knight like him kissing an odious serpent like me.

I knew the clock was running down, so I

went at him from two angles. One hand under his shirt, the other one into the gap at the top of his pants. I didn't even touch bare skin there, because he was wearing boxer shorts. He made a sound that I assumed was *wait.* Then he was back on his knees next to me, like he was in time-out. His left hand on top of his head. His right hand hovering out in the air. Open, then clenched.

The situation was complicated and frustrating, but Gentry was hairy and sweaty and hard-dicked, and those are my three favorite things about men. Everything else is negotiable.

Once I thought of it as negotiating, it wasn't complicated. It was really simple. We were on a swing going back and forth. Not enough. Too much. Not enough. Too much. In between: a minute of just right.

When we swung toward not enough, it was this insanely hot high school heavy petting. Like musical chair sex, and I didn't know when the music would stop.

When we swung toward too much, I couldn't even touch him.

But the in-between, the just right? Oh my god. An absolute free-for-all.

The next time he kissed me, he didn't waste time petting my legs. He pushed his hand between my thighs and said, "Sooth, my lady, thy cunt *is* wet."

That word coming out of his mouth made me laugh so hard I started crying a little. He took his hands off me and rocked back on his heels with a serious frown on his face.

"My lady. Art thou well? Have I wounded thee?"

"I'm fine, but I can't believe you said *cunt.*"

I expected him to apologize, but he said, kind of defensively, " 'Tis a good English word," which made me start laughing again. I was definitely still buzzed.

I rolled onto my side to look at him. He was kneeling there, looking at me, and for once I knew exactly what he was thinking. He was taking inventory of what he wanted to do to me.

"I don't mind if you say *cunt,*" I said. Honestly, I could respect a man who would drop the c-word while his hand was in it.

"I would do more than say it."

"Then come here and do it."

Finally, I got him to lie down with me. So there wouldn't be any confusion about whether he had permission, I opened my legs for him, and he went straight for it with his sword hand. Two fingers in me and his thumb digging into that little cushion of fat over my pubic bone. Holy fuck, he had a grip on him.

We went round and round for I don't know how long, before he unlaced his pants, and I actually got him in me.

Too much.

During one of those too much minutes, lying next to each other, breathing hard, not touching, I realized I was waiting for him to say *yea*. I wasn't waiting for it to be over, like I usually did with men. I was waiting for his mouth to come back to mine. My skin felt flushed and prickly. Ready.

"Now?" I said.

"Nay, my lady." He had his face buried in the pillow and his voice was hoarse. Where his hand was lying between us, every time I inhaled, the little hairs on his knuckles brushed against my belly.

He turned over to face me and opened his eyes.

Shifting his hand, he traced his thumb from my hip bone down the front of my thigh to my knee. I went goosebumps all over. When I rolled onto my back, he followed, kissing me. I took his hand and put it between my legs, because we kept circling back to that moment when I was the sword.

I was so close to getting off — something that almost never happened for me with men — that I didn't know what to do. Except I didn't want it to be over yet, so I said, "Wait." That way I could lie next to him, feeling him waiting. His breath was warm on my shoulder when he said, "Now?" but I waited a little longer before I said yes.

When I came, he had his mouth against mine, but we were breathing so hard it wasn't really a kiss.

After that, I wanted what I always wanted: a few minutes to be inside my body by myself. When I pushed Gentry's hand away, he let me go. We laid there next to each other for a couple minutes, and I felt this quiet calm, like I hadn't felt in ages. I stretched and my hip popped.

He wasn't done, but I wasn't sure if he wanted to be or not.

"Do you want me to?" I didn't offer anything, because I figured he could show me what he wanted. Instead, he started stroking himself off, which I understood. Sometimes it was easier to take care of yourself. After a little bit, he reached over and put his left hand on top of mine, so we held hands while he jerked off. I thought that was sweet, but I wondered what the hag, the nag, and the douchebag had to say about it.

CHAPTER 27
GENTRY

While the sky was still dark on Sunday morn, I lit the fire and cooked that Lady Zhorzha and I might break our fast. I made small bread with eggs and ham baked upon them, and brewed coffee. I meant not to wake her, but ere 'twas ready, she rose and came forth from my pavilion.

"Hey," she said.

"Good morrow, my lady."

She came to the fire, near enough that I smelled her warmth and saw the red marks of sleep on her arms. Lo all the uncertainty I spent my night hours upon departed as quick as mist under the sun.

"Art thou hungry?"

"I could eat," she said. "But I need to pee first."

"I left thee a pot for such matters."

"Yeah, no. I'm not gonna pee in a pot and have you empty it. Can I just go squat in the woods like any self-respecting bear?"

"Yea, Lady Bear, as it pleaseth thee."

She laughed and betook herself into the trees. When she returned, I poured the water I had heated that she might wash. Then I whetted my blade and made to shear the night's beard.

"You're seriously going to shave with that big knife?" she said.

"Yea, but 'tis only a middling knife."

She seated herself near me, and I was uneaseful under her gaze.

"Okay, if that's how you shave, what the heck are you doing to your hair? I've been wanting to ask that for as long as I've known you."

My hairs weren too recent cut short, but I acted it for her. I clutched a handful where it grew upon my crown and made as though to pass my blade twixt head and hand. She laughed so that I dared not look upon her, for the firelight gilded the shape of her breast and roused flames in mine own bosom.

"The sound of scissors 'pon my head liketh me not," I said.

"Okay. That explains a lot."

Our ablutions finished, I took our repast from the fire.

"If it thee liketh, we might break our fast atop the hill and see the sunrise."

"Let me put some clothes on," she said, for tho she was warm next the fire, the morning was chill.

"My cloak hangeth in the pavilion, if thou wilt wear it."

Lady Zhorzha drew it over her chemise and laced her shoes, while I packed our meal in a basket. Upon the hill, I spread the blanket and we ate in quiet but good fellowship. In the east, the sun painted the sky in red. All was still but for the stirrings of deer and turkeys, and only a whisper of smoke rising from the trees revealed our camp below.

"Do you come out here every weekend?" she said.

"As oft as I may, but less than I wish. For my lord Bombardier requireth much of me, and my mother and sister needen me. And thee, my lady."

"You don't have to look out for me all the time. In the last two years, I only desperately needed your help like twice."

" 'Tis no hardship that I should see thee every day," I said.

To my perplexity, she laughed.

"I jest not, my lady. To hold thee in my protection is both duty and pleasure."

"I wish LaReigne was under someone's protection. It makes me crazy not knowing

284

where she is or if she's safe. The marshals act like if she had a relationship with this guy, she's safe. Like those aren't exactly the guys who kill you."

Lady Zhorzha shivered, but she drew not my cloak to cover her shoulders and arms. I had no comfort for her, but the quiet eased me, and I hoped it served her also. She rose and walked to the edge of the bluff. The sun arrived in all its heraldry and lit her hair like a watch fire, like the quick leap of a spark upon dry grass.

I went to her, and for once, those within me all weren silent. They offered no warning and no guidance, so that I followed only mine own heart. I went down upon my knee to Lady Zhorzha and, finding me there before her, she offered her hand. I envied Sir Rhys' ease in that passage of a lady's hand to his lips, but I possessed it not. Still I took her fingers into mine.

"Mayhap thou art a phoenix, for thy hair is like fire," I said.

She laughed and pressed my hand.

"It's beautiful here. I wish I could stay here. I wish I could bring Marcus here." She was heartsore to be parted from her little page. The night past, she had gone up the hill to call him, but his grandfather rebuked her and would not allow her to speak with Marcus. She had been much distraught. "But I can't stay, can I? I need to figure out what to do, and I have no clue what that is. I feel so fucking helpless," she said.

"What wouldst thou do? Wishest thou return to thy mother?"

"I don't know. We always fight, and I'm no use to her, but I can't just hide out here and wait for . . . I don't even know what I'd be waiting for. We have to go back to Wichita anyway, don't we?"

"I vowed we should return ere the midday meal, for my aunt, the lady Bernice, needeth my help," I said.

"I know you have things to do. You don't need to worry about me."

She released my hand and, all the while she paced the hilltop in her fiery splendor, I kept watch. She spake not to me of the battle that raged in her, but ere the sun rose above the trees, she returned to me.

"I think I need to go see my uncle," she said.

"My lady, I shall take thee wheresoever thou wilt."

"No. I can't ask you to do that. It's all the way in Missouri. Plus, I haven't seen him in a long time. He acted really weird when I called him, so I don't even know if it would be safe to take you with me."

"If it be not safe for me, how can it be safe for thee?" I said.

Lady Zhorzha put out her hands as though she meant to place them upon my breast. I braced myself, but she did not lay hold of me.

"My uncle is — He used to be involved with some really bad men and maybe he still is. I wouldn't feel right taking you there."

"Fear not for me, but give me leave to stand at thy side."

"Ah, thy pride revealeth thee," Hildegard said. "Thou speakest like a braggart, not one content to serve. Thou wouldst that she see thee as a great warrior."

"More like she shall see thee as a preening cock," Gawen said.

" 'Tis not preening to declare I am unafraid to meet her enemies."

"I'm not saying you're afraid," Lady Zhorzha said. "But maybe you should be."

CHAPTER 28
ZEE

Rhys said they sometimes fought with real weapons, and on Sunday morning, they did. It was crazier than MMA, because it was seriously three guys in armor with swords and shields waling each other. Or anyway, Gentry waling on Rhys and Edrard, while they tried to defend themselves. After two hours, they took a break, and Rhys looked pissed when he pulled his helmet off.

"What the hell is wrong with you?" he said. When Gentry didn't answer, he knocked on Gentry's helmet and said, "Are you in there?"

"I am here, Sir Rhys." Gentry took off his helmet and picked up his bottle of water. He was dripping with sweat and red in the face, but completely calm. Rhys was the one who seemed out of control.

"Did I do something to piss you off that you're trying to kill me?"

"Nay," Gentry said. He didn't look mad

to me, but I didn't know him that well. His left hand was relaxed, and his right hand was closed around the metal water bottle. Rhys looked over at me, like it was my fault.

"Whatever it is, maybe we could discuss it without weapons?" Edrard said.

"I am not angry with ye, my brothers. I am sorry if I was too fierce."

"Shit." Rhys laughed.

"What's going on with you? You're acting a little crazy." Edrard laid his gloved hand on Gentry's armored shoulder. So that was allowed.

" 'Tis not madness, but the Witch claimeth my blood be not hot enough."

I hated the idea of Gentry feeling he had to prove to the Witch or to me that he was brave enough. Had I started it by talking about going to see Uncle Alva? By saying Gentry ought to be afraid?

"I don't know where the Witch is getting her information, but your blood is plenty hot enough," I said.

"I hear the voice of experience." Rhys was back to leering.

"Well, I'm glad you're not having a feud. I don't want my husband hurt," Rosalinda said. "Why don't we go ahead and have breakfast?"

"Nay, I promised my lady mother I would

return ere noon." Gentry was already un-buckling his armor, but he stopped when he got to where my headband was tied. This time he'd asked me for it.

"Without breakfast?" Rosalinda said

"We already had breakfast," I said, since Gentry didn't answer.

"But we always break fast together on Sunday." Apparently me being there was screwing up traditions.

"Sorry. Gentry cooked."

He raised his head when I said his name, and came toward me, holding out my head-band. I wasn't sure how to feel about how he was acting, so I didn't move, and he eventually closed the gap between us. I took the headband and put it back on. When I was done wrestling with my hair, he was still standing there.

" 'Tis common that a knight might receive a kiss from the lady for whom he hath stood champion," he said. That's what he'd been thinking about. How to say that. Whether to say that.

"You can kiss me." I was pretty sure he'd meant for me to kiss him, but I didn't want to overstep.

"Where, my lady?" He brought his head up a little and smiled.

Oh, jokes. We were making jokes.

"Right here." I put my finger up to show him where, mostly to tease him, and got a clean-shaven but sweaty kiss on the cheek.

"Aww," Rhys said. "Our little boy is growing up."

Chapter 29
Zee

After Gentry got home from work on Tuesday morning, he took me to pick up my car from the police impound. From there, I drove straight to Mom's house, which was worse than I remembered. The hutches were still standing in the yard with their doors hanging open. Smaller pieces of furniture were lined up beside the porch, and the stack of dead microwaves had toppled over and blocked the front steps. Everywhere else — every square inch of dead grass and weeds — was covered in cardboard boxes and trash. Like a tornado had hit the house.

Sitting in my car, staring at the mess, I didn't even know where to start. Movers? Gasoline and matches?

When I walked into the front room, the shock of seeing it almost empty was nearly as fresh as it had been on Friday. There were maybe a dozen cardboard boxes that she'd managed to drag in herself. Or maybe a neighbor had.

"I told you not to come back here," she said, after she lit a fresh cigarette off her butt.

"Are you still having a temper tantrum?"

That fast, I failed at the resolution I'd made not to snap at her.

"Go away. Just leave me alone to die. It's what you want to do."

"When's the last time you ate?" I said.

"What do you care?"

She picked up the remote control and turned the sound back on her TV show. The cordless phone charger was there on the side table, but the cradle was empty, which explained why she hadn't answered all weekend. I went to see if there was any food in the house. Someone had brought the mini fridge and the one working microwave and set them up in front of the sink. Mom yelled something I couldn't hear, so I went back out to her.

"— cares more than you do," she was saying.

"Who does?"

"Kevin. He helped me bring some of my things in." Mom waved her hand at the boxes scattered around. Kevin was the same neighbor who got her cigarettes and brought her garage sale treasures, no matter how many times I asked him not to.

"Gentry and I tried to bring things in, but you wouldn't —"

"Oh, I know. I'm not allowed to have an opinion about anything. I'm just supposed to sit here and smile like a doll, and be grateful for anything you do," Mom said. To prove she wasn't a grateful little doll, she picked up the pack of cigarettes and butt-lit another one. She was using a Peter Rabbit Melmac cereal bowl as her ashtray.

"Where's your phone, Mom? I tried to call you a bunch of times."

"I wouldn't know. Maybe Mr. Mansur can tell you what he did with my phone."

She took a big drag off her cigarette and did a French inhale. Then she turned the volume up on the TV. Some Hollywood doctor was talking to a thin blond woman about *superfoods.* Some berry that would *just melt the pounds away.*

Back outside, I walked up and down, looking in boxes. After almost half an hour, I saw the cordless phone's antenna poking up out of a box of paperbacks. I grabbed the phone and an armful of books, and carried them back inside.

"What did you bring those in for?" Mom said, when I set the romance novels on the side table next to the phone. Like they hadn't come out of her house.

"So you can have something to read."

"Those old things? I've already read those."

"Okay. Well, here's your phone. I thought I might call some movers today and maybe a cleaning —"

"Mind your own business! If I want movers or cleaners, I'll call them. I certainly don't need your help." She stubbed out her cigarette in the middle of Peter Rabbit's face and picked up one of the books. "Don't you worry about me."

She read while I stood there trying to decide what to do. The phone nook was still unburied, and the poster board with Uncle Alva's phone number and address. I tried to think practical thoughts, and what I kept coming back around to was that Uncle Alva knew Craig Van Eck, because he'd been in Van Eck's gang, the White Circle. And Van Eck knew Barnwell and Ligett, because they were also in his gang. To me, it looked like Uncle Alva was already three steps closer to LaReigne than the marshals were.

He'd told me not to call him, but if I showed up at his house, he would have to talk to me. Plus, going to see him seemed less crazy than staying and fighting with my mother. In the ten years since I moved out, nothing had changed. Wasn't that the definition of crazy? Doing the same thing over and over, thinking you'll get a different result. I might as well have stuck my head in Mom's oven as think anything was going to change.

I went outside and locked the front door behind me. Then I got in my car and drove. I went past Marcus' school, but it wasn't recess time. I drove out to the Gills' house, and circled around their fancy lake. I drove by the restaurant where Kristi was probably getting ready to work my lunch shift.

Before I could think about it too much, I drove past Toby's house to see if his car was there. Then to the Juarez Bakery, where I bought those pink conchas he liked. I knew he would still be in bed, and when I knocked, it took him almost five minutes to open the door. Just a crack, to peek out and see who it was.

"What the fuck are you doing here, Red?" he said.

"I brought you breakfast." I held up the Juarez bag.

Maybe if he'd seemed mad at me, I would have done the smart thing and left, but he only looked surprised. Deep down, I wanted him to send me away, because if I was making a list of people I was scared of, Toby was at the top. Once, this woman had come to Asher's, begging for a fix. No money. Making a scene. Asher had told Toby to get rid of her. Toby had punched her so hard her teeth went rattling across the floor like loose gravel. Then he'd thrown her down the stairs.

I should have left, but when Toby opened the door a little further, I didn't wait for an invitation. I went into the living room and sat down on the couch. It was the only place to sit. He stood there barefoot, wearing nothing but a pair of old gray sweatpants. I set the pastry bag on the table and, after a minute, he sat down next to me and opened it.

"Seriously, though, what do you want?" he said while he was eating the first pan dulce.

"Can you get me a gun?"

He laughed, spraying crumbs on his coffee table. For a minute, he looked at me without saying anything. He had a couple of nasty bruises on his knuckles.

I shouldn't have come to Toby.

"You for real?" he said.

"Yeah. Can you get me a gun?"

He stuffed another big bite of concha in his mouth and nodded. I stayed on the couch while he went into the bedroom, and a few minutes later he came back with something wrapped in a dirty rag. It was nothing fancy. A 9 mm.

"How many crimes has this been used in?" I said.

"Ha-ha. Fuck, I dunno. I got a couple of them. I can let you have that one."

"How much?"

"Oh, come on. We ain't that kinda friends, are we?"

"Last I checked, we weren't any kind of friends," I said.

"Come on, Red. You know I like you, even when you're being a bitch to me. You know what I want."

Toby liked me too much to take my money and just enough to want to see me on my knees, sucking his dick. Like I knew he would, he put his hand around my throat while I did it, and it still wasn't as bad as having sex with Asher.

I only wanted the gun because I wanted to feel less scared, less helpless. Wherever I was going and whatever I was going to do, I didn't want to be unarmed.

"You're pretty good at that," he said after it was done.

I shrugged, because my mouth was full and I wasn't about to swallow.

I picked up my shirt and bra, which he'd

made me take off, and carried them down the hall to his bathroom.

"You're not gonna use my toothbrush, are you?" he yelled.

Like putting his toothbrush in my mouth would be an improvement over his dick. I spat in the sink and took a big slug of his mouthwash.

After I gargled for a minute, I got dressed and went back out to the front room. He was still lounging on the couch with his sweatpants down around his ankles. I re-wrapped the gun and put it into my purse.

"You know how to use that, don't you?" he said.

"Yeah, I know how to use it."

"Well, whatever you plan on using it for, keep my name out of it."

Like I'd want to tell anybody how I got a gun from Toby.

I drove out to Cabela's and bought a box of ammo. Not target ammo, but the serious shit that's meant to blow a hole in some-body. Then I went to the bank to empty the household account, because it wasn't like I needed to pay the rent or utilities on the apartment anymore.

After that, I did the only thing I could think of: I went back to the Franks' house.

Charlene and Elana were doing math

problems when I walked in without knocking. She kept telling me to. I carried my purse back to the guest room and counted my money. At least I had the Colorado money and the weed money, even though that was supposed to go to my medical bills. Add in the household money, and I had four thousand dollars. I put it, the gun, and the ammo into the secret pocket in my backpack with the last ounce of weed. Then, because I still felt gross, I brushed my teeth and gargled with the mouthwash in the bathroom cabinet.

Since we came back from camping, Gentry and I had only seen each other in passing, and his bedroom was empty as I walked by. I thought about taking my stuff and leaving, but I owed Gentry something, at least a thank-you. Also, I really wanted dinner and a place to sleep. Story of my life.

"Are you looking for Gentry?" Charlene said, when I went back out to the front room.

"He's outside sleeping," Elana said.

"Does he always sleep outside?"

"As long as the weather's good," Charlene said. "He has trouble sleeping. Always has."

I went to the patio doors and looked out. Sure enough, he was lying in the middle of the backyard with his shirt off. When Trang got home from school, he woke Gentry up, and they went for a run. After that was dinner, and then family TV time, which Gentry spent on the floor reading a book.

"Gentry? Could I borrow another book? I finished the other one," I said, thinking I might get him alone that way.

"Gladly, my lady."

He jumped up, and I followed him to his bedroom, where some of the shelf space was used for books instead of weapons and armor.

"What liketh thee?" With his book tucked under his arm, he squatted down to look at the bookcase under the window between the beds.

"I don't know. What's your favorite book?" I said.

I didn't understand what he said, but it sounded like *Vain Laurence Olivier O'Leon.*

" 'Tis there. *Yvain.*" He pointed at a row of books lined up on the dresser behind me.

"Hey," Trang said from the doorway. "I was gonna FaceTime with a friend for a little bit."

"With thy lady?" Gentry said.

"Well, I'm trying to talk her into being my lady."

"We shall not keep thee from thy noble task."

"I'm just getting a book." I pulled down one that said *Yvain* on the spine, but when I opened it, the actual title was *Yvain ou le chevalier au lion.* "Okay, I'm almost a hundred percent sure this book is not in any kind of English."

Gentry came to me and took it out of my hand. He said, "Nay, 'tis Old French."

"And you speak Old French?"

"I know not if I speak it well, but certs I can read." He said something else that was a bunch of random sounds to me. It didn't sound snooty like I thought French would, but then he didn't have a fancy accent when he spoke Middle English, either. So he sounded like himself in Old French, too, except saying words I didn't understand at all.

"He knows Old German, too," Trang said.

"Here, my lady." Gentry put the book back and took out another one. Also *Yvain,* but this one in English.

We took our books, and Trang closed the door after us. We stood there facing each other, me pointed toward the front room and Gentry pointed away. I thought about stepping past him and going back to where his family was, but I'd wanted to be alone with him, so I turned around and led him to the guest room.

Only I didn't want to be *alone* alone with him. I worried that he might want to fool around, and I didn't think I could stomach that after sucking Toby's dick. I sat down on my bed and left it up to Gentry to close the door, if he wanted. He left it open, but came and sat on the bed beside me.

I took a pillow and put it behind my back so I could lean against the wall. I handed him the other pillow and he did the same thing. Then we sat on the bed next to each other with our bare feet hanging off the side, both of us reading.

It reminded me so much of LaReigne it made my stomach hurt. We read together a lot when we were kids. Something to do on a cold or rainy day. Or when Mom was feeling strict and wouldn't let us leave the house. We would curl up together on her bed and take turns using each other as a pillow. One of those things we never did once we were adults.

I put my hand on the bed to shift my weight a little, and I left it there until I needed to turn the page in my book. When I went to put my hand back on the bed, though, Gentry's hand was in the way, and I accidentally touched his pinky finger with mine.

"I'm sorry." I thought it was an accident,

so I moved my hand, but the next time he turned his page, he put his hand back on the bed close enough for our pinkies to touch again. It reminded me of those dating games I wasn't any good at, but I didn't imagine Gentry was any good at them, either.

"Do you want to hold my hand?" I said.

I figured I'd get some variation on *I am thy servant,* but he said, "Yes."

He scratched his neck for a couple minutes, but after he finished, he put his hand on top of mine where it was on the bed. We stayed like that until I had to turn the page. Then I put my hand on top of his. Whichever one of us needed to turn a page, that person's hand went on top, like the slowest hand stacking game in the world.

Gentry read faster than I did, so his hand was on top more often. It was pretty banged up, covered in scrapes and bruises. He had a big scar on his thumb, and the nail of his ring finger was black. His palm was calloused, from sword fighting and castle building, I guessed.

I was trying to think of what to say — *Thanks for everything* and *I'm going to do something reckless in the morning* — when Charlene came pushing Elana down the hallway.

"Sir Gentry, will you read me a bedtime story?" Elana said.

"Certs, my sister. Wilt thou hear it also, Lady Zhorzha?"

"No. I'm gonna keep reading my book," I said.

From the way Charlene smiled at me, I knew it was the right answer.

Like he had before, Gentry closed his book without a bookmark. Then he stood up, still holding my hand, and bent over it. I wasn't sure if it was because Charlene and Elana were watching, but he held my hand for nearly a minute, before he lowered his head and pressed his lips against my knuckles.

"I shall sleep ere I labor for my lord Bombardier, so I bid thee good night, my lady," he said.

I let that decide me. In the morning, I would get up and go to Missouri.

CHAPTER 30
ZEE

I didn't take any THC drops at bedtime, because I was worried about oversleeping, but if I'd slept better, I would have gotten out of bed and left on time. Instead, I was still packing when I heard the front door open and Gentry saying good morning to Elana and his parents. Trang was already gone, and I should have been, too. I carried my backpack out to the front room, planning to say thanks and goodbye. Gentry was standing in the kitchen with a glass of orange juice.

"Lady Zhorzha," he said. "Preparest thou to depart for the house of thine uncle?"

Somehow I'd thought since we didn't talk about it the night before, he wouldn't remember we'd talked about it at all. It probably would have been better to lie to him, but I couldn't bring myself to do it.

"Yeah, I thought I'd leave this morning so I can get there before dark."

"What road wilt thou follow?" Gentry set down his juice, took out his phone, and opened the map app like we were going to discuss roads and travel time. Which was why I couldn't lie to him. He was so good.

"Well, have some breakfast before you go," Charlene said, as she carried dishes from the dining room to the sink.

"I'll just get something on the road," I said.

"I'll pack you something." She started digging around in the cupboard for a plastic container. She was going to do it anyway, so I set my backpack down and decided to go to the bathroom one last time before I left.

When I came back to the kitchen, Charlene had stopped in the middle of packing me breakfast, and Bill had come in from the dining room. They were frowning, and Gentry had his sword hand clenched.

"Gentry tells us you're going to visit your uncle in Missouri. Do you have more than one uncle?" Bill said. It felt like a trick question.

"Um, no," I said.

"Then this is the uncle they mentioned on the news?"

"They mentioned my uncle on the news?" My heart did this weird floppy thing, because all I could think was that something had happened to make this all more complicated. I couldn't even imagine what that would be, unless they'd arrested Uncle Alva.

"Well, when they were talking about your sister, about the situation at El Dorado with the escape, they mentioned that your father and your uncle . . ." Bill lowered his eyes, like he was embarrassed.

"Oh, that they were in El Dorado? Or that they robbed a couple of banks?" Even though it had been years since anyone had brought it up, that old prickly defensiveness came back fresh. I refused to be embarrassed, but it always got my hackles up.

"Are you sure that's a good idea?" Charlene said. "Going to visit him?"

"You don't think he's connected to what happened with your sister?" Bill said.

I picked up my backpack before I answered, because I was stumped for what to say. There wasn't anything neutral enough to describe what I was hoping to get out of my uncle, and like hell I was going to tell Gentry's parents anything. If Uncle Alva knew something — *if* — it was worth finding out. Because I didn't trust the police or the marshals to get LaReigne back safely. I could imagine the headline: HOSTAGE KILLED IN POLICE RAID GONE WRONG. Shit like that happened. Branch Davidian shit.

"Well, he's family," I said. "So, yeah, I'm going to visit him."

"At what hour wilt thou depart?" Gentry said.

"I don't have a schedule. I'm gonna try to talk to my mother again before I go."

"I shall be ready ere the hour turns." Gentry put his phone in his pocket and came around the kitchen island. By my math, the hour was going to turn to nine in fifteen minutes.

"You don't need to go," I said.

"Thou mayest need me yet."

"It doesn't sound like she invited you, honey." Charlene laughed.

"I am her champion."

I thought he was speaking to his mother, but he frowned and lifted his head. Not to look at her, but listening. That was the Witch above his head.

"I don't think that's a good idea, son." Bill looked more comfortable being embarrassed than he did disapproving.

"Nay, I cannot leave my lady go alone."

"I —" I wasn't sure what I was going to say, but Charlene cut me off.

"Gentry, I'm not going to forbid you to go," she said.

"I am glad, my mother, for it would distress me to defy thee."

"Son," Bill said, "I appreciate that you want to help Zee, but you may have done as much as you can."

"And what about work? You've got no business gallivanting around and missing work." Charlene could say she wasn't going to forbid him to go, but to me that sounded like he was being forbidden.

"I shall call to my lord's quartermaster to tell him I will not come for some while."

"Gentry, son, this is like — do you remember how we discussed Battle of the Nations? And why we didn't let you go?" Bill said. He leaned down until his elbows were resting on the countertop, so he could give this very stern, fatherly look to Gentry, who was looking at my knees.

"Yea. Because ye believe I am not ready to be tested in battle."

Bill laughed. "Battle is the one thing I do think you're ready for. The rest of it — being out in the world, dealing with people out there who won't accept you — that's what we're worried about."

"Let's sit down and discuss this," Charlene said.

Rhys had joked about it, but I don't think the Franks liked the idea of *their* little boy growing up.

CHAPTER 31
GENTRY

"If I say yea and ye sayen nay, 'tis no discussion," I said. 'Twas as the Witch said: I needed heat in my blood if I would stand as champion to my lady. Tho we discorded, I would not show uncourtesy to my mother and father, so I bowed to them ere I went to my room. I called the quartermaster and, tho 'twas with little warning, he offered no harsh words, for I was always dutiful in my service to him.

I took from my cupboard a satchel and filled it with what I might need. 'Twas my habit to bathe, but I would not delay Lady Zhorzha. Little time remained, so I returned to the great room, my satchel in hand. My lady had placed her own bag upon her back and stood in the front hall with my mother and father.

"How dare you judge the choices I have made for my son," my mother said to her.

"Mrs. Frank, I am not judging you. I'm

saying I feel like I'm in the middle of an argument that has nothing to do with me. It's not my job to tell Gentry what to do." I knew many things more harsh had been said, that Lady Zhorzha called my mother *Mrs. Frank* and not Charlene.

"I think you need to leave," my mother said.

"I understand. Thank you for everything. You all were really kind to Marcus and me."

Lady Zhorzha turned to the door and saw me there. I would look upon her eye to eye, to show her my resolve, but 'twas she that dropped her gaze.

"Be this the hospitality ye taught me?" I said to my mother and father, for it angered me to hear them say such things.

"It's okay," Lady Zhorzha said. "You've been really great and I appreciate it, but I don't want to cause problems. I'm gonna go. I'll talk to you when I get back, Gentry. Okay?"

Ere I could speak, she crossed the threshold. I followed her to the porch.

"Gentry!" my mother called. She was not wroth, but she was uneaseful.

"My lady," I said. "Wilt thou give my regards to thy mother when thou seest her?"

"Yeah. I'll tell her you said hi. Thank you." Lady Zhorzha crossed the street and forthwith drove away.

When I returned to the front hall, my father laughed. I knew not why, but it me angered. For in all ways I shewed him the respect he was owed, but was I to be shewn no respect? Had I not done all that he hoped for me and yet more?

"I don't want you to pout about this," my mother said. "You know I'm right."

They waited, for they would hear my answer. I had come to them a child whose native tongue was a scream. I learnt to speak. I earned proof of my learning, and took up a trade. I was accountable to myself, and oftentimes for Trang and Elana.

From thence I had started, and I grew into a man. They knew all this and still they doubted. I knew only that if I was not ready then, I never would be.

A knight tethered to his father's keep was more akin to a dog. Much as 'twas an oath I swore to be my lady's champion, 'twas also that I desired to prove myself. I believed I was worthy, but were I not tested, I could not know. I was Yvain, ever in the shadow of Sir Kay and Sir Gawain. Were I to wait til I was granted leave to go, I should have no adventures. I should live no life but a very narrow one.

"My lady mother, I would not distress

thee," I said. "But thou hast no fair reason to keep me from this journey."

"I absolutely forbid it. You barely know that girl. And her uncle? The whole situation is . . ."

Where my mother found not the word she sought, my father supplied it: "The situation is troubling. The fact that you don't see it is a damn good reason to keep you from going."

"Where's Gentry going?" Elana said, and came forth from the dining hall, for we had made such a noise she could not keep her mind upon her studies.

"Gentry isn't going anywhere, except to bed, and then to work tonight," my mother said. Were her will enough, it might have been so, but 'twas not.

"Nay, my lady, I go this hour to Missouri that I might help Lady Zhorzha."

"Absolutely not! You are not going."

My mother clenched her hands fistwise, and I feared she would pierce them with her nails, for I knew them to be sharp. Yet I would not be made to obey like a dog or a child. I gathered my satchel and made sure of my keys in my pocket.

"Son, this has gone too far," my father said.

"Don't think you can disrespect me when

you live under my roof," said my mother.

"Charlene, let's not go there."

"Oh, we're already there. Your son needs to know he can be out on his rear just like Carlees, if he can't obey my rules."

I recalled well those months when in his youth Carlees went out from hearth and home. They weren dark times, for he was sore missed. To hear such words cast me down. I wished not to be unsheltered and unloved.

" 'Tis not love thy mother would deny thee, but freedom," the Witch said. "She would fright thee with her rebuke."

"Such a knight as to be frighted by his mother's plaints," Gawen said, ever eager to shame me.

"I am not afraid," I said. Tho I willed it not, I put my satchel upon my shoulder that I might lay mine hands upon my neck.

"You're upsetting him," my father said.

"Let him be upset," said my mother. "He needs to think about this."

As though I gave it no thought.

"If thou wilt send me out of thy keep for it, I doubt not thy right. I mean no scorn, ne for thee ne for my father, but methinks I am a man, and may do as I see best. I shall see you upon my return," I said and bowed to them.

315

When I went out, my mother remained within, but my father followed after.

"Your mother is very upset," he said.

"And I am sorry, for I would not distress her, but I swore to serve Lady Zhorzha in all ways."

"I know, son. I understand an oath like that is important. Just promise me that you'll be careful." He put out his hand to me, and I clasped it ere I departed, but I made him no promise, for what knight ever vowed ride under a banner of caution?

I made straightaway for the dragon's lair, lest I miss my lady. Mayhap the dragon was as wroth as mine own mother, for 'twas very little time I waited ere Lady Zhorzha came forth. She walked not to where I stood, but to her own car, and thence looked at me.

"I didn't expect to see you," she said. "Your mom seemed really mad."

"She is ill-pleased, but she cedeth 'tis my right to do as I will."

"Are you sure about this? Because I really don't want to drag you into something."

"My lady, when I swore to be thy champion, 'twas ne poesy ne chatter. I stand ready and eager to serve thee. Tho 'tis better we should travel in my truck, for I think it more well-proved."

"Probably so." Mayhap her hip pained

316

her, for she leant against her car and lifted her foot from the ground. I waited that she might say what she wished, but she spake no more. I perceived I must lay upon our keep the next stone, tho 'twas heavy.

"If thou wilt not have me as thy champion by cause thou hast no faith I can protect thee, I will say no more. If thou wilt not have me at thy side for mine own protection, thou art unjust. I am no child. I am strong enough to carry thee, and I am not afraid."

"I know you're not a child. But I don't know what's going to happen," she said. For some moments, she was silent, her gaze upon the sky beyond me. Much akin to me when I am folded within myself.

"Is it thy desire to go alone?"

She looked upon me then, and I looked back, tho 'twas a privity that bared me to her utterly. For the nonce we weren two together. Bonded, as the black knight said.

"No," she said.

"Come, dear lady, my steed awaiteth."

She laughed and opened the door of her car to take up her satchel. Then she came to me in all seriousness. When I opened the door and put forth my hand, she took it that I might help her up.

CHAPTER 32
ZEE

While Gentry slept, I drove, rehashing my argument with his mother in my head.

"He is not mature enough," she'd said.

"He doesn't seem all that immature to me. Except for the part where you still treat him like a kid," I'd said. I wasn't proud of that, but I'd been thinking of how she called Gentry and Trang *the boys.* Trang *was* a boy, but Gentry was almost as old as me. I'd wanted to ask, *What exactly is so immature about Gentry?* Before I could, she accused me of being judgmental and told me to leave.

Okay, he lived with his folks and shared a bedroom with his kid brother, but I was twenty-six years old, and had been sleeping on my sister's couch. He had a better job and a nicer car than me. And he had a mortgage. If he wasn't an adult, then what was I? I didn't know, but I still didn't like causing a fight between him and his parents.

I was glad they'd made up before he left.

I'd planned to drive the whole way while he slept, but after we crossed into Missouri, we stopped for lunch, and Gentry drove from there. While he was asleep, I'd driven with the radio off, and we went on like that once he was driving. No music and not talking except to point out which roads to take. It didn't bother me as much as it had before. It felt okay being quiet together.

I knew we were in the right place when we passed the old amusement park. When I was little, it had seemed like Worlds of Fun, which we couldn't afford to go to. Now, it looked like something out of a horror movie, where there was a psychotic clown waiting for you in the burned-out fun house. I was going to make a joke about it, but Gentry was focused on driving, and every time I talked to him, he slowed down to pay attention to me.

It was a good thing we weren't just relying on my childhood memories, because once we left the main highway, there were no landmarks I recognized. When we reached the place where Google Maps said we were supposed to be, there was nothing there except a pile of junk. Old tires, a rusted-out washing machine, and a mountain of old beer and oil cans.

We drove on until a muddy creek crossed the road at the bottom of a ravine. On the other side, there was a cattle gate with a NO TRESPASSING sign. If there hadn't been tire ruts leading through the gate, we would have turned back.

"I'll get the gate," I said.

"Nay, my lady."

Gentry put the truck in park and got out, looking back the way we had come. Then he unhooked the gate and swung it open, riding it with his foot on the lowest bar. After we pulled through, he got back out and closed the gate. I wondered if we should leave it open in case we needed to make a quick getaway, because I kept thinking about Uncle Alva saying, *Don't call me again.* I focused on why I was there. Find LaReigne. Get Marcus back.

Further on, the woods thinned, and we passed a trailer, a metal shed, and a few more piles of junk before I saw the house. Like everything else, time hadn't done it any favors. I remembered it as a Victorian mansion. A big, white house with lots of candy-colored trim and a long screened-in veranda. Whatever the house had been, it wasn't a Victorian mansion, and it hadn't been white in a long time. The porch had sagged and half the screens were torn out.

The only thing that jibed with my memory was that under the eaves, I could still see where the shingled siding on the second floor had been purple, green, and pink.

There wasn't anything to indicate what was driveway and what was yard, except the circle of gravel a dog had scoured with his chain. When Gentry pulled the truck in, the dog ran to the end of his tether and barked at us in a hoarse voice. I thought that might make Gentry hesitate, but he reached for his door handle. I tried to stop him, because I figured my uncle probably wouldn't shoot me for trespassing, but Gentry wasn't about to let me go alone. We walked up to the house side by side, with the dog barking, Gentry clenching his hand, and me testing out different versions of reintroducing myself.

Before we could set foot on the porch, the door opened and Uncle Alva stepped out. As he came down the stairs, I saw he had one of those .410 revolvers on his belt.

"Well, goddamn, girl. If you ain't a sight for sore eyes," he said. Instead of getting run off the place, I got a hug that smelled like old-man sweat, bourbon, and cigarettes. He pulled back and held me by the shoulders to look at me. "I didn't have no idea how much you turned out looking like your grandpappy."

I laughed, because Mom always said I didn't look like anybody in our family. As for Uncle Alva, he looked as run-down as the house. He was missing all four of his bottom front teeth.

"I'm sorry to just show up here, but you didn't give me a chance to tell you I was coming when I called," I said. He laughed. Either he believed me, or he appreciated a good lie.

"Whyever you come, it's good to clap eyes on you. This your man?"

"This is Gentry Frank. This is my uncle, Alva Trego."

They shook hands in that super serious way Gentry had. Physical contact required all of his attention. I was glad he didn't say anything, because as soon as he opened his mouth it would produce about ten other questions I hadn't come all the way to southern Missouri to answer.

"You're sure welcome here," Uncle Alva said. "Come on in."

We followed him up the steps and into the kitchen, where I braced myself for chaos. The piles of junk outside weren't a warning, though, because the inside of the house was neat. It could have used a good scrubbing and a few coats of paint, but the counters were bare, and the kitchen sink was empty. The linoleum was stained and worn out, but swept. If the marshals had come to search this house, it wouldn't have taken long.

"Sit down here and let me get you a tonic."

We were sitting at the kitchen table drinking cans of store-brand pop when the screen door swung open, and a tall, skinny guy in camo pants and no shirt walked in.

"You see you got company?" he said. Then he looked at Gentry and me sitting at the table.

"You're about as useful as a Mason jar full of toenail clippings," Uncle Alva said. "This is your cousin Zhorzha and her man — I forgot your name already, son."

"Gentry Frank, sir," he said, before I could answer for him.

"This is your cousin Dirk, who you won't recognize, I imagine. He wasn't but about four years old last time you saw him."

"Well, holy shit," Dirk said. "You come all the way from Kansas? What're you doing in these parts?"

"I came to see Uncle Alva," I said.

A minute later, my other cousin, Dane, came up to the house. Him I knew, because he was only a year older than me. Nine to my eight when our fathers went to prison. He was even taller than Uncle Alva or my dad, and he had a little blue teardrop tattooed next to his right eye.

"Goddamn, I'd recognize that hair anywhere," he said. "This is a helluva surprise."

"For a couple reasons, I guess." I stood up, and he came around the table to hug me.

"What does that mean?" he said.

"You never mind these boys," Uncle Alva said. "They don't keep up on the news. Unless it has to do with baseball or boxing."

"There something going on?" Dirk said.

"Let's don't talk about it right now," Uncle Alva said. "How about some supper? You come to stay a bit, ain't you?"

"If you don't mind," I said.

Dane went into town and came back with stuff to cook out: bratwurst and hamburgers. Since I was female, they put me in charge of the coleslaw and potato salad, but Gentry was the one who sharpened the old knives, sliced all the vegetables, and peeled the eggs. Dane and Dirk tromped in and out, like cooking on the grill was some manly chore.

"Well, shit, you're a regular hand in the kitchen. Bet you make a mean cake, too," Dirk said to Gentry, trying to stir up some shit, but Gentry was off in his own world.

I hoped he could stay there, but as soon as we sat down to dinner, Dane said, "So, what do you do, Gentry?"

Gentry finished chewing and swallowed, before he said, "I build flying machines."

"Flying machines? Like airplanes?"

"Yea." I willed him to leave it at that, but he didn't. "For the Duke of Bombardier. At present, 'tis my duty to rivet wings upon Learjets."

"Are you fucking with me?" Dane said.

"No, seriously. He builds planes for a living," I said.

"Well, he also talks like a goddamn weirdo." Dirk waited to see if Gentry would rise to that, but he took another bite of his dinner.

"So what does bring you all the way out here?" Dane said.

"She's here cuz she needs her family at a time like this," Uncle Alva said.

"A time like this?"

"LaReigne's been kidnapped." It was the first time I'd said it like that, and it felt so stupidly melodramatic. "And Mom's having some kind of a nervous breakdown or a temper tantrum. She won't talk to me."

"Damn. I'm sorry to hear that," Uncle Alva said. "I don't reckon things been easy for her these years."

"What do you mean by *kidnapped*?" Dirk said.

"She was volunteering with a prison ministry at El Dorado, and they had two inmates —"

"Oh, holy shit! I heard about that, about the prison break. LaReigne's one of the hostages? Shit, I woulda paid more attention to that on the radio if I'd known it was my cousin."

"Those are the guys tried to blow up that Moslem church a couple years back, right?" Dane said. I nodded and he snorted. "She's prolly fine. They're good old boys, I bet you."

"Yeah, good old boys who just, you know, already killed their other hostage," I said. I hadn't had much appetite to begin with, but sitting there with half my dinner left on my plate, thinking about Molly Verbansky, I couldn't swallow another bite.

"Oh, you know what I mean. They ain't likely to kill her. Unlike you with that hair, looking like you got a poodle in the woodpile, LaReigne looks like good Aryan blood. And with our granddaddy being in the Klan, she's practically a KKK princess."

Dirk thought his brother's joke was pretty funny, because they both laughed. I didn't say anything. Molly was a white woman, too, for all the good it did her.

"Ain't the only danger a woman's in," Uncle Alva said in a low voice. "So Zhorzha needs her family."

After we finished eating, Dirk and Dane went out on the porch to smoke, like they'd never heard of washing dishes. Uncle Alva stuck around to help Gentry and me clear the table. Maybe they didn't usually sit down to family dinners, because the only dishes in the drying rack were a single plate and a fork.

"Why don't you two go out on the porch and I'll take care of the dishes," I said. I was used to doing that when I was a guest, but I also needed to get Gentry out of the habit while we were there. He didn't care if Dane and Dirk sniped at him doing *women's work,* but them sizing him up made me uneasy. Since I'd brought him there, I needed to make a place for him that Dane and Dirk would respect.

"Go on," I said again, because Gentry was there at my elbow, like he was trying to cut in on a dance. "Go. I'll bring you a beer when I'm done."

He tilted his head to the right. Whoever he was listening to must have given him the same advice, because he nodded and went outside. Then it was just Uncle Alva and me. He sat down at the table, so I dried my hands and turned around to look at him.

"I came because I need to talk to you," I said. "I need your help."

"I figured as much when you called. I'm sorry I was so short with you, but you never can be sure who's listening."

"I know. I'm sorry I didn't think about that, but I need you to help me find out where LaReigne is."

"Girl, it don't work like that," he said. "I can't just pick up the phone and call the KKK."

"I think it works like this — if anybody knows anything, it's Craig Van Eck, because Barnwell and Ligett were part of his gang. And you know Craig Van Eck, because you and Dad were in his bullshit white brotherhood gang, too. White Circle, whatever it's called."

Uncle Alva laid his hand on his forearm and smoothed out his shirtsleeve, so I knew he had the same tattoo as Dad. The same as Tague Barnwell.

"Lord, yes," Uncle Alva said. "I know Van Eck. I wish I could answer otherwise, but I was part of his gang when I was inside. Wasn't much choice about it, if you wanted to serve your time without taking a knife in your side or a dick up your ass. That's how it works. They tell you they're protecting you from other inmates, but it's like any other protection racket. All they're selling you is protection from them. You don't join, you're fair game. But that's all done. Van Eck hasn't heard nothing of the Trego boys since your daddy died. I don't owe Van Eck nothing, and he don't owe me nothing."

"That was only six years ago. You're telling me you don't know anybody who's gotten out since then who knows somebody who knows somebody who might know where Barnwell and Ligett would go to hide out? Nobody?" It all came gushing out, because I was tired and frustrated.

"You trying to get me killed? You don't think they'd come after me if I was passing information to the cops?"

"Oh my god, Uncle Alva. Do you think I'd go to the cops? I know we haven't seen each other in a long time, but you think I'm that crazy?"

"What the hell you planning on doing if I can find out where LaReigne is?" he said.

"I'm gonna go get her."

"Just go in there guns a'blazin'?"

"If I have to," I said. It was total bullshit, except that I'd brought a gun with me. Still, I had no clue what I would do. I was hoping Uncle Alva might have an idea.

"Girl, I can't be part of that."

"You don't have to be part of it. I just —"

"We can't talk about this tonight." Uncle Alva got up and went to look out the screen door. "I'd ruther not talk about it at all, but we'd best wait til tomorrow, when we can have some privacy."

I nodded, even though he couldn't see me, because I was grateful he hadn't refused outright. I finished washing up the dishes, and while I was drying the cookie sheet the bratwursts had been brought in on, Uncle Alva said, "I hope that son of a bitch ain't about to bite him."

I went to the screen door to see what he was talking about. Out in the yard, Gentry was making his approach to the dog. He walked slowly, with his hands held out in front. The dog got up from where he was lying and trotted to the end of his chain. Gentry stopped a few feet away.

"Is he a biter?" I said.

"What dog ain't?"

I reached past Uncle Alva, pushed the screen door open, and stepped out on the porch, where Dirk and Dane were watching Gentry and the dog, too.

"What's the dog's name?" I said. What I really wanted to ask was *Can you call him off?* I knew Gentry just well enough to be nervous about what he might do.

"Don't have a name," Dane said. "Dirk bought him for fifty bucks offa this nigger over by Rolla. Used to be a fighting dog, I guess, but —"

"He's a good guard dog, because he don't like nobody," Dirk said.

"Oh, good. You got a guard dog you can't call off. What happens if he decides to eat some Jehovah's Witnesses?" I said.

"I guess I'd have to shoot'm." Dirk grinned at Dane.

I went down the steps and started across the yard to where Gentry was squatted in front of the dog. When I came up behind him, I could hear him doing the medieval version of *Who's a good boy.*

"Thou art a noble beast. 'Tis right thou shouldst bristle, for thou knowest me not. But I bring thee meat that we might make amity twixt us."

"Be careful," I said. He had one of the leftover bratwursts from dinner in his hand, and he nodded before he tossed a piece to the dog. For a couple seconds, the dog went on standing at full alert, before he lowered his head and sniffed the meat. He looked at Gentry and me, growling the whole time. Then he picked it up and ate it.

"Yea, I hear thee. A bit of meat maketh not fast friends," Gentry said. "How do they call him?"

"Dog. They bought him from some guy, and I guess they don't know his name."

For once I could read Gentry's facial expression pretty clearly. He wasn't impressed. He threw another piece of meat, and that time the dog gave it one quick sniff before he gulped it down. Up close, I could see how skinny he was. Whatever they were feeding him, it wasn't happening often enough. He was some kind of pit bull, big, but stripped down to muscle and bone. Gray or dingy white, with brindle on his neck and back legs. He had a ropey pink scar on his left shoulder and a limp on that leg. His head was about the size of a microwave and somebody had cut his ears off down to his skull. He was a sad, ugly dog.

" 'Tis wrong he hath no name," Gentry said. "And to see his chain so short liketh me not."

"I'm not a fan of it, either, but don't get any ideas about making friends with him. My cousin says he used to be a fighting dog."

"He is a noble beast all the same." Gentry tossed out some more bratwurst, and then he gave me a piece. I didn't want to be a part of the whole thing, but I threw the meat to the dog.

"You're not very pretty, are you?" I said. "But you're a good boy, right?"

"Ah, the beast would be tamed to a lady's hand." Gentry smiled. "He waggeth his tail for thee. Not for me."

The dog had so little of a tail nub left, I don't know how Gentry could tell, but I didn't take the next piece of meat he held out to me.

"Just try not to get bit, okay?"

He nodded, so I left him to it and walked back across the yard. The whole situation was making me agitated. All I wanted was a chance to talk to Uncle Alva and, for whatever reason, he expected me to wait until tomorrow.

He was sitting on an old steel rocking chair on the porch, and I sat down on one end of an empty double glider. Dirk stood at the top of the steps, leaning against a pillar, watching Gentry. I could tell he didn't like seeing the dog practically eating out of Gentry's hand, but I guessed that dog was ready to give his loyalty to the first person who was nice to him. Whose fault was that?

After he'd given the dog the last piece of sausage, Gentry came back to the house.

When he reached the top of the porch steps, I thought Dirk was going to say something to him, but instead he stuck his foot out to trip Gentry. Gentry pitched forward, but caught himself pretty easily on his hands and pushed himself back up.

"Oops." Dirk grinned.

Back on his feet, Gentry turned to Dirk, looked him up and down, and cocked his head to the right, listening. Who was on his right?

"Nay, Master Dirk. If thou wouldst put a man upon the ground, 'tis done thusly."

Dirk laughed, about two seconds away from a smart-ass remark he wouldn't get to make. Gentry swung his leg, caught Dirk behind the knees, and cleared his legs right out from under him. From the opposite direction, he swung his arm and checked Dirk across the chest. Dirk hit the porch floor flat on his back, hard enough to rattle the kitchen windows.

"Like so," Gentry said.

Dane had been about to light a cigarette, but when Dirk landed, Dane's mouth dropped open and the cigarette fell out. In the total silence that followed, Uncle Alva started coughing. Gentry walked across the porch and sat down next to me on the glider.

I was feeling the first unraveled edge of panic, when Dirk let out a low wheezy breath. He wasn't dead.

"Well, that was educational," Dane said. He picked up his cigarette, put it between his lips, and lit it.

"At least one of you boys learned something," Uncle Alva said, and I realized that in the middle of his coughing, he was laughing.

Dirk groaned and mumbled, "I think maybe I broke something."

"Serve you right if you did, you goddamn jackass," Uncle Alva said.

"Would you like a beer?" I said to Gentry.

"Yea, my lady."

I wouldn't have been offended if he'd slapped my ass when I got up. I'd been worried about him establishing his place, and after what he'd done to Dirk, did he need anything besides a woman fetching him a beer?

When I came out with the can of beer, Dirk had managed to sit up, propped against the porch railing. At least his back wasn't broken.

"I don't suppose *you* learned anything from that," Uncle Alva was saying to him.

"Like what?"

"I like to think there's two lessons what a

half-smart man could take away from this."

"Oh, now you're gonna hear it," Dane said.

"My thanks," Gentry said, when I handed him the beer. He had his head down, so I wasn't sure if he was paying attention to my uncle and my cousins.

"First of all," Uncle Alva said. "You'd do well to remember that a man has a sacred obligation to his guests. Same as he has a duty to his host. You see how them things go together."

Dane rolled his eyes, but Gentry nodded. Uncle Alva was speaking his language. Dirk was still checking to see if all his limbs worked. He must have bitten his tongue, because he had blood on his lips.

"What's the other lesson?" Dane said.

"Don't think just cuz a man's a head shorter than you that you can whoop him. Boy's built like a brick shithouse. He ain't afraid of that dog, and he ain't afraid of you. If you'd bothered to take his measure, you wouldn'ta tangled with him. You was so busy yukking it up, you didn't see him taking your measure. He didn't come at you til he'd looked to see whether you could be took."

"Nay," Gentry said. " 'Twas to assure myself a fair fight, but I mistook thy son for my equal. I repent if I wounded him."

Uncle Alva crowed laughing while Gentry took a drink of his beer.

I figured Dirk would try to brush it off, but he seemed to be genuinely hurting. After he'd sat on the porch floor for twenty minutes, Gentry offered him a hand up. I dragged another rocking chair down the porch for Dirk, and then I suggested what was pretty much my go-to icebreaker: "Do you all wanna get high?"

I got the weed out of my backpack, but the pipe had gone missing, probably down by the fire ring at Mud Manor. I used Gentry's knife to turn an empty beer can into a pipe, which we all passed around. Gentry and Uncle Alva only took a few puffs, but Dirk hit it hard. We made peace without too much more trouble.

After we were all a little buzzed, Dane went in and opened one of the windows in the front parlor so he could listen to the Royals game on the radio.

Dirk started a long, rambling story about somebody Dane played football with in high school committing suicide. Dane took up the rest of the story, about the dead guy's sister borrowing five hundred bucks from him. It turned into a rant about users, and if I was reading between the lines, it had to do with the dead guy's sister dating a black guy instead of Dane.

"That's where the dog come from," Dirk said. "I bought him off her nigger boyfriend for fifty bucks."

"Yeah, and I'm still out five hundred bucks and you got a nigger dog don't even like you," Dane said.

" 'Tis not my wish to offend ye who aren my hosts, but I will not bear that word," Gentry said. He wasn't looking at Dane or Dirk, but he had a serious expression on his face. I felt like shit, because I'd been listening to them talk that way and never said a word. I'd spent too much time around people like that. People like Toby and Asher.

"You got a problem with me saying *nigger*?" Dane said.

"Don't be an asshole," I said.

"My mother is a lady of color, and I will not hear a word that impugns her or her people."

"Yeah? Or what?"

"Say it again and I shall meet thee on the field of battle," Gentry said.

"I don't recommend that," Dirk said to Dane.

"Mind your mouth," Uncle Alva said. "This is my house, and I won't have you insulting my guests." I'd thought he was asleep in his chair.

"Your guests." Dane snorted, but he didn't say it again. After the baseball game was over, he went inside and switched to a country music station.

"So for real? Your mama's a colored lady?" Dirk looked at Gentry like that changed everything Gentry had said and done.

"Yea. And she is worthy of all esteem." I don't think it occurred to Gentry to explain that she was his adoptive mother.

"Well, shit. No offense, man. I didn't know." Dirk looked embarrassed, and after a minute, he said, "Come on, Zee. Get up and dance with me."

He was stoned, I could barely two-step, and then he started getting overly friendly.

"Don't put your hand on my ass, you pervert," I said.

"Or what? Is your boyfriend gonna knock me down again?"

"Okay, first of all, I'm your cousin. So gross. And two, yeah, if I tell him to, he will."

"He take orders from you?" Dirk took a step back from me and looked at Gentry. "You take orders from her?"

"Yea. I am the lady's champion. 'Tis my honor to do her bidding." He wasn't drunk or stoned, but he looked relaxed, leaning back on the glider with his sword hand closed around a can of beer. I went to sit next to him.

"Boy, you pussy-whipped, ain't you?" Dane said. "Between her and your mama. Pussy. Whipped."

"I know it not," Gentry said.

"You don't know what that means? Means you letting a girl boss you around. Cuz you afraid of her. Afraid of her pussy."

"I'm pretty sure it's the opposite," I said. "I bet you're the only one here afraid of a cunt. I know Gentry's not."

Dirk laughed, which pissed off Dane even more.

"Lord, girl, you got a mouth on you," Uncle Alva said. "Now, these boys is up to all hours, but I need to get some shut-eye. Let me make up the guest room for you two."

Gentry shifted on the glider and turned his head toward me. Were we having a moment?

"Oh, you don't need to do that," I said. "We have a tent. We can set it up in the yard."

"I don't think that's a good idea," Dane said. "You'd better sleep in the house. We got all kinda critters out here."

"I am well-armed," Gentry said.

"I ain't saying you ain't, just that you

might get more than you bargained for."

"What? Do you have bears? Mountain lions? Isn't that what the guard dog is for?" I said, but Uncle Alva cleared his throat.

"No. Dane's right enough. You'd best stay in the house."

It felt like they were talking in code, but unless I was willing to keep pushing, we were sleeping in the house. I followed Uncle Alva upstairs, and he brought out some sheets from the linen cupboard in the hall. They were musty like they'd been in the closet for years, but there weren't any bugs or mouse shit in them. Same for the mattress in the guest room. It was probably older than me, but I didn't see any bugs in the seams as I made it up.

A few minutes later, Gentry came in carrying his big rucksack and a sleeping bag. I wondered what weapons he had in the rucksack, and whether he was planning to sleep alone in the bag.

"Now, I'm just downstairs in the back room, if you need anything. The boys got their own trailer, so they don't sleep up here. You'll have it to yourself," Uncle Alva said and, after he went downstairs, Gentry and I were alone.

On a scale of one to ten, with the old amusement park being about a seven, Uncle

Alva's house was maybe a four on the horror movie scale. When I went to brush my teeth, I wasn't bracing myself for a ghost to look back at me from the old mirror over the sink, but it wouldn't have surprised me. I wondered how long it had been since anybody had slept up there. On the way back from the bathroom, I peeked into the bedroom that had belonged to Aunt Tess and Uncle Alva, and my grandparents before that. A layer of dust covered everything. I didn't imagine Uncle Alva had slept there since Aunt Tess died. I wondered if her clothes were still hanging in the closet, but that was strictly ghost territory, so I went back to the guest room lickety-split. At some point that evening, Uncle Alva must have given the guest room a sweeping and dusting, because it wasn't that bad.

Gentry was sharpening a knife, so at least he was prepared for horror movie developments, but he came back from his turn in the bathroom smelling like toothpaste and soap and looking freshly shaved. That explained the knife sharpening.

He looked at his phone and sighed. Then he said, "I must call my mother."

"Do you want some privacy?"

"Nay." I still thought maybe I should leave, but his end of the conversation was a lot of *Yea, my lady* and *Nay, my lady.* He told her we were staying with *Lady Zhorzha's kin.* "Yea, all is well. My lady's uncle, Sir Alva, hath made us welcome." That was kind of true.

There wasn't anybody for me to call, so I laid back on the double bed and looked at stuff on my phone until he hung up. Then we were alone, together, in that creepy, drafty heap of a house. With just the one bed. Uncle Alva only put us together because he thought Gentry was *my man,* so I considered offering to make up one of the other beds, but he had his sleeping bag, and I didn't want to be alone when the ghosts showed up.

Plus his T-shirt and his boxers were a little too tight around his thighs and his arms, and that made sharing a bed more interesting. I got up and turned off the overhead light, so the only light left was his little camping lantern. Then I curled up on the bed with my legs uncovered. For a minute, Gentry stood with his back to me, looking at my reflection in the mirror over the dresser. Then he turned around and came across the room to stand next to the bed. Left hand on top of his head. Right hand clenched. Relaxed. Clenched.

"Come to bed," I said.

"Nay, I shall sleep there and keep the watch." He pointed to where he'd unrolled his sleeping bag near the door.

"Well, you can sleep on the floor, but I wasn't really talking about sleeping. What stories haven't you told me?" When I scooted over, he sat down on the edge of the bed.

"A great many, but I would hear a tale of thine," he said.

"I don't know any stories."

"Tell me how thou wast wounded."

"You wanna hear about my wreck? It's not very interesting." In addition to being boring, it was kind of awful, so I told it like a fairy tale. Like Melusine.

"Once upon a time, there was this girl. Her mother was a dragon. Stop me if you've heard this one. One day a prince, the Prince of Merriam, came around and acted like he wanted to make her a princess. She wasn't interested in being a princess, but she figured it might be better than being a scullery wench. So she went back to his castle with him, and for a year and a day —" That was something LaReigne had taught me. A Wiccan thing that was like marriage. Hand-fasting. As soon as I thought about LaReigne, I got this nervous hitch in my stomach. LaReigne was out there alone. Worse

344

than alone. With some piece of shit who'd taken advantage of her.

"My lady," Gentry said. He'd been sitting on the edge of the bed, but he laid down next to me. "Art thou —"

"So for a year and a day, they were together. Then the dragon's daughter found out she was going to have a baby, and the prince got pissed off and acted like the dragon's daughter was trying to trick him into making her a princess. Except she never wanted to be a princess, and she thought the prince was acting like a royal shitbag. In fact, she thought maybe she should just ditch the prince and keep the baby. For the record, babies are nice. Princes, not so much.

"So the prince and the dragon's daughter had a big fight, and the prince took her . . . carriage keys away to keep her from leaving. So she hopped on the prince's horse and rode away, and he came after her in the carriage. He rode up on her ass so close that when some other asshole swerved his carriage into her lane, she couldn't slow down fast enough, and she got her front tire clipped and wrecked the . . . horse. Then the prince got what he wanted, because she didn't have the baby, and he got to go home to his mommy and daddy. The dragon girl's sister came to rescue her, and later she met a knight at physical therapy, and you know what happened next. The end."

"But she was ne a dragon ne a princess," Gentry said. "She was a phoenix."

For a second I got teary-eyed, because that was exactly why I'd got the tattoo. To cover up my surgical scars and the massive stretch of road rash down my leg, but also to remind myself that I was going to rise from the ashes. I never told anybody that, and the fact that he got it seemed like the nicest thing.

"Yeah, it turned out she was a fire bird instead of a fire lizard, and she went and flew around the shitty prince's castle and cursed him, and she was never seen there again."

He laughed, which made me laugh. We laid there for a while not talking, until I said, "Can I touch you?"

"Yea, my lady."

He was lying on his back, so I looked him over, trying to choose where. I picked the two scars under his chin and ran my thumb over them. Then I brought my hand back to my own space.

"That's a dog bite, too?" I said.

"Yea."

"So, Miranda didn't get rid of her dogs,

even after that happened?

"Nay, they weren not her dogs. She was but fifteen years old. They weren the dogs of her stepfather," he said.

"She was only fifteen when she had you?"

"Nay, she was but twelve when I was born. I was three when the dog bit me, and she had no power to make her stepfather give up the dogs."

"Oh my god. She was twelve?" I took back some of the horrible things I'd thought about Miranda, because that would fuck you up, having a baby when you were twelve. "Who's your father?"

"I know not," he said. If it bothered him to talk about it, I couldn't tell.

"Okay, just be honest. Why did you take me to Miranda's house that night? It was because you thought I was too white trash to take to your real house, wasn't it? You didn't want Charlene to meet me, did you?"

"My lady, nay. In truth, I took thee thither for the same reason I first wished to know Miranda. It granted me more freedom. If I said to my lady mother, *I go out,* she would say, *Where will you go? Who will you see? What will you do? When will you return?*

"If I said to her, *I go to see Miranda,* she dared not question me, for she felt it was not her place to query my right to see the

347

woman that gave birth to me. The night I took thee to Miranda, 'twas with the same desire. That I be not questioned. That thou be not questioned. *How do you know Gentry? How did you meet Gentry?*

"Above all, I desired my mother not take thee aside to tell thee I am autistic. To tell thee of my voices. I longed for thee to know me ere thou heard such things."

"Yeah, she did do that," I said. "But I kinda get why she thinks she needs to."

"Lady Charlene meaneth always to care for me, in the way she thinketh best."

"So what's up with your other family now? Is Brand in prison yet?" I meant it as a joke, but Gentry didn't laugh.

"I know not. I saw them not after that night," he said.

"Wait. What? You haven't seen them since that night?"

"I could not bear it. They cared not for me, and they shamed me before thee. Thou wert wroth with me."

"I was not ever mad at you. Things were just complicated," I said. I held out my hand like I was going to touch him, but I waited until he nodded, before I touched the bite scars on his shoulder.

"And you're not afraid of dogs, even though that happened?"

"Nay. I was a child and knew naught of dogs. Now I ken I must earn their respect."

"Was that the plan tonight?" I said.

" 'Twas only to make amity with the dog. And methinks him hungry."

"Yeah, I don't think they feed him enough. Probably some stupid bullshit about making him tougher. I wish people wouldn't get an animal if they're not going to take care of it."

" 'Tis why I have no dog, tho I would. I am not worthy yet." He rolled onto his side and looked at me. My face, my mouth. I wondered if he was going to kiss me.

"What do you mean by *worthy*?" I said.

"Once a man earneth a dog's devotion, 'tis nigh impossible to undo. A dog giveth his loyalty even to a man that beateth him and starveth him. I must be worthy ere I accept a dog's trust." He said it with a level of sincerity I didn't think I'd ever managed about anything.

"Well, if you're not worthy of a dog, I definitely am not worthy of a champion," I said.

" 'Tis not for thee to be worthy. 'Twas for me to become worthy. When I was a boy of fourteen, the Witch told me I would be given the honor of protecting a lady. For eight years, I waited."

"But why me? Seriously, I have never done anything to deserve a champion."

"When first I saw thee, thou wore a blouse of green," he said. "Thy leg was braced and thy physic had caused thee great pain. The Witch said, *There is she.*"

"I think the Witch might be a little daffy. Like what if she just randomly picked me?"

"Nay. Ever she speaketh truth."

I wasn't sure what to think about that, because the Witch lived inside his head, and he was the only one who could hear her. She was part of Gentry, but not Gentry.

"I'm pretty sure you're worthy of a dog," I said.

"Mayhap someday, but not this day, when it is still my labor to be worthy of thee."

CHAPTER 33
ZEE

I wondered if the push-ups Gentry did while I was sleeping were part of becoming worthy of me.

"Are you seriously doing calisthenics?" I said, when I woke up around midnight.

" 'Tis not my custom to sleep at night."

I couldn't complain about it, because he was being quiet. Pant. Push. Pant. Push. Then he switched to sit-ups, and I fell back to sleep. I woke up later to this feeling that people were fighting. The sound of people arguing traveled the way no other noise did, but even when you couldn't hear it, you could feel it, like static electricity from a thunderstorm.

"Gentry?" I said, but he wasn't there.

I got out of bed and went to the door, not thinking about shoes or pants. With the door open, I could hear the sound of men raising their voices. Gentry was standing at the end of the hallway, to the side of the window that looked out over the front yard. When I went to him, I was groggy, and my arm bumped against his chest. He stepped back and let the curtain flutter closed.

"Sorry." I backed up to give him more space, but he stepped forward, so that my arm touched his chest again. Then he put his left hand on my waist, in this very particular way that would have made me laugh in a different situation. Like I was a piece of equipment with a handle there.

He lifted the edge of the curtain, so we could look out. In the front yard, there was an old Lincoln Continental parked behind Gentry's truck. A guy I didn't know was leaning against the driver's door, looking at his phone. Another guy with a beard was standing next to Gentry's truck, arguing with Dane. The dog paced back and forth at the end of his chain.

I couldn't make out what they were arguing about, but the guy raised his hand, gesturing to Gentry's truck. Then he pointed his finger at Dane, almost in his face. Dane shook his head. They went through that a few times, the way meth heads do. Repeating the same gestures and accusations.

Finally the bearded guy smacked his hand on the hood of Gentry's truck. The dog let out a low *woof.* Dane went on shaking his head. A minute later, the two strangers got into the Lincoln and backed down the driveway toward the road. Dane walked across the yard toward the trailer parked in the woods. Then it was just the dog standing by himself under the light of the single bulb that hung off the side of the barn.

I didn't hear Uncle Alva stirring downstairs, so I guessed that was a regular enough occurrence that it didn't disturb him. Gentry and I went back to the bedroom, but I was too awake to go back to bed. That was the effect arguments had on me. I went to the window and looked out at the side yard. From there I could see a light on in the trailer, but nothing else. I walked back to the middle of the room, where Gentry was standing with his arms crossed.

"Will you kiss me?" I said, thinking at least sex would be a distraction.

He uncrossed his arms and kissed me, but carefully, like he was thinking about something else. I paced around the room in the dark trying to work out the stiffness in my hip. Then I picked up my phone and went through the gestures. Checked messages. Looked at Facebook. Read some news websites. Watched a video of a baby pangolin to cheer myself up.

By the time I'd done all of that, my heart had slowed down, so I laid on the bed and closed my eyes, trying to think relaxing thoughts. There was something I'd meant to ask Gentry, but I couldn't remember what it was. Then I saw it. Him on the porch, tilting his head like he was listening to a voice, but on the right. I opened my eyes, and looked at Gentry in the middle of the room, head down, scratching his shoulders with both hands.

"Who are you listening to on your right side?" I said.

" 'Tis the black knight." The way he said it gave me a chill. "He is ever at my ear when I joust. He helpeth me fight."

"He told you to knock Dirk on his ass, didn't he?"

"Yea. Art'ou wroth with me?"

"No. He deserved it," I said. "I'm glad you did it."

I closed my eyes again, wondering exactly how many voices were talking to Gentry. Sometimes he didn't pay attention when people talked to him, but who could blame him with all that going on inside his head?

"The black knight told me I must trust thee," he said.

"Trust me?" I'd never thought about whether anyone trusted me or not. I didn't have any power over anyone, so what did it matter if I was trustworthy? Except for Marcus. I had to be trustworthy for him, but maybe I'd failed at that.

"Yea. The black knight said . . ."

Gentry walked over to the bed and rested the knuckles of his right hand against my thigh for a minute. Without even asking.

"He said what?"

"He said if we two would be bound together, I must trust thee." He slid his knuckles up my leg until he got to the hem of my nightgown. I thought he might pull it down to cover me up. "That if my oath to thee was not idle words, I should lie with thee, and we would be bound together."

"The black knight told you to have sex with me? As part of your oath?"

"Yea, my lady."

I'd never thought of sex that way. Sometimes it was a chore, and a lot of times it was something to barter, like having a little money, even when I was broke. I relaxed my legs and Gentry pressed his hand between them, with just my panties separating us. I wondered, if we hadn't had sex, would I have said yes to him coming to Missouri with me? Probably not, and I was glad not to be there alone.

"You want to come to bed and bond some

more?" I said.

"Weren we elsewhere, somewhere safe, I would grind thee as a millstone grindeth grain to flour, but not here."

I laughed, because he had the best dirty talk. Weird but filthy.

"No, probably not a good idea," I said.

"Tho they be thy kin, my lady, I trust them not."

Gentry was right. I trusted Dane about as far as I could throw him.

CHAPTER 34
ZEE

In the morning, Gentry cooked breakfast. Omelets, hash browns, and biscuits that he made from scratch. I'd hoped it would only be Gentry, Uncle Alva, and me, but Dirk came up to the house as we were sitting down. He seemed excited at the idea of getting breakfast, and since Dane wasn't there, he didn't act stupid about Gentry cooking it. Uncle Alva had told me to wait til the morning to talk, so I hoped that was coming, but after he mopped his plate clean with half a biscuit and finished his coffee, he pushed back from the table.

"I gotta go into town for an appointment," he said.

"How long will you be gone?" I said.

"I expect for a couple hours. Ain't nothing changed since you was last here, so you make yourself at home."

After they left, Gentry went upstairs to sleep and I wandered around the house. In the front room, Uncle Alva had the same record player that had belonged to my grandmother: an old console about the size of the couch. When I was a kid, there'd been a picture of my grandfather in his Klan robes hanging in that corner, but now there was just a square of wallpaper that wasn't as sun-faded as the rest.

I looked around for some books, but all he had were old Reader's Digest Condensed Novels. Since I'd already started it, I went out to the truck to get *Yvain*. The dog was sleeping, sprawled out like he was dead, but when I came down the steps, he jumped up and trotted toward me, dragging his chain.

"You mind your business, buddy, and I'll mind mine," I told him.

Out of curiosity, I took a peek behind the truck seat at what Gentry had stored back there. The usual stuff, like a roadside kit and the jack, but also a chain mail shirt, an axe, and a sword. I unsnapped the strap that kept the sword in its sheath and slid it out halfway. Unlike the "real swords" he and Rhys and Edrard fought with, this was a *real* sword. Like the one that hung over his bed, but a lot smaller. Shiny and sharp and dangerous looking.

"What do you want anyway, coming around here?" Dane said behind me.

I slid the sword into the sheath and slammed the seat back into place. With one hand I grabbed my book and with the other, I pushed the lock button down on the door. When I turned around, Dane was right there, so that I had to sidestep to close the door. I didn't often have to look up at people, but Dane was at least half a foot taller than me.

"Like I said, I needed to get away and see family."

"You ain't seen my dad for almost twenty years, but now he's family? You know he had to find out from the prison chaplain that Leroy died. Y'all didn't even invite him to his brother's funeral."

"That was my mom's business. Not mine," I said, which wasn't totally true. I hadn't tried to get in touch with Uncle Alva when Dad died.

"But here you are, coming around like you're looking for something. What are you up to? You know he ain't got no money. You can't get nothing off him."

"I didn't come looking for money."

"Right. You just need your family at a time like this."

I took a step sideways, planning to walk around Dane, but he cut me off.

"Why don't you get the hell out of here

and leave us be?" he said.

"Because Uncle Alva asked me to stay."

"Because he can't see what you're up to."

"What am I up to?" I said. To show him I wasn't afraid, I took a step closer to him. Sure, he was taller, but he wasn't that much bigger than me. His hygiene wasn't great, either. Between his BO and his breath, I wished I'd kept my distance. His eyes were red and raw looking.

"You're stirring up trouble. Go on home and wait for the cops to find them two jailbirds and LaReigne."

"Oh, you didn't forget that my sister's been kidnapped?"

"That's your problem," he said. "Ain't nothing Dad can do about that. So you need to mind your own business, and stay outta ours."

"Do you remember what my dad used to say? *I was born on a Thursday, but it wasn't last Thursday.* Do I look stupid? People coming around at night. You up all night. The stink. The fact that you have fewer teeth than your father. Meth much? I don't give a shit what you're up to. Doesn't interest me at all. I'm just here to talk to Uncle Alva."

"You ain't fucking talking to him! You need to go in the house, get that weird-ass boyfriend of yours, and get the fuck out of here."

"Or what?" I said. "Are you threatening me, you peckerwood?"

"You goddamn right I'm threatening you!"

He was shouting by then. We were both shouting. He reached out and put his hand on my chest, pushed me until my back was pressed against the side of the truck. I lost my grip on *Yvain,* and the book landed in the gravel.

"You don't get the hell off my property, I swear to god, you'll wish you had."

"It's not your property," I said.

"It will be. Old man ain't gonna live forever."

The things I wanted to say. I had a whole mouthful of them, but looking past Dane, I saw Gentry, more wild-haired than usual, coming across the yard, not even pussyfooting on the gravel in his bare feet. We'd woken him up. He was scratching his neck with his left hand, and his right hand was in a fist.

"Tell you what," I said to Dane, wanting to end the argument before it got worse. "When your dad comes back, I'll ask him what I want to ask him and then I'll go."

"Master Dane," Gentry said, about fifteen feet away and still coming. Dane let go of me and turned around. "I will not allow thee to outrage thy cousin."

"Fucker, don't come at me. You gonna find out I ain't a pussy like my little brother."

"Come. Let we two fighten. I am ready to meet thee."

"I ain't gonna fight you, faggot." Dane backed up to put more distance between Gentry and him, but Gentry closed the gap, so they were only a few feet apart. It worried me how Gentry kept his head tilted to the right as he looked Dane over, like he and the black knight were doing the math on how to fight Dane.

"Put thine hand upon the lady again, and I shall fight thee whether thou wilt or not."

Dane took another step back, and Gentry took two steps forward. I put my arm out, not close enough to touch Gentry, but to signal him to back off. From what I could see, Dane didn't have a gun on him, but I didn't want to find out.

"I'm serious," I said. "When Uncle Alva comes back, we'll talk, and then I'll go. You're the only one trying to make trouble, Dane."

He took a few more steps back, shaking his head. He pointed at me and then at Gentry.

"You — you better not fuck with me. You have your little chat with Dad, and then get the hell outta here."

Dane kept backing up, like he was worried Gentry would jump him from behind. Then he finally turned around and headed toward his trailer.

"You okay?" I said, but Gentry didn't answer. He walked around his truck, running his hand along it. I figured he was having a conversation with one of his voices, so I left him alone. He went around the truck a second time, and stopped at the rear quarter panel, a few feet away from me.

"Thou art well?" he said.

"Yeah. I'm fine. I'm sorry we woke you up."

He squatted and picked up *Yvain*. After wiping the dust off on his T-shirt, he held the book out to me in both hands, like an offering.

CHAPTER 35
ALVA

That damn girl looked just like my daddy, with that same wide mouth and wild copper hair. Built like she could hunt bear with a stick, she was like the ghost of my daddy in more ways than one. Come to call me to answer for my misdeeds, remind me of the obligations I needed to put to paid before I died.

With the land paid off and the boys grown, I wasn't particular broke up at the idea of dying. I was ready to meet my maker and, knowing what Tess had went through, I wasn't of a mind to put myself through that, no matter how bad the coughing got. All the same, I figured it was best to know how much time I had left to put things in order, so I gone to see my doctor.

After my appointment was done, I had Dirk drive me to the convenience store up the other side of the valley.

"Why you wanna go there?" he said.

"Because they don't know me."

"Why you need to go somewhere they don't know you?"

"Just drive, boy."

I swear, he was dumb as a box of hammers. I made him wait while I went into the store and bought a prepaid phone. Clerk was one of them Paki fellas. Wasn't even sure if he spoke English, seeing as how he didn't say a word to me. Took my money, gave me my change. When I come out, Dirk looked over at the phone package like he figured to ask me another stupid question, but he musta thought better of it.

The first call was the easiest. To a man I did six years with. Like me, he'd moved on after he served his time, but he hadn't got himself as far away from Van Eck as I had. We spent a few minutes shooting the breeze til I worked my way around to telling him why I'd called.

"Maybe you heard what happened to my niece, who was took hostage over at El Dorado while she was volunteering," I said. "I'm real worried about that, you can imagine."

"I can. I can. Tell you what, I'm a mite busy right this minute, but I'll call you back," was his answer.

"I'll count on that." There wasn't no good

to come of talking on a landline, so I give him the prepaid number and we said our goodbyes. An hour later, the prepaid rang, and, like I figured, he had some idea of who I ought to call next.

Wasn't a fella we served with, but one whose son I looked out for. Lost four teeth and took seventeen stitches from a guard to protect that boy, because Van Eck told me he was like a nephew to him. The boy's father was somebody important in one of the big Arkansas conclaves. Nobody to mess with, but my lungs right on schedule fired up to remind me that being alive was mayhap a temporary condition. If somebody wanted to come around some night and shut me up from asking the wrong questions, they might be doing me a favor.

This fella, Janzen, he acted like he didn't have no truck with me, til I was forced to remind him how I helped his son.

"I appreciate that but," he said.

"But what? This my family I'm talking about. Just like your boy. I'm trying to make sure my niece is all right. See if I can't negotiate to get her back without involving no police."

"Negotiate?" Janzen said, and he seemed a mite more interested in talking to me.

"I don't aim to get something for nothing,

and neither do I aim to cause no trouble. I just wanna find my niece. That's my late brother's daughter."

It gone on that way into the afternoon, til I was down to the last prepaid card I had.

"I'm gonna have to call you back," said a man who wouldn't tell me his name. He'd called me, got my number from someone else. Somewhere in there I'd spoke to someone who'd told me this man with no name was a Fury with a secret grudge against his Titan, who was married to the no-name man's sister.

"Whatever help you can give it'd go a long way toward easing my mind," I said. After I hung up from the Fury, I laid down to rest, but Dane come stomping through the house and pounding on my door.

"What the fuck are you up to?" he said, and walked into my room without an invitation. I knew he'd been cooking that crap and likely smoking it, as he had the stink of it on him. "Dirk said when he took you into town you bought a burner phone, and all afternoon you been shut up in here making phone calls. Who are you calling?"

"What the hell business is it of yours?"

"It's my business same as always, if you're bringing trouble around here. Jimmy T. was real pissed last night, finding out we had company. He don't like that our *guest* is somebody the cops might be interested in talking to."

"Why the hell'd you go and tell Jimmy T. that? It ain't like he's watching the news."

"I agree with him," Dane said. "The cops could come around anytime, wanting to talk to her. That's what Jimmy T. don't like about it."

Ever since he'd gone into business with that man, it was *Jimmy T. wants this* and *Jimmy T. don't like this.* Worse than listening to a man bellyache about his wife. Made me ashamed I'd raised a son who was so far up some meth head's ass.

"Seeing as how it's my home, I reckon I'll bring trouble here if I like," I said.

"What I don't get" — Dane gone to running his hands through his hair like it was on fire — "is why you're putting your ass on the line for her. You're acting like you owe her something."

"I don't know exactly where I went wrong, son, but apparently I failed to teach you one real important lesson."

"Oh, goddamn. You and your lessons." He turned around like he meant to walk out, but he didn't.

"Family comes first," I said. "If our family is a problem for your business partner, you need to get you a new business partner. Because I ain't gonna take Jimmy T.'s feelings into account ahead of my family."

"That sounds real high and mighty, but what good does it do us to put her first? What's she ever done for us?"

"Son, that girl — those two girls — sacrificed their daddy for us, that's what. They grown up with no daddy at all, because Leroy took the blame for all of that."

"You gonna act like I didn't grow up without a daddy? You was gone for six fucking years."

"Yep, I served six years, but you know what I didn't serve? I didn't serve no goddamn life sentence, which your uncle Leroy did. Maybe you think I shoulda been here wiping your ass them six years, but I did come back. And I done my best for you and your brother. Them girls never did get their daddy back. That girl never got to see her daddy again except on the other side of a prison visitation room. So that's what she done for us."

"That was on him. He was the one who planned that," Dane said, so flippant-like, I wanted to smack him. But then who'd let him believe those lies, if it wasn't me?

"You don't know the first thing about what happened, but mayhap it's time I set you straight."

The thought of telling those old secrets put a twist in my guts, but I reckoned the truth was part of what I needed to confront before I died. Maybe I'd die a mite easier, if the weight of them secrets wasn't pressing down on me no more. I'd carried them for so long, it was like I couldn't hardly stand up straight.

CHAPTER 36
ZEE

Avoiding Dane seemed like the best idea, so I spent the rest of the morning lying in bed next to Gentry, reading while he slept.

Yvain was some trippy shit, but I could see why Gentry liked Yvain. He was a good guy. Not a show-off like Sir Gawain or a conceited jerk like Sir Kay. I wasn't all that sympathetic when Yvain killed Sir Esclados and then hung around the castle like a stalker and made googly eyes at Laudine, Esclados' widow. Apparently, though, that was how chivalry worked. You could kill a guy and that was okay, as long as it was a fair fight between two knights.

Yvain didn't really get into trouble until he broke his promise to Laudine. By that point, she'd gotten over her dead husband and married Yvain, even though he was the knight who'd killed her husband. Yvain was madly in love with Laudine, but he wanted to go off and have adventures with Sir

371

Gawain and King Arthur. So he promised his wife that he would come back before a year and a day.

"Oh, Yvain," I whispered, because I knew he was going to fuck up. I wasn't even halfway through the book, so no way was he going to get back to Laudine on time. It reminded me of my mom and dad. The day Dad was sentenced, he'd promised he was coming back. Swore it up and down, even though he wasn't going to be eligible for parole for twenty years. It didn't work out. He never made it back, and I didn't think Yvain would, either.

I knew someone was downstairs but not who, until I heard Uncle Alva coughing. He sounded bad, and it made me wonder what kind of appointment he'd had that morning. After a few minutes, Dane raised his voice, and then Uncle Alva raised his. That went on until I couldn't stand it anymore. I closed the book and got up. I went out to the stairs, trying to be as quiet as I could on those creaky old floors.

"You was gone for six fucking years!" Dane was saying.

More back and forth, and then Uncle Alva's voice rose up all wobbly, old-man angry: "It was *my* fault that all gone south!

I'm the one shot that goddamn bank guard!"

I'd been standing about halfway down the stairs, but I had to sit down. I could barely breathe, and my skin felt tight all over. Almost my whole life I'd believed my father was a murderer, that he'd killed some poor rent-a-cop who was just doing his job. I'd spent years trying to make that balance out against all the good things I knew about Dad. Like the fact that he'd robbed a bank to try to get decent medical care for his sister-in-law, who was dying of cancer.

Except he wasn't a killer. That was a lie. He'd confessed to it to save Uncle Alva, and he'd let me and LaReigne and Mom carry that lie around all those years. There was no way Mom knew, because she couldn't keep a secret for shit. Even after his liver crapped out and he knew he was dying, Dad had kept that from us to protect Uncle Alva.

Dane came stomping through the front room, right past the foot of the stairs. I didn't want him to see me, to know I'd been listening, but I couldn't stand up. It didn't matter, because he went straight through the dining room and never even glanced at me. After he was gone, Uncle Alva started coughing again. I grabbed the railing and pulled myself up.

I went upstairs and laid on the bed next to Gentry. The whole room felt like it was spinning, that was how much my world had changed. I laid as still as I could, but maybe my heart was beating so hard it woke Gentry up.

"My lady," he said in a groggy voice.

"Will you put your arm around me?" It was easier for him to touch me than to let me touch him. I rolled over on my side with my back to him and, after a minute, he put his hand on my waist. That was enough to hold me together.

We were like that for an hour, maybe longer. Long enough that my shirt, between my side and Gentry's palm, got damp with sweat. Then I heard someone coming up the stairs.

I slid off the bed and went across the room to where my backpack was sitting on the dresser. I unzipped the side pocket, to feel where the gun was. Gentry must have heard the creak of the stairs or sensed something else, because he sat up and swung his legs over the side of the bed. He cocked his head to the right, listening.

"Zhorzha?" Uncle Alva said. "You awake, girl?"

"Yeah, what's up?" I took my hand out of the backpack, and left the gun there.

"Just thought we might could have that talk."

That talk. I opened the door far enough to look out at him.

"Sure. I'll be down in a minute," I said.

He nodded and started down the stairs. I watched him go, with this mix of anger and sadness and hope. He looked so frail going down the stairs, holding on to the railing with both hands. He hadn't seemed that weak last night.

After he was gone, I went down the hall to use the toilet. I planned to go downstairs alone, but when I came out of the bathroom, Gentry was waiting for me in the hallway. He had his boots on, and a red crease across his cheek from the pillow.

Downstairs, Uncle Alva was sitting at the kitchen table with a cup of coffee and a newspaper folded up in front of him. He'd taken off the button-down shirt he'd worn earlier and was in an old wifebeater. The tattoo was there, like I knew it would be, and, above it, a strip of medical tape held some gauze at the crook of his elbow. That kind of appointment.

I sat down across from him, and Gentry went to stand at the back door, staring out through the screen with his arms crossed.

Uncle Alva unfolded the newspaper and

slid a big, old waxed manila envelope across the table to me. I started to untie the rotten shoelace wrapped around it, but he tilted his head toward Gentry, whose back looked like a wall. Now that I'd seen him in his armor, I could picture him that way all the time, even when he wasn't wearing it.

"You trust him?" Uncle Alva said.

"Yeah. He brought me this far." I didn't say, *More than I trust you.*

After what he'd told Dane, I wondered what kind of crazy secrets Uncle Alva was offering me. I was not expecting ten stacks of hundred-dollar bills with yellowed bank bands around them. I pulled out one bundle and looked at the date on the top bill. 1996. I flicked through the stack, looking at all the dates. Nothing after 1999.

It was money from the first bank robbery.

"Jesus Christ," I said, and for a while I couldn't get any other words out. When they finally came, they were in a crazy jumble. "What is — why are you giving me this? Is this — you've had this all along? You asshole! All this time?"

"Keep your voice down. The boys don't know, and they don't need to know."

I was quiet, until the urge to yell had mostly passed.

"Why give it to me now? There were probably a hundred times in the last fifteen years this might've been helpful. Like when I got hurt. Or for LaReigne to go to college."

"Girl, you think I was holding out on your mama? Shit, if you knew how much money had gone through her hands. Them ladies novels. All them goddamn figurines. She spent what money she had on crap that didn't add up to nothing. That there, I kept that back for you girls, like my brother asked. Only now I guess you need it."

"I need more than money. It won't do me any good if I can't find her," I said.

"You seem pretty damn sure she didn't run off with them two fellas."

I took out my phone and pulled up the home screen. "This is your great-nephew. He was born after Dad died. This is Marcus, LaReigne's son." My voice cracked. "She may have done a lot of stupid things, but she did not abandon him. She wouldn't do that, not after what we went through when we were kids."

Uncle Alva was quiet, looking at Marcus' picture and tapping his pack of cigarettes on the kitchen table.

"How much is this?" I said.

"It's a hunnert thousand. Fifty thou for each of you."

"Let me ask you: did LaReigne — does

LaReigne know about this?" I meant *Is it remotely possible that the assholes who took her knew about the money?*

"Might could be. I reckon over the years it's possible your daddy told her, but she never asked me about it. He didn't dare tell your mama, and I reckoned if I gave it to you while she was alive, you'd end up spending it on her."

"Why are you giving it to me now?" I said.

"Because there's a small chance I know somebody who can tell me where them boys are holed up. That information ain't gonna be free. And *if* I can find it out, you ain't gonna be able to waltz in there and say please. You'll need something to bargain with. Them boys might be inclined to swap your sister for this money. I'd do it myself, but I don't know that I got it in me."

"Have you — do you think —" I couldn't even get out what I wanted to ask.

"I don't know yet. I made a few phone calls to some folks who might know. I'm waiting to hear from a few more folks. I know you'd like to have answers today, but I can't guarantee that's gonna happen."

"Well, I don't think Dane is going to be okay with me staying."

"That goddamn boy. Don't mind him. You're welcome here." I thought the conver-

378

sation was over, because he tapped a cigarette out of the pack and lit it before he said, "There's another thing I need to say to you, and mayhap you won't be inclined to stay after you hear it, but I need to say it."

"I know. I heard what you told Dane. About my dad and the robbery. About the guard."

Uncle Alva took a long drag off his cigarette, with his hand shaking. Then he started coughing. He coughed until his eyes watered, or else he was crying.

"I'm sorry, girl. Ain't no way to make up for that or justify what was done. I just — you deserve to know the truth."

"It is what it is," I said, because if I didn't manage to swallow that feeling of betrayal, I was going to cry or scream. Uncle Alva managed another puff off the cigarette, and then he pointed at the envelope of money.

"Better put that someplace safe," he croaked.

CHAPTER 37
GENTRY

My lady was troubled, for 'twas a great sum of money her uncle had committed to her, and upon her shoulders alone lay the matter of her sister's safety. I was ready to take up any task she might wish, but for the nonce 'twas naught for me to do but feed her. I made our even's meal of what was in the house, and we supped in silence.

After, we went into the front room, and Sir Alva put upon the television that we might watch the news. 'Twas there Dane found us. I rose to greet him, full ready for his wrath, but he abided in the doorway.

"Hey, cuz. You still here?" he said.

"Yep. She's still here," Sir Alva said. "Still my house. Still ain't your business."

"You taking off tonight?" Dane spake without heeding his father.

"Boy, leave your cousin alone."

Once I saw Dane would keep peace, I set myself again beside Lady Zhorzha. Her hands lay together upon her lap, one holding fast to the other. The cloth of her trousers was worn through at her thigh, shewing the milk white of her skin and the blood black of her fire bird.

"Thine heart is fouled with lust," Hildegard said.

" 'Tis not his heart," Gawen said, and then to me: "Thy touch affronteth her not. Last even she was eager to open her thighs to thee."

Sooth, she had received my touch tho I asked not, but I presumed not she should again, so I reached not for her hand. Hildegard believed I had naught but lust in my heart, but in truth I was much concerned with how I might serve my lady. While I pondered it, Sir Alva rose from the couch and walked up and down in a manner most uneaseful.

When first I met him, I thought of him as a hermit, alone in some high place, deprived of company and comfort. Now I bethought myself of Raymondin, who pined for Melusine but never again saw her. Like Sir Alva, he was a man bereft of his wife, left to raise up two sons. Tho Sir Alva's castle was in decline, it remained, mayhap a testament to the labors of his wife. Mayhap also a prison for a man whose heart was sore wounded.

Sir Alva stopped and took his phone from his pocket.

"This peace cannot last," the black knight said. I rose to my feet, my hackles abristle. Dane's shoulders weren tight, his hands fist-wise at his sides.

"I'll take this in my room," Sir Alva said.

"What the fuck are you doing, Dad?"

Sir Alva answered not and, after he departed, Dane wandered the floor and slapped his hands upon his shanks.

I kept watch, and Dane came anon to stand before my lady.

"We had a deal. You said you were gonna talk to Dad and then you were gonna go," he said. "But you're still here, sitting around like you don't plan to leave."

"Uncle Alva is helping me with something," Lady Zhorzha said. "I'll go when it's done."

"You'll fucking go *now.*"

He stepped closer so that we stood nigh toe to toe. I watched his hands and set my shoulder that I might be ready for him. Ere we came to blows, the kitchen door opened and Dirk called out.

"Hey, where are you all?" He entered the room and observed we three. "What's going on?"

"What's going on is Zhorzha's getting ready to leave," Dane said.

"Already?"

"She ain't going nowhere," Sir Alva said. He came from the hallway, his phone yet in his hand.

"I think maybe I better go," my lady said. She made to rise, but could not. When I put out my hand to her, she took it, and I pulled her to her feet. Once aright she was unsteady and leaned upon me.

Sir Alva inclined his head toward the hall, and he alone among us in that room held no tension in his body, for methinks he was weary to his bones.

"Come on back to my room," he said to my lady. "I got some news for you."

CHAPTER 38
ZEE

"He ain't nobody to us, and I aim to keep it that way," Uncle Alva said, when I asked what the guy's name was. *The Fury,* that's what Uncle Alva kept calling him, and it took me a couple minutes to realize the guy with no name was a Klansman. Whatever relief I'd felt finding out my father wasn't a murderer, it was watered down by knowing that my grandfather had seen nothing wrong with lynching and cross burning.

"How do we know we can trust him? That he's not just scamming us for ten grand?" That was what the Fury wanted: ten thousand dollars in exchange for information on where Tague Barnwell and Conrad Ligett were hiding out.

"No way to be dead certain, but he was sent to me by a man who knows him, and wants to see we're dealt by honestly."

"And what does that guy expect to get out of it?" I said, because I was still choking on the thought of giving somebody ten thousand dollars for information.

"Debt paid. He owes me."

I might have felt bad that he'd called in that favor for me and LaReigne, except right then Uncle Alva didn't look like he had much longer to get paid. He was sitting on the edge of his bed, bracing his hand on his knee like he needed it to hold himself up. Someone banged on his bedroom door.

"What the fuck are you two whispering about in there?" Dane yelled.

"Mind your own goddamn business!" Uncle Alva answered.

"How is this going to work?" I said, since we were out of time. "Is the Fury going to call us? How does he get his money?"

"He's coming here."

"It is my goddamn business, whatever you're getting up to." Dane rattled the knob, but Uncle Alva had locked the door.

"*Here?* Because that doesn't seem like a good idea to me. I promised Dane I was leaving, and I think I better."

"You're fucking around with this because you don't know how dangerous it is," Dane said. "You need to come out and see what's on the news."

We couldn't talk with Dane yelling anyway, so I opened the door, even though I figured it was bullshit. Gentry was standing in the hallway with Dane. I left them there and went out to the front room, where Dirk was watching the news.

"They found her dead," he said. "The other hostage."

"I know." I felt the most cold-blooded relief that it was just more details about Molly Verbansky. Cause of death was manual strangulation, and the news people talked like the police were sure Molly had helped with the prison escape, because she was "romantically involved with Conrad Ligett." For the first time, they started hinting that maybe LaReigne wasn't innocent, either. All that told me was that the police cared even less about her safety than before.

"You see?" Dane said, standing in the doorway with Uncle Alva and Gentry. "Those are the kinda men you're messing with. And you think you're gonna track 'em down and get your sister back?"

"We're gonna go into town and get a motel room," I said.

"Why don't you head back to Kansas, get a motel room after you cross the state line?" Dane said.

Uncle Alva doubled over coughing, and the look Dane gave him was pure contempt.

"Come on, Gentry," I said.

We hadn't unpacked much, so it only took a few minutes for us to get everything put back in our bags. I don't know what was said while we were gone, but when we got downstairs, I could see it wasn't anything good. Uncle Alva was standing at the kitchen sink. Dirk was at the back door, and Dane was out on the porch pacing up and down, smoking a cigarette.

"Just be cool," Dirk was saying to him.

"Do you fucking know what they're up to?"

"I know there's no sense getting into a fight about it."

When I stepped outside, Dane stopped pacing, but he didn't say anything as Gentry and I went down the steps. Uncle Alva came after us, and together we walked across the yard to Gentry's truck. Dane stayed on the porch, smoking and glaring. The sun was going down, but the outside lights hadn't kicked on yet.

"I hate to see you go like this," Uncle Alva said. Because I didn't know what else to do, I hugged him. The butt of his gun pressed against my hip bone.

"I'll call you and let you know where we're staying," I said.

"I reckon that'll suit. Better than having somebody come around here while Dane's bent outta shape."

I let go of Uncle Alva and nodded. He turned back toward the house and, while Gentry put our bags in the back of the truck, I went around to get in on the passenger side. As I circled the hood, Dane came walking across the yard. Before he got to me, he took a drag off his cigarette and pitched it.

"Don't you fucking do it," he said. "I told you to go back to Kansas, and you damn well better."

I ignored him and reached for the door handle.

"You seen what they did to that other woman. You think some Klansman is gonna sell out his brothers? More likely he's coming to kill you. Maybe come around here and kill us, too."

"I thought they were *good old boys*," I said.

"I swear to god you better shut your smart mouth."

Dane grabbed my arm and turned me around. I don't know what he planned to do, but as soon as he touched me, Gentry came around the truck at full speed.

"I warned thee," he said.

"And I'm warning you. You better get this bitch of yours under control before I —"

Gentry grabbed Dane's elbow and did something to it that made Dane shut up and let go of me immediately. Then he turned and took a swing at Gentry.

They were completely mismatched. Dane was tall and lanky, and Gentry was short and stocky. I would have been afraid for Gentry, because Dane had better reach, but Gentry had a real boxer's stance, and when Dane swung, Gentry dodged it. I backed way the hell up, because I didn't want to catch a stray fist, but Gentry never even tried to punch Dane. He plowed into him, his right shoulder in the middle of Dane's chest, and slammed him into the truck. Dane brought both his hands up, but before he could do anything, Gentry jabbed his left fist into Dane's side, practically into his back. Both of Dane's arms went floppy, and Gentry caught him around the waist and lowered him to the ground.

"Oh, damn!" Dirk said, as he ran across the yard. When he got to us, he squatted down and looked into Dane's face. "I told you, man. I warned you not to mess with him."

Dane didn't answer. He was slumped against the truck's rear wheel with his legs crumpled up under him and his hands limp at his sides. He looked pale and sweaty.

Gentry was shaking his left hand like it hurt, which it probably did. His right hand was in a fist, but not the clench and release he did when he was anxious. Just a loose fist. Turning away, he took a dozen steps across the yard to where the dog had watched the whole thing. The dog came as close as his chain would let him, so they were only a foot apart. Gentry stretched out his left hand. The dog sniffed it for a few seconds and then licked it.

"Gentry," I said, but he wasn't listening.

"You all right, bro?" Dirk looked at me. "Shit, he really done him. Right in the liver."

"Gentry!" I tried again.

Dirk and I got Dane on his feet, and when I put my arm around him, I felt the gun tucked in the back of his belt. I pulled it out and handed it to Dirk. Then we walked Dane over to the front porch and lowered him down to sit on the steps.

"I swear. Here I thought you was the stupid one," Uncle Alva said to Dirk. "At least you learnt your lesson."

For a couple minutes, the three of us stood around Dane, but when Gentry walked up, I knew the peace would be over as soon as Dane could get on his feet.

"I'll call you, Uncle Alva," I said.

Gentry drove and I looked at Yelp, trying

to pick a motel. There were only four in town, and they were all little run-down motor lodges. Thinking about the Fury, who wouldn't even tell us his name, I picked the motel on the highway south of town. Maybe he wouldn't like it being so visible on the main road, but in my mind that made it safer. Dane was an asshole, but that didn't mean he was wrong about the Fury's intentions.

While Gentry carried our bags into the room, I went down to the ice machine. When I got back, he was pacing up and down, having a conversation with his voices. Clench, release, clench, release. I put some ice into a hand towel, but I had to follow him back and forth a few laps before I got him to stop and take the ice. His hand was swollen but not too banged up. The upside of not punching people in the face. He let me wrap the towel around his knuckles, but then he went back to pacing.

I called Uncle Alva, and while I listened to the phone ring, I felt this sinking dread. What if he'd changed his mind? What if Dane had done something to him?

After about a dozen rings, someone picked up.

"It's me," I said, half expecting to hear Dane. Instead, I got thirty seconds of coughing before Uncle Alva spoke. I told him what motel we were at and what room we were in, even though it made me nervous to say it.

"The Fury says he's coming Saturday, but he don't know what time. Stay close and keep your phone with you."

I felt better after I hung up. Not *not* nervous, because I was nervous as hell, but not as helpless. So much of the time I felt like I couldn't help anyone, but maybe I could help LaReigne. I didn't know what to do for Gentry, who was still going up and down. I said his name about ten times, trying to be loud without sounding like I was mad. Finally, he stopped at the foot of the bed where I was sitting.

"Gentry? Are you okay?" Then I tried to say it how he would: "Are you well?"

"I know not, my lady."

"Does your hand hurt? Do you think you broke something?"

He unwound the wet towel, straightened his fingers, then made a fist.

"Nay," he said. "But ere this day, I never struck a man in anger."

"So you learned to box and beat the shit out of people with swords for fun?"

"Lady, 'tis not for amusement but to ready myself for a day I might see battle." He was looking at his hand, frowning. Not like he'd never punched somebody and hurt his hand, but like hitting Dane was a whole new thing. I got up and took the towel, planning to put some more ice in it.

"Okay, well, think of it this way," I said. "You saw battle today. Turns out all that practicing paid off. You were prepared."

He nodded, but there was more pacing, until he finally stopped and pulled his phone out of his pocket. I wanted him to have a distraction from whatever he was thinking about, but I worried about who he was texting.

"You're not going to tell your parents what I'm doing, are you?" I said.

"Nay, my lady. 'Twould distress my mother, and betray thy trust."

"Yeah, somehow I don't think you're a very good liar."

He smiled and said, "I am able, when I must. I have lied to thee twice and thou knew it not."

That cracked me up. I think he expected me to ask what he'd lied about, but two lies? That was a drop in the bucket of the lies men had told me.

"I'm gonna take a shower," I said.

I planned to take the longest shower in the world, like I never got to take. I was in there for a solid hour and, even though the hot water still hadn't run out, I finally turned it off. I'd scrubbed everything I had to scrub, washed my hair, sang all the Patsy Cline songs I knew, and my hands were getting pruney. Since I'd turned the bathroom into a steam sauna, I used the motel's blow-dryer on my hair, hoping it would cut back on the frizz. It was kind of soothing, hanging my head down, the blow-dryer buzzing in my ear, but when I turned it off, I heard how quiet the room was.

"Gentry? Gentry?" No answer. I poked my head out into the room to check on him. He was sitting on the bed, cross-legged, with his hands on his knees, and his eyes closed. Meditating. Or praying. "Gentry?"

"My lady?" he said, but he didn't open his eyes.

"You okay?"

"I am. I thank thee for asking. Art thou well?"

"I'm very clean anyway." I didn't know how I was feeling.

I went back to the bathroom sink to comb out my hair. I hadn't combed it in weeks, and it made the frizz worse. Gentry came and stood next to me, watching me try to unfuck my hair. After a few minutes, I gave up and tossed the comb on the counter.

"What do you think?" I held my arms out, so he could see me in my full glory. Bare-ass naked, half freckled, half ghostly white, thighs thick as hell, that scorched bird trying to take flight off me, and a massive poofy triangle of orange hair.

"Methinks thou art Venus from the sea."

"Maybe I am a water nymph instead of a phoenix," I said. "I do like showers."

"Mayhap thou art many things I have ne seen ne heard of."

I laughed and he smiled. I liked to watch him look at me in the mirror. It used to bother me that he never looked me in the eye, but now I knew that was just how he was. He wasn't shy or squirrelly, but he was getting whatever information he needed by looking at other parts of me. Even though he'd been all knightly goodness about not watching me swim, he wasn't embarrassed about looking at me. Not touching, just looking. Maybe waiting for an invitation.

I reached for my hair band on the bathroom counter, but he put out his hand, so I gave it to him, wondering if he meant to help me put my hair up. Instead he slid it up his arm, like he was taking my favor before a joust.

"To see thy hair loose upon thy shoulders liketh me best."

"I wanna say something nice about you, but . . ." But honestly, the nice things I wanted to say, most men wouldn't take them as compliments. I liked that he was strong but not hard. I liked that if his hand was somewhere I didn't want touched, I could move it. I could say *Stop* or *Do it like this,* and unlike every other man I'd ever fucked, Gentry didn't get offended. "But your hair is seriously messed up. I like your prick."

"Then I shall use it to lay siege at all the gates of thy keep," he said.

"Oh my god. You are so fucking filthy."

I only meant to tease him, because he made me laugh, but he stopped smiling and got a serious look on his face.

"I fear I am, my lady. I fear Hildegard be right that I polluted my oath to thee."

"You haven't polluted any oath to me. Or do you think the black knight was wrong?"

Gentry was still frowning, but when I held out my hand, he took it.

"Nay, my lady."

"I don't, either," I said.

As for him laying siege to all the gates of my keep, we gave it a shot.

Chapter 39
Rhys

The first text message I got about the situation was from Edrard: *Did you know Gentry was going to Missouri?*

When?

He's there now. They drove over on Wednesday.

They?

He and Lady Zoroaster, Edrard texted. Then: *Ducking autocorrect.* Then: *Lady Zee.*

Later, when Gentry started a three-way text with Edrard and me, it took me about twenty texts to catch up. They were talking about going to find Zee's sister, who I guess was missing.

Like a search party? I said.

Kind of.

Nay, Gentry texted. *Tis a negotiation for her return.*

Come on. It'll be fun. I'm taking my bow, Edrard said.

An armed negotiation? I said.

Lady Zhorzha needeth an escort for the negotiation. Tis better we should be an armed escort. Tho thine aid would be much valued, my brother, if the journey thee liketh not, I shall not press thee.

That was Gentry's way of saying I was being a chickenshit, and for an hour I didn't answer him.

On the other message thread, Edrard said, *It'll be cool. A little change of pace.*

What does Rosalinda think?

She's pouting about it. I think she's jealous of Zee. Idk why.

I couldn't tell if he was joking or that oblivious. I was trying to decide how to answer Gentry when my boss popped up over the top of my cubicle.

"Doing anything fun this weekend?" he said.

"Oh, the usual." I fumbled my phone into my pocket, because we weren't supposed to have them out, and pulled up the next work ticket on my monitor.

"Now what is it you do again? Like live action D and D, is that what it is?"

"No, it's called *buhurt.* It's historically accurate medieval combat."

"But that's basically LARPing, right?"

"No. It's not LARPing," I said. I was sick of people acting like we were out in the woods cosplaying. "You wanna see a video of it?"

"Yeah, sure."

It was against the rules, but he was my boss, so I took my phone out and pulled up a video from a one-on-one joust. For a couple seconds, my boss leaned down to watch it and then, without even asking, he took the phone out of my hand.

"You're the tall one, right?" he said.

"Yeah."

"Son of a bitch!" He laughed. "Who's the guy in the black armor?"

"That's my sparring partner, Gentry."

"Your man Gentry is nuts. Dude is a berserker."

"Yeah, well, that's not exactly the goal," I said.

"That's some hobby you got there." He handed the phone back before the video ended. Before I beat Gentry, because that was the time I clocked Gentry with my shield hard enough he went down like a post. We'd taken him to the hospital, but it turned out he didn't have a concussion. He'd just got his bell rung.

"Butt hurt? That's not really what it's called, is it?" my boss said.

"Buhurt."

He walked away laughing, and there were

forty minutes left on the clock, so I started on the work ticket. My phone was still out on the desk, so I saw the text notification from Edrard pop up.

Ok seriously. Are you going?

I hesitated for a minute, but it was 4:23 on a Friday afternoon and what else was I doing?

Sure, I said. *How do you feel about leaving in the morning?*

Edrard picked me up at dawn. He had his truck loaded down with way more equipment than we could possibly need. It wasn't like we were actually going into battle, but he seemed to be having fun, so I didn't burst his bubble. Rosalinda called him twice as we were leaving town, and the second time he put it on speakerphone, so I got to enjoy the sound of her seething with rage.

"I'll be back Sunday night," Edrard said. "Why don't you go visit your folks?"

"I don't want to go see my folks," she snapped.

I didn't blame her, because Rosalinda's family were long-denim-skirt-wearing Evangelicals. Her younger sister was the only member of her family who came out for Rosalinda and Edrard's handfasting, and she acted like I was trying to seduce her because I flirted with her. So I parked her next to Gentry, who'd sat there being chivalrous and nonseductive for the whole day.

I reached over and muted Edrard's phone for a second.

"Just ask her if she wants to go," I said. Edrard gave me a look of horror. "Just invite her."

I unmuted the phone and after a second, Edrard said, "Sweetie, do you want to go?"

"No! I don't want to go to Missouri and look for Zee's stupid sister." She delivered that in a snarl, but it was the answer I'd expected. Rosalinda was a homebody, and there was no way she wanted to go watch her backup knight in shining armor serve that red-haired minx.

End result, Rosalinda stopped calling, and two-thirds of the Three Musketeers hit the road for southern Missouri, where we made a few dueling banjo jokes the further we got off the main highway. Gentry had texted us the motel information, so when we got into town around noon, we went straight there.

It looked like one of those by-the-hour motels on Broadway in Wichita and, when Gentry let us in, the room was all paneled walls and cheap furniture, with a funky smell.

"Damn. This place smells like a whore-house," I said, while Gentry and Edrard shook hands.

"That's really flattering," Zee said. She stepped out of the bathroom wearing nothing but a T-shirt and panties. I stared at her, because she had this enormous tattoo that covered her whole thigh. Honestly, it wasn't attractive, but it was pretty compelling. Shocking, too. Was that the goal? To surprise you? To make you stare?

She walked across that nasty motel carpet in her bare feet, and picked up a pair of blue jeans off the foot of the bed. Instead of going back into the bathroom to get dressed, she pulled them on with the three of us there in the room. Hiked up her T-shirt and fastened them.

"Why don't we go get some lunch?" I said.

"You all can go," Zee said. "But I need to stay here in case they show up."

"They?"

"My uncle and a friend of his might be coming."

"I shall stay with thee," Gentry said.

"I can stay with you while they go get lunch," I said, but Zee ignored me.

"Well, hey, why don't I just go get us some lunch?" Edrard said.

" 'Twould be well met."

Gentry reached for his wallet — he always paid Edrard's way — but Zee waved him off. She got up and went to a backpack on the dresser and unzipped it. Took out a fifty-dollar bill and handed it to Edrard. We decided on pizza, since we'd passed a place on the way into town. Edrard left to get it, giving me a look like I should come with him, but not when things were getting interesting.

Zee was sitting on the bed further from the door, so I sat down across from her. She was messing with her phone and didn't look up.

"Sorry about barging in while you were getting dressed," I said. "We didn't know you were sharing a room."

"Why wouldn't we be?"

It was a room with two beds, though, and they both looked slept in. Plus, the way Gentry acted when he sat next to her on the bed, a good foot apart, with his hands on his knees, I didn't think there was any way he'd summited Mount Zee.

The whole situation had me thinking about awkward love triangles, because whatever her operating system was, she had me intrigued. I couldn't figure out why Gentry had latched onto her, because she did not fit into his chivalrous little world.

She had a mouth like a sailor and a body that was more Rubens' *Venus* than *The Lady and the Unicorn*. Still, for whatever reason, Gentry was really into her, and I didn't want to be the person who made a mess of his romantic delusions.

The two of them sat there, messing with their phones, until Zee turned her head and looked at Gentry, then back at her phone.

"Are you two texting each other right here in front of me?" I said.

Zee snorted, finished typing something, and put her phone away. Then she got the backpack off the dresser and carried it into the bathroom.

"So, how are things going with her?" I asked. "Sir Percival still a virgin?"

Without answering, Gentry followed Zee to the bathroom. Nothing weird about that.

They'd been in there for maybe five minutes when someone knocked on the door. It was way too soon to be Edrard back with the pizza, so I got up to see who it was. Zee came out of the bathroom and shook her head at me.

"Will you do me a favor?" she said.

"Certs, my lady." I winked at her, but she gave me a kill look.

"Sit right there and keep your mouth shut."

"Really? That's —"

"Seriously. Don't say a word. Can you do that?" she said.

I made a little zipping motion with my hand over my mouth. She must have already given Gentry that speech, because when he came out of the bathroom, she didn't say anything to him. She went to the door and he followed her.

"Hey, Uncle Alva," she said when she opened the door. She hugged him for a second and then stepped back to let him in. Him and a guy behind him, whom she didn't hug. Her uncle was tall, but sort of stooped over, with a scraggly goatee. The other guy was average-sized but with one of those big mountain-men beards. Younger than me if I was guessing. While Zee closed the door, he looked around the motel room. At Gentry. At me.

The whole thing felt super sketchy, even before Zee turned around and I realized she had a gun stuck in the front of her jeans. Then I looked more closely at the uncle and the other guy, and realized they both had guns, too. Theirs were in holsters and not stuck in their waistbands, but I was in a motel room with three people with guns.

"Let's make this quick," the bearded guy said.

"Do you wanna see the money?" Zee said.

"Yeah."

If Zee having a gun surprised me, I definitely wasn't ready for Gentry to reach into the cargo pocket on his shorts and pull out a stack of bills. He passed it to Zee, who handed it to the bearded guy, who flipped through the bundle of money and nodded. When he passed it back to Zee, she returned it to Gentry.

"All right. So here's the deal." The guy reached into his back pocket and pulled out an actual paper road map. He unfolded it and laid it on the dresser. Zee's uncle stayed where he was, but Zee and Gentry went to stand next to the guy.

"There's an old cabin here, back up in the woods. Originally belonged to Craig's grandparents. Here about ten years ago, his ex-wife sold it to some people who put it in a trust. It's complicated, but the folks who own that trust are friendly with the wizard" — I swear he said *wizard* — "who supports Craig. On paper, it don't look like it's connected to him. That's where they are. And it's pretty far out in the country, not easy to get to, and not many folks around."

"That's a pretty big circle," Zee said.

"Yeah, well, I've only been there twice, so it's not like I can give you coordinates."

"I bet a satellite map would help," I said.

Zee shot me a glare.

"Like he said," the bearded guy said. "You look at satellite maps, you'll be able to find it. It's the only thing for miles around."

"You sure that's where they are?" Zee's uncle said.

"They're there."

"How do you know?" Zee said.

I'd been trying to keep an eye on the big picture, but I kept coming back to where everyone's hands were in relationship to their guns. Zee's uncle had his hands down at his sides. The bearded man kept his arms crossed, so that he was like Gentry's mirror. Zee had her thumb in the pocket below where the gun was tucked into her waist-band. It made me nervous, but I guess I was the only one.

"Because I spoke to a man who's with them. And he seems to think they'd be better off without your gal. Save themselves some trouble. Now, I'm not about to get in the middle of this, but if you go there, I bet they'd talk to you for the right amount."

"What's your friend's name?" Zee said.

"Same as mine. None of your business. Now, I think I've done what I agreed to do."

Zee looked at her uncle and, when he nodded, she held out her hand to Gentry.

Just like he had before, he took the wad of cash out of his pocket and gave it to her. She gave it to the bearded guy, and he walked out, leaving the map behind.

After he was gone, Zee took the gun out of her waistband and set it on the dresser. For almost a whole minute her uncle coughed, and then he said, "I wish I could do this for you, girl. I truly do."

"I know. It's okay," she said.

"You take care of her, son," the uncle said to Gentry. "I know you can handle yourself in a fight, so I ain't worried about that, but you tread careful."

"I shall, sir." Gentry put out his hand and they shook.

After the uncle left, Zee and Gentry stood next to each other looking at the map.

"Am I allowed to talk now?" I said.

"If you have to," Zee said.

"What the hell was that?"

They didn't answer and, before I could ask anything else, Edrard came back with lunch. Zee folded up the map, and he put the pizzas on the dresser.

"How fareth Dame Rosalinda?" Gentry started passing around pieces of pizza, so I guessed we weren't going to talk about the bearded guy.

"Well, she wasn't very happy about Edrard coming here," I said.

"Understatement. I suspect my name will be mud when I get home," Edrard said.

"I'm sorry," Zee said around a bite of pizza. "I didn't think you two would come."

"All for one and one for all, right?" That's what I said, but I was seriously disturbed by the whole thing. Ever since I got the diversion for my DUI, I'd been keeping my head down, being extra careful. This wasn't anything like careful.

"I thank you, my brothers," Gentry said.

We ate our lunch talking about jousts and armor upgrades. Zee sat there eating, listening to us. When Edrard went to get another piece of pizza, he finally noticed what I'd been thinking about all along.

"Why is there a gun here?" he said.

Zee picked it up and set it next to her backpack. Like that solved the problem.

"Yeah, I have to say, Zee having a gun is just the tip of the iceberg, but maybe we could start there," I said.

"She hath arms, for these Knights of the Ku Klux Klan are ne to be trusted ne to be trifled with," Gentry said.

"Wait. That guy was KKK?" I said.

"What guy?" Edrard swiveled to look at me.

"While you were gone, Zee's uncle came

here with a guy who's apparently in the KKK. So what the hell is going on?"

"What did Gentry tell you?" Zee said.

"That we were going to get your sister," I said. "I assumed she needed convincing to leave a bad boyfriend. Or he needed convincing."

"My sister is LaReigne Trego-Gill. She was taken hostage in the prison escape from El Dorado last week."

"You're serious? And you somehow think you're going to do what? Go negotiate with white supremacists who murdered people and kidnapped your sister? And then what are you gonna tell the police about how you got her back?"

"We'll drop her off in the country and she can walk into town and tell the police she escaped," Zee said.

"Yeah, I'm sure nothing could go wrong with any of that."

Zee looked annoyed and Gentry was scratching his neck, but I couldn't get a bead on Edrard. He looked uneasy, but he wasn't saying anything.

"Look," I said, "if that guy is KKK and he actually knows where your sister is, we need to call the police. They're the people equipped to deal with this."

"You don't have to be a part of this. But

we're not getting the police involved," Zee said.

"What do you think we are? Navy SEALs?"

"No, I think you're exactly what you are." She managed to make it sound like an insult. "It was not my idea to invite you along, and Gentry, no offense, but I don't think this is a good idea."

"My lady, with all respect to thy view, 'tis better we should be four than two. I am thy champion, and they aren my brothers-at-arms."

"I appreciate that. I do. But I don't want to drag a bunch of people into this," she said.

"Oh, now that's occurring to you," I said. "That maybe you shouldn't take a bunch of amateur knights to a negotiation with the Klan. Exactly what are you going to say to convince them to let your sister go?"

"We're not going to negotiate," Zee said. "We're going to ransom her."

I wondered where the money had come from, and obviously she had money, since she'd given a bunch of it to the bearded guy. The Klansman. I hated to admit it, but I was starting to agree with Rosalinda. Zee wasn't our kind of people, and she was getting Gentry mixed up in something danger-

411

ous. He wasn't even paying attention to us. While we were talking, he picked up Zee's gun and very calmly popped the clip out of it. Then he ejected the bullet from the chamber, like he was in a movie.

"When last was this cleaned?" he said.

"I don't know," Zee said.

Gentry opened his big rucksack to get a rag and a bottle of oil. He started taking the gun apart and cleaning it, while Zee watched.

"You know how to use a gun?" she said. "What happened to swords and armor, Sir Gentry?"

"I am no fool, Lady Zhorzha. I build flying machines. Yea, I ken the workings of a gun. My father taught me."

"Well, I think you should wipe it all down, including the bullets, so it doesn't have your fingerprints on it. You know, in case it gets used."

Gentry nodded and went on cleaning the gun.

"So, we're talking pretty casually about shooting people. Did I read that right?" I said.

"I'm sorry he brought you all the way out here without telling you what was going on," Zee said. "If I'd known, I would've stopped him."

"I mean, I kind of knew," Edrard said. Which was complete bullshit. At no point had he mentioned white supremacists or hostages or anything like that. He had such a fear of missing out, he would go along with anything. "But do we know for sure where your sister is?"

"Yea, we haven a map," Gentry said.

He put the gun back together and gave it a last wipe-down before he put it in Zee's backpack. Then he went to the bathroom and washed his hands. When he came back, Zee got the map, Gentry got his iPad, and, like we hadn't been discussing the KKK at all, the three of them started looking at satellite maps and discussing what roads to take. Talking like they were really going to do this, until I thought my head would explode.

"Josh, will you listen to me?" I said. "While you were gone, her uncle came here with a guy who is apparently in the Klan, and brought that map. Please, will you think about that? Her uncle knows people in the Klan."

"Yeah, that's kind of how prison works. You make friends with the people you make friends with," Zee said. "Including white supremacists sometimes, which is not my favorite thing, either."

"I was here. I saw the guy, Josh. These are not fancy-pants college campus Nazis in fitted suits. These are real, backwoods, cross-burning racists. The kind of people who tie you to their tailgate and drag you to death. Just for fun."

" 'Tis all the more reason I would see them returned to their prison," Gentry said.

"Then let's call the police. I didn't sign on for some crazy vigilante shit." I hadn't signed on for being the only one thinking rationally, either, but there I was.

"It's not like her uncle is still in the KKK," Edrard said, like that was the whole point of what I'd said. "Is he?"

"No. He never was. He was friends with these people in prison, because he had to be."

"Gentry," I said, but we'd lost him. He was in full-blown campaign mode, scribbling notes on the map with a cheap motel pen. We weren't getting him back anytime soon, which in some ways made it easier to say what I needed to.

"Zee, I haven't known you very long, but I feel you may have missed an important element, so I need you to listen to me really carefully. Gentry is my friend. I care about him."

"We all do," Edrard said, but I thought it

was more likely that Zee saw him as a convenience. Someone to use.

"Okay, great. We all care about him," I said. "I know you've known him the longest, Edrard, but I've known him for nearly five years, long enough to say very firmly that he is not all there. I'm not saying that because he's autistic, so don't even with that. Autism spectrum disorder is one thing. Plenty of people on the spectrum function really well. Gentry does fine. He has a job. He has his hobbies. But let's be honest, he also has half a dozen invisible friends who talk to him in his head. Please, will you think about that for a minute?"

Zee gave me a glare that was so malevolent it made me glad Gentry had put her gun away.

"You don't have to be that way about it," Edrard said.

"I guess he probably does," Zee said. "I guess that's how he sees Gentry."

"Oh, don't get all high and mighty with me like I'm being mean or something. You cannot possibly believe he's capable of making the kinds of decisions that are involved in this. He has no business going on some half-assed rescue mission with you. You need to call the FBI or something, and give them that map."

Gentry looked up from his trance and said, "My lady, we musten go this even."

"I know. They won't stay there. We have to get there before they leave," she said.

Like I hadn't said a word.

"Josh, are you really —"

"Stop calling me Josh," Edrard said. "What are you trying to do?"

Before I could answer, someone knocked on the door. As if it were a totally normal thing to do, Zee took the gun out of her backpack, tucked it into the back of her pants, and went to answer the door.

"Hey, cuz," said the guy she let in. He was tall like her and her uncle, but a pimply, gap-toothed kid whose eyes were too close together. Top-quality inbreeding. He shook Gentry's hand, saying, "My man."

"Master Dirk, well met," Gentry said.

Then because we were there and he was looking at us, Edrard and I introduced ourselves.

"What are you doing here? Is everything okay?" Zee said.

"Yeah, but I got to thinking, if you needed another hand, I'd go. I mean, we're family and all."

"I think that's a great idea," I said. "We can go home, and Zee and Cousin Dirk can go do whatever crazy thing they want to do."

"Thou art under no obligation, Sir Rhys. If thou wishest, thou mayest go at once." It was maybe the first time I ever heard Gentry sound annoyed. He was so phlegmatic that even hearing him raise his voice was a surprise.

"Gentry," Zee said. "Can I talk to you for a minute?"

He tilted his head the way he did when he was having one of his internal conversations.

"You see?" I said to Zee, but she was watching Gentry like she was waiting for him to finish a phone call. Like it was totally normal.

CHAPTER 40
ZEE

I took Gentry into the bathroom, but once we were alone in there with the door closed, I felt stupid. I should have said what I wanted to say in front of everyone.

"My lady, thou art troubled," he said.

"Yeah, I don't think your friends want to go, and that's probably a good thing. Maybe just Dirk and I should go."

"Sir Rhys and Sir Edrard may do as it please them, but I am thy champion, and methinks more ready to do battle than Master Dirk."

"I keep thinking about what you said about never hitting anybody in anger before, and I'm afraid this might turn out to be more of that," I said.

"I am not afraid." He'd had his head down, but he lifted it and said, "May I kiss thee?"

"Now? No. You need to seriously think about this." It was nice to say no and have him listen, but I didn't want to hurt his feelings.

"Nay, I hear thee, but thou speakest naught I know not already," he said. Not to me, because he cocked his head to the right. If it had to be one or the other, I'd take the black knight over that bitch Hildegard any day. Gentry took a step closer to me, so that he was actually in my personal space. Face-to-face, looking down at him from only a couple inches away, I watched his eyelashes flutter when he blinked.

"It's not that I don't like kissing you, but that this is serious," I said.

"I ken 'tis no light matter, my lady. I swore to serve thee howsoever I might, and I would kiss thee to remind thee I am bound to thee by my oath and my flesh."

And I had let him make that reckless oath both ways. I'd opened my legs right up, and let him make some solemn vow to me that I barely understood.

"Is it okay if I touch you?" I said.

"Yea."

I brought my hands up to his jaw, to hold him. Then I kissed him straight on, my lips against his lips. The most sincere kiss I had ever given anyone in my life. The same way he shook hands. Before we could get distracted, I let go of him and stepped back.

"Okay," I said. "Whatever you think is best."

"My bond to thee abideth. If thou goest, I shall go."

"Then you're going."

Rhys, on the other hand, was not going. When Gentry and I came out of the bathroom, Dirk was leaning against the dresser, eating a piece of leftover pizza. Rhys and Edrard were huddled together, whispering. They broke apart when we stepped into the room.

"Please, tell me you talked some sense into him," Rhys said.

"I am sensible of the danger," Gentry said, but that was all.

I didn't say anything. I laid my backpack out on the bed and started deciding what to leave and what to take. Gentry did the same.

After a minute or so, Edrard unzipped his bag, and he and Gentry started talking about what weapons to take. Dirk picked up an axe from the things Gentry had laid out on the bed.

"Holy shit. Y'all are some crazy motherfuckers. All's I brought was this."

Dirk pulled a 9 mm out of his belt. Dane's, if I was guessing. Like he had with my gun, Gentry took it apart and oiled it. While he was wiping down the bullets and reloading them, Rhys had a meltdown.

"Jesus fucking Christ! You cannot do this!" he said.

"You don't have to go, if you don't want to," Edrard said.

"I swear, I'll call the police. You walk out that door, I will call the police and tell them what you're doing."

"What wilt thou tell them, Sir Rhys?" Gentry didn't even look up to say it.

"That you're going on some half-assed rescue mission, armed with guns and swords."

"What do you think they'll do?" I said, as I loaded the money into my smaller back-pack.

"Stop you."

"Yeah. They'll probably arrest us, so if that's what you want."

He wasn't going to do it, but he stood there for a few minutes before he came up with his next threat: "Fine. I'll call Gentry's parents. Let's see what Mr. and Mrs. Frank have to say about this plan."

I wondered if Gentry was about to hit somebody in anger for the second time in a week, because he had his jaw clenched when he turned to Rhys.

"Thou must do as thou wilt, Sir Rhys, but I called upon thee to help me, for I believed

421

thou wert true and brave. Call me not thy brother, if thou wouldst be my nursemaid."

Gentry was probably the nicest guy I'd ever met, but I was relieved to find out that wasn't all he was.

"Edrard, you're not really going, are you?" Rhys said.

"Yeah, I'm going. Gentry is my brother and, for once, I'd like to go do something without you or Rosalinda making me feel like a bumbling idiot."

Rhys sat down on the edge of the bed, watching Edrard and Gentry pack. Once we were finished, I did what I knew had to be done.

"Give me your phones," I said. "We can't take anything that can be used to prove we were there."

"Oh, shit, for real?" Dirk said.

"I didn't even think of that." Edrard took out his phone and looked at it.

Gentry didn't hesitate. He laid his phone on top of his iPad on the dresser. Whatever notes we needed were on the map. I turned my phone off and added it to the stack. Dirk shrugged and did the same. Edrard fretted and sent one last text message before he gave his up.

"We'll stop at Walmart and buy a couple burner phones, so we can —"

"And you're just going to leave me here?" Rhys said.

"The room is paid for tonight," I said.

"We'll come back and get you," Edrard said. He looked embarrassed, but then he was Rhys' ride.

We drove straight south out of town, Gentry and I in his truck, Dirk riding with Edrard. We made two stops, at a Walmart across the Arkansas state line to pick up a pair of burner phones and, once we got to Murfreesboro, to get some dinner. In the parking lot of a Sonic, we double-checked our plan. The map was at least fifteen years old, and it had been unfolded and refolded until the seams were worn white. But between it and the satellite images we'd looked at, we knew where we were going.

I was so grateful to Gentry, because I had no idea how to plan something that looked like military strategy. He had marked the place where we would leave the county road and take an old fire road running through some heavy woods. It was high ground above the cabin, which had been a little gray square on the satellite maps. He'd also drawn the route we would take on foot to the road that led to the cabin.

" 'Tis nigh half a mile, my lady. Mayhap

'twould be best if thou waitest here," he said, and put his finger on the map where we were going to leave the trucks.

"Wait there? Are you for real? I'm not fucking waiting there." It was the first time I'd ever been mad at him.

"I would not for the world put thee in danger."

"Oh, but you in danger is fine? And which one of you is going to do the talking? Because I know you're not, Gentry." I felt bad saying it that way, but he didn't look offended.

"Nay."

"Yeah, I think she better go," Dirk said.

" 'Tis nigh half a mile," Gentry said again. "Wilt thou be able to walk it, my lady?"

"Yes," I said, but I already knew I wouldn't be doing it sober. My stomach felt so tight I thought I might vomit up the hamburger I'd eaten. When I took out my THC drops and offered them around, Edrard and Dirk took some. Gentry was too busy plotting to be nervous.

"We shall reach it ere the sun sets and I shall search out the place that we might come upon them unawares. 'Tis to our advantage, for the sun shall set behind us. Master Dirk, thou shalt come with us, but remain here, where the trees given cover to

424

the road. If we needen help, we shall call for thee. Sir Edrard, as ever with thy mighty bow, thou shalt remain here, upon high ground."

I know I gave Edrard a doubting look, and he blushed.

"I'm no good at hunting," he said, "because I don't like killing little animals. I'm actually a really good shot, though. At a hundred yards, I can hit a three-foot target zone with my compound bow. I'll be good for sniper cover."

"Yea, and so shall we use thee as proof we comen not alone," Gentry said.

Except for when he'd tried to convince me not to go, Gentry hadn't clenched his hand or scratched his neck. The closer we got, the calmer he was.

"So, we ready?" Dirk said.

"Yea, but hence we travel under the dragon banner," Gentry said.

"What's that mean?"

"No quarter. No mercy." That was Edrard and, hearing the nervousness in his voice, I wished so hard that he'd stayed home. I wanted to wish that Gentry had stayed home, too, but I couldn't have done it alone. And Dirk? He acted like we were in a video game.

"Hard-core, man," he said and laughed.

CHAPTER 41
ZEE

Gentry was so relaxed he didn't even do a drive-by. On the first pass, he turned off the highway and, a few miles further on, he left the county road for the fire road, with Edrard a few car lengths back. For once, I had a job to do. I had the bolt cutters that Gentry apparently always carried in the back of his truck, and I was the one who jumped out and cut the chain on the gate. We drove in probably another half mile, until the dirt road turned into not much more than a gap between trees. When Gentry cut the engine, Edrard pulled up beside him.

Even with the THC drops, I was a nervous wreck, and Gentry must have finally felt his nerves, because he started scratching his neck. After he finished, he got out of the truck and folded the seat forward to get his weapons. My heart hammered like crazy, watching him buckle a leather harness on

426

over his T-shirt. When he was done, that sharp, shiny sword was strapped to his back, ready to be drawn over his head. He pulled a loose blouse on to hide it, and traded out his Timberlands for the soft leather boots he'd worn at Bryn Carreg. Dressed that way, he looked like a woodsman, all in green and brown, with another knife and a small axe strapped to his belt. He squatted down and rubbed a little dirt on his bare skin to take the shine off.

While he was getting changed, Dirk and Edrard had gotten out of the other truck and walked over to us. We didn't talk, because by then we'd gone over it enough times there was nothing to discuss. Gentry took one of the phones, tucked it into his pocket, and walked off to reconnoiter. After he was gone, Edrard got his bow and arrows ready, and I braided my hair to keep it out of the way.

Then I double-checked the money. Including what I'd started with and what Uncle Alva had given me, minus what I'd paid to the Fury, I had ninety-four thousand dollars. I wasn't about to offer that up front, because I thought there was a good chance I'd end up haggling with them. So I'd split the cash into two piles: fifty thousand in one Sonic bag and forty-four thousand in another. I locked them both in Gentry's truck. Finally I chambered a round on my gun, put the safety on, and tucked it into the back of my jeans. Then all we could do was wait.

It was so quiet out there; I didn't hear any sounds of civilization. Not even road traffic. I didn't have a watch, so I kept pulling out the phone and checking the time. Gentry had made us promise that if he wasn't back in half an hour we would leave, but looking at Edrard, I knew we weren't going to do that.

After twenty minutes, I started to get this gnawing dread like I had never had before in my life. Maybe because nobody had ever taken that kind of risk for me. Gentry was out there walking around in the woods, spying on guys I knew were killers. I looked at the phone again. Twenty-four minutes.

Gentry came walking out of the trees to the west of where he'd gone in. He was deep in conversation with the black knight. Not saying anything out loud, but nodding and gesturing. Edrard, Dirk, and I gathered around him, but it was a few more minutes before he was done. He bowed, first to the black knight, then to me.

" 'Tis better than we hoped. I saw but four men. Two in the barn that standeth to the north. They aren at work upon their truck, and much distracted. Another man hath gone into the house. One sitteth upon the porch to keep watch, armed with naught but a shotgun."

"Did you see my sister?" I said.

"Nay, my lady." He pulled out his burner phone and thumbed it on. "But when I spied into the window, I saw this."

"Oh my god. You looked in the windows?"

"Yea, for I would see as much as I might, and they keepen no watch upon the south."

He'd taken the picture through a gap at the bottom of the curtains. I could make out the shape of a couch and an old TV and a rocking chair. Tossed over the back of the rocking chair was a piece of pink fabric. None of those men owned a size extra-small pink fleece jacket with fairy wings embroidered on the back, but LaReigne did. She kept it in her car, and there was no reason for it to be there unless she was, too.

Relief and fear had a little tug o' war going in my heart. She was there, she was alive, and we were about to do something probably stupid and dangerous to get her back.

"My lady, art thou ready?"

"Yeah," I lied.

"Master Dirk? Sir Edrard?"

"I'm ready," Edrard said.

"Shit, yeah, let's do this thing." Maybe Dirk was bluffing, but he sounded surer of himself than Edrard and I did.

Gentry passed his phone to Edrard, and we all fell in line behind him. Edrard peeled off first, when we were still a hundred yards out, to take up his position on the high spot Gentry had picked out for him. I called Edrard's phone and, when he answered, Gentry, Dirk, and I walked on with the line open.

When we reached the road that went to the cabin, we left Dirk to stand watch. The sun was at the top of the trees, and we were only forty or fifty yards from the cabin. Gentry stepped out into the middle of the road, so I did, too. Then we started walking.

At twenty yards, the man on the porch finally noticed us. He stood up and lifted the shotgun he'd had across his lap. It was only a shotgun, though, and at that distance, I wasn't worried. When we were ten yards away, I recognized the man on the porch. Conrad Ligett. He yelled back into the house through the open screen door: "Scanlon! Get out here."

Gentry and I stopped about fifteen feet from the front porch. The man named Scanlon stepped outside and, for a minute, he and Ligett just looked at us. We obviously weren't cops, but we weren't obviously anything else, either.

"You folks need to get on outta here," Ligett said. "You're trespassing and about to get yourselves shot."

"I'm here to get my sister, LaReigne."

"I don't know nothing about that. Get the fuck off my land."

"I'm not expecting anything for free. I'm willing to pay to get my sister back." I'd practiced it in my head during the drive, but it was happening so fast I wasn't sure I was saying what I'd planned to say. I felt like there was a time delay between my brain and my mouth.

"What makes you think your sister's here?" Scanlon said.

"Because that fucker is here." I pointed at Ligett. "Conrad, right? You've been on the news. If you're here, I figure my sister's here, too. I'm willing to pay you all fifty thousand dollars to get her back. It's cash. Used bills. Unmarked. Untraceable."

"Fifty grand?" Scanlon said. "Fuck if you have fifty grand. I bet you don't have a hundred bucks to your name."

"Let me show it to you."

"Yeah, why don't you do that?" Until then, Scanlon had had his gun down by his side, but he brought it up and pointed it at us. Gentry tensed up beside me.

I pulled the phone out of my pocket and opened the photos app. I took a dozen steps closer to the cabin porch, Gentry right next to me, and held the phone out.

As crazy as it was, we'd taken the pictures in the Sonic parking lot. I'd laid the cash on the hood of Gentry's truck and posed with it. One pic with the fifty thousand, another with the almost ninety-five thousand, in case I needed it.

"That photo was taken today. There's the money," I said.

"What's to stop me from shooting the both of you and taking it?" Scanlon was still pointing his gun at me, and I hoped I didn't look as terrified as I felt.

"Because if you shoot me, my friend up on the hill is gonna put a couple arrows in you, and burn this place to the ground."

Scanlon laughed, so I handed the phone to Gentry. He put it to his ear and said, "Prove thy aim is true, Sir Edrard."

About twenty seconds later a flaming arrow dropped out of the sky and hit the dirt in the space between the cabin and the barn. Even though I knew it was coming, it made me jump. The second arrow landed ten feet closer to the cabin. Scanlon stopped laughing. Gentry handed me the phone and went over to stamp out the flames from the arrows. He was grinning when he walked back to me.

"So like I was saying. I'm offering you fifty thousand dollars for my sister. Here's how it works. You bring her out here. She and one of your friends walk back up the hill with us. We give your friend the money, he walks back down here, and we drive away."

"Shit, I guess it's true, all them rumors about your daddy ending up with that bank money," Scanlon said. It didn't surprise me there were rumors at the prison. Everybody liked to think somebody had succeeded where the rest of them had failed. I wondered again if that was why they'd picked LaReigne. Had they thought they might be able to ransom her? If I'd waited, would they have come to me or Uncle Alva eventually?

"Oh, you think we're gonna let you walk away and call the cops?" Ligett said.

"If I wanted to call the cops I'd have done it an hour ago, and my friend with the bow and arrows can call them right now. Except I want my sister back alive, and I don't think the cops can help me with that. If she's here, let me see her."

"Well, I'll say this: you're a helluva a lot

smarter than your sister, but I bet this is the stupidest thing you've ever done," Scanlon said.

"It's really simple. You want the money? Let me see my sister."

"I don't —" Ligett started to say, but Scanlon cut him off.

"All right. You come on inside, but your boy stays out here."

"It me liketh not, my lady." When I looked at Gentry, he was scratching the back of his neck with both hands. He could draw his sword from that position, and I wasn't sure if that made me less nervous or more nervous.

"It's okay. I have the phone. If I need help I'll tell Edrard and he'll let you know."

Gentry lowered his hands and nodded.

I went up the stairs like an old lady, because my hip was so tight I could barely get my foot up each riser. The steps creaked under me and, when I got to the top, Ligett reached out like he meant to frisk me.

"Don't fucking touch me," I said. "You got a gun. I got a gun. Let's play nice."

For a minute, I thought that was going to be the deal breaker, but Scanlon shook his head at Ligett and said, "It's okay if the lady wants to bring a gun. She's not gonna shoot the place up."

Inside, the cabin smelled like stale cigarettes and mildew and onions.

"Go on ahead. Door on the right." Scanlon pointed for me to go down the hall ahead of him. When I stopped at the door he'd indicated, he said, "Go on in."

The sun was coming down fast, and it was dim in the hallway, so that when I opened the bedroom door, all the light coming through the curtains made me squint. I stepped inside, Scanlon closed the door behind me, and there was LaReigne. She was lying on the bed with her shoes off. When she saw me, she sat up, and the book she'd been reading fell out of her hands. The cover had a shirtless man in a kilt on it.

"Oh my god! Zee!" she said. "What are you doing here?"

"I'm here to get you. Let's go."

"What do you mean you're here to get me? Did you bring Marcus?"

"No. I didn't bring Marcus," I said. "Come on, put your shoes on so we can go."

She got up off the bed, but she was staring at me like she couldn't believe I was there. It hit me, then. She was safe. I grabbed her and held on to her as tight as I could, and for a minute, she didn't do anything, because she must have been in shock. Then she laughed and put her arms around me. Most of my life, I'd felt like an ugly giant next to her, but right then I felt strong. Strong enough to protect her. We held on to each other, until I remembered Gentry was outside waiting for me. I let go of her and looked around the room for her shoes. They were on the floor next to a chair covered in clothes. Just like at our house.

"Oh my god, Zee. How are you here?" she said.

"It's a long story, and we have a long drive home, so I'll tell you all about it."

She sat back on the edge of the bed and I squatted down to put her shoes on her, like she was Marcus.

"But how?" she said, while I tied her shoes. "How did you even know where we were?"

"I promise, I'll tell you everything, but we need to go."

"It's not like we can just walk out of here. They have guns. There are more of them than us."

"How many are there?" I said.

"Four."

"Okay, well, there's five of us."

"Who's with you?" She was still sitting on the bed, looking at me like I was crazy. Had they drugged her? She was acting like she was drugged.

"Gentry, a friend of his, and our cousin Dirk," I said. "I have money to pay them, so we need to get the hell out of here, okay?"

"I need to talk to Tague first. He —"

"The fuck you do."

I grabbed her hand and pulled her up to standing.

That was when we heard the first gunshot.

CHAPTER 42
GENTRY

"The sword upon thy back is no child's baton," the black knight said.

I spake not but gave him my accord. I knew well 'twas no trifle.

"They aren not noble men. The one called Ligett, he meaneth to harm thee."

The black knight was aright, for tho Scanlon would speak of money, Ligett was full of malice. In his shoulders he held ill intent, where he paced upon the stoop before me. The two knaves whispered one to the other. Tho I heard them not, I kenned well enough what they spake of, for Ligett looked to where Sir Edrard's arrows had fallen, and thence toward the woods, as tho to seek the place my brother held.

Scanlon entered the house and Ligett alighted from the porch and strode toward the woods. As he passed me, he said, "You stay right fucking there, pal."

I stayed, but soon the trees would hide

him from Sir Edrard's sight, and so I raised my hand to warn him.

" 'Tis nigh dark," the black knight said. "Soon thou shalt lose thine advantage. Now is the time to leave, for Scanlon is ill-prepared to fight."

I mounted the stairs and approached the door to look within, but the sinking sun made havoc of shadow and light. As I laid my hand upon the door to open it, the sounding of a gun came behind me. Another came soon after, certs from the woods, but the echo and resound left me hard-pressed to ken the very place.

I stepped free of the door, drew my sword, and was at the ready. Aside the door, I squatted and, ere I had been there a nonce, a man burst from the barn door and ran toward the woods, carrying with him a long gun. From above, Sir Edrard dropped three arrows to the path, and 'twas only by hap that the man was missed by the bolts.

Within the cabin, I heard the footsteps of Scanlon. He ran to the door, loudly and without caution. Mayhap he meant only to fright me, but he thrust the door open with his foot and fired his gun. When he rushed out, I heaved up from where I squatted and struck full force my shoulder upon his flank. The blow sent him to the ground.

"He means to kill thee if he is able," the black knight said.

Sooth, as quick as he landed, Scanlon gained his feet and raised his gun to fire once more. 'Twas but a breath betwixt us and I hastened it to close.

"You fucking idiot. You really brought a knife to a gunfight." From pride, Scanlon scorned against me. 'Twas misguided boldness, for he might have wounded me, had he forborne to speak, and fired his gun. Ere he did, I swung my blade and smote his arm with enough might that he dropped the weapon. Scanlon cried out and blood flowed forth.

I made to subdue him, and grappled his neck to cut his breath, and with it his will to fight. I might have mastered him, but from the trees there came more gunshots, and from the barn came the fourth man, the one called Tague Barnwell. He carried not a long gun, but a pistol. I struck Scanlon upon his temple with my pommel, and twisted his wounded arm that I might use him as a shield.

There was naught to be gained by retreating and so I advanced, Scanlon before me til we came to the rail of the porch where Barnwell approached.

"This be no tournament. Thy rules aren

for naught," the black knight said. "If thou fightest not for thy life, certs thou wilt it lose."

Scanlon ceased his bemoaning, and I felt in his back that he meant to fight. Where before his shoulder was drawn tight to protect his injured limb, he lowered it, for he meant to lunge right. Had I followed the black knight's entreaty, I might have spared myself all harm, but as I forced Scanlon from me, I felt a burning wound upon my thigh. I heard it not, nor anything, aside the black knight's admonishment and mine own breath. I ought have done it sooner, but the deed lay clear before me, once I was wounded.

I swung my blade and cleaved Scanlon's bared neck. His blood was as a warm bath upon my arm and, as he fell at my feet, I leapt down upon Barnwell, ere he could fire his gun.

On the ground, breast-to-breast with me, his gun was of no use, but my blade found his foot, and I drove my head into his chin. 'Twas well for me the wound to my leg was a distant thing, for pain made Barnwell a fool. He grasped my sword with his hand to draw it from his foot, thereby wounding himself a second time. He cried out, I knew not what, and seeing how poorly he fared, he ceased his futile defense and attacked. He hit his arm hard upon my elbow so that I must release him, and ere I regained my hold, he pushed me hence. To free his gun, he meant, but he was unready when the moment came.

I was ready. The movement of his arm as he made to steady his gun twisted his trunk all unarmored toward me, and I thrust my sword into him. Under his ribs, through to his back, until my hilt pressed flush against him. His arms dropped, the gun with them, and I held him up til the weight upon my blade was too much. He fell upon the ground, and when I drew my sword from his body, blood poured into the soil. His mouth opened in a cry, and tho I would hear his last words, none came, only the sound of pain.

I tossed his gun from his reach, but left him lie in peace, for he could no more menace me. Tho Barnwell still had breath, certs I had killed two men. I knew not how I lived while their lifeblood drained away.

" 'Twas well done," the black knight said.

" 'Twas necessary," the Witch said.

"If thou wert as steady with the thrust of thine other blade," Gawen said.

Hildegard said naught but a prayer:

God that is mightful
Speed all rightful
Help all needful
Have mercy on all sinful

I echoed it that I might remember these fallen men had souls as frail as mine. Then I lifted my hand to signal Sir Edrard but there came no arrow in answer. All round me was a great pall of silence that set my raised hand atremble, but the hand that held my sword remained resolute. I turned to the cabin and mounted the steps to find Lady Zhorzha and her sister.

CHAPTER 43
ZEE

The scary thing was how the gunshot came from two places at the same time — outside and the open phone line in my pocket. One loud, one quiet, like a firecracker and a pop gun going off at the same time. I fumbled the phone out of my pocket and almost dropped it.

"Edrard? What's going on?" I said, but he didn't answer.

There was another gunshot, and with the phone to my ear, the secondary pop was louder. I wondered if it was closer to Edrard.

I said his name again and heard a bunch of scrambling noises.

"I don't know," he said, breathing hard. "It's too dark to see anything. I'm going up to bring one of the trucks down the main road. Hang on."

I was going to tell him to wait, but before I could, there was another gunshot, so close it sounded like it was inside the cabin. I pulled LaReigne down next to me in front of the dresser. It wouldn't be much protection but it was something.

"We can't go out there," LaReigne said.

I hadn't come all that way to get her shot, so we stayed where we were. Edrard must have put the phone in his pocket, because I couldn't hear anything.

Three more gunshots came right together. Or maybe more than three. I couldn't keep track anymore. Someone started screaming. A man screaming, which I'd never heard in my life. I told myself it didn't sound like Gentry, but would I recognize anybody I knew from the sound of them screaming in pain?

After a few minutes, the screaming stopped and there was nothing but silence. I pulled myself up with the edge of the dresser and went to open the bedroom door. The hallway was empty. I took the gun out of my waistband and flicked the safety off, because if I was ever going to need a gun, it was then.

"Come on. We need to go." I snapped my fingers at LaReigne.

"Lady Zhorzha! Art'ou well?" Gentry shouted from outside.

"Oh, thank fuck, Gentry. Yes. We're okay."

Hearing his voice, hearing that he was okay, made me so shaky I had to put the safety back on the gun.

I took LaReigne's hand and pulled her after me, down the hall and across the front room to the door. When we got there, Gentry came up the stairs, his sword in his hand, and stepped over the body lying on the porch.

The body.

Lying.

On the porch.

I think the only thing that kept me from freaking out was the weed. Whatever LaReigne was on, it did not help her. She started saying, "Oh my god! Oh my god!" and then: "Where's Tague?"

The body was the guy they'd called Scanlon, with a huge gash in the side of his neck. He was very dead.

"We musten go, my lady, and swiftly." Gentry held out his hand, but I didn't take it, because he was covered in blood — his hands, his sword — of course, he'd killed Scanlon. There was a hole in the left thigh of his pants, with blood seeping out of it.

"Oh, Jesus Christ. Did you get shot?" I said. That's how stupid I was. I'd brought him to that place and gotten him shot, and I was surprised?

" 'Tis not horrible, but we musten go."

With the gun still in my right hand, I put my left arm around LaReigne's waist, and lifted her over Scanlon's body. Then I stepped over him and pushed her toward the porch steps.

Once I had her moving, I thought we were going to be okay, but she kept turning and looking around. We only made it a few feet from the cabin before LaReigne came to a dead stop and started shrieking from the bottom of her lungs.

"Tague! Tague! Tague!" That's what she was screaming, and that's how I knew who was lying in the grass next to the cabin. La-Reigne twisted her arm out of my grip and ran back to him. He was such a bloody mess, I couldn't even tell what was wrong with him. LaReigne got on her knees beside him, still screaming his name.

Gentry was ten feet ahead, waiting for us to catch up. I stuffed the gun into my jeans and went to get LaReigne. I was strong enough to lift her, but she started swinging and kicking, so I ended up dropping her, practically on top of Tague, who moaned.

"We have to go," I said. "We have to go *now*!"

"I'm not leaving him!" LaReigne said.

"What did you do, sissy?" I said. My

stomach bottomed out, the same way it did right before I laid that motorcycle down on my leg, when I realized I was going to wreck. When I knew there was no going back and maybe no going forward either. "Did you help them? What did you do?"

"I didn't do anything. But Tague says this is a chance for us to start over. Leave his past behind. Leave my past behind." She was crying, but she said it in this dreamy, faraway voice.

"Leave what behind? Marcus?" Anger was always safer than fear. I knew what to do with anger. I smacked the side of her head, hard enough to make her pay attention to me.

"No," she said. "Tague promised. Molly's going to bring Marcus to me."

"How? How is Molly going to bring him to you?"

"She was supposed to pick him up and bring him to me that night, but when she got to the apartment, you weren't there. She's going to try again next —"

"No, she isn't, because Molly's *dead.* Somebody *murdered* Molly."

"No, she stayed behind in Nebraska. Conrad's going to go meet her."

"Nobody's going to meet her!" I yelled. "One of your boyfriend's buddies murdered her. Or maybe he murdered her. Maybe you're next. And did you think I would hand Marcus over to some stranger? Because fuck that really fucking hard."

"It's okay. I've got you," LaReigne whispered to Tague. Where she had her hands pressed to his side, blood was seeping out between her fingers.

"We're leaving now. Right now."

"No, I can't. We'll figure out a way. You don't understand, Zee. Loudon is going to get paroled and as soon as he does, I'll have to share custody with him. I can't do that."

"You won't be sharing custody with anybody, if you don't come with me right fucking now. We can still figure something out, but only if we go," I said.

"I can't leave him." She was crying and looking down at Tague, so I grabbed a handful of her hair to turn her head and make her look at me.

"You're not leaving Marcus! They took him away! The Gills took him away! So you are fucking coming home and getting him back!" That was all I could think of: if she went to prison, the Gills would get to keep Marcus. It made me feel like my heart was on fire. "You don't just get to abandon your family."

As soon as I let go of her hair, she went

back to looking at Tague and saying, "It's okay. It'll be okay."

I took ahold of the waist of her jeans with both hands to move her, but she fought so hard I had to squat down and dig my heels in to keep ahold of her. Gentry was pacing, waiting for us, scratching his neck and holding his sword. I really, really wished that he would finish Tague off, because I felt like maybe Tague being good and dead would clarify a few things.

"This is not *Beauty and the Beast*! He's not going to magically change from a fucking Nazi into a prince, just because you love him," I said.

"He's not a Nazi. He's made mistakes, but he's a good man. I love him. He's going to take care of me the way Loudon never —"

"Loudon? Fuck you! I took care of you. I took care of you and Marcus."

"You smothered me. You don't even have your own life. You were there all the time! I never got to be alone."

"Because you needed me! Because you and Marcus are my life," I yelled. "When did *I* get to be alone?"

"Well, you can be alone now!" LaReigne said.

"My lady." Gentry raised his voice enough

to cut through our shouting.

Hearing how freaked out he was killed my anger. LaReigne dug her fingers into the grass, still trying to get away from me. I let her go. Then all I had left was fear.

"Please, LaReigne. If you stay here, you're going to prison. Even if you didn't help them escape, it's going to look that way. When the cops show up and you're here crying over this piece of shit, it won't matter whether you're innocent. I don't even care if you are, but you can't stay here. Please."

Maybe I would have gone on begging her until the cops showed up, but we heard more gunshots from the woods. They were close together, rapid-fire, and they echoed back across the valley.

"Lady Zhorzha, by the oath I made, I beg thee come with me," Gentry said.

Thee. That meant just me. Whether he meant it that way or not, I knew he was right. If I stayed, I was going to end up in prison, too. Nobody would believe I'd come there to rescue LaReigne. They would think I was in on it. And if I went to prison, Mom would be alone in the world, Marcus would grow up in the Gills' house, and I would never get to see him again.

Gentry gave me his hand and pulled me

to my feet. We left LaReigne there with her head down next to Tague's, crying and whispering to him.

Where we went into the woods, I could see there'd been a fight. There were broken branches, scuff marks in the pine needles, and blood. More blood. Twenty or thirty feet further, Conrad Ligett was lying face-down in a puddle of blood. It wasn't Dirk or Edrard, so we kept going.

Even with a bullet in his leg, Gentry was faster and stronger than me. I'd wrecked my hip fighting with LaReigne, and my foot was numb, so every step of the way, Gentry was pulling me and holding me up, and all the time blood was running down his leg.

I'd told him I could walk from the truck to the cabin, but for some stupid reason I'd never thought about the fact that I would have to walk both ways. Thinking I should tell Edrard we were coming, I pulled the phone out of my pocket. Somewhere along the way it had gotten disconnected, so I re-dialed the other burner number. There was no voicemail, so it kept ringing as we got closer to the trucks. Finally, he picked up.

"Jesus Christ," Dirk said. "Where are you? You gotta get up here. They shot Edrard."

"Go. I'm coming as fast as I can." I let go of Gentry's hand and he ran ahead of me.

I was still dragging myself up the hill when I heard Gentry's voice over the phone.

"Edrard, my brother," he said. Like a coward, I hung up before I could hear anything else. A couple minutes later, I got there anyway and saw what had happened.

Edrard was lying next to the open door of his truck, with Gentry and Dirk kneeling on either side of him. Gentry had pulled his blouse off and was pressing it against Edrard's stomach, but there was so much blood. We'd left Tague and Scanlon at the cabin, and Dirk must have killed Ligett down the hill. The fourth one — Gentry had said there were four — had followed Edrard to the trucks. Edrard had put two arrows in him, one in his leg and one in his shoulder. Not to kill. The guy had an AR-15 kind of rifle, and even with two arrows in him, he'd managed to shoot Edrard. Dirk must have finished the guy off with a bullet to the head.

Out of the cab of Edrard's truck, I grabbed anything that looked like it could be used as a bandage — an old beach towel, a T-shirt — and tossed it out to Gentry, who was doing the only thing he could, applying pressure to the wound. I did the only thing I knew to do. I unlocked Gentry's truck and got a tampon out of my backpack. It wouldn't do anything for Edrard, but it would work for Gentry. I'd read it in some survivalist book that said as the tampon swelled up, it would put pressure on the bleeding arteries. I knelt down next to Gentry and ripped open the edges of the hole in his pants. I didn't ask him. I just unwrapped the tampon and jammed it into the hole in his leg. Based on the sound he made, it hurt a lot, but he didn't stop me, so I pushed it in until the string was hanging out.

I thought it might bother me, but I'd been practicing for that ever since I got my period for the first time. I just didn't know it.

"We have to get him in the truck and get him to the hospital," I said. Without even talking about why, the hospital in Ashdown was one of the things Gentry had marked on the map. "Dirk, you go with Gentry. You'll go west into Oklahoma, then head back to Missouri. I'll take Edrard to the hospital."

"Nay. He is my brother. I shall take him," Gentry said.

"No. Whoever takes him is going to have to answer a lot of questions."

"Yeah, she's right," Dirk said. "Gunshot wound, they'll have to call the cops."

"The cops are going to be coming soon

454

enough. Maybe LaReigne already called them," I said.

"Where is LaReigne?" Dirk said.

"She's not coming. She's staying here with that asshole."

"Holy shit. I wondered, you know."

"Oh, shut up. You didn't wonder shit," I said. "Now, come on, we need to get Edrard in the truck."

We tried. Even though Edrard screamed, even though the edge of the bath towel shifted and I could see his insides, we tried to move him. Gentry was strong enough, he could have done a fireman's carry, but not without killing Edrard. After we gave up, Gentry went back to pressing the soggy bath towel over the place where the blood seemed to be coming out fastest. Dirk and I watched. The sun had set and the only light was from the cab of the truck.

"Call 911." I took the phone out of my pocket and handed it to Dirk.

If we hadn't done so much planning and talking, it might have been a problem when the emergency dispatcher answered, but Dirk didn't have any trouble giving directions. The highway, the county road, how many miles, the fire road.

"There's two gunshot wounds. Two people hurt. One of them real bad," he said, and then, "I ain't nobody. Just send an ambulance."

He disconnected before the dispatcher could ask him anything else. When he handed the phone back to me, I saw he had a big gash on his arm. A bullet graze?

"Now what do we do?" Dirk said.

I looked down at Gentry, who had his head bowed like he was praying. He was bloody up to his elbows.

"We have to go. We're all going to get arrested otherwise." I hated myself for how crass I sounded, but if we stayed, we were going to prison. I would be abandoning Mom and Marcus as much as LaReigne was.

I put my hand on Gentry's shoulder.

"We have to go, Gentry. Do you hear me? We have to leave. I know that's really shitty, leaving Edrard, but you need to come with us."

He didn't look at me, so I tightened my grip on his shoulder, trying to will him to come back from wherever he was.

"We have to go," I said. "Come on."

He raised his head, and I thought he was finally hearing me, but he looked up. Toward the Witch.

"I know what I swore. Yea, I ken it well, but I will not leave him. He is my brother."

"Please, Gentry. Remember about Melusine? How she told Raymondin to ride out of the woods and tell no one what he had done? This is like that."

"I would it were, my lady. For tho my oath be but ash and salt, I cannot go with thee for I cannot leave my brother," Gentry said.

I should have been crying and begging him to go, but I was thinking of what I needed to do to protect myself. I found the other burner phone where Dirk had dropped it while we tried to move Edrard. I looked around to be sure there was nothing else that could place me there. The gloves I was wearing were bloody, but I hadn't left any fingerprints behind.

"I have to go, Gentry." I put my hand on his shoulder, hoping he knew I was there. "I have to go, because of Marcus and my mom."

"Heap on me curses, if thou wilt. Always have I done what thou bid me. Ever I trusted thee and here I am!" He shook my hand off his shoulder. "Here lieth my brother. With him lieth my trust in thee, hag!"

Right up until he said *hag,* I kinda thought the next words out of his mouth might be *odious serpent.* He was talking to the Witch, but I deserved it. He had trusted me. I was the one who'd brought him there. It was my fault Edrard was lying there, maybe bleeding to death.

I had the keys to Gentry's truck, so Dirk and I got in, and I backed it down the fire road, wishing I could go faster, but knowing it was more important to get out of there without running into anything. After I backed through the gate, I put the truck in park and slid out of the cab.

"What are you doing? We gotta go," Dirk said.

"One thing."

I pushed the seat up and popped the lid off Gentry's roadside kit. Like I figured, the medieval Boy Scout had a pair of road flares. I tossed one to Dirk, and we cracked them and laid them at the edge of the county road to mark the turnoff for the fire road. When the ambulance came, it might make the difference in whether they got to Edrard in time. Back in the truck, I buckled my seat belt, turned on the headlights, and pulled out on the road like a law-abiding citizen.

The ambulance, and the cops with it, would come from Ashdown, to the south, so I drove west toward Oklahoma.

CHAPTER 44
ZEE

We took the long way back to Missouri, on a bunch of little two-lane roads through Oklahoma, leaving a trail of trash behind us on the way north. In the dark, we took the scenic route past Broken Bow Lake, where Dirk tossed the guns out into the water, piece by piece. After that, it was a bloody T-shirt in one trash can, bloody gloves somewhere else. A broken burner phone here. The other there.

Throwing things out should have felt like I was lightening the load, but nothing could do that. I was pretty sure I would be carrying the feeling of leaving Gentry and Edrard behind for the rest of fucking forever.

We didn't stop until the big truck stop north of Smithville. I cleaned up there, and bought new clothes to replace Dirk's bloody ones. Cheap sweatpants and a truck-stop GOD BLESS AMERICA JESUS T-shirt.

"What happened?" I said, while he

changed in the parking lot. I didn't want to know, but I had to. It was my doing.

"I was down by the road, keeping watch like Gentry said, and that guy came at me."

"Did you shoot first or did he?"

"It happened so damn fast, I don't know," Dirk said. "He was shooting at me, I was shooting at him, and then he didn't shoot back. That's how I knew I'd killed him. I never killed nobody before."

"Did you shoot the other guy? At the trucks?"

"Yeah, but it was too late. He'd already shot Edrard before I got there."

I didn't ask anything else, because Dirk sniffled like he was trying not to cry.

We cut across the northwest corner of Arkansas, through a town called Siloam Springs, heading back toward Missouri. It was nearly three o'clock in the morning, and Dirk was asleep beside me, when I saw the sign: GENTRY 9 MILES.

I would have driven a hundred miles out of my way to avoid passing through a town called Gentry, if I'd known it was there, but I was driving without a map. I didn't know where to turn off, and I didn't dare turn back.

Nine miles later: GENTRY CITY LIMITS.

I felt so shaky I pulled off into the parking

lot of a grocery store on the main street of Gentry, Arkansas. I rested my forehead on the steering wheel, trying to convince myself that raw feeling behind my eyes was just tiredness. Only sleep couldn't undo the horrible, stupid thing I'd talked Gentry into doing. That was all I could think of: Gentry surrounded by cops, with a bullet in his leg, and covered in Edrard's blood.

After ten minutes, I got back on the road. Half an hour further, I stopped for gas and bought a tub of disinfectant wipes. While the tank filled, I wiped down the inside of the truck, trying to get rid of any physical evidence of the horrible, stupid thing.

By the time we pulled up to the motel, I knew what to do. Dirk would get in his truck and go home. I would go into the room, pack up anything we'd left, and wipe everything down. Part of that was paranoia, but the cops were going to come around, and the less there was for them to find, the better.

In the daylight, Dirk's wound looked a lot worse, scabbed in black and deeper than I'd thought.

"Fucked if I'm going to the hospital," he said. "That's how you get arrested."

"Why don't you go home, and after I pack up, I'll bring some bandages and stuff out to the house?"

Dirk nodded and opened the truck door, but didn't get out. After a minute, he said, "I'm sorry it didn't work out how we figured."

"Me, too."

As he walked across to his truck, he held his left arm close to his body, so I knew it must hurt.

I braced myself for how I'd feel when I saw Gentry and Edrard's stuff, but I'd forgotten one big thing. I didn't brace myself at all for the possibility that when I opened the motel room door, I would hear the shower running. Rhys was still there, because we'd left him there. Because Edrard was his ride home. If I'd had anything in my stomach, I would have puked it up right there. Not that it would have been a new experience for that motel carpet. I'd thought I would have ten or fifteen minutes to be alone and lose my shit, but now I was going to have to deal with Rhys.

He'd slept in the bed closest to the bathroom, the one I'd slept in the night before. Gentry had pulled the bedspread up over the pillows on the other bed. His big rucksack was propped against the headboard, with all of our phones zipped into the side pocket. I needed to start making phone calls, but first, I peeled back the bedspread and leaned down to sniff the pillow. Of course, it didn't smell woodsy like Gentry, because he'd barely slept there the night before. It didn't even smell like sex, even though we'd used that bed. Like all motel sheets, it smelled like bleach.

I unzipped the pocket and took out our phones. Dirk's I stuck in my back pocket, still powered off. I turned mine on and waited for it to catch up. A few texts: Julia at the restaurant, a few people I sold to, Toby, who said, *You didn't go and do something stupid did you, Red?* There were voicemails from Emma and Mom's doctor, but I didn't listen to them.

When I looked at Gentry's phone, I almost cried. His home screen picture was of him and Trang and Edrard in armor. He was so trusting he didn't even have a passcode to keep anyone out. There were two missed calls, both from his parents' house the night before, and texts from Trang and Carlees, checking on him.

I left those, but I deleted his text threads with Rhys and Edrard. I knew the cops could find out when texts were sent, but maybe not what was in them, and the texts with Rhys and Edrard had just a little too much information. Even in Gentry's phone

I was Lady Zhorzha Trego, and I didn't only delete the text thread between us, I deleted myself.

I knew I ought to call Charlene — I owed her that — but when I scrolled through RECENT CALLS, it was Carlees' number that I hit. Carlees, who had smoked pot with Gentry when they were teenagers. Carlees, whose last text to Gentry was *Bruh how mad is Mom?*

The shower was still running when Carlees answered, and even knowing that Rhys could interrupt me at any time, I did what I had to do.

"Hey, Gee, you —"

"Carlees?" I cut him off before he could say anything else. "My name is Zhorzha Trego. I don't know if Gentry told you about me."

"Oh yeah! Lady Zhorzha, it's good to talk to you. Is everything okay with my baby brother?"

"I don't think so." Then I told the lie I would have to tell to anyone who was willing to hear it. I said, "I think Gentry's done something dangerous, and I don't know what to do."

"You're for real? Did he get himself hurt in a joust again?"

"No, it's a lot worse than that. He was

supposed to be back by now, but he isn't. He's been gone all night."

"Well, sometimes he goes out in the woods to be alone," Carlees said. He sounded less worried than when he thought it was a joust.

"I think he went to try to make a deal with some very dangerous people down in Arkansas, and I don't know what happened."

"Oh, shit. That's was what he was talking about." For a second I thought the lie was already dead in the water. Maybe I'd been stupid to think it would ever work. "He said he was maybe going to get your sister back. I thought he was just talking, you know. I thought he meant he wanted to, not that he was going to."

I kept it vague, because I couldn't tell Carlees where Gentry got the information about Barnwell and Ligett. I couldn't tell him I'd had anything to do with planning it.

"The only thing I know is that he went to Arkansas. Somewhere in Little River County. He wouldn't let me go with him," I said. I was a pretty good liar, but that sounded flimsy as hell to me.

"Jesus. Yeah. He'd want to protect you. And he was supposed to come back this morning?"

"I thought he'd be back hours ago, and I

465

don't know what to do. I'm in Missouri right now. I was going to call the police down there or hospitals, but since I'm not family, I wasn't sure they would tell me anything."

"No, it's good you called me and not our mom. I'll call the sheriff down there and see what I can find out. I'll let you know what I hear," Carlees said.

"Okay, thank you." I knew I wasn't going to hear from Carlees again, and I didn't think I could stand to. He wouldn't be so nice once he knew what had happened.

I was sitting there, looking at Edrard's phone, when the bathroom door opened and a woman said, "What the — who — uh, Rick?"

I stood up and turned around, just as Rhys came out of the bathroom with a towel around his waist. The woman was in a towel, too, with another wrapped around her hair.

"Jesus Christ, Zee. I was seriously getting worried," he said. Then he looked at the stuff I'd gathered up to pack. "Where are Gentry and Edrard?"

"I don't know. They didn't —" I had to take a deep breath, because I wasn't ready for how big the lie needed to be. "They wouldn't let me go. They left me in Murfreesboro. They left me there and they never came back."

"What are you talking about? They left you?"

"They decided it was too dangerous. They didn't want me to go. I was supposed to wait for them, but they didn't come back."

"God, if they were smart, they ditched you there and drove back to Wichita," Rhys said. As shitty as that was, it was true. They should've done that. "How did you get back?"

"That's what I'm telling you. They left me with Gentry's truck, and the two of them went in Edrard's truck, and they didn't come back. I just called Gentry's brother. I didn't know what else to do."

"Wait, what about your cousin?"

"He stayed in Murfreesboro with me," I said.

Rhys started pacing up and down, still in his towel, while the woman stared at him, then me, then him. I went back to packing.

"This is your fault," he said. "This is all your fault."

"I know. Of course, it's my fault."

"We need to call the police and tell them what kind of crazy-ass thing you talked Gentry and Edrard into."

"Rick, do you think we should —"

"Will you shut up, Tiffany? I need to think."

Tiffany winced, but instead of getting mad, she shuffled back to the bathroom and, after a minute, turned on the blow-dryer. I stuffed a few more things in Gentry's bag and zipped it up.

"I'm calling the police." Rhys picked up his phone off the dresser. "You can explain it to them."

"Yeah, well, I hope you don't mind getting arrested, because they'll arrest you, too."

"Why would they arrest me?"

"You were here when we planned it," I said.

"I fucking was not!"

The hair dryer cut off and Tiffany said, "Rick, is everything okay?"

"Dry your goddamn hair, Tiff," he said.

She turned the dryer back on, maybe just as white noise to drown us out.

"You planned it," Rhys said. "And you and Gentry both told me not to call the police."

"For the same reason I'm telling you not to call the police now," I said. "I'm going to have a lot of questions to answer anyway and, unless you want to answer a lot of questions, you should stay out of it."

"You deserve to go to jail."

468

I couldn't argue with him, so I did something I hated myself for. There was going to be a lot more of that in my future.

"Please, I am begging you not to call the police. If I go to jail, there's going to be nobody to take care of my mother, who is disabled, and nobody to take care of my nephew, who is only five. Because if Gentry and Edrard didn't come back, I don't think my sister is coming back. For all I know she's dead. And I can't —" I couldn't cry on command and I was too scared to cry for real, because I wasn't sure I could stop if I got started. I took a step closer to Rhys, who backed up against the dresser like I'd threatened him. I took another couple steps until we were face-to-face.

"I can't abandon them. Please. What do you want? Money? I can get you some money. Do you want me to beg you?" I got down on my knees, even though I wasn't sure how I would get back up. A bolt of pain ran up my leg, and a muscle spasm followed it, so that it felt like my phoenix was coming to life. "Okay, I'm begging you. Whatever you want. Just please don't call the cops."

Rhys looked down at me the way men like him always looked down at me. Somewhere between contempt and curiosity with a side of maybe. Honestly, I think if Tiffany hadn't been there, he would have made me suck him off.

"Jesus Christ. We have to call somebody," he said, but he put his phone back on the dresser. *We* meant me.

"I already called Gentry's brother. Should I call Rosalinda?"

"God. I guess so. I need to get out of here. If we're not telling the police, I'm going home. I can't have anything to do with this. Whatever happens with Gentry and Edrard, this is your fuckup. This is on you."

"I know. I'm sorry."

"Tiff, are you ready to go?" he yelled.

The hair dryer turned off and she said, "Sure. I can be ready in a couple minutes."

Apparently Tiff was the same kind of sucker as LaReigne. She'd driven all that way to let Rhys talk like shit to her.

To give them a chance to get dressed, I went out and got in the truck. I'd brought Gentry and Edrard's phones with me, but in the end I couldn't bring myself to turn Edrard's phone on. I imagined the kind of text messages his wife had been sending him for the last twelve hours. Surely she'd been expecting to hear from him. In Gentry's contacts she was under *D* for Dame Rosalinda.

I was prepared for her to think I was

Gentry, like Carlees had, and when she answered, she said, "What have you done with my husband?"

I told her exactly what I'd told Carlees, but it was harder, knowing how badly Edrard had been hurt. She yelled at me, but after I told her I didn't know what happened, she got so quiet.

"If they got arrested will he get to call me? He probably doesn't even know my number if he doesn't have his phone. Who should I call?"

"Hang on," I said. "Let me see if I can find a number."

I left her on the line and pulled up the Internet, to look up the number for the Little River County sheriff. I gave her the number four or five times, because she kept jumbling them up when she repeated them back. It made me feel like a monster. An odious serpent. I had come to her house and stolen her husband, and now I was toying with her.

It was close to half an hour before Rhys and Tiffany came out of the motel room. I wondered if he'd called the cops, or Gentry's parents, or Rosalinda, but when he came and stood at the truck window, I didn't ask him any of that.

"If anything has happened to them, it'll

471

be your fault," he said. "Girls like you, it's how you operate. Take a nice guy like Gentry and use him. But if something happens to him, you'll have to live with that."

"I know."

He got into Tiffany's car and they drove away.

Girls like me. I wished I was the kind of girl Rhys thought I was. Girls like me, though, girls actually like me, we weren't master manipulators. We were garbage fires of failure.

I went back in the motel room and finished packing. After I loaded the bags into Gentry's truck, I wiped down the room and the keys, and left them on the dresser. Then I stripped the sheets off the beds and bundled them up. The housekeeping cart was parked a couple rooms down, so I carried the sheets over and stuck them in the laundry bag.

The housekeeper came out of the room she was working on and gave me a funny look. She was an Indian lady in a sari and a Justin Bieber shirt. By the time I got in the truck and started it, she'd gone back into the other room.

At the Walmart, I bought what I'd promised Dirk: rubbing alcohol, bandages, and aquarium antibiotics. Plus a case of beer and a frozen lasagna.

Standing in the checkout line, I was behind a woman with two daughters. Like some fantasy version of Mom, LaReigne, and me. I looked at the family-sized lasagna in my cart, and it seemed stupid and sad to me. My family was smaller. Again. Pretty soon maybe a single-serving lasagna would be all I needed.

CHAPTER 45
ALVA

I figured I'd best get rid of that burner phone, but before I could, it gone and rang again. Shot me bolt upright in bed, even though I'd knocked out half a bottle of bourbon trying to get to sleep. My cough was always worse at night. The clock said it was half gone two. I got the phone outta my night table and that no-name Fury said, "What the hell happened? What did you get me into? I thought your people were going to negotiate. *Ransom,* that's what you said."

"That's what I said." My heart was hammering in my chest, but my brain was like a mess of cotton.

"I'm hearing there are men dead down there. What did you get me into? What am I supposed to do if folks start asking me questions?"

His voice gone up higher and that, more than anything, shook me. He sounded like Dirk, young and scared. *Men dead,* and I hadn't heard nothing from Dirk nor Zhorzha one.

"I didn't get you into nothing," I said. "You got your money. I don't know your name." He didn't answer, but he went on breathing heavy in my ear. "If you got any sense, you'll hide that cash and ditch that phone, just like I'm gonna do with this one."

"I never talked to you."

"No, sir."

"Okay," he said, but he was on the line breathing til I hung up.

I put my boots and sidearm on before I went out to the shed. I didn't know too much about cellular phones, but I took a screwdriver and a hammer to it, until I got it separated into a bunch of little electronic parts. I took the whole mess out into the woods and buried it.

By the time I was done it was near four o'clock. I stood out on the porch, listening to an owl down by the creek, thinking how the world had got bigger and shrunk up at the same time.

Didn't reckon I was likely to get back to sleep, so I gone into the house and put the kettle on, brewed up some coffee. Then I took down my mam's Bible and done what she always called *witching*. Stood it up on its spine and let it fall open where it would.

The verse I got come from the Book of Joshua: *And it shall come to pass, that when they make a long blast with the ram's horn, and when ye hear the sound of the trumpet, all the people shall shout with a great shout; and the wall of the city shall fall down flat, and the people shall ascend up every man straight before him.*

The story of Jericho wasn't nothing to set my mind at ease, and I done what I always did, gone looking for some kind of comfort out of the Psalms.

Around nine o'clock, I brewed a fresh pot of coffee, and I was drinking that and reading the Bible when Dirk pulled up in the drive. He'd left alone and he come back alone, wearing clothes I didn't recognize, with blood dried down his left arm.

"What happened to you, boy? And where's your cousin?" I said.

"The motel. She's coming later."

Men dead, that's what the Fury had said.

"You need to get that arm seen to."

"Later. I just wanna sleep for a while." Dirk gone into the front room and a couple minutes later, I heard Patsy Cline on the record player. That was always one of my mam's favorites. I wondered if he remembered that, or he'd been told enough times he thought he remembered. Family stories

476

were funny that way, how they carried on long after they stopped being facts. When I gone in the front room, he was lying on the sofa with his arm over his eyes. I left him be.

Zhorzha wasn't too much further behind him, looking tired but not bloody. She come in carrying grocery sacks and a case of beer, like we was set to have a barbecue.

"I guess Dirk told you what happened," she said.

"Dirk ain't said ten words to me, but that Fury called me in the middle of the night. Said folks got killed. Truth be told, I ain't had the stomach to turn on the news for fear of what I might see."

She wouldn't look at me. Spent a good ten minutes fussing around lighting the oven and putting a tinfoil pan in there. When she finally come to the table, she put a can of beer in front of me and opened up one for herself.

"I almost got Dirk killed. He got shot. Did you see?" She dug around in another of the grocery sacks and pulled out some first-aid supplies.

"Yep, he's in there bleeding on your grandmam's good divan, I reckon."

"When he wakes up, I'll clean up his arm," she said.

"And your man?"

"I left him. His friend who went with us, he was pretty badly hurt, so Gentry stayed."

"You think them Klansmen are gonna deal kindly with them?"

"He and Dirk took care of them."

"Sweet Jesus, girl. You gone in there and killed them boys?"

"We didn't plan to. We tried not to. They shot first. Anyway, I hope they shot first, because otherwise it was Dirk."

"Well, he ain't the brightest, but he don't got a hair trigger, neither. That's more Dane's style," I said.

"I'm sorry. I really fucked things up. Do you think they'll come here, the people you talked to?" She took a big swallow of beer and grimaced.

"If they do, I'm armed. I don't go nowhere without this." I patted my sidearm. "Besides, ain't much benefit to let it be known they talked to me. Get them killed quicker than me. We won't hear from that Fury again."

"I hope you're right."

I'd thought ten-thirty was a mite early to start lunch, but the lasagna wasn't ready til noon. By the time it come outta the oven, Dirk was up. Zhorzha bandaged his arm and counted out them antibiotics.

"You sure it's safe to take that shit?" he

478

said, when she put the pills in front of him.

"Yeah, I've taken them plenty of times. Unless you know another way to get antibiotics without going to the doctor." She picked up the bottle and pretended like she was reading off it. "Possible side effects: may grow gills and flippers."

"Jesus, fine." He tossed the pills back with some beer and then we was ready to eat.

We gone through lunch, not talking about nothing serious, but after we ate, I reckoned we had waited as long as we could. I gone into the front room and turned on the news. Dirk come and sat down in the rocker, but Zhorzha stood in the doorway, swirling her beer around in the can. We didn't have to wait too long for the news to come around to the story. Folks love a good story with blood and suffering.

"The manhunt for escaped mosque killers Tague Barnwell and Conrad Ligett ended in Arkansas last night, with the death of Ligett and the arrest of Barnwell. Authorities have not released details about the circumstances surrounding the arrest, but local sources say three other men are dead, and another man and a woman are in custody at this hour."

That was all they had, and the same old mug shots of Barnwell and Ligett.

"What do you make of that?" I said.

Zhorzha was standing there, beer in one hand, her other hand clutched over her stomach.

"Shit. I guess Edrard didn't make it. That's a goddamn shame. He seemed like a real good guy," Dirk said. He got himself puffed up the way men do when they want to talk tough. "He took a couple slugs in the gut. That's why we had to leave him, you know."

"Hush," I said to him. Zhorzha looked peaked as hell and none too steady on her feet. "Girl, you ain't gonna faint, are you?"

"No," she said. For once Dirk took his cue from me and kept his mouth shut.

"Y'all got your story straight? Them federal marshals, they're gonna circle back around with more questions."

"I didn't go," Zhorzha said. "That's what I'm telling them. I don't know what happened."

"Exactly. I don't know nothing," Dirk said. He got up and gave Zhorzha a hug, before he gone into the kitchen and out the back door.

"Is your man likely to tell them otherwise?" I said.

"I don't think so, but what about LaReigne?"

"What about her?" I said. "You ain't so much as said her name til now. I was starting to think she fell off the edge of the world, except I'm guessing she's the one they got in custody."

"She wouldn't leave. I went there to get her, and I got Gentry's friend killed, and she wouldn't leave. She's in love with that piece of shit, and she stayed there with him."

"It may not matter much what she says about you. And maybe she gone off and done something stupid, but that don't mean she forgot it's her job to protect her little sister."

"Except she abandoned us. For that asshole. Why would she do that?"

Zhorzha finished her beer and stared down into the empty can, like the answer was in there.

"Well, she takes after your mam. Dot woulda done anything for your daddy, right up to and including breaking him outta prison, if she coulda figured out how. For that matter, LaReigne takes after me and your daddy. Consider the goddamn reckless thing I did for Tess, and he helped me. I reckon you got more of your grandpappy's sense than we did."

"Are you kidding me? Did I or did I not just drive down to Arkansas and get people killed, trying to ransom my sister? I'm just like you all."

I laughed, which wasn't the kindest thing I coulda done, but it did tickle me.

"Shit, girl. I was trying to cheer you up. I didn't want you driving all that way home alone, feeling like you made a huge mistake."

"I did make a huge mistake." She crunched the beer can in her fist and leaned her head against the doorframe like it was too heavy to hold up.

"That's the way of the world. If there ain't nobody in the world you care enough about to do something crazy for, that's gotta be an empty feeling. What I did for Tess, it was dumb as hell, but it come from how much I loved her."

"And you think that makes it okay that LaReigne abandoned her family for that bastard. That she helped them, and those prison guards got killed?"

"No," I said. "But it means something that you love your sister so much you done what you done."

CHAPTER 46
ZEE

When I'd parked the truck the day before, the dog had walked out to the end of his chain to look at me. On Monday morning, after I said goodbye to Uncle Alva, the dog was standing in the exact same spot, waiting. As close to the truck as he could get. When I opened the door to get in, he took a step closer, so that his chain was stretched tight. I put out my hand the way Gentry had, and the dog sniffed it.

"Are you hungry? Did anybody feed you while Dirk was gone?"

When I touched his scabby head, he squinted his eyes but didn't move. Before I could change my mind, I took ahold of the hook on his collar and thumbed it open. The chain hitting the ground spooked him enough that he tucked his flanks and rolled his eyes at me. I jerked my hand back, but the dog didn't do anything except scuttle a few feet away from the chain. Then he trotted straight to the truck and hopped up in the cab.

I headed back up to the house, leaving the truck door open. When I walked into the kitchen, Uncle Alva was sitting at the table with his glasses up on his head and his eyes closed.

"Tell Dirk I'm taking his dog," I said. "And tell him not to get another dog if all he's going to do is chain it up out there."

"I been thinking about getting me another beagle. You know, them Snoopy dogs. We used to have one. You remember?"

"Yeah. Beelzebub. You told us you stole him from the devil."

"That wasn't no story, girl. They're good little guard dogs."

"Well, you can get you one now." I unzipped my backpack and took a stack of cash out of the envelope. I laid a few bills on the table. "This is for Dirk, so I'm not stealing his dog. Plus, he needs new boots because we tossed his."

"So you didn't lose the money?" he said.

"Do you want it back?"

"Lord, no. Ain't no good to me. Only thing I ever wanted it for was your aunt, and she's long gone. Besides, you'll need it. Lawyers ain't cheap."

I nodded, but I slid the rest of that bundle

of bills across the table to him. That left me with eighty-four thousand dollars.

"You should keep this, just in case," I said.

"I'll hang on to it for you. Or for LaReigne's little boy." He didn't pick it up, though. I wondered if I'd ever get to a place where I could be that indifferent to ten thousand dollars.

"Okay. Thank you. And I'm sorry." It was what I'd said when I left five minutes before. *Thank you. I'm sorry about how things turned out.*

"Take care, girl," he said, just like he had before, but as I was walking out the door the second time, he added something else: "Don't be a stranger."

The dog was still in the truck cab, standing in the seat. On the drive through town, he hung his head out the window. When I pulled onto the highway, though, I rolled up the window, and the dog settled down in the passenger seat.

I drove all the way through to Parsons without stopping, but I figured the rest area on the other side of town was as good a place as any to let the dog out to pee. He stuck with me, even came inside when I went to the bathroom. It surprised me, because I hadn't exactly made friends with him, but maybe he figured if I was driving

Gentry's truck that made us friends by association. We walked up and down a little so I could stretch out my hip, and I stopped to look at the historical plaque about the Bloody Benders. Nice to know there was at least one family in Kansas that was more fucked-up than mine.

While we'd been walking around, another car had pulled in, and as we headed back to the truck, I saw they had a dog, too. Some kind of bulldog, I thought, right as Dirk's damn dog went running toward it snarling and snapping. The woman screamed, "Oh my god! Oh my god!" Sounded just like La-Reigne.

If the woman had been alone, I think it would have ended pretty badly, but her husband picked up their dog, and then Dirk's dog stood in front of them growling. The whole time I was trying to get there, but I couldn't go very fast, let alone run.

"That dog needs to be on a leash!" the woman screamed at me.

"You can't just have a dog like that running loose!" the man said.

"You need to get your dog under control!"

I got ahold of the dog's collar and, when I pulled on it, he yelped and tucked his tail end.

"I'm sorry. I just bought him from this

486

guy who had him out on a chain. I didn't even think about not having a leash for him. I'm sorry. I didn't know he would do that." When I pulled on the dog's collar, he came with me, all hunkered down and trembling. Big scary dog shaking like a leaf. As soon as I opened the truck door, he jumped in the cab, looking happy again.

I got in the truck, but before I could start it, the guy with the bulldog came jogging over. He'd left his dog with his wife, but I figured he was coming to lecture me some more. Unless I was going to ignore him, I had to roll down the window.

"Hey, I wasn't sure how much further you had to go, but since you just rescued him, it'd be a shame if anything happened. We've got an extra leash, if you want." He held it up to show me. "You're welcome to it. That way you can get him home safe."

"Thank you." I reached out the window and he put the leash in my hand. "I never had a dog before, so this is kind of new for me."

"What are you calling him?"

"Oh, uh. Leon." It was lying there on the dashboard, where it had been for the trip to Arkansas and back. *Yvain, the Knight with the Lion.*

"Leon. That's a great name. Good luck

with him."

The guy walked back to his car, and waved at me as they drove away.

I sat there, wondering why a random stranger had given me a dog leash.

"Who even does that?" I said to Leon. He really was the saddest, ugliest dog. It was a stupid thing to cry about, but I was tired, and LaReigne was in jail, and Gentry was in jail, and Edrard was dead, and I missed Marcus, so I cried. After twenty minutes of watching me cry, Leon must have gotten bored, because he laid down in the seat. Not on the passenger side like before, but right next to me, with his giant head on my leg.

Even though my foot fell asleep about twenty miles down the road, I didn't make him move his head, and we drove the rest of the way to Wichita like that.

I didn't know who else to call, so I called Julia from the restaurant, since they were closed on Mondays. Once I offered to pay her, she agreed to meet me at the Franks' house, so I could drop off Gentry's truck.

I parked it in the street, hoping not to be noticed. I'd wanted to do it under cover of darkness, but I knew that would look suspicious. I moved my stuff first: my purse and backpack. Then I put the leash on Leon. He looked at me, but didn't move.

"Come on." I pulled on the leash, and he walked across the seat and jumped down. When I opened the back door of Julia's car for him, though, he just looked at me.

"Oh, you weren't kidding about the dog," she said. "He doesn't have fleas, does he?"

"No." I had no idea.

"Get in," I said to Leon. I was starting to feel like I'd made a terrible mistake. I'd brought him all the way from Missouri, and maybe he'd only come with me because I was driving Gentry's truck. I tried to nudge him into the car, but he wouldn't go.

"Hold on," I said to Julia. I closed the door and walked across the street to the Franks' house, with Leon following me on the leash. I rang the doorbell, feeling sick with something right in between fear and shame.

Charlene's sister, Bernice, answered the door, so I could guess what had happened after I called Carlees. He would have called the sheriff in Little River, and then he would have called his parents. They would have asked Bernice to babysit, while they drove to Arkansas to take care of Gentry. To clean up the mess I made.

"Zee?" she said, and kind of squinted at me.

"I brought Gentry's truck back." I held out the keys, but she was looking at Leon.

"Is Gentry with you?" She looked at me, then out at Gentry's truck, then at Leon again.

"No. I just brought his truck back," I said.

As soon as I passed the keys to her, I turned around and walked to Julia's car. I opened the back door and got in. That worked, because Leon jumped in after me. As Julia pulled away, Bernice was standing on the front porch with her cellphone pressed to her ear.

At Mom's house, I had Julia pull in behind my car. She stared at the disaster in Mom's front yard, but I pretended like it wasn't even there. I took out the half ounce of weed and the hundred dollars I'd promised her and passed them over the front seat to her.

"Thanks," I said.

"No problem. You know, after all this dies down, I'm sure Lance will be okay with you coming back to the restaurant."

"That's okay. I don't think I'm coming back."

I walked Leon over to my car and, while I was unlocking the door, I thought about

490

how Gentry and I had stood next to it, and how I'd been a coward or a weakling. If I'd been braver or stronger, when he asked if I wanted to go alone, I would have said "Yes" instead of dragging him with me.

I opened the front passenger door for Leon, and he got in without any fuss. When I drove away, Julia was still parked there, staring at the mess in Mom's front yard.

I went down Broadway until I came to one of those run-down motels with a sign that said PET FRIENDLY. Leon had been happy enough riding around in the car, but to get him into the motel room, I had to drag him by the collar. He acted like he'd never been inside before. I ordered a pizza, and while I waited for it to be delivered, I put Leon in the tub and washed him with motel soap. He didn't fight me, but he stood under the running water with his head down, not even looking at me. Once he was toweled off, he ran out to the room and hid between the bed and the wall, like he was worried I had something worse planned for him. After the pizza came, though, he jumped up on the bed without even waiting for me to invite him. I split the pizza with him, right down the middle.

Then I knew why I'd brought Leon with

me. Because he needed to be taken care of, and I needed someone to take care of.

CHAPTER 47
DEPUTY EVANGELISTA

Three to the morgue, two to the hospital, and two to jail. A pretty typical headcount for a meth deal gone bad, except there was no meth lab. The only thing in the barn was a stolen SUV with half of a new paint job. We found a little weed in the house, but not enough for three men to end up dead over. We weren't going to be able to question the two injured until they came out of surgery, and the woman wouldn't say anything except, "I want a lawyer."

The kid with the sword was an interesting possibility, though. We were thinking PCP at first, because he was wacked out, sitting in the interrogation room, covered in blood, talking to himself a mile a minute.

"I hear thee! I hear thee! What boon is it to me? Thou art as good to me as a bucket of water to a drowning man. Yea, I defied thee. 'Tis on my head. I hear! Yea, I pray thou art right, for if I am to go to hell, I shall not spend eternity in thy company."

It went on like that for two hours. Zelker and I watched him, thinking eventually he'd wind down. Off and on the whole time, the kid kept clenching his shoulders up around his ears and cracking his neck. He'd do that for ten minutes, and then bang his head on the table. After the fifth or sixth time, I started to worry he was going to give himself a concussion.

Then he started saying, "Nay, it itcheth not," and a lot of crazy stuff I couldn't really understand.

"Seriously, what do you think he's on?" Zelker said.

By then we knew we had those two escaped convicts from Kansas, one dead, and one in the county hospital trying to die. We were working on identifying everybody else, so we decided to take a run at this kid. Fingerprint him, swab his hands for GSR, take a blood sample, see if we could get a statement.

Once we were inside with him, I started with a trade-off.

"You got an itch you need scratched?" I said.

"Nay, it itcheth not," he said. He was staring at the wall, with his jaw clenched.

"You sure? We could undo those cuffs, if

you tell us your name."

"I am called Gentry Frank."

"There. Easy enough." I unlocked the cuffs, planning to give him his right hand free.

"I pray thee, my lord, my left hand," he said.

So I kept his right hand cuffed to the table. For a second, he rested his left hand flat on the top of his head. Then he brought it down to the back of his neck and started scratching. Ten solid minutes he scratched his neck.

"That can't be good," Zelker said, but the kid actually looked more relaxed the longer he scratched. He'd spent two hours shouting at himself and banging his head on the table, but after ten minutes of scratching, he was calm.

"Okay, Gentry Frank. I'm Deputy Evangelista and this is Deputy Zelker. Do you want to tell me what happened tonight?"

He took a deep breath and started in like he was reciting something.

"Sir Edrard and I gone there this night to rescue the lady LaReigne from the knaves that kidnapped her. He armed with his bow, I armed with my sword, we came upon them unawares, but ere we could make away with their captive, they would fight us. We fought and tho Sir Edrard be valiant, he was sore wounded."

I looked at Zelker like *Are you hearing this shit?*

"That is one crazy-ass story," Zelker said.

" 'Tis no lie." Most people tried to sell their lies with eye contact, but the whole time we'd been in with him, Gentry Frank never looked us in the eye. Like he couldn't.

"Maybe we could try it again from the beginning," I said. "Only this time in regular English?"

An hour later, it was pretty clear we weren't going to get that. If he was lying, it wasn't to protect himself, because he admitted that he'd stabbed two men with the sword we had in evidence. He couldn't or wouldn't tell us about how anybody else had ended up dead.

"What about this guy with an arrow in his leg, an arrow in his shoulder, and a bullet in his head?" Zelker slid the picture across the table to Gentry. The look on the kid's face never changed, but he kept squeezing his right hand into a fist.

"I know not. I was not there when he was slain."

"What about this guy? Conrad Ligett. Two bullets in him. Were you there when he was slain?" I said.

"Nay. I know not how he was slain, but Barnwell, I slew him, and another man."

"Well, Barnwell isn't dead," Zelker said.

"He yet lives?"

I figured the kid would look disappointed or something but he kept his poker face.

"Yep. So, you know who Barnwell is? And Ligett?" I said.

"Yea. I saw them upon the news. They aren knaves and men of murderous intent. 'Tis no great harm that they should be slain."

Zelker laughed, and I shook my head at him.

"And that's what you went there to do?" I said. "To kill them? That was your plan?"

"Nay. 'Twas my intent to negotiate for the lady LaReigne's freedom. 'Twas not I who struck the first blow."

That was all we could get out of Gentry Frank, and after he'd given us the same version three times, he asked for some water. Zelker got up to get it, but he stopped at the door and looked back at Gentry with a frown on his face.

"Where did all that blood come from?" he said.

I got up and went around the table, where I could see there was a puddle of blood under Gentry's chair. I'd thought all the blood on him was from his friend, but that would have long since dried up. The blood on the floor was fresh.

So I recuffed him, loaded him in a patrol car, and drove him over to the county hospital. They put him in one of the back cubicles, where I cuffed him to the bed. Not that I thought he was going to cause trouble, because he seemed pretty calm. Not much like the kid who'd been banging his head on the table. Once the doctor cut his pant leg open and started messing around with his leg, Gentry went back to scratching his neck and talking to himself.

"I know well thou art wroth for I defied thee, but speak." Then he turned right around and said, "Wilt thou not cease plaguing me? I have prayed. I will pray, but I would hear the Witch."

"What is that?" I said, when the doctor tossed a big bloody wad into the basin.

"Tampon."

"He stuck a tampon in his leg?"

"Good wound packing in a pinch," the doctor said.

"My brother, Sir Edrard, be he here?" Gentry said, ignoring the doctor rooting around in his leg with a forceps.

"Yeah, he's here."

"How fareth he? Well or ill?"

"I can go check on him. Doc, you know I need that slug for evidence."

"I know."

I figured a little show of goodwill might get Gentry to open up some more, so I left him there with the doctor, and went to check on his friend.

Turned out I wasn't going to have any goodwill to offer, because his friend had coded about fifteen minutes before, and they couldn't resuscitate him.

Final count for the night: four to the morgue, two to the hospital, and that pretty blond woman crying in a jail cell. I was glad when the U.S. marshals showed up to take it all off our hands.

CHAPTER 48
ZEE

In the morning, while I walked Leon up one stretch of Broadway and down the other, I made plans.

First, I had to get on the straight and narrow as much as I could. I hid the THC drops inside the lamp base in my motel room. That envelope of cash was pretty incriminating, too, so I put some in a new checking account and the rest in a safety-deposit box. They tell you not to store cash in safety-deposit boxes, but you can't deposit eighty thousand dollars in a bank account without answering a lot of questions, either.

At Mom's house, things were worse than they had been. It had rained at some point while I was gone, and the whole front yard was a swamp of ruined furniture, rotting cardboard boxes, garbage, and bloated romance novels.

Hanging on the front door was a yellow

piece of paper from the City of Wichita: a notice of abatement telling Mom she had thirty days to clean up her front yard. Otherwise the city would clean it up and fine her. One of her neighbors must have called out the city inspector. I didn't blame them for wanting the mess gone, but the date on it was the day after the cops had searched the house. That only gave me three weeks to solve it.

I took out my phone, looked up dumpster rental companies, and called the first one. I rented the biggest roll-off dumpster they had, knowing Mom would never forgive me. We might make peace someday, but she was never going to get over me parking a twenty-foot dumpster in her driveway.

"Where have you been?" she said, when I went inside. "I have been absolutely frantic wondering where you were."

"You could have called me." I could have kept my mouth shut.

"I thought I had the wrong number."

"I wrote my number right there on your list. Right there." I walked across to her phone list and tapped my number. I'd even written *Zhorzha* instead of *Zee*. Mom ignored me.

"I talked to LaReigne yesterday, and she needs help hiring a lawyer. She's in Arkansas right now, but she's going to waive extradition so she'll be closer to home. It's unbelievable. They're charging her as an accomplice! She's been through hell and back, and they have her sitting in a jail cell, instead of letting her come home to her family. It's criminal. She needs to be with Marcus. With us. And don't you nag me about my phone bill. You know they only let them call collect."

"I know, it's a scam," I said. "What did she tell you?"

"What kind of question is that? You know she can't talk about anything on those phones."

I'd long since memorized Mom's rant about the Department of Corrections listening in on phone calls, because I'd had to hear it every time she talked to my father. I went to look at the situation in the kitchen: the leaking sink, the garbage disposal, the dead fridge that was blocking the back door. I needed to hire an electrician, a plumber, and a couple guys to throw stuff into the dumpster.

"Are you listening to me?" Mom yelled. I hadn't been, but I went into the front room, because if I ignored her for too long she would come into the kitchen, and catch me making plans.

"I didn't hear you."

My phone rang, but it wasn't a number I knew, so I didn't answer.

"I said she needs a better lawyer than a public defender," Mom said. "Your father's lawyer was fresh out of law school. He'd never even been to trial. There has to be something we can do to scrape up a retainer. I'm going to call your aunt Shelly. She's always complaining about money, but she certainly has more than we do. And I can always take out a second mortgage on the house."

I stood behind Mom's chair, waiting to see if the person calling would leave a message. I wasn't surprised when the voice-to-text popped up.

Miss Trego, this is U.S. Marshal Boyd Mansur. Please return my call at your earliest convenience.

"You need to stop pouting and help me figure out what we're going to do!" When I didn't answer, Mom squinted over her shoulder at me. Then she put her hands on the arms of her chair like she was going to stand up. "What are you doing?"

"What I'm going to do is go to the Goodwill and buy you a couple china hutches and a bookcase. I'll get some guys to bring them into the house, and you can fill them up. Everything else has to go," I said.

"I told you to leave it alone. I'll get it cleaned up."

"Mom, please. We only have three weeks. If we don't take care of this, the city is going to come, and they are going to throw everything away."

"Don't you worry about it. Come here."

When I didn't do it fast enough, she snapped her fingers at me and held out her arms. I bent down over her, and she put her arms around me. I wasn't sure if it was a hug or if she wanted me to help her up out of her chair.

"We have to help your sister. With a decent lawyer, there's no way she'll serve time," Mom said.

The way she could flip from one subject to another, I knew we were never going to have a real conversation about any of it. Nothing I said was going to sink in.

"Mom, I know you hope that, but you need to be realistic."

"Or at least not much time. Help me up."

"If the prosecution can convince a jury that LaReigne was in love with him, the jury's going to believe that she helped him," I said. I bent my knees a little deeper and pulled hard enough to get Mom out of her chair. Hard enough that my back and my

504

hip lit up.

"So what if she helped them? She can't have been very much help! It's not like she's a criminal mastermind."

"It doesn't matter how much. If she helped them at all, that makes her an accomplice to at least two murders." I didn't want to be angry at Mom, but I was. She had stood by Dad for so long because she could twist everything around until it fit with what she wanted to believe. Mom still had her arms around me, and it felt like she was trying to hold on to me and push me away at the same time.

"That wasn't her fault. She didn't kill those guards. I just need my baby to come home. I want LaReigne to come home."

"I want LaReigne to come home, too," I said, but it was a lie. "But I don't know if that's going to happen."

"Don't you say that." Mom pushed me away, and I was glad to get free. "If you move in, we can use your rent money. That might be enough to hire a better lawyer."

"No," I said.

"Excuse me?"

"I'm not moving in." I thought of how Leon was so stubborn, and in my mind, I put my head down and tucked my tail.

"Can we please not go through all that

drama again?" Mom said.

"I'm not going through any drama, and I'm not moving in. You can call Aunt Shelly, and you can call the bank, but I'm not giving you my rent money."

"This is not the time to be selfish! Your sister needs your help, Zhorzha! You owe her that!"

I thought about that pile of cash in the safety-deposit box. *Lawyers ain't cheap,* Uncle Alva had said, and at the time, I'd nodded, but as I walked out of Mom's house, with her yelling after me, I made up my mind. I wasn't going to spend a dime of that money on a lawyer for LaReigne. To get Mom's yard cleaned up, yes. To hire a family court lawyer to get visitation with Marcus, yes. But for LaReigne, no. I didn't care if half of it was supposed to be for her. She chose Tague Barnwell. Let him hire her a lawyer.

I went back to my motel, took Leon around the block, and fed him some real dog food. Then, even though it was only noon, I took a big dose of THC and got in bed. There was a *Bewitched* marathon on TV, and I laid in bed with Leon next to me, watching *Bewitched* and making lists on my phone. I'd already made a huge list of things to do for Mom, but I started one for myself, too. I needed a lawyer, a job, a veterinarian, and a place to live with a yard.

Toward the end of the afternoon, when I was looking at houses for rent, my phone rang again. I let it go to voicemail and a few minutes later, there it was: *Miss Trego. Boyd Mansur. We need to talk.*

CHAPTER 49
ZEE

Mansur's voicemails started out polite, but I knew he would get around to threatening me eventually. A week later, while I was standing out in Mom's yard watching the truck driver park the dumpster, I got the message I couldn't ignore.

Miss Trego. Boyd Mansur. I would prefer not to issue a warrant for you as a material witness, but if that becomes necessary, I will.

After I signed for the dumpster, I called Mansur back.

"So let's talk," I said. "I don't know anything, but I guess you need to hear it from me personally."

"Why don't I come to your mother's house, so I can talk to you both? Two birds, one stone."

"That saying is actually *kill* two birds with one stone. Are you trying to kill my mother?"

"Miss Trego, I don't wish to distress your

mother or you, but I do need to talk to you both."

I didn't want to meet him at Mom's and he wouldn't talk in public, so I went to his hotel room, which was a lot nicer than mine. He had a suite at the La Quinta on Kellogg, and it even had a little kitchenette and a table, which was where we sat.

"Before we talk about anything, I have one question," I said. "Are you going to arrest me? Because I'd need to find somebody to take care of my dog."

"No, Miss Trego. Unless you plan to make an unexpected confession to something pretty substantial, I'm not going to arrest you."

I knew he was getting ready to lay some shit on me, because he set up his laptop. The first thing he showed me was black-and-white footage from a surveillance camera, showing LaReigne standing outside a door.

"There's LaReigne," Mansur said, and paused the video. "Waiting at the rear door to the education building, where the volunteer ministry meets. Normally this door would have been locked, but your sister's ministry group got permission from the chaplain to use the yard for part of their . . . ritual. This is just as the riot started and

509

after the first corrections officer was killed in the education building. At that time, a few inmates and the volunteers locked themselves in a classroom. All of the volunteers except Molly Verbansky and LaReigne. I want you to look at the time stamp on it — seven-sixteen P.M. — because here's footage from a different camera at the same time."

He clicked PLAY and the video switched to two people standing at a chain-link fence. A woman, so probably Molly, and a man with something in his hand.

"That's Conrad Ligett, using a pair of wire cutters that Molly Verbansky smuggled in — we're not really sure how."

"Is this for real a prison?" I said. "I'm not kidding, my nephew's grade school is more secure than this."

"Normally, the alarm would have been raised by now, but we believe the riot in the main building was part of a diversionary tactic. And the corrections officer who would have raised the alarm about the situation in the education building had just been killed." Mansur paused the video to give me a minute to feel like shit for joking about a situation where two people ended up murdered.

"Notice that Ligett is cutting a hole in a

fence next to the parking lot, while your sister stands at this door." He went back to the video of LaReigne and clicked PLAY. "Conrad Ligett and Molly Verbansky are on the south side of the education building. Barnwell is in the building, about to kill the second guard. What is LaReigne doing?"

"She doesn't know what to do," I said. I hated myself for trying to defend her, but she was looking back and forth in two directions, like she was confused. And if my story was that I didn't know anything, then I had to pretend I still believed LaReigne was innocent.

"But it's obvious what she should be doing. What any sane person would do in this situation is run across the yard to the main building. She could have gotten there easily, but she didn't. Why not?"

"Maybe she was scared."

"So scared, she stayed there instead of running to get help?"

"Wasn't there a riot in the main building?" I said.

"In one of the cell blocks. Not at the entrance nearest LaReigne. When I look at this, I see LaReigne waiting for Barnwell. Because she was in on their plan. That's the only reason she wouldn't have run away. You know what else she did that night?"

"No."

"She left everything in her car. Why would she leave her purse, her phone, even her car keys in her unlocked car in the parking lot of a prison?"

"It wasn't unlocked," I said. "Her car has one of those keypad locks on the door. She always puts her keys and her purse in the trunk."

Mansur frowned and then went on like I hadn't said anything. That's what they would do in court, too.

"She knew she was going to need those things later, and she knew she wouldn't be going back through the security checkpoint when they left the prison. Your sister parked her car on the other side of the fence of the education building, on the opposite end of the parking lot from where she entered the prison. But once Ligett cut the hole in the fence, her car was right there and the keys were in it."

"Yeah, except that —"

"And here she is, running toward that hole in the fence, holding hands with Barnwell."

Maybe that's what the video showed. Or maybe it showed Tague holding her by the wrist and pulling her after him. Or I wanted it to show that. I wanted her to look like she was trying to get away from him, but no matter how much I squinted, she was still running toward the fence with Tague. She wasn't trying to get away. She wasn't fighting him. Not the way she fought me. Maybe she hadn't planned to go with him, but she went with him, and in the end, she stayed with him.

"Why didn't you show me this before?" I said.

"Because we didn't have all this information yet, and we were still very much in the middle of a manhunt. Would seeing this have changed something for you?"

I couldn't answer him, because if I talked too much I was going to cry. And if I cried, I was going to lose control. I'd gotten Edrard killed and Gentry arrested, because I'd trusted LaReigne to be better than me. My whole life looked like a mistake now.

"Is that all you want?" I said, when I was sure I was calm enough. "For me to admit I was wrong about my sister?"

"Oh, I'm just curious how it all fits together, and I think you can help me figure that out. For example, the young man who was at your mother's house with you, the one you insisted didn't know anything, he managed to locate two fugitives the U.S. Marshals Service couldn't find. I wonder how he came by his information."

"Not from me."

"He says the same thing. He says, and I'm quoting —" Mansur opened a file folder and looked at a sheet of paper. *"I may not tell thee whence I learned the place the lady La-Reigne was kept by these knaves.* He really said *knaves."*

"That's how he talks."

"However he talks, he's been charged with a whole raft of things, including obstruction of justice and three counts of murder."

My chest felt so tight, I couldn't take a breath. I pushed back from the table, trying to get some air. I sucked in enough to say, "Murder? For those assholes?"

Mansur pulled a photo out of the file folder and slid it over to me. Someone wearing blue plastic gloves was reaching from off camera to force Gentry's chin up for his mug shot. He had a welt on his forehead, a black eye, and smear of blood across his cheek. I assumed the cops had done that to him.

"He's an odd kid," Mansur said. "But considering what he did to Barnwell and this other man — Paul Scanlon — he's not a lightweight. Not sure how he'll fare in the Arkansas penal system, having killed two local white brotherhood types. Probably won't be easy for him."

"You think that's funny? I bet you're the kind of creep who laughs at prison rape jokes." In the last week, I'd chewed my nails down to the quick. The only thing left to chew on was my cuticles.

"I'm going to be very blunt with you, Miss Trego. I believe you know exactly where his information came from, because you're the one who gave it to him. What I would like to know is how you —"

"You think I knew where my sister was, but instead of going to see her, I sent Gentry to fight these Nazi assholes to get her back, even though you also think I knew she helped them escape? How does that make any sense? If I knew she helped them escape, why would I think she needed rescuing?"

"I admit it doesn't entirely add up, but you knew something, didn't you? Because you went to Missouri with Gentry Frank."

"I went to Missouri to visit my uncle, and Gentry went with me," I said.

"Your uncle, Alva Trego, who has a connection to Craig Van Eck, the ringleader of the White Circle at El Dorado?"

"*Had* a connection. My uncle hasn't had any contact with those people since he was paroled. He's a law-abiding citizen."

"In my experience that's a pretty rare

outcome for someone like your uncle."

"You don't know anything about him."

"I'll know more after I talk to him," Mansur said, but he was wrong. He wouldn't get anything out of Uncle Alva. I hoped he wouldn't get anything out of Dirk, either. "So you went to Missouri with Gentry Frank? How did you end up driving Mr. Frank's truck back to Wichita? Mr. Frank's aunt, Bernice Betts, she identified you as the woman who returned his vehicle."

"Yes, I returned his truck. I didn't know what else to do. Gentry left his phone with me, I didn't know where they went, and he and Edrard never came back."

"By *Edrard* you mean Joshua Kline? Who was killed in Arkansas?" Mansur flipped over another page in his file folder, I think just to see me flinch, but there was no bloody picture.

"He was introduced to me as Edrard," I said.

"According to you, they left you in southern Missouri, drove away, and you didn't hear from them again, so you drove Mr. Frank's truck back to Wichita."

"Exactly."

"And Richard Bowers?"

"I don't know who that is." I could guess. The girl at the motel had called him Rick.

516

"Becky Eddiger identified him as a friend of Joshua Kline's who might have gone to Missouri with him. She wasn't sure. He says he didn't go. What do you say?"

"If he did, I never saw him. And I don't know who Becky is," I said.

If Rhys claimed he never went to Missouri, it meant he was sticking to the lie. Mansur made an irritated little pout with his mouth, and flipped a few pages in his file folder.

"Apparently all of these people are members of a . . . historical medieval combat group, and the . . . Society for Creative Anachronism. They all have pseudonyms. You may know Becky as *Rosalinda*?"

"Yeah. Edrard's wife. I met her a couple weeks ago at Gentry's castle."

"His castle," Mansur muttered. "Ms. Eddiger was under the impression that Frank, Kline, you, and possibly Bowers, were going to Missouri on *some kind of crazy mission*. That was how she described it."

"I went to Missouri to see my uncle. Edrard came later to see Gentry. They left. I never saw this other guy."

Mansur looked at his notes some more, while I waited for the other shoe to drop. For him to say, *According to your sister you were there.*

Except LaReigne wasn't just my sister. She was our father's daughter. I was guessing she hadn't spoken to the police at all.

CHAPTER 50
CHARLENE

Gentry had always been a problem for the courts. When he was three, and bumped from foster home to foster home, because no one could handle him. When he was eleven, and had his knightly misadventure.

I'd thought that was behind us, but after he was arrested, we lived it all over again. Every morning when I looked around the breakfast table at Bill, Trang, and Elana, I wondered what we would do as a family. Maybe the worst part was trying to maintain communication with Gentry, when he was in Arkansas, and we were trying to hold our lives together. Phone calls were impossible. He would answer questions, but only if I asked the right ones. He wrote letters, but they told me nothing about how he was coping. I didn't want empty reassurances. I wanted to know the truth, and Gentry's truth filtered through Middle English and bounced off Gawen told me nothing useful.

According to our lawyer, Gentry was still a problem for the courts.

"Obviously, they won't want him to take the stand. The feds haven't even subpoenaed him for Barnwell and Gill-Trego's trials," Ms. Howell said. She had come highly recommended by a church member, and I generally thought she was wonderful, but it soured my stomach every time she said *Trego.* As we learned more about the investigation, it was clear Zhorzha knew nothing about how those men escaped from prison. However innocent she was on that front, she was directly responsible for Gentry being a party to the deaths of three men, albeit none of them good men, and none of them innocent. Zhorzha was the reason Gentry was in jail, waiting to go to trial.

"Wouldn't it be risky for him to testify anyway?" Bill said. After years of my nagging him to lose weight, he finally had. Now I worried the stress was killing him.

"Only for the prosecution," Ms. Howell said.

"How so?" I said.

"Gentry? Gentry?" Ms. Howell leaned across the table and tapped her pen in front of him. He nodded. "Can you tell me about how you know LaReigne Trego-Gill?"

"Certs. She be the elder sister of Lady

Zhorzha Trego."

"And what's your relationship with Zhorzha?"

"I am her champion. I am sworn to protect her."

Ms. Howell smiled when she turned back to me. I never knew how to take those smiles, pitying but kind. I took hers in silence, because we needed her help.

"If he testifies, there are a few possible outcomes. One: The jury doesn't understand him or the jury finds him funny. Two — and this is the one the feds are worried about — the jury sees an earnest young man with a disability, who is being prosecuted for what is essentially a good deed.

"Furthermore, because he was injured, it might be difficult for the prosecution to argue that what he did wasn't self-defense. We may end up negotiating for an obstruction of justice charge or a mayhem charge. Worst-case scenario, manslaughter."

"Is there any way to get them to lower his bail?" I let Bill ask, even though we'd stayed up a ridiculous number of nights trying to figure out how to scrape together the bond money. We couldn't.

"Not while he's charged with three counts of murder. They know they can't convict on that, but it keeps him locked up until the trial."

Just hearing it said — *murder* — made me sick.

I held out hope that we could reach a plea deal that would allow Gentry to serve his time in a mental health facility. Anything to keep him out of prison. While he was awaiting trial, he was housed at the county jail, but several times they took him to a diagnostic facility to assess whether he was competent to stand trial. Of course, he understood what he'd done was against the law, but according to Ms. Howell, the prosecutor worried there might be room for a diminished capacity plea, because of his voices.

In the end, I wouldn't have to hear *murder* again, because Ms. Howell negotiated a plea deal. One count of obstruction of justice and two counts of assault with a deadly weapon, which meant Gentry wouldn't have a felony on his record. As part of that deal, Gentry would go to the state hospital, rather than to prison.

Bill and I went down to Arkansas together to meet with Ms. Howell and Gentry, who looked terrible in his orange jail scrubs. His hair was getting shaggier every week, and he clutched a manila folder of paperwork to his chest like a shield. I longed to hug him, but physical contact had become even more difficult for him while he was locked up. I made do with telling him how glad I was to see him. He bowed to me, then to Bill and Ms. Howell.

She explained the plea agreement more remedially than was necessary, because Gentry's silence was so often mistaken for a lack of intelligence. After she finished, he held out his hand for the papers. He read it through twice, before he passed it back to her. She flipped to the page he would need to sign and laid a pen on top of it.

"Would ye have me sign it?" he said to his father and me.

"Yes, Gentry. I think it's the best thing. Don't you, Bill?"

"I suppose your mother's right. Because your other option is a trial, and I don't know about that."

Gentry nodded, but he stood up and walked to the other end of the room. He'd stimmed on and off while reading the plea, but now he was doing it in earnest. Squeezing his right hand into a fist, while frantically scratching his neck with his left hand, until I knew, from experience, he would end up drawing blood.

"Is he okay?" Ms. Howell said.

"He just needs a few minutes. Gentry —"

"Nay," he said, loudly enough that Ms. Howell jumped in her seat.

I smiled to reassure her, but she was staring at Gentry, who was pacing and scratching, and having a rather heated discussion with Hildegard, if I were to guess.

"Plague me not, harridan," he said. "Thou hast no more wit than a stone. And a stone hath a use, more than thee."

"Should we call someone?" Ms. Howell said.

"Son," Bill said. "Calm down. You're scaring Ms. Howell."

"Nay!" Gentry came back to the table and did something I hadn't seen him do in years, something he'd been taught in ABA therapy. He put both his hands on the table and forced them flat with his fingers spread out. They'd been trying to stop him from stimming, even though that was actually useful to him. Flattening his hands like that had never helped him, and it made me uneasy to see him do it. He was breathing too fast when he picked up his folder and took out a few photocopies stapled together.

"Read thou this?" he said to Bill, and then to both of us: "Read ye this and ye bidden me agree to such a thing?"

"Do you know what he means, Bill?" I said, but before he could answer, Gentry slapped the pages down on the table between Ms. Howell and me.

"It's an article I sent him," Bill said. "About diminished capacity plea deals."

"Is't true?" Gentry said. "If I plead as ye would have me, they might give me physic I need not? They might keep me as long as they will? This tells of men held ten years and more, with no hope of freedom."

"It is one of the risks with this type of concession," Ms. Howell said. I don't think she had quite recovered from Gentry's outburst, because she couldn't look at him. "It requires him to show progress in his treatment. If he doesn't, they would be able to incarcerate him for as long as they deemed necessary. For public safety."

"Of course, he'll make progress," I said. I waited for Bill to say something, but he'd picked up Gentry's article and was flipping through it. "And if he goes to trial and gets convicted, what then? He'll never get another aeronautics job. Not with a felony. What will he do?"

"I got him the Bombardier job. He can get another job. No, he'll never get security clearance for military work with a felony, but there are civilian jobs. Besides, maybe he'll be acquitted," Bill said, and then the thing he kept saying to all his friends: "Hell, he ought to get a medal for what he did."

At one point, I almost agreed with him, but in that moment, it made me angry. Unreasonably, irrationally angry at Bill. At Gentry. At myself.

"Gentry, I want you to sign this. I think it's the best option you have," I said.

"I will not." I wanted to believe he was talking to Gawen or the Witch, but he was looking at my hands where I had them laced together on the table.

"Do you understand what it would mean for you to go to prison? It's not safe. It's —"

"My mother, I know it well, but I will not go to a mental hospital. Let those who suffer an illness of the mind do so and prosper of it, but I do not and I will not."

Gentry went to the door, and I knew from the set of his shoulders there was no way to convince him.

That morning, as Bill and I had been driving the nearly eight hours from Wichita for the umpteenth time, I'd held on to the hope that we would go home with things decided. Instead I went home in tears, knowing we would come back for another meeting. As many meetings as it took to convince Gentry to take the plea deal, or to prepare him for trial. I was so upset when I left that I forgot to tell him I loved him.

For the longest time, I'd worried that I was overprotective of Gentry. I'd sheltered him too much and kept him from finding his own way. Now I felt like I hadn't sheltered him enough. I should have kept him on a shorter leash. I should have kept him under my wing, like the mother hen Bill always accused me of being.

Instead, I'd let Bill teach him about guns like they were harmless toys. I'd let Gentry take boxing lessons. I'd let him go to all those tournaments, and learn to joust, and hang all those swords in his room, like it was a hobby. Like it was model trains instead of learning how to kill people.

When we got home, Bill went to pick up Trang and Elana from Bernice's, and I went around the house, doing a few chores and trying to calm myself before they got home. Trang had left his baseball cleats in the laundry room, so I carried them back to his room to put them away. There, I looked at the swords in a way I never had before.

In the beginning, when Gentry was a teenager, it was all wooden swords and rubber axes, pretend weapons. The claymore hanging over his bed was the first real sword he'd bought with his summer lawn-mowing money. Hardened steel, double-edged blade.

The handle was wrapped in leather and almost a foot long. It was a sword meant to be wielded with two hands, and it took me both hands to lift it down from the wall.

Gentry had left his bed neatly made as always, and I stood in the middle of it in my shoes, trying to steady myself enough to get down while holding that ridiculous sword.

I wasn't sure what I was going to do with it, but it wasn't staying in my house.

CHAPTER 51
GENTRY

The Witch spake not to me tho I cried out for a word. Let her curse me as readily as Hildegard, or mock me as Gawen did, if only she would speak. She left me to be torn between them like a bone twixt two dogs. In her silence, 'twas the black knight who counseled me.

"Speak not what might harm Lady Zhorzha," he said. "If thou art in truth her champion, hold thy tongue."

Tho my mind was confused, I heeded him, and spake only those things that had been wrought by mine own hand, and what I knew of Sir Edrard's courage. For he could no more suffer the consequences, and I would have it known that he was true and valiant to the last. Of Lady Zhorzha, Master Dirk, and Sir Alva, I was silent. Many a time, I told the ilk tale of my journey to Arkansas, first to the sheriff's men, then to Mansur, then to the lady Howell, my father, and my mother. I was heartsore to distress her and recalled my father's words when I was a boy. If I would be noble, he said, I must strive to do her honor.

Certs, to give her grief was dishonor, and I knew she grieved when I would not do as she asked. She bade me say I knew not what I did, that I was ill, for then the court would send me to some safe place. I might have done it, ere I read how I could be kept there and physicked beyond my wish. As ever, she desired to protect me, but I accorded not with her desire. My mother went from me in tears, and I could offer her no comfort.

In truth, I was glad when they had gone, and I was returned to my cell, where there was what silence I could have. I made my prayers to appease Hildegard, and I told tales to soothe Gawen. Sleep would not come in that room where the window was no more than an archer's loophole, but there weren hours enough to exercise myself. I passed many weeks thus, and each week the lady Howell came with my father, or my mother, for they could not often come together, and leave Elana and Trang with my aunt. It shamed me that I was such a burden unto them, and I bade them not surrender so much for me. 'Twas also that I wished to speak alone with the lady Howell, for she was mine advocate and not my mother's. It liked her not, but she came as I asked, and soon I made her know my intent.

I would not plead to be locked away safe for some unnumbered years, but to spare my father and mother, I would plead. For I did those deeds by mine own hand, and by pleading, I would free myself sooner. The lady Howell spake with the prosecutor, and returned to tell me what he offered. If I vouched my guilt for slaying Paul Scanlon, I should serve no more than five years.

That week 'twas my mother that visited, and she was wroth with the lady Howell, and with me, and with God, methought, for she cursed us all.

"Lord, don't test me! I won't allow you to do this!" she cried out with fierce feeling. I knew it well, for oft she had turned it upon me when I was a stubborn boy.

"Mrs. Frank, honestly, this is a good offer," said the lady Howell. "He'll probably only serve two to three years. At the rate things are going, he won't even go to trial for another eighteen months."

"I don't care. He cannot go to prison. Do you hear me, Gentry? You're not taking this plea deal."

"My mother, I hear thee, but prison be not Battle of the Nations," I said. "Thou canst not forbid me go, as thou didst then."

I readied myself for her wrath, but she wept, and still I could not give her what she longed for. After some while, she drew from her purse her kerchief and dried her eyes. When she laid her hand upon the table, I gave her mine.

"Gentry, please, listen to me," she said, and her voice in its hoarseness reminded me of the lady dragon. "I know you take what the Witch says very seriously, and I understand why, but you can't trust her to help you make decisions like this. She doesn't know any more than you do. She's not psychic."

"Sooth, I know it. My mother, rememberest thou when first the voices spake to me?"

"Of course, I remember."

"And I was frighted, for I knew them not. And thou said, *Fear not. They aren part of thee. They aren thy voice.* I say to thee, it is so. If I rely upon the Witch's wisdom, 'tis myself I rely upon. This is my choosing."

I told her not that the Witch was silent. She spake not to me since I broke my vow to protect Lady Zhorzha. 'Twas I alone that chose this path, the sooner to be free.

Tho til the last, my mother tried to sway me from it, I made my plea. I went before the judge, and there I swore a true confession of what crimes I committed. My lord asked, kenned I my plea and felt I remorse for what I had done? I assented I did, tho in truth I thought my crimes not very horrible.

At last, I was delivered to the place of my servitude, where I was put into a barber's chair still shackled. The first cold dread crept into my belly when the clippers with their gnashing metal teeth were put to my head. Tho I longed to be brave and stoic, I was not. I cried out like a small boy, like the small boy I had been when the therapist would do what she called *desensitizing.* I never could be made insensible, for 'twas not a battle to be fought, but a torment to be endured. My gaoler called for another to restrain me, and they scorned against me, as I was put to the blades.

The place was called Malvern, a name that struck fear into my heart. Malvern cometh of the Welsh *moel bryn,* meaning a bald hill, and in my mind I saw Bryn Carreg, its stones tumbled down to strip the hill bare. I saw my dreams turned to rubble and dust.

CHAPTER 52
ZEE

The City of Wichita used a Bobcat to clear Mom's front yard, while she stood on the porch, screaming and crying. When they were done, there were no waterlogged china cabinets, no boxes, no books, not even any grass left. Just a patch of dirt with a few broken bits of china here and there.

Mom didn't speak to me for a month.

I went back to waiting tables at the Cantonese place, and I picked up some shifts at a biker bar, where I got my ass grabbed ten times a night. With both of those, I could keep Mom and me afloat without dipping into the money from Uncle Alva. I moved that, a hundred a week, into a savings account for Marcus. Not enough to make anybody suspicious, but it would add up to fifty thousand dollars by the time he was eighteen.

I hired a lawyer, who took my retainer in cash and started filing paperwork to get me visitation with Marcus. Because the Gills and I were all nonparental relatives, the lawyer thought I had a good chance.

I rented a house off Craigslist. A little run-down bungalow on Seneca with scuffed wood floors, a pink-tile bathroom, and a fenced yard for Leon. I furnished it with a bed, a dresser, and a coffeemaker. When I wasn't working or sleeping, I laid in bed and read, so that was all the furniture I needed. I wondered if this was what prison was like. It was what I deserved.

I still had Gentry's *Yvain* book, but I put it away after I got to the part where Yvain overstayed his year and a day, just like I knew he would. Laudine had given him a magical ring to protect him, but she sent a servant to get the ring, and to tell Yvain not to come back. After he realized how badly he'd screwed up, Yvain wandered off into the woods like a crazy person. *A whirlwind broke loose in his brain, so violent that he went insane.* If I let myself think too much about what I'd done, I might go insane. *He hated himself above all else,* the book said, and that was how I felt. I drank too much and smoked too much, trying not to think about it.

I'd never lived alone before, and sometimes it felt like being the last person on earth. At night it was worse. I started taking Leon for walks along the river when I came home from the bar shift at three o'clock in the morning. Leon helped me remember that I had obligations, that I couldn't wander off into the woods like a crazy woman.

I thought I might go on that way forever, until the social worker, Ms. Alvarez, called to schedule my home visit. She gave me a list of what she wanted to see, including *where the minor child will sleep.* So I bought a bed, a dresser, and some toys for Marcus' bedroom. Plus a table, two chairs, a couch, and a coffee table. By the time I was done, it looked like a house instead of a prison cell.

Ms. Alvarez looked at everything, marking stuff off a checklist on her clipboard. She even opened the kitchen cabinets to see what kind of food I had. When she finally came back to the front room, I shooed Leon off the couch, so she could sit down.

"The dog is yours? He lives here?" she said.

"Yeah. This is Leon."

I snapped my fingers at him and he came slinking over to me. When I squatted down to pet him, he rolled onto his back. The Internet said that was a submissive display.

"Is he good with children?"

"Yeah, I mean, you can see he's — Somebody used him as a fighting dog, but he's really a big baby."

I rubbed his belly while he laid there looking sheepish and pathetic. Right then I realized that Leon was the dog equivalent of me: shabby and broke down and ugly with his hacked-off ears. The kind of dog you pay fifty bucks for and chain out in your yard. Why would a judge ever give me visitation?

"Is everything okay, Ms. Trego?" the social worker said.

I'd worried so much about not looking like a stoner and the house being clean, but I'd never even thought about Leon.

"If it's a problem for me to have him, for Marcus to come visit —" I couldn't say it without crying. "I can get rid of the dog."

"Oh, no. I don't think that's necessary. He seems very docile. And as long as you're supervising properly, there's shouldn't be any trouble over you having a dog in the home."

When she reached for her briefcase, Leon jumped up and slunk away behind the couch.

Two weeks later, my lawyer called to tell me I had a date for family court. I thanked him and told him how happy I was, but after I got off the phone, I was so shaky I had to lie down on the floor where I was standing.

Nothing good had ever happened to me in a courtroom. Just the idea of going to court, and having a judge look down on me, made me feel sick. It made me want to go to bed and never get up. The only thing worse than thinking about going to court was thinking about the judge saying no, because what I couldn't stand was the thought of never seeing Marcus again.

By the day of my family court hearing, Mom was back to speaking to me, and I wished she wasn't. She called me first thing in the morning and asked me to come over and help her with something. She wouldn't tell me what, and the only way to stop her calling was to go.

I went, expecting some kind of crisis, but she was in her recliner, watching TV. When I leaned down to hug her, she said, "Honey, is this what you're wearing to court?"

The whole thing felt like a trap. Like I was Leon exposing my belly. I straightened up while she was kissing my cheek.

"Yeah, this is what I'm wearing. Why?" Why did I ask?

"Just those pants are awfully tight and you've got pills on your sweater."

I'd tried. I used actual bobby pins to put my hair up, and I'd put on lipstick, but I guess neither of those things outweighed my fat ass or my Goodwill sweater.

"What do you need help with?" I said.

"One of us needs to meet with your sister's lawyer. I worry that he's not doing enough for her."

One of us. Since only one of us ever left the house, that meant I was supposed to meet with LaReigne's lawyer.

"Is that why you wanted me to come over?"

"I would rest easier if you met him. You could go after court." The way she said it, I knew she'd gone behind my back and told LaReigne I would.

So I was a nervous wreck walking into family court, knowing as soon as I was done there, I would have to see LaReigne for the first time since I left her in Arkansas.

"Aunt Zee!" Marcus yelled and, before the Gills could stop him, he ran down the aisle to hug me. In four months he'd grown so much, and he had a junior accountant haircut to go with his khakis and button-down shirt, but he smelled like Marcus. My Marcus. Like crayons and grass and somebody who hasn't been washing behind his ears. I wasn't prepared for it.

It was the best day and the worst day I'd had since Arkansas. Even while I was hugging Marcus and crying into his hair, I thought about Gentry. Maybe he didn't hug people, but he was surely missing his family, and that was my fault. As much as I wanted Marcus to be happy, I didn't deserve to be as happy as I felt.

Not that I got to keep that happiness, because after the hearing, I said goodbye to Marcus, and drove to the county detention center in El Dorado. LaReigne's lawyer met me in the parking lot. His name was Ben, and he looked like he was about fifteen years old: scrawny with a giant Adam's apple.

"Is this your first real trial?" I said.

He laughed and then coughed.

"No, of course not. Don't worry about me, Ms. Trego. I'm going to do everything I can for LaReigne."

Not *Lauren* or *Lorraine.* LaReigne. He was already half in love with her. The ones who were going to fall for her always got it right.

The meeting was in a locked cubicle the size of a bathroom, with a table and four chairs. Ben and I were standing there when they brought in LaReigne, not even cuffed. Just walking next to a corrections officer, carrying a file folder. I'd prepared myself

540

for seeing her in jail scrubs, but I wasn't ready to see her with all the blond grown out of her hair. She hadn't been brunette since we were kids.

"So is this an ambush?" she said, once we were in the room together, like I'd tricked her into meeting with me.

"I thought you wanted me to come, but I can go," I said.

"Don't be silly. I'm glad to see you." She held her arms out for me to hug her. I didn't want to, but I put my arms around her. It was like hugging someone I barely knew. She felt smaller and softer, and she smelled different. Not like when we were kids, when we'd both smelled like Mom's house — musty and smoky — but not like the grown-up LaReigne, who'd smelled like perfume and makeup. Now, she smelled like prison. Unless Ben pulled off a miracle, maybe she always would.

I let go of her and pulled out one of the chairs at the table to sit down. Ben stood behind me, waiting for LaReigne to pay attention to him, but she didn't.

"What's the special occasion you're dressed up for?" she said after she sat down across from me.

"Mom didn't tell you? I had family court this morning."

"Well, you look really nice," she said in this fake-ass voice.

"How did it go?"

"Loudon got arrested in Oklahoma on another DUI and driving on a suspended license. So the Gills will keep custody of Marcus. My lawyer says he's pretty sure the court will grant me some kind of visitation. But you're probably not interested in all the details."

"Of course I'm interested! How can you even say that? Ben is working on me being able to call Marcus for his birthday."

"The Gills' lawyer has made it clear we'll need a court order," Ben said. "That's our next step, unless your sister gets visitation, and then —"

"She'd have to get a landline first," LaReigne snapped.

"I want to talk to you alone," I said to her.

"I can't do that," said Ben, sitting down in the chair next to mine, across from LaReigne. "This is as private as it gets, because this is a confidential meeting between client and attorney. Regular visitation is monitored."

"You can say whatever you want in front of Ben. It's okay," LaReigne said.

"No, it's not. He's your lawyer. Not mine.

Maybe anything I say he'll use to try to help you."

"I assumed you wanted to help her," Ben said.

"Not if it's going to get me in trouble." I'd sat down at the wrong angle, and I couldn't get comfortable. When I stood up, LaReigne's eyes got wide.

"Please, don't go," she said.

"I'm not going. My hip's just bothering me." Once I was on my feet, though, I wanted to leave.

"I was hoping we could discuss the trial," Ben said.

"Don't. I'm not testifying. You could subpoena me, but you'd be sorry if you did." I hadn't come there to talk to him, so I said to LaReigne, "I'm doing what I can. I'm taking care of Mom. I'm trying to make sure Marcus will be able to see you. And I put more money in your commissary account."

"I don't want your money," LaReigne said in a tiny hurt voice.

"I don't know where you think the money comes from, but Mom doesn't have any. I'm the one who pays her phone bill, and I'm the one who puts money in your account."

"Zee, please, don't be mad."

I started to say, *I'm not mad,* because it

was so much more than that. I felt like a firestarter, like I could burn everything down just by thinking about it. *Hothead,* that was what Mom always called me.

"Did you even Google it?" I said.

"Google what?" She gave me a confused look like she couldn't understand why I was angry. Like my anger was random.

"What Tague Barnwell did. Did you even Google it before you decided to fall in love with him?"

"That's not how love works!" she said. "I know you don't understand anything about it, but normal people don't decide to fall in love. That's why it's called —"

"Okay, fine, I don't know how it works. So you accidentally fell in love with him. Not your fault. But did you know what he'd done when you decided to run away with him? Because it took me like sixty seconds on the Internet to find out that he murdered five people. He would have murdered more if he was better at building bombs. One of the people he killed was a little boy. His mother was trying to protect him, and a bullet went through her shoulder and into his head. He was only four."

There was so much heat in me that it dried up any tears I had for that little boy.

"That wasn't Tague," LaReigne said, sniffling. "That was Conrad."

"Even if that's true, did you fail to fucking notice the part where while you were running away and making plans with Tague that Conrad was escaping from prison, too? Was that just an afterthought?"

"I'm sorry," LaReigne said. Whatever that meant. Not, I guessed, that she was sorry she'd done something so fucking stupid. "You don't need to testify. You don't even need to come to the trial. I appreciate everything you're doing, but will you do me one favor?"

I didn't say yes or no, but I didn't leave. She opened the file folder on the table in front of her and handed me an envelope. There was one word written on it: *Tague.*

"What is this?" I said.

"Please, you can hate me all you want, but please, will you deliver that to him? If I mail it, they won't give it to him, but you can go to his trial." I was so shocked, I didn't know what to say and, since I didn't say no, LaReigne kept talking. "I know I'll never see him again or talk to him again. I accept that. But please, will you do me this one favor?"

CHAPTER 53
RHYS

Somebody must have given my name to the police, because a U.S. marshal came to interview me. I kept waiting for the guilt to kick in and make me confess what I knew, but my drive for self-preservation was too strong. After an hour of saying, "I don't know," repeatedly, I said, "There are white supremacists in the SCA, and some of the HMB groups. Not a lot, but some. People who think the Middle Ages were full of white people."

"Do you believe Gentry Frank is involved with them?" the marshal said.

"No, that's not what I meant at all. Gentry would never get involved with people like that. I'm just saying maybe that's how he got the information about where those guys were."

After that, it seemed like every news site did a think piece or an exposé about the SCA, historical medieval battles, and white supremacists. Some of them played Gentry and Edrard up like heroes. These two plucky kids armed with only a sword and a bow who went to rescue a hostage. Other pieces made them out to be the punch line to a joke. These two idiots who went to fight white supremacists armed with only a sword and a bow.

Somebody must have given the news outlets pictures of Gentry and Edrard from a tournament, because they started running a photo of them in armor. Edrard looked like a jolly elf, laughing and wearing ribbons in his beard. Gentry looked every inch the brooding killer, all in black with a bloody nose, staring past the camera.

Once, I saw an interview with Gentry's biological brother, Brand. He looked nervous but eager to get his fifteen minutes.

"Well, you know he's got autism, and he's like schizo or something," he said, grinning at the female reporter. "He's pretty weird and he talks like *Oh my lady dost think something.* Like that."

A few times, I saw Zee on the news, when some reporter was trying to get her to make a comment. She never did, unless you count words that have to be bleeped on television.

I got calls from reporters, too, but I never agreed to be interviewed. I wanted less to do with the story, not more. When Gentry's lawyer called me, wanting to talk about testifying at his trial, I was floored. Obviously, as a friend, I owed him something, but I didn't plan to pay that debt by perjuring myself.

Plenty of times, I'd thought about calling Zee and talked myself out of it, but that night I did. I got her voicemail.

"This is Zhorzha Trego. If you're law enforcement or someone connected to the legal system, please leave me a message. If you're a reporter, no, I don't do interviews. If you're a criminal law student, I still don't do interviews. If you're a creep who's in love with my sister, get a life. If you're calling for some other reason, leave a message."

I'd forgotten how sexy her voice was. Husky, half bored, half amused. I hung up and sent her a text, asking her to call me. It was almost midnight when she did, and I could hear bar noise in the background.

"For real, this is Rhys?" she said. "How'd you get my number?"

"Gentry gave it to me that weekend at Bryn Carreg. I was trying to hit on his girlfriend, and he gave me your number."

"I wasn't his girlfriend, and he's trusting like that," she said. As though I were the one who'd taken advantage of Gentry's

548

trusting nature.

"His lawyer called to ask me to be a character witness for his trial. Did she call you?"

"You're kidding, right? You think anybody would want me as a character witness?" She laughed. Then to somebody else: "Yeah, that keg's almost empty."

"So, it's just not your problem?" I said.

"I didn't say that, but you're his friend, and I'm the person who fucked up his whole life."

"And what the hell am I supposed to say in court?"

"I don't know," she said. "Maybe you could say that Gentry is a really kind, decent person, who was trying to help somebody. Look, I gotta go."

"Wow, it's true what they say. Redheads really don't have souls. I cannot believe —"

She hung up on me.

I worried about it for nothing, because a couple weeks after Gentry's lawyer called me, I read in the news that Gentry had taken a plea deal. There wasn't going to be a trial.

CHAPTER 54
ZEE

I should have said no. I didn't owe LaReigne any goddamn favors. After what she'd done, I didn't owe her anything, but I tried to remember that not everything is about what you owe or what you pay. If nothing else, that was the lesson I should've learned from Gentry.

So I took the envelope and I carried it around in my purse for two months, waiting for the trial to start. Every once in a while I'd take it out and look at it. *Tague.* Sometimes I thought about opening it and reading the letter. A few times, I thought about throwing it away.

The first two days of Tague's trial, I had to work.

The third day, I stayed in bed with Leon and a pile of books.

I made myself read farther into *Yvain.* A noble lady found him wandering in the woods and helped him get better. For a second I thought he was going to cheat on his wife, but no, he just helped the noble lady and went on his way. Then halfway through the story, the lion finally showed up! Reading that, I understood what Gentry meant about being worthy of a dog's devotion, because Yvain's lion was so loyal that he went into battle with him. When he thought Yvain had died, the lion tried to kill himself.

Yvain was trying to get home, but on the way he volunteered to be a champion for a woman who was getting screwed by her sister over some land. Next thing I knew, Yvain and Gawain were planning to joust to settle the argument between the two sisters. They were best friends, but they were really going to fight each other to the death. *I wonder how a Love so great can coexist with mortal Hate?* That was how I felt about La-Reigne. As much as I loved her, I hated her that much, too.

The fourth day of Tague's trial, I had to go, or admit I wasn't going. Honestly, I'd hoped it would be over on the third day. They had surveillance footage of him murdering a corrections officer, and Kansas doesn't even have the death penalty. How hard could it be to send him back to prison for the rest of his life?

I went, and I spent the morning watching the back of Tague's head. Every once in a while he would turn to look at his lawyer, but he didn't take notes, because he couldn't. That was part of the defense's argument: he wasn't a threat to society anymore. They had medical testimony about exactly where his spine had been severed by Gentry's sword, but the end result was that he was paralyzed from the chest down.

The closer we got to lunch, the more nervous I got. I'd decided that at the recess, I would get up, walk to the railing behind the defense table, and hand LaReigne's letter to one of Tague's lawyers.

By the time the judge called the recess, my foot was asleep and my hip was locked up. When I stood up, I could barely walk. I shuffled out into the aisle, but before I could take two steps, I saw her.

Rosalinda.

She was wearing a baggy blue sweater, a long denim skirt, and tennis shoes. Instead of a medieval head scarf, she had her hair pulled back into a braid. Her eyes were red from crying. I turned around, I hoped, before she saw me. Using the rows of benches for support, I limped out of the courtroom and pushed through the crowd outside.

Down the hall on the left was the bathroom. I went into the first stall and pulled the letter out of my purse. Whenever I'd thought about getting rid of it, I'd imagined I would read it first, to see if there was some truth in it that LaReigne was keeping from me, but I didn't. I left it in the envelope when I tore it up. Half and half and half and half until I had a stack of torn squares too small to tear again. I dropped them into the toilet and flushed.

After a couple of minutes, I pulled off a piece of toilet paper to blow my nose. I flushed that, too, sending LaReigne's letter a little further on its journey to the sewer. Right as I stepped out of the stall, the bathroom door opened and Rosalinda walked in.

CHAPTER 55
ROSALINDA

I wondered if Zee thought I followed her to the restroom to fight her. I'd never so much as slapped someone, and I definitely couldn't imagine doing it to her. She was a foot taller than me and she looked like a girl who knew how to fight. Except when I walked into the restroom, she looked scared.

"I didn't think I would see you here," she said.

"He's the only one who's going to stand trial. He and your sister."

In some ways that was the hardest part. The man who killed Edrard was dead. Edrard had killed him, but I still had an empty place in my soul. I'd convinced myself that seeing Tague Barnwell's trial would fill it up, which wasn't very Christian of me.

Another woman came into the restroom, and I had to step aside to let her in, but after she went into a stall, I stepped back to make sure Zee didn't escape.

"I'm sorry. When they went, I didn't know what — I should have stopped them." Zee put her hand over her mouth. "I'm so sorry."

"I bet you are, since your sister's going to prison," I said. Whenever I thought about it, I got angry. I knew I needed to forgive, but no matter how much my father prayed over me, I couldn't let go of it. I didn't know how to let go.

"She sent me here today. To pass him a note. But I couldn't do it."

"Is that supposed to make me feel better? That your conscience is bothering you? Because it doesn't. It doesn't do me any good for you to feel guilty."

Zee nodded.

Other women went in and out of stalls, flushing, and washing their hands, while Zee stared at my feet. Almost like Gentry, except it was shame that kept her from looking at me.

"I need you to take me out to Bryn Carreg. Gentry's place," I said. "I need someone to take me, and I don't have a car."

"Do you — like right now? You want to go right now?"

"No. I have to go back in when the recess ends."

"When do you want to go?" she said.

"I'll call you."

When I handed my prayer journal to Zee, she stared at it like she didn't know what to do.

"Just write your number down," I said. "I don't have a cellphone."

Finally, she scrawled her number in the middle of a random calendar page and handed the journal back to me. I let her go. After the recess I didn't see her in the courtroom.

At almost three o'clock that afternoon, the defense rested, and the judge sent the jury to deliberate. Most of the spectators left then, but my brother wasn't coming to pick me up until six, so I stayed and worked on my weaving.

The bailiff came back at four o'clock. Then two lawyers came scurrying in. The jury had a verdict. There was a half-hour crush of lawyers and reporters hurrying to get set up. Finally, the deputies wheeled Tague Barnwell back into the courtroom, and the jury filed in.

I wanted to feel free, but when the jury foreman said, "We find the defendant guilty," I didn't feel anything. Six times the foreman said, "We find the defendant guilty," and none of them made me feel any differently.

When my brother picked me up, he didn't

even ask how I was, so I said, "It's over."

"Yeah? What's the verdict?" He didn't care, though. Like my father, he thought I was a fallen woman, because I'd run away from home and lived with Edrard without being married. They thought this was my punishment.

"Guilty," I said. I might as well have been talking about myself.

"Good. Because you need to get this out of your system and do something useful. Mom and Abby need your help at home."

"Okay."

I was obedient and contrite, because that was the price of coming home. I bowed my head at dinner, while Dad prayed over me. When he said, "Lift up Becky and come back into her heart. Forgive her for her sins," he meant my whole life was a sin that I needed to atone for.

If I had obeyed Dad, I would have gotten married right after high school and had kids, like my sisters did. Instead, I'd gone into strangers' homes to babysit to pay for three semesters of college. Because I wouldn't, my father had picked the man he thought I should marry, and invited him to dinner. Week after week, for two years, while the sand ran out in the hourglass of my father's patience.

Then a girl in my theater class invited me to the Renaissance Festival in Bonner Springs. After I saw the ladies in their tippet sleeves, and the knights in their armor, I never wanted to go back to my old life. I didn't want to wear modest clothes or get married or have four kids.

The night of Tague Barnwell's verdict, while my nieces got ready for bed, I read my Bible like a good aunt. After the lights were out, I waited until they were asleep before I cried. For Edrard. Not for me. Because even though I hadn't done what I was supposed to do, it was what I'd wanted. It was what I still wanted.

After everyone was asleep I took my prayer journal into the kitchen. Zee had the handwriting of a third grader. Big sloppy sixes and scribbled twos. I picked up the phone and dialed, liking the idea of bolting Zee out of bed in the middle of the night. A sliver of terror cutting through her sleep. Except she answered after two rings and she sounded awake.

"I just got home from work," she said, when I asked if she'd been asleep.

"Where do you work?"

"At a bar." That was all she said, and I remembered I hadn't exactly treated her like a friend when I saw her at the courthouse.

"Can you go this Saturday? Out to Bryn Carreg."

"We'd have to go early, because I work in the afternoon." Then like she was talking to someone else in the room, she said, "Yeah, I know, Leon. We're gonna go here in a minute."

I gave her my folks' address, and then we hung up. I sat holding the phone, trying to imagine where she was, who was with her, but all I knew was that she wasn't alone. Not the way I was, awake in a house full of good Christians sleeping the sleep of the innocent and the righteous.

CHAPTER 56
ZEE

When I went to pick Rosalinda up on Saturday, she walked around to the passenger side of my car, staring into the back seat the whole way.

"Is the dog coming with us?" she said.

"This is Leon. I didn't want to leave him cooped up at home."

"This is the Leon you were talking to the other night?"

"Yeah," I said, even though I didn't remember that. I'd been pretty high when she called. "I know he looks scary, but he's safe. If it's a problem —"

"No, it's fine," she said, but when she got in the car, she kept looking over her shoulder at Leon like she thought he was going to come over the center console and eat her.

After we got on the highway, he laid down and went to sleep. Rosalinda opened her bag and took out a long roll of what looked like belt webbing, with a pattern in it. It reminded me of the trim on the dress Gentry had given me. The dress that was somewhere with his camping stuff in his truck.

"I'm going to work on my weaving, if you don't mind," she said. "I'm trying to get a bunch of things ready for the holiday season for my Etsy shop."

"You have a shop on Etsy?"

"I used to make decent money, but it's been harder since . . . because I have to borrow my brother's phone to upload pictures and stuff, and I can't always get to the post office."

"You really don't have a cellphone?"

"It's money we don't have. Besides, I'm always at home," she said. "I didn't finish college, so I can't get a regular job. The weaving and some babysitting are the only jobs I've ever had."

"I didn't go to college." I didn't know why she was telling me that stuff, but I thought we could try to have a conversation. "You could always wait tables."

"I don't think my dad would like that."

I was going to ask how old she was, but I didn't want it to sound like a smart-ass remark. Still, I figured she was old enough to get a job her father didn't approve of.

We didn't talk after that, until I saw a red-tailed hawk perched up in the top branches of a pine tree.

"There's a hawk," I said to make her look up from her weaving.

"Oh." That was all she said, but a few miles further, there was one on a road sign past Udall. She pointed and said, "There's another one."

That fast we saw another, up on an electrical line, twisting his head around, looking in the grass for something to eat.

"That's three," I said.

She folded her weaving up in her lap, and from there on, that was all we said to each other. Four, five, six, seven. To keep track of how many hawks. By the time we reached the pull off for Bryn Carreg, we were up to thirteen, plus three turkey buzzards and a bald eagle fighting over a deer carcass.

In six months, the weeds had grown up around the carport, so the only place to park was the shoulder. We were far enough out in the country I didn't bother with Leon's leash. I just opened the back door and let him out. I put my purse in the trunk, and I offered to put Rosalinda's in, too, but she clutched it to her chest and shook her head.

As I came around the other side of the car, I saw a metal sign half hidden by the weeds. It had a real estate company name and phone number on it. FOR SALE in big red letters. *84 Acres, Pond* was painted underneath that.

It made everything worse. Five years Gentry had worked on his castle, and I destroyed it all in a week. Following Rosalinda up the path to Mud Manor, I thought about Gentry carrying the tent ahead of me, inviting me into his life. Look what he got for it.

I'd worried I wouldn't be able to keep up with Rosalinda, but she had to stop a few times to catch her breath. Leon ran ahead of us, chasing things.

"I don't miss this hill," Rosalinda said, panting as we came up the last stretch. The weeds hadn't taken over Mud Manor, because there was too much shade, but a bunch of vines were climbing up the side of the house. "I still don't know how Gentry hauled all the construction materials up here."

"Did he build this, too?"

"Oh, he built this first, so I wouldn't have to camp out. I mean, Edrard helped, but Gentry did most of the work."

"That's nice."

"It really was. I'm sure it doesn't look like much to you, but this is my real home," she said. I thought about Rhys telling me she had a crush on Gentry. I wondered if that was true, or if it was homesickness. Either way, I felt bad for her.

I assumed she'd come to get her things from the house, but she walked around the fire ring and started up the path to the hill of good cell reception. I whistled for Leon and we followed her.

It had been so beautiful in the spring, all green and shimmery. Now the valley was hazy from range burning, and the trees were starting to look bare, but a few still had bright orange leaves. For maybe ten minutes, Rosalinda and I stood on the hill looking down on all those long stretches of brown grass. Then she reached into her purse and pulled out a plastic bag full of gray powder.

"He always said he wanted his heart buried on this hill. His parents acted like I made that up, but his father finally agreed to give me some of his ashes. Maybe part of his heart is in here. Or for all I know, his father gave me a handful of ashes out of their fireplace."

"How come they decide whether you get his ashes?" I said.

"Oh, we weren't married. We were only handfasted."

"I think that counts." I didn't actually have an opinion about marriage, but my opinion about Edrard's parents was they'd acted like assholes to Rosalinda.

"I don't know what to say," she said. "The only prayers I know are a bunch of Old Testament stuff Edrard wouldn't appreciate."

"You could sing something."

I was sorry I'd suggested it, because she picked this song that was so fucking sad, she only got partway through it before she cried. After she gave up singing, I helped her untie the knot in the plastic bag. She tested for the wind direction, tipped the bag over, and the breeze scattered the ashes down the side of the hill. Then Leon hiked his leg to the limestone outcropping behind us. Amen.

"I'm going up to the castle, if you want some time to yourself," I said.

She nodded.

On the way up, I heard something flapping in the wind. The edge of one of the tarps had come loose, so it popped back and forth at the top of the east tower like a blue flag. Someone had cleared out Gentry's stuff. The only things left were some scaffolding, tumbleweeds, and the bones of a little critter. Leon sniffed it over and hiked his leg to the doorway.

"Quit pissing on everything," I said, but he gave me the look that was basically a dog shrug. When I went up the steps, the big goof came after me, his claws scrabbling on the stones. About halfway up, he changed his mind and went back down.

At the top of the tower, I had to lean way out to grab the edge of the tarp. Down below me was the whole state of Kansas again. All winter brown, except for those splotches of fire orange. It made my throat tight knowing Gentry might never get to see that view again. I let go of the tarp and took out my phone. Stretching my arm out as far as I could, I took a panoramic picture of as much of the horizon as would fit.

I took one last look for myself, long enough to see Leon trotting down the hill toward the ponds. I called for him and, for the first time, he turned at the sound of his name. I didn't know anything about tying knots, but I managed to get the tarp fastened. Whether that did any good, I didn't know, but at least it was done.

When I got back to Rosalinda, she was sitting on the ledge, staring out at the horizon.

"I'm sorry," I said. I couldn't remember if I'd told her that. "It's my fault what happened to Edrard, and I'm sorry."

"I don't blame you." I wasn't expecting her to say that, and she didn't sound angry. "The thing is, Gentry would have followed you to the ends of the earth. Edrard couldn't even be bothered to help with the housework. What he did, that wasn't because of you. He did it for Gentry, for brotherhood. Maybe it was stupid, but it was also incredibly brave."

We walked back to the car without talking. I popped the trunk to get my purse and, while the trunk was open, I uprooted the FOR SALE sign and put it in. Then we got on the road to Wichita.

"Would it help if you had your own phone?" I said, after we'd been driving for a while. Now that I'd thought about the FOR SALE sign for thirty miles, I was ready to think about something else. "I could get a phone for you on my plan for like fifty bucks a month."

"Why would you get a phone for me?" She looked at me like I'd invited her to join a coven of lesbians.

"Why wouldn't I? I'm just saying, would it help you? With your Etsy store? Not having to count on your brother for so much. Because it's not that expensive. I can afford that."

"Seven," she said. We were up to seven hawks on the drive back. She was quiet for probably ten minutes, until she said, "I could pay you back eventually."

"You don't have to. It's not a loan."

"That's a lot of money for you to just give me."

"Let's say a year," I said. "We'll do it for a year, and either you'll be able to afford it yourself next year, or we'll work something else out."

A year was only six hundred bucks. It wasn't a lot of money, and it didn't do a thing to make me less sad about Edrard, but at least I was doing something useful for somebody. When we got to town, we went by the Verizon store and she picked out a phone. With taxes, it was forty-eight dollars a month. The same as it had been when LaReigne and I had a phone plan together. Mine was the first number that went into Rosalinda's phone.

"If you need anything, you can call me. Like if you need a ride to the post office. Or whatever," I said, when I pulled up to her folks' house to drop her off.

"Okay."

I was relieved that she didn't say thank you, because she didn't owe me anything. It wasn't charity.

"Why did you take the FOR SALE sign?" she said.

"Because it's not for sale." Some things weren't for sale.

CHAPTER 57
GENTRY

My cellmate was called Nate, and upon our meeting he was quick to make jest of me.

"Shit, we got Prince Valiant up in here," he said, when first I spake to him.

I took it not amiss, for his hands weren open and he rose to greet me, not to oppose me. Sooth, Nate and I weren well matched. He minded not that I paced, and I minded not that he snored. 'Twas no worse than to share a room with Trang.

Malvern was a place of small chambers and smaller windows, but after some weeks, I began to think I needlessly borrowed the Witch's superstition over the name. Among what was called *general population,* there was the yard, there was daylight, there was chapel on Sundays, and Nate would hear tales and tell them also, so we might while away our time of penance. I wrote letters that my family might know I thought of them. I would write to Lady Zhorzha, but I knew not where my letters would find her, nor whether they would be welcomed. To my great shame, I remembered not her words on parting. Nor mine own.

There weren some queds and knaves who would offer me offense, but they frighted me not. I would meet a push with a push and a blow with a blow.

When I had been there nigh a month, Nate was called to take physic for a tooth that troubled him, and I remained alone. Two men came to the open door of the cell and demanded I know not what, for I was speaking with Gawen and heard them not. Seeing how the first man drew his elbow close to his body, I sat up, for I knew he meant to strike me. Were he quicker he might have done so.

He swung, keen to land his blow when I was unready, but I grasped his hand and, pulling him with it, laid him upon the floor. He rose and made to strike me again, but 'twas much diminished and landed upon my shoulder. I meant to end the skirmish as quick as I might, and struck my elbow upon his throat with some force. He fell prostrate and the other man, who by a venture had come to fight me also, instead bore his friend up and retreated.

"I heard some of those Aryan boys got it

in for you," Nate said upon his return, when he learned what had betiden. "Dude named Scanlon saying you killed a blood relation of his. That true?"

"Mayhap. For my brother and I fought and slew three men that weren numbered among those who call themselves Knights of the Ku Klux Klan. One was called Scanlon."

"You for real killed you some KKK motherfuckers? Shit, I guess that makes you an honorary nigga around here."

Sooth, I was sore in need of a friend in that place, and Nate seemed to me an honorable man. His crime was the manufacture and sale of a controlled substance, for which he served a sentence longer than mine own, but he was ne a man of violence ne a liar. I was alone in that place, but he took me in among his brethren, and invited me to sup with them. In the yard, they kept their own place, where they lifted weights and played at cards. When I slept in the sun, I was safe among them, but 'twas Nate's certainty that Scanlon would seek to fight me again.

"Dude come at you, figured you for an easy mark," Nate said. "He won't make that mistake again. Next time, he'll come around with a couple bigger dudes. Killers."

"I am trained in melee combat," I said.

"You understand," said Vernon, he that was first among Nate's brothers. "We can't buck for you, man. Not at this juncture. If it turned into a brawl, the warden would come down on us. Nothing personal, but you gotta fight this one yourself."

"Nay, I ask it not of you. Ye musten guard yourselves."

"You, too, my man. You gotta keep your head on a swivel," Nate said.

"Certs. The black knight be ever vigilant."

"Shit. The black knight." Vernon was not alone in his laughter, for Nate and his brothers weren much amused that I carried the black knight with me.

Later, when we awaited lights out, Nate returned to the matter of Scanlon.

"You can't let him off easy next time. None of that chivalry shit. When those Aryans come for you again, whoever comes for you, you gotta give them a real beat-down. Knock they teeth in. You go for blood, so they don't mess with you again," he said.

It liked me not, but Nate spake truth. I came to Arkansas under the dragon banner and under it I would remain for the length of my sentence in Malvern. No mercy, no quarter.

When Scanlon came for me again, he brought with him two men. One called Bobby, who had no teeth to be knocked in, and one called Orvis that stood nigh six and a half feet tall, and was made of a great deal more cunning than was Scanlon.

"I got it on good authority that you're the man who killed my cousin Paul," Scanlon said. He would make himself heard that day, though his voice was damaged by the last blows we exchanged.

"Sooth," I said. "I slew thy cousin in fair combat. He came well-armed and might have slain me, but could not."

"What the fuck is this?" Orvis said. "Speak some fucking English."

"That don't mean shit to me," Scanlon said. "All I know is this fucking nigger lover's gonna answer for Paul's death."

Answer, I did.

They three pressed me to a corner, as tho they would stop my escape, but in truth, it gave cover to my back, that they could not attack from all sides. Certs my life was forfeit if I failed, so I fought as tho I meant to rend their limbs from their bodies.

I wished I had a lion to come to my aid, as did Yvain, but 'twas I alone. Tho they beat me and wounded me, I spared them not and gave them what hurt I could. Bobby was no more than a flea, and I felled him with a blow to his knee that made him cry out, and he would fight no more.

As Orvis made to crush me with his fists, I grappled Scanlon as I had his kinsman before him. Once I made him fast, I smote his head upon the wall, a dozen times or more, til blood stained the stones of Malvern.

Then I faced the giant alone.

Had we fought full armored, we should have shattered our shields and bent our blades. The battle burned hot, for the gaolers wished our feud ended and stopped it not.

Orvis and I traded blows til our arms tired. Unlike Yvain and Gawain, we had no love between us, and Malvern was no place for honor. I fought on, tho my sides heaved with effort, and my breath was like a knife, where Orvis broke my ribs.

Ere 'twas done, methinks we both would have given much to quit the field, but we could not fight to a draw. If I bested not Scanlon's giant, I would have no peace, and the giant's pride allowed him grant me no quarter.

I found one blow more in my hands than had the giant in his. I found his jaw softer than my skull. I found the virtue to advance, when he retreated. At last, he lay upon the ground, a bloodied heap, while I stood firm upon my feet. I, conqueror, and he, conquered.

I was taken first to the infirmary, where my arm was put back into its socket. 'Twas the same as was injured before. My ribs were bound and my nose and fingers splinted. My head was declared not too badly broken, tho I had used it to break the teeth and nose and fists of a giant. Thence, I was forsent to what they called *Segregation,* where there weren no windows and none but those within me to speak to.

In a short while I kenned not day, night, nor the passage of time. The black knight laid plans as tho like Edmond Dantès, we weren entombed within le Château d'If. He was aright in one thing. If I could tame ne my mind ne mine heart, I would make my body submit. Hour upon hour, I built muscle, strained sinew, said my prayers upon a bank of sweat and pain. Let Hildegard say what she might, in that place where there was dark but no night, I thought long on Lady Zhorzha's milk-white thighs and the flame twixt them. I had beaten a giant, but I surrendered to lust.

My flesh was gratified, but my mind ran to confusion. Let the Witch be silent, but she would hear me. I cursed her, cursed the day she first spake to me, cursed even the day she set me to be Lady Zhorzha's champion.

When those curses brought no solace, I cursed myself. For I failed Lady Zhorzha. For I failed Sir Edrard. For I failed my mother and father. I was Yvain in the woods, gone mad, and my hair and beard grew to suit my madness. I knew not how to gain an audience with Lady Zhorzha or the Witch, nor how to plead my case.

In my weakest hour, thrown down into the pit, he that was called Dr. Kimber came to me again. I met him first when I was sent to be *assessed,* and he had declared me an *interesting case.* I made the plea that brought me to Malvern, rather than submit to his physic. For I recalled the therapy of my childhood, when I was treated as a dumb beast that might be yoked.

"How are you, Gentry?" Dr. Kimber said. "I thought you might finally be ready to talk to me. Segregation can be a great time to set your priorities and make changes. A chance to start over."

For some while, I could do naught but scratch my neck, seeking calm. 'Twas my wish that he should go, but he remained, and would have me speak. I knew not how to greet him when my mind was undone, and so first I repeated the prayer Hildegard offered up.

Jesu, with Thy precious Blood
And Thy bitter Passion
Aid me to be right and good
Grant me Thy Salvation

"It's good that you have your faith," Dr. Kimber said. "It can help you get through your time here, but I'd like to see you do more than just do time. I'd like to see you make progress. I could make things a little easier for you.

"Part of the reason you're here is that you live too much in your fantasy world. You need to come back to this world, and we don't speak Shakespearean English here."

I dared not tell him nigh two hundred years lay twixt Shakespeare and my tongue, and I should not speak at all, if I was not allowed to speak as I would.

"Tell me about this person you're so angry with. I was here yesterday and heard you begging them to talk to you. You seemed pretty upset. I'm curious what you think this person can tell you."

Dr. Kimber came in the guise of a confessor, but 'twas for his own curiosity that he would peer into my soul. I dared not speak to the Witch aloud, but I made my daily plea.

"Give me some sign, some word. 'Tis mine own fault that Sir Edrard is dead. Had I listened to thee and come alone to Arkansas, he would yet live. Only tell me what I am to do now."

After months of silence, the Witch spake: "This physician is a fool and easily fooled to thy gain."

"I know segregation can be hard, but it's possible I can get you out of here sooner, if you're willing to work with me. Gentry, do you hear me? Are you okay?" Dr. Kimber said.

"Yes," I said. "I am okay."

'Twas a devil's bargain, for after that, he came each day. In trade for playing his games, for taking his physic, anon I was given my clothes and my razor and then a book to read. My sojourn there was marked as *good time.*

True to his word, Dr. Kimber shortened my time of solitary penance, and the gaolers returned me to my cell. Tho small, 'twas blessed with a window and sunlight.

"Look at that," Nate said in greeting. "Sir Lancelot done eighty days and don't look too much worse for wear."

Tho my mind was at ease, I had slept poorly in the dungeon. In the yard, the sun was as a white-hot coal upon mine eyes, but a blessing. I lay down upon the asphalt and rested with none to keep watch, for the word had been given out that Scanlon and the Aryans would try me no more.

CHAPTER 58
ZEE

I don't know what I would have done if
Charlene had answered the door, but I got
lucky, and it was Bill, holding a coffee mug.

"Zee," he said, looking at the FOR SALE
sign. "Would you like to come in?"

"If that's okay."

I thought if I could get in the door, we
could have a conversation, but while we
were still standing there, Charlene came up
behind him.

"What is this nonsense?" she said when
she saw the sign.

I'd only brought it to the door, because I
didn't know what else to do with it.

"I think Zee has something to say to us,"
Bill said.

"Well, I've got a few things to say to her."

"Now, Charlene —"

"Don't you say it. Don't you tell me to
calm down or be nice, Bill. Because my son
— our son — my baby boy that I spilt tears

and sweat and blood for — is sitting in a prison in Arkansas because of this girl."

I'd never heard anybody say *girl* like it was a dirty word, but she did. She said a lot of other things, too. Like *trash* and *user* and *selfish* and *ugly,* and then she circled back on *trash,* but she was losing steam, because there was maybe half a minute of silence between her saying, "Curse the day you ever set foot in this house" and "Whatever you have to say, I'm not interested in hearing it."

"I'm interested in hearing it," Bill said, and pushed the door open far enough for me to step inside. I left the sign propped up against the side of their house.

"Goddamn you," Charlene said to Bill, who led me into the dining room. She must have been in the middle of cooking dinner, but the table wasn't set yet. A stack of plates and silverware were waiting on Trang.

"Okay, Zee," Bill said, after we were sitting down.

"I want to say that I'm sorry, even though I know it doesn't do you or Gentry any good. But I don't want you to think I'm not sorry, just because I haven't said it. And I'm sorry for coming here, because I know I'm not welcome, but I wanted to ask about the FOR SALE sign, because I don't want

Gentry to sell his land and — and the castle." That was really as far as I'd gotten in figuring out what I needed to say. "Because I know how much it means to him, and what happened is my fault."

"You damn right it is," Charlene called from the kitchen, which would have been funny if I didn't think she'd be happy to slap me silly. She came to the doorway and glared at me. "And how dare you go out to Bryn Carreg? What right do you have to go out there?"

"None," I said. "But Rosalinda asked me to take her there to spread Edrard's ashes."

"Oh, you went out there to help scatter the ashes of a man you got killed?" Charlene took a deep breath and said, "That could have been my son!"

"Charlene," Bill said.

"Our son!"

I nodded, because it was all true. Charlene took another breath and snorted it out. Then she turned and went back to the kitchen. Because Bill didn't say anything, I tried to go back to what we'd been talking about.

"It's bad enough Gentry is being punished for trying to help me, but I couldn't stand for him to get punished by losing Bryn Carreg, too," I said.

"I think you know that's not the kind of people we are." Bill crossed his arms on the table and leaned toward me. It made me wish Charlene would come back. I could stomach her yelling at me, because I'd spent most of my life with my mother yelling at me. I wasn't sure I could take Bill being kind and fatherly.

"I know," I said. "But I don't know why you're selling his land."

"Well, it's a simple matter of economies. I cosigned the loan for Gentry, because he was only nineteen, but he has been solely responsible for the mortgage and the taxes. We've been doing that out of his savings, but that's about to come to an end. We can't afford to keep paying it without his income. He understands it has to be sold."

"I can pay it," I said.

"Oh, the shit is getting deep in there." Charlene slammed a cabinet in the kitchen and something metal fell on the floor.

"I think that's a very noble gesture," Bill said, "but the property taxes come due on December first, and it's quite a bit of money that has to be paid all at once."

"I can pay it."

Charlene came stomping into the dining room and tossed two things onto the table in front of me. An envelope from the tax assessor in Chautauqua County and a loan payment book.

"Sure, you go on ahead and pay it," she said.

Bill didn't say anything, so I looked at the tax bill first. Almost four thousand dollars, which wasn't as bad as I'd expected. The next coupon in the payment book was for November first, in a week. Five hundred and eighty dollars. I rounded up and did the math in my head. The mortgage and taxes were about eleven thousand dollars a year.

Rosalinda's phone had been practice for the idea of giving away money. The fifty thousand for LaReigne would go to Marcus. I wouldn't touch that. But I had thirty-four thousand dollars for me in the safety deposit box. That would almost pay off my medical bills, but it would also pay three years of the mortgage and taxes on Gentry's land. And I could add to that. I could pick up a few more shifts, or if worse came to worst, I could do the run for Toby. I just had to keep everything afloat until Gentry got on his feet again. I put the tax bill back in the envelope and stuffed the coupon book in there, too.

"I promise I'll pay it," I said. It was all I'd come there for, so I pushed my chair back from the table and stood up. "Just, please, don't tell Gentry. You can tell him whatever you want, but don't tell him I'm paying it."

"You're sure?" Bill said.

I nodded and said, "Thanks."

I didn't wait for them to walk me to the front door. I knew where it was.

When I got to the foyer, I heard Charlene say, "She's never going to pay that."

"We'll see, I guess," Bill said.

As I went down the sidewalk, the front door opened behind me and Trang called my name. I waved at him over my shoulder, but kept walking. He came after me, crunching through the leaves, all the way to the car.

"I'm glad to see you," he said. "Gentry asked me to give you this, but I didn't know where to send it."

He held out an envelope that had my name written on it. *Lady Zhorzha Trego.* I didn't want it. Some of the worst anxiety I'd had in the last six months was about someday seeing Gentry or hearing from him. I could pay the mortgage and the taxes on Bryn Carreg, as long as I never had to open that envelope and read that letter, but Trang was holding it out, so I took it.

"It's a visitation form. So you can be on the list to go visit him. He wanted to mail it to you, but we didn't have your address."

"Why would he want to see me?" I said, even though I could think of a few reasons, and they were none of them good. The way I felt about seeing LaReigne, I figured that was how Gentry would feel about seeing me. He'd stopped seeing Miranda and her kids because they'd been rude, and I'd done a lot worse. I could never live up to Gentry's standards.

"You're kidding, right?" Trang laughed. "He's your champion. You're his lady. You respect him for what he's good at."

"I still don't think —"

"My mother threw his sword out. The big one over his bed. She took it and got rid of it. I know she's upset, but she doesn't care at all about chivalry or his knighthood. You do, and that matters to him. So yeah, he wants to see you."

"Okay," I said, even though I didn't mean it. I just wanted to escape without crying.

Trang stuck out his hand, so I took it. Except instead of shaking my hand, he bent over it, like Gentry would have.

"Fare thee well, Lady Zhorzha. We shall meet again."

"Thank you, Sir Trang."

He laughed and shook his head.

"Not yet, but one of these days." He let

go of my hand and waved at me as he jogged back up to the house.

I was such a coward, it took me two days to open that envelope. Like Trang had said, it was a visitation application form for Arkansas Department of Corrections Inmate No. 1489736, housed at the Ouachita River Unit at Malvern, Arkansas. In the middle of the form was a section for me to fill out. Name, address, phone, driver's license, and a bunch of security questions. I knew how it worked. I would fill out the form, send it back, and the Arkansas DOC would run a background check on me. Assuming they decided I was okay, I would be added to Gentry's visitors list.

I came home every day for a week and looked at the form on the kitchen counter but didn't mail it, because according to the instructions, I was supposed to mail it back to Gentry. Could I stick it in an envelope and send it by itself? Or did I have to send a letter with it? I couldn't think of anything to write. *Hey, sorry I totally fucked up your life. XO, Zee.*

When I was a kid, Mom made us write letters to my dad every week. *Just tell him about what you're doing,* she always said, but it felt awful to send him a letter full of things he couldn't be there for. This was worse than that, because at least it wasn't my fault my father had gone to prison.

Maybe I never would have mailed it, but I kept thinking about Gentry's sword, about his mother throwing it out. Because I knew she loved him, and I knew she didn't want to hurt him, but she'd taken something he cared about and thrown it away. Every day for a week, I looked at that visitation form, and I thought, *I'm not much, but I'm not nothing.* I could do at least as good a job of caring about him as anybody else. If I could pay his mortgage and taxes, I could go visit him.

CHAPTER 59
MARCUS

Aunt Zee got a dog. She said he was Sir Gentry's dog, but he could be my dog, too. Leon lived at her house and slept in her bed, but when I threw his ball out in the backyard, he brought it back to me. I had my own room at Aunt Zee's house, but if I got up in the middle of the night, I could crawl into Aunt Zee's bed, and sleep with her and Leon.

I wished I could live with Aunt Zee all the time. She didn't get mad if I made a mess or if I was noisy, and we had fun. But I only got to visit her every other weekend. Sometimes we went to a movie or skating or to the playground, but sometimes we stayed in our pajamas on Saturday and played Go Fish and ate donuts and petted Leon.

Then one Saturday we drove a long way, at least two hours. I kept asking Aunt Zee where we were going, but she wouldn't say.

"It's a surprise," she said, but it wasn't a

good surprise.

"I don't want to go to prison." I didn't want to cry like a baby, either, but I did. Why did she want to take me there?

"You're not going to prison. We're here to see your mom."

"I don't want to," I said.

"Why not? Don't you miss her?"

"Yes, but she's bad!"

"She's not bad. Who told you she was bad?"

"Grandy and Grammy. Grandy says Mommy is bad bad bad. Daddy said a bad word I'm not allowed to say, but Grandy says that Mommy killed people."

"Oh, bullshit!" Aunt Zee yelled so loud it scared me, and hit the steering wheel with her hand. "What does Grandy say about your dad? Did Grandy tell you that your dad killed somebody?"

"No, he didn't! He made a bad decision. That's what Grammy said."

"Your mom made a bad decision, too. Your dad's bad decision got somebody killed. And your mom . . ."

"What about Mommy?" I said.

"Well, your mom's bad decision got people killed, too. She was trying to help someone, only that person was a liar and killed some people. Which is a bad thing, but she didn't know that would happen. She isn't any worse than your dad. They both did bad things."

"You take it back," I said, because it made me sad. If Mommy and Daddy were that bad, maybe they would never get to come home. Grandpa Leroy never got to come home.

"I'm sorry, buddy. It's a really hard, complicated grown-up thing. Come on, blow your nose."

Aunt Zee got a tissue out of her purse and put it up to my nose, so I hit her arm.

"I'm not a baby!" I said.

"If you're not a baby, you know it's not nice to hit people."

"I'm sorry." I was sort of. She gave me the tissue, so I wiped my own nose. Then I cried some more, because I was scared to go to prison. Grandy and Grammy never took me to visit Daddy, because it was a *bad environment.* We only talked to Daddy on the phone.

"You know, sometimes good people do stupid things and go to prison," Aunt Zee said. "Not everybody in prison is bad."

"Like who?"

I thought she would say Mommy, and I would know she was a liar, but she said, "Sir Gentry."

"Sir Gentry is in prison?" I didn't know knights could go to prison, but it made me sad, because I liked him.

"Yeah, that's why Leon is our dog, because Sir Gentry is in prison. But he's still a really good person."

"Did he do something bad?"

"Yes and no. He broke the law, but he was trying to do something good. It just didn't turn out right."

That scared me, because what if sometime I tried to do something good, but it didn't turn out right, and I had to go to prison?

That first time, we didn't go see Mommy. Instead we drove home, took Leon for a long walk, and ate pizza.

I thought maybe we wouldn't have to go again, but my next Saturday with Aunt Zee, we went to Topeka again. I yelled at her, and even though I didn't want to cry, I did. She gave me like ten tissues out of her purse, because I snotted a bunch.

"Did you get it all cried out?" Aunt Zee said, when we got to Mommy's prison.

"I don't wanna go."

She was quiet for a long time, and I hoped she would start the car like last time, but she put the car keys in her purse.

"Ten minutes," she said. "We'll go in and sit with your mom for ten minutes. You don't have to talk to her or anything else, but I want you to spend ten minutes. After that, we can go to the rain forest, okay?"

"What rain forest?" I said. Because there aren't any rain forests in Kansas. Those are only in South America.

"The Topeka Zoo has a rain forest. The website says they have toucans and snakes and giant bats. If you'll go see your mom for ten minutes, we can spend the rest of the day at the zoo."

"Okay."

She said ten minutes, but we walked through all the chain-link fences, and down sidewalks and hallways. There were policemen and police ladies, and Aunt Zee had to give them paperwork, and we walked through a big machine that scanned us, and then we waited in a hallway for a long time. None of that counted for our ten minutes.

Finally, one of the police ladies said, "Visitors for LaReigne Trego-Gill," and that meant we could go into a room that looked like the cafeteria at school. Aunt Zee took my hand and we walked across the room to a table, where there was a lady in a gray sweatshirt with short brown hair. She was crying and Aunt Zee hugged her, but I didn't know why until the lady said, "Marcus, baby. I'm so glad to see you." It was

Mommy, but she looked different. Not just because her hair wasn't blond, but because her face looked fatter.

"Come give me a hug," she said, but I hid behind Aunt Zee.

At the other tables, there were more ladies in gray sweatshirts talking to people. There were other kids, too, and I wondered why their moms were in prison.

"Just give him a minute," Aunt Zee said. After she sat down, I stood next to her so she would put her arm around me.

"How's school?" Mommy said.

"Okay."

"Just okay?"

I nodded.

"Mom says you got a dog, Zee."

"His name is Leon," I said.

"What kind of dog is he?"

"Big and ugly."

"He's a pit bull," Aunt Zee said and rolled her eyes at me.

"But you always say he's *big and ugly*."

"Yeah, but that's not what kind of dog he is. That's how he is."

"I don't care if he's big and ugly. He's a good dog."

"Yes, he is," Aunt Zee said.

"He's part my dog, too. And part Sir Gentry's dog."

Mommy glared at Aunt Zee. Then she said, "Did you bring some money for the vending machines?"

"Do you want something?" Aunt Zee said.

"I thought Marcus might want a pop."

"Can I, Aunt Zee?"

"Sure." She got out her change purse and dumped a bunch of coins on the table. Then she leaned over and whispered to me, "Will you ask your mom if she wants something?"

"Do you want something out of the vending machine?" I didn't look at her when I said it, though.

"No, baby. All I want is a hug."

I didn't answer her.

Aunt Zee slid the coins off the table into my hand and said, "Get whatever you want."

I walked all by myself to the other side of the room where the vending machines were. I could have run there — I was a fast runner — but I walked as slow as I could. Heel, toe, heel, toe. I put the coins in as slow as I could, too, using up all the nickels first, because the longer I took, the quicker the ten minutes could be over.

CHAPTER 60
ZEE

When I was recuperating from my motorcycle wreck LaReigne had given me this book about Mount Everest. I guess it was supposed to be motivational. People rising above difficulties and challenging themselves to climb the highest mountain. All I remember about Mount Everest is that the altitude is so high, there's not enough oxygen, and it's like one hundred degrees below zero. It's so dangerous that when people die on Mount Everest, they leave them there. There's one body they call Green Boots, and he's right on the main route to the top of the mountain. Everybody has to walk past his frozen, mummified corpse that's been there for two decades. How's that for motivational?

I thought it was a pretty good description of how relationships are. Everywhere you go, you leave behind the corpses of your failed relationships. If you're lucky you can shove the body down into a crevasse, so you don't have to look at it, but some bodies you can't get rid of. You have to walk past them all the time. I doubt that's what I was supposed to get out of the book, but there it is.

That's what I thought about bringing Marcus to visit LaReigne. He would be twenty-six years old before she was eligible for parole. I didn't want her to be a corpse he had to walk past for the next twenty years, but I didn't know what the answer was. I thought about how I had promised him we would all be together again, and there was no way to keep that promise. I didn't agree with Mom that it was my *duty* to make sure LaReigne had a relationship with Marcus, but I did think he needed to have a relationship with her. I just thought it should be on his terms, which was why she was pissing me off so much.

As soon as he was on his way to the vending machines, LaReigne said, "I don't see why he can't give me a hug when I haven't seen him in so long."

"Do you have amnesia?" I said.

"What's that supposed to mean?"

"Do you not remember how hard this was when we were kids? Because I remember being terrified, and you're acting like he's supposed to be thrilled to see you." I was trying not to lose my temper with her, but she wasn't helping me.

"And what's this nonsense about *Sir Gentry's dog*? Isn't Gentry in prison?"

"Marcus knows Gentry's in prison. Just like his mommy and daddy."

"If it weren't for me, his Aunt Zee would be, too," LaReigne said.

"Yeah, and I'm the only one who's ever going to bring Marcus to see you, so stop wasting your breath threatening me."

For a minute, we looked at each other, and then LaReigne blinked and smiled like everything was fine. I'd seen her swallow her feelings like that a hundred times with Loudon. I didn't know what to think about her doing it with me.

"I was starting to think you were never bringing him to see me. Mom says you've had visitation for three months."

"Did she tell you I only get him every other weekend?" I said.

"That's six times he could have come to see me." She was still smiling, but it was fake.

"I tried to bring him two weekends ago, but he cried so much I felt like shit, so I didn't make him come inside. He cried this time, too. Seriously, do you not remember that?"

"I was older than you," LaReigne said.

"He's almost the same age I was."

"How's money? I know Mom's phone bill is a lot, but it's hard to get her off the phone once she gets started."

Like that was all on Mom. She only accepted the charges when LaReigne called. I was trying to think of a way to suggest maybe she didn't need to call Mom so often, when Marcus came back to the table with three cans of pop hugged against his chest. A can of orange, a can of Coke for me, and a can of Diet Coke. That was what LaReigne always drank. When he slid it across the table to her, she didn't even thank him. If it wasn't some grand gesture, she didn't know what love looked like.

"Thanks, buddy," I said. Even though I didn't really want the Coke, I opened it and took a drink.

"Is it time yet?" He put his knee on the bench next to me, but didn't sit down.

"Time for what?" LaReigne said.

"We're going to the zoo. To see rain forest bats," he said.

"Here in a minute," I said.

"You're going already? I get two hours for visitation and you've only been here fifteen minutes."

"We'll stay longer next time." I meant we'd try to stay longer next time. LaReigne gave me her sad, disappointed face, but I pushed myself up to standing and took another drink of my Coke. Then I put my hand on Marcus' shoulder and squeezed it. "Do you think you can give your mom a goodbye hug?"

I did it first, to show him it wasn't a big deal. When I let go of her, Marcus was hanging back at the table, but after a minute, he nodded. Still holding on to his pop, he took a couple steps closer and let LaReigne hug him. After maybe twenty seconds, he pulled away from her.

"I'll see you Saturday after next." She was trying not to cry.

"Probably not," I said.

"What do you mean *probably not*?"

"I don't think we'll come on our next weekend."

"Why the hell not?" Supposedly I was the one with the bad temper, but there was a flash of LaReigne's.

"Because it's not fair to him. Or me," I said. "It's four hours of driving on the only full day we get to spend together."

"And Leon is cooped up at home while we're gone," Marcus said.

"And what about me?" LaReigne said.

"You'll be okay." Marcus shrugged.

It was a crappy note to leave on, but I felt like I'd gotten lucky, because she didn't get a chance to ask me about giving Tague her letter. I hadn't decided if I was going to tell her the truth.

When we got back to the car, Marcus looked relieved. I gave him my phone to find directions to the zoo.

"When are we going to visit Sir Gentry?" he said. I was glad he was focused on my phone, so he wouldn't see me looking T-boned.

"Well, you can't."

"Why not?"

"You have to be a relative or you have to be eighteen. And you're not either one."

"Oh. Will you tell him I say hi when you go visit him? And tell him I'm helping you take care of Leon. Okay?"

"Okay," I said.

CHAPTER 61
ZEE

I got there early, like the Arkansas DOC website said to, and went through all the checks. My car, my purse, me. They even swabbed my hands for drugs, so I was glad I'd quit smoking weed and was only taking drops for my hip. The system at Malvern was a lot more thorough than at Topeka, and different from when I was a kid. When I was little, the visitation area at El Dorado was a long counter with partitions and glass, to keep prisoners and visitors from touching. I remembered how Mom and Dad would put their hands up on either side of the glass, like they could somehow feel each other through it.

The visitors' room at Malvern was full of square metal picnic tables, with a mesh bench seat on each side. As soon as I was cleared, I filed into the room with everybody else, and found my assigned table.

I was there for five minutes, watching

inmates come in and hug their families, before Gentry came through the door with a man in a sport coat. They stood at the doorway for a few minutes, the man in the sport coat looking at me and talking to Gentry, who was looking down at the floor. Finally they walked over to my table and Gentry sat down.

For some stupid reason I'd thought he would look the same, but his hair was cut down to his scalp. Either they were making him get a buzz cut or he was doing that himself with a razor, but he looked like a skinhead. Someone had broken his nose, long enough ago it was healed, but not quite straight. I'd expected him to look smaller, the way LaReigne did, the way my father had, but if anything Gentry was bigger than I remembered. The muscles on the tops of his shoulders bulged so that he almost didn't have a neck, and the arms of his jumpsuit were stretched tight. He was pale, though, almost as white as me. I didn't imagine they let him sleep outside.

He wouldn't look up, so I had to try to figure out how he was feeling by looking at his hands. They were both palm down, pressed flat to the tabletop, the left one relaxed, the right one tense enough that his knuckles were white, and the scar on his thumb stood out purple. I didn't know what that meant.

"Hey," I said.

He shifted in his seat, raised his left hand to tug at the collar of his T-shirt, and then started scratching the back of his neck. The guy in the sport coat stood next to our table, but I ignored him until he said, "Gentry, can you put your hand down and introduce me to your visitor?"

I tried to give him a look that said, *Can we get some privacy?*

"Gentry? Who's your friend?" he said.

Gentry dropped his chin closer to his chest. He put his left hand back on the table, but his right hand tightened into a fist around his invisible sword.

"Gentry." The guy snapped his fingers, which made Gentry flatten his sword hand back out on the table.

"Hello," Gentry said in a voice I didn't recognize. "This is Lady Zhorzha Trego. This is my psychologist, Dr. Kimber."

"I'm so pleased to have this opportunity to meet you, Zhorzha. And not a little surprised." The doctor gave me a cheesy smile and made me shake his hand.

"Oh, you thought I was a voice like Gawen," I said, and got my hand back from him.

"I admit, I did not expect *Lady Zhorzha* to turn out to be —"

"Lady Zhorzha is a waitress. She lives in Wichita. We met at physical therapy," Gentry said.

His voice gave me the nervous giggles. Like a cross between my cousin Dirk and Keanu Reeves — half redneck, half surfer dude. Was he messing with the doctor or with me?

"Very good," Dr. Kimber said and then, like Gentry wasn't even there: "But we are trying to encourage Gentry not to use unnecessary titles."

"I don't see how my title is unnecessary, since I prefer to be called Lady Zhorzha," I said. It was a lie — I'd always felt weird that Gentry called me that — but it was a true lie. Gentry was allowed to call me whatever he wanted.

Dr. Kimber frowned. Maybe he thought I was a dominatrix.

"Part of what we're trying to do during Gentry's time with us is to encourage him to speak more normally, so he can better adapt to his surroundings."

"Okay." I didn't want to make trouble for Gentry, so I kept what I really thought to myself.

"Well, it's nice that you've come to visit,

Zhorzha. I'm sure Gentry appreciates it," the doctor said, and made me shake his hand again. Then he left us alone.

"I'm sorry." It was the only thing I could think of to say, and then we were quiet for a few minutes. "That's all I really wanted to tell you, that I'm sorry, because this is all my fault. Especially what happened to Sir Edrard. I'm so sorry about that. I know he was like your brother."

Gentry looked over his shoulder to where Dr. Kimber was standing across the room, talking to one of the corrections officers.

"I'm gonna go. I shouldn't have come," I said.

When Gentry turned back to me, he brought his chin up from his chest. His right hand slowly squeezed his sword, and the world tilted back into balance.

"Nay," he said. "Thou art welcome, my lady. My heart is gladful to see thee, tho I know not how to answer thine entreaties for forgiveness, for most urgently I would ask thy forgiveness."

"Oh, crap, Gentry. You freaked me out with that surfer redneck voice. Why would you even ask for — what is there for me to forgive?"

"I neglected my oath to thee. I was thy champion, and I abandoned thee."

"No. You didn't. You were so brave. And you did what you had to do," I said, but he shook his head. "How are you? Are you okay here?"

"I am well. This place be full of knaves and godless motherfuckers, but I fear them not. And the time is short enough. Mayhap only two years more."

"Why are they trying to make you talk funny?" That was how it felt, and not because he said *motherfucker*.

"Dr. Kimber desireth that I speak as he speaketh. He biddeth me also take physic to silence my voices, but no physic has yet been made as will quiet Gawen."

I knew he was making a joke, but I couldn't laugh about it.

"And how farest thee, my lady?"

"I put money in your commissary account, because that's what the women in my family are good at. I don't mean — I'm not saying you're like my father. Anyway. I brought you a couple things. Marcus drew this for you."

I took out the envelope the guards had let me bring in and unfolded the drawing for Gentry to look at.

"He still talks about you showing him how to sword fight. For his birthday, I got him one of those Playmobil sets with the k-nights." I said it with the *k*. "He wanted to draw this for you, since he can't come see you."

Gentry leaned forward to look at the picture, and I think he smiled.

"How is thy nephew?"

"It's pretty confusing for him. The court gives me visitation two weekends out of the month, and maybe I'm going to get him for the whole month of July this summer, because his grandparents are going to France. Sometimes we go see his mother, but he doesn't like it, which I get. I was that way about going to see my dad. And Mom, she can't go see LaReigne. Or she won't go, I guess. She won't leave the house, which is a wreck. Every time I try to do something about it, she gets mad at me."

"Thou mayest not command a dragon do thy bidding. She hath her own ways in her own time," he said.

It made me laugh, when I usually wanted to cry thinking about Mom. There was something about her as a dragon that made it easier to let it go. How could I make a dragon do anything?

"What be this?" Gentry put his finger down on the corner of the picture, where Marcus had drawn Leon. It looked more like a ghost couch than it did a dog.

"That's your dog," I said.

"I have no dog."

"You do if you want him. Do you remember the dog you made friends with at my uncle's house?"

"I remember it well."

"After I went back to my uncle's house, I took the dog. He's living with me."

"Methinks 'tis thy dog," Gentry said, and he was definitely smiling. I didn't know what Leon thought, whether he was my dog. Maybe I only wanted him to be Gentry's dog, so I would have something of Gentry's.

"I named him Leon, kind of after Yvain." After I butchered the title in French, Gentry said it right. *Le chevalier au lion.*

"My lady, tell me true. *Yvain,* it thee liketh?"

"I haven't finished it yet. And I know, it's been a long time, but I'm kind of scared to, because I'm afraid Yvain's going to get himself killed. He's the nicest guy, but kind of a sucker, and he's reckless." As soon as I said it, I remembered I was talking about Gentry's hero. "I mean, he's noble and very brave, but I can't do sad endings right now."

"Nay, all is well. Sir Yvain liveth."

"Oh, that's good." I really was relieved.

"And his lady wife forgiveth him. *For one must have mercy on sinners,* the story says. I fear thou wilt not forgive me, for I shall not return ere a year and a day."

I wasn't sure what he was asking me for. Forgiveness? To wait for him?

"Since it's my fault you're here, I totally forgive you," I said.

"Dame Rosalinda writ me that thou carried her to Bryn Carreg. 'Twas kind of thee to go in my stead. She said ye two scattered Sir Edrard's ashes upon the northern hill."

"Yeah. Better cell reception up there." I was a jackass for making the joke, but I was shitty at serious conversations, and we'd gotten to the serious stuff so fast.

I opened the envelope again and took out the other thing I'd brought. I hadn't been able to figure out how to print a panoramic picture, so I ended up with three pictures taped together. I unfolded them before I laid it out on the table, but I couldn't bring myself to look at Gentry looking at the view from his tower. I couldn't keep my mouth shut, either, because him sitting there looking at the picture without saying anything was killing me.

"I don't know if they'll let you keep this, because I know they have rules about how many photos you can have, and this is really three instead of one. I'll try and figure out how to get it printed on one piece of paper."

He still hadn't said anything so I kept talking. "I didn't think it would be so pretty in
the fall, but the leaves — the trees with the
bright orange leaves, I don't know what they
are, but they're beautiful."

"They aren sugar maples," he said, sounding kind of soft but not sad. I glanced at
him, but he was still looking at the picture.
"When I return, I shall tap them for syrup.
And sledge more stones for the tower. I
would most earnestly thank thee, my lady,
for I know 'tis by thine hand Bryn Carreg
was saved."

"Oh. They weren't supposed to tell you
that."

"Brother Trang cannot be trusted with a
secret, and God's blessing upon him, for I
am glad to know. It giveth me hope."

I imagined he needed hope, because he'd
had his whole life planned out, and I'd
ruined it. We were quiet for a while, and I
caught myself doing what I'd done as a kid,
what Marcus did, watching the clock, like
my visit was an hour-long prison sentence.

"But thou hast not said how thou farest,
and 'tis a matter dear to my heart. Art thou
well, my lady?"

I didn't mean to cry. My father always got
so mad and accused my mother of manipu-
lating him when she cried. At least Gentry

didn't do that. I knew it was bad, that I had completely lost my shit, because a woman at the next table came over and handed me a little package of tissues.

"Girl, you gotta get that all out at home," she said. "Your man don't need to see that."

"I'm sorry," I said to Gentry. "I can't ever make this up to you."

I forced myself to stop crying, because it was selfish.

Gentry waited until I got myself under control again, before he said, "My lady, thou needst not stay if it giveth thee pain. I know 'tis a long journey."

"It's not by wagon, Sir Gentry. And I don't have to drive the whole way back today. I'll spend the night at Uncle Alva's. Turns out he doesn't have lung cancer like he thought. It's emphysema, so he's not going to die anytime soon."

"I am glad to hear it," he said. "But methinks it paineth thee to come to this place. Thou owest me no debt, for 'twas my honor to serve thee. I would that I were thy champion still."

"Aren't you? I thought you were always going to be my champion." I wished I hadn't said it, because it seemed like I was asking for something impossible.

"Thou hast not a new champion, my lady?"

"I don't need a new one. Didn't I swear no matter what happened, I wouldn't send you away?"

"Yea, thou made such an oath, but I hold thee under no obligation."

"I wanted — I want to come see you," I said. "It's stupid, but I had this idea that I'd come and see you and you'd hold my hand. Or something. I don't know. I'm not any good at this."

"Thou offered me not thine hand."

His hands were still on the table. One palm down, one in a fist, so they were like rock and paper, missing scissors.

Both my hands were tucked under my thighs, pressed between my legs and the metal bench. I'd put them there like I was trying to keep them safe. I pulled them out and wiped them down the front of my jeans. When I plopped them down on the table in front of me, they were red, and the palms were waffled from the patterns in the bench.

Gentry unclenched his sword hand and reached across to put it on top of my left hand. Then he lifted it up and put his other hand underneath mine. It didn't look or feel like any other time I'd held hands across a table. He squeezed his together, like he was making mine into a sandwich. Then like he'd just invented holding hands, he ran his thumb along the webbing of my thumb. We didn't talk for a long time. I didn't know what to say, and he was staring over my head, maybe having a conversation with someone else. The Witch?

He nodded and then he looked at me. My hair, my mouth, our hands together on the table.

"Lady Zhorzha," he said. "This be how a tower is built. Lay first the foundation stone. Then upon it, lay the next stone. Up and up, one stone, then another, til thou hast built a tower to keep thee and thine safe."

He meant for our hands to be like the tower's stones, and my right hand was the only one not on the pile. I laid it on top, so that all our hands were stacked together.

"It's not a very tall tower," I said.

"This tower shall keep out a foe that is broad but not high."

I laughed, because I felt like I was in danger of more crying, which wouldn't make either of us feel better. I squeezed his hand between mine and he squeezed back.

"What's going to happen?" I said. "When you get out, what will you do?"

"When first I came to this place, I thought to give myself over to quiet things. To prayer. To art."

"Are you an artist?"

He smiled and shook his head.

"Nay. Master Marcus hath more skill than I. Nor am I restful in such labors, for I miss the grip of a sword. And I am ill-suited to be a priest, for I long to spend another night in my pavilion with thee." For the first time ever, his hand felt sweaty between mine.

"But what can I do for you now?" I said.

I knew in another minute, Gentry would have to let go of my hand. Too much. Until then, I curled my fingers around his.

"Wilt thou come again?" he said. "Come again and lay thine hands upon the table, that thy champion may look upon thee and be content."

CHAPTER 62
CHARLENE

I swore I wasn't going to be ashamed. Not of what Gentry had done, and not that he'd been in prison. I invited everyone I could think of to his welcome-home party. Everyone at church, all the neighbors, everyone I knew through the foster system.

Well, I didn't invite *everyone.* I didn't invite Gentry's biological family, and I didn't invite Zhorzha. I assumed Gentry would invite her, but I hoped she would have the decency to stay away.

Because it had been so long since we managed to have family photos, I hired a photographer my sister, Bernice, had recommended. After the photographer arrived, I sent Trang to round everyone up for pictures. When I went into the family room, there was Zhorzha, coming in from the backyard with Gentry.

I must have stopped in my tracks a little too quickly, because Bernice said, "Oh, she

617

did come," like it was a good thing. "And she dressed up for him."

"In a dress that's six inches too short," I said.

"It's hard for us tall girls to find things that fit," Janae said.

"I'd like to douse her hair with a gallon of coconut oil." Why had no one taught that girl about leave-in conditioner?

"Aw, but look," Bernice said.

I looked. Zhorzha and Gentry had gone to stand at the kitchen bar, not any closer than casual acquaintances would have, but Zhorzha had her hand on the counter with Gentry's on top of it. While I watched, Zhorzha laid her other hand on his, and he added his other to the pile. Then she pulled her hand out from the bottom and put it on the top. They laughed, the first time I'd heard Gentry laugh in a long while.

"He sounds happy," Bernice said.

"Why can't you two let me be aggrieved in peace?" I said.

"Because it's not who you are," Janae said.

"Oh, it's who I am, make no mistake."

"Nothing good's going to come from holding on to that anger," Bernice said.

"Do you blame me?"

"Don't play yourself. After all the things you've done for me, how can you —"

"Now wait. The Lord knows I love you, but I have never done anything like that, and I never would. Not even for you," I said.

"Okay, everybody," the photographer said and clapped his hands. "Let's put the sisters on the love seat here. Then spouses behind and kids around."

Bernice tugged on my hand to lead me to the love seat. We did what we always did, smiled at each other to check for food in our teeth. Then she leaned in close and said, "What about the time you drove down to Tulsa to put the fear of God into Prester?"

"That was different," I said. "He'd hit you. And I didn't get anyone else hurt."

"Seems to me you got lucky. If I remember right, your roommate was driving the get-away car that night."

"That isn't the same," I said.

"Cheryl and David, on that side, next to Bernice. And Elana, on this end with your mom," the photographer said.

Once Elana got her chair situated, it was just a matter of fitting everyone else in. Bill and Carlees in back, because they were the tallest. Janae and her girlfriend filling in between Bill and my niece and her husband.

"Trang, let's put you —"

"Will you get Gentry?" I said to Trang, because I didn't want to end up shouting to get his attention. I'd wanted everyone dressed up for the pictures, but none of Gentry's dress shirts fit him anymore. Too tight in the arms and shoulders. He was wearing what he liked best: a black T-shirt.

Trang went to talk to Gentry, and then the two of them took up their places behind Elana. The rest of the party quieted down like civilized folks to let the pictures be taken.

Zhorzha stayed at the kitchen counter, sitting on a bar stool with her hands on her knees, keeping her skirt pressed down. Obviously she was also uncomfortable with how short her dress was.

"All right, everyone look at me," the photographer said. Then, like he was playing the crowd for laughs: "I'm talking to you, Charlene."

Bernice squeezed my hand, so I looked, and the photographer snapped pictures.

I was still annoyed that Zhorzha had come to the party, but I felt a little bad. It couldn't be any fun for her, surrounded by strangers, and worse than strangers: people who knew all about her. It wasn't as though I'd held my tongue when it came to my opinion of Zhorzha. *Redhead* was the nicest thing I'd called her.

It would have been so much easier for her

to walk away. Nobody had made her pay the mortgage on Bryn Carreg. Nobody had made her visit Gentry. Nobody had made her come to the party, but she showed up. Not because she wanted to be there, but for Gentry. Her loyalty to her sister had brought her nothing but grief, and yet there she was, taking another chance on loyalty, on trusting another person. She could have stayed home, but she came for Gentry, who also didn't want to be there. He would be looking down like he did for every family picture.

"Zhorzha," I said, and then louder: "Zee, come be in the picture."

"No, it's for family. I don't —"

"Yes, and I want you to be in it."

"Okay, let's put you next to Carlees," the photographer said. After all, she was taller than Gentry.

Zee didn't look happy, but she got down off the bar stool, still pressing her skirt to her thighs, and came to stand with us.

"My lady," Gentry said. When I looked over my shoulder at them, he'd put his hand into hers. I predicted they would both look awkward in the photos, but they would look awkward together.

"You two don't have to stay after the pictures," I said to them. "I know you don't

621

want to be here."

"Aren't we having this whole party for him?" Bill said.

"Don't be silly. This party is for me. He can celebrate any way he likes."

"Okay," the photographer said. "Big smiles, everybody."

Bernice gave me a smug look and squeezed my hand again.

CHAPTER 63
GENTRY

Nigh three years to the day, Lady Zhorzha and I returned to Bryn Carreg. 'Twas bright April, with all things turning to green but the air still full of winter chill. Deep in the woods, rimes of snow clung to the ground, bedded on pine needles.

"Are you sure you don't want me to carry anything?" my lady said. She walked before me a few paces, but turned back to ask again.

"My lady, knowest thou, if I need thee to carry aught, I will ask thee."

I would remind her that she carried things for me I could not. I would remind her that 'twas by her labor Bryn Carreg was still mine, but such words dis-eased her, so I spake them not.

I raised the pavilion upon the hill beside the tower, tho 'twas not my custom, for there was no protection from the wind. Yet I desired we should sleep in sight of the work that lay before me. Soon enough I would have other work, the building of flying machines if my father could make it so. Some other thing if not. For the nonce, I longed to finish the eastern tower, and lay as many stones as I might upon the southern tower ere winter returned.

While I began setting the scaffolding that would serve me to lay courses of stone, Lady Zhorzha swept out the leaves that had blown into the towers and bailey. Marcus and Leon weaved in and out, seeking rabbit nests and other matters of great import to boy and dog. Weren they inclined, I would train them together on the hunt. 'Twas a thought that called to mind Sir Edrard, and I longed to see him, knowing I could not.

"What else can I do?" My lady's shadow fell across where I worked upon the scaffolding. 'Twas work made easier with two, but if I looked upon her, I would be reminded that we two carried the blame of Edrard's death.

"Thou might clean also the bathing pond, for it will be choked with leaves. The net may be found with the other tools in the eastern tower."

"Okay." She went away, calling for Marcus: "Come on, come help me!"

"Leon!" Marcus shouted, and they three

went down the hill. For some while I was alone with my labors and my grief. In such time the desire to be alone passed.

"Thy moody countenance will send her from thee as surely as sharp words or a heavy hand," Gawen said.

"He would be better parted from her," Hildegard said. Some days, methought to take once more the physic that silenced her, but it quieted also the black knight.

"She cometh of her own will and might go of her own will," I said, tho in truth I would not have her go.

"So might thou. Go to her if it thee liketh," the Witch said. "Thou art free."

I had not yet laid the planks upon the scaffold, but I climbed it that I might see Lady Zhorzha. Aside the ponds, she and her nephew had gathered a mound of leaves, branches, and other things that had fallen in the water over three winters. They two stood at the lip of the bathing pond, where she held the net braced upon the ground like a shepherd's crook. At my lady's bidding, Marcus ran up the hill toward the keep. When he departed, my lady lay down the net and took off her blouse. As I watched, she stepped out of her shoes and brought her hands to the clasp of her trousers.

Two things stirred in my breast: a great longing to see her disrobed under the bright sun, and a great uncertainty. The water was too cold for bathing. What meant she do?

I climbed down from the scaffolding and ran out of the bailey. As I went down the hill, I met Marcus.

"Did thine aunt send for me?" I said, and turned him back to accompany me.

"No. She told me to go up to the tower."

"Wherefore?"

"I dunno. I was supposed to get something but I don't remember what."

I made haste ahead of him, for my lady no longer stood at the edge of the pond. I saw her not, nor whither she had gone.

When I reached the pond, my lady's garments lay aside her shoes. Ere I called for her, Lady Zhorzha's head broke the surface of the pond. She took a great gasp of air and coughed it out.

"Oh, fuck, that's cold!" she said, but to herself alone, for she knew not that I was there, until she drew her hair back from her face, and opened her eyes.

She looked upon me and I upon her. I knew not what to say, for fear I broke some unspoken vow in spying her at her bath.

"Aunt Zee, are we going swimming?" Marcus said.

"Oh my god, no. I told you to get me a towel." My lady's teeth chattered together. "They're in the basket in the tent."

At the center of the pond the water reached nigh her chin, but after Marcus went, she crossed to where I stood. As she stepped from the water, her hair lay in dripping strands upon her breasts and shoulders, and water-beaded leaves clung to her skin like faerie jewels, for she had gone into the pond all unclothed. Steam rose from her flesh like mist at sunrise. I drank her up from the crown of her head to the curve of her hip, til I saw what she bore in her hand.

'Twas my sword. The first true sword I owned that long hung above my bed in my father's keep. When I returned from Malvern, the sword was gone, and Trang knew naught but that my mother it took. Just or unjust, I asked her not, for my mother had endured much by cause of my folly.

Yet there was my sword, some rusted but whole. Lady Zhorzha grasped the hilt in both hands and lifted it clear of the steps, tho 'twas too heavy for her to hold it aloft. When she reached the top step, she brought the point to rest in the grass.

I knelt to her, as I had knelt many years before when I was knighted. She laughed, I knew not why, but 'twas a glad sound. Her right hand remained upon the hilt, and with her left, she grasped the blade to lift it before her.

"Your sword, Sir Gentry," she said. When I raised my hands, she put it into them.

ACKNOWLEDGMENTS

My sincere gratitude to the following people:

Liberty Greenwood, my favorite traveling companion and my favorite stay-at-home companion.

Robert Ozier — friends who keep showing up are the best friends.

My agent, Jess Regel, who continues to take a chance on my weird ideas.

My reckless but brave editor, Tara Singh Carlson, and the wonderful people at Putnam: Helen Richard, Sally Kim, Ivan Held, Alexis Welby, Ashley McClay, Meredith Dros, Maija Baldauf, Joel Breuklander, Anthony Ramondo, Monica Cordova, Nayon Cho, Katy Riegel, Brennin Cummings, Jordan Aaronson, Elena Hershey, Bonnie Rice.

The early readers and supporters of this book: Kell Andrews, Liz Michalski, Barry Wynn, Lisa Brackmann, Colby Marshall,

Jenna, Tracey Martin, Erin Mansur, Kelly Haas, David and Nick.

Renee and Bogi Perelmutter, who have been readers, consultants, emotional support, and the source of my dinner on many occasions.

Kris Herndon, my mermaid sister and the cofounder of my secret undersea volcano lair.

Matt Hyde and the staff of 715, for the celebratory dinners and all the happy hours.

V.K., Jo Nixon, and Tom, for their assistance in creating a version of Middle English that is accessible to modern readers. Any errors or anachronisms aren mine own.

Robert T. Corum, Jr., professor emeritus of French at Kansas State University, who first introduced me to Yvain.

The Consortium for the Teaching of the Middle Ages and the Early English Text Society for making Middle English texts more readily accessible.

Ruth Harwood Cline for her beautiful English translation of Chrétien de Troyes' *Yvain*.

My Purgatorians and YNots, two of the most supportive writing groups a person could ask for.

Clovia Shaw, a fellow daughter of a

dragon, who always shows me the world from a slightly different angle.

ABOUT THE AUTHOR

Bryn Greenwood is a fourth-generation Kansan, one of seven sisters, and the daughter of a mostly reformed drug dealer. She earned a MA in Creative Writing from Kansas State University and continues to work in academia as an administrator. She is the *New York Times* bestselling author of the novels *All the Ugly and Wonderful Things, Last Will,* and *Lie Lay Lain.* She lives in Lawrence, Kansas.

The employees of Thorndike Press hope you have enjoyed this Large Print book. All our Thorndike, Wheeler, and Kennebec Large Print titles are designed for easy reading, and all our books are made to last. Other Thorndike Press Large Print books are available at your library, through selected bookstores, or directly from us.

For information about titles, please call:
  (800) 223-1244

or visit our website at:
  gale.com/thorndike

To share your comments, please write:
  Publisher
  Thorndike Press
  10 Water St., Suite 310
  Waterville, ME 04901